DÉJÀ KARMA

Vish Dhamija is the bestselling author of eleven works of crime fiction, including *Unlawful Justice*, *Bhendi Bazaar*, *The Mogul*, *The Heist Artist*, *Doosra*, *Prisoner's Dilemma* and *Cold Justice*. He is frequently referred to in the Indian press as the 'master of crime and courtroom drama'. In August 2015, *Glimpse* magazine called him 'India's John Grisham' for stimulating the genre of legal fiction in India. Vish lives in London with his wife, Nidhi.

DÉJÀ KARMA

VISH DHAMIJA

PAN

First published 2023 by Pan
an imprint of Pan Macmillan Publishing India Private Limited
707 Kailash Building
26 K. G. Marg, New Delhi 110001
www.panmacmillan.co.in

Pan Macmillan, The Smithson, 6 Briset Street, Farringdon, London EC1M 5NR
Associated companies throughout the world
www.panmacmillan.com

ISBN 978-93-90742-40-0

1 3 5 7 9 8 6 4 2

Typeset in Adobe Garamond Pro by R. Ajith Kumar, New Delhi
Printed in India by Gopsons Papers Pvt. Ltd., Noida

In memory of

RUCHIRA PATHANIA

(1968–2014)

See you later, Ruchira

Author's Note

IN INDIA, THE TERMS 'LAWYER' AND '*VAKIL*' ARE OFTEN used colloquially while the official term is 'advocate' as prescribed under the Advocates Act, 1961. Hence, before some advocate decides to take me to court over this, I confess I have taken the liberty of informally using 'advocate', 'lawyer', 'attorney', 'solicitor' and 'vakil' in both their singular and plural forms to break the monotony of repetition. I have refrained from using 'counsellor' and 'barrister', as the former sounded too American and the latter very British.

Judges in the Supreme Court and High Courts of India are addressed as 'My Lord/My Lady' – a legacy of the British. India being a constitutional democracy, the Bar Council passed a resolution to refer to judges as 'Your Honour' or '*Janaab*'. To preserve the dignity of democracy, at all times I have addressed the judge by these terms.

At any given point in time, there are over three crore (30 million) cases pending in the Indian courts. Which means, had I adhered to the true timetable for the hearings of this trial, this book could have gone on forever. I have, therefore, fast-tracked the case to bring it to a swifter conclusion.

HINDUISM WAS DESIGNED TO BE A PHILOSOPHY, A WAY OF LIFE. It was never supposed to become a religion, but it inadvertently developed into one. One the simplest of religions, it lets you declare yourself a follower of the faith without even having to perform any rites. The Hindus believe in karma. And reincarnation. Most people equate Hinduism with paganism and a profusion of gods, but that isn't the case. True, Hindus are polytheistic and recognize the trinity of Brahma, Vishnu and Mahesh (commonly known as Shiva). The Creator. The Protector. The Destroyer.

Brahma is a demiurge in the truest sense of the word: the creator of the world, yet he became a subordinate god due to a curse. Fact is, who needs the creator after the creation? Vishnu is the antipode of Brahma. The pantheon of deities – Krishna, Rama, Ganesh et al. – are all avatars of Vishnu, worshipped to protect the believers. Shiva – the god of destruction – is undeniably the most feared and revered of all gods, worshipped in very few forms: as Himself, Nandi (the trusted bull He rides), Vasuki Naga (the serpent wrapped thrice around His neck to represent past, present and future), *Trishul* (His weapon) and the *Lingam* (the phallus). Shiva, supposedly, has a third eye on His forehead, which, if He opens, can destroy everything. But Shiva does not wish for an apocalypse. He does not destroy because He wants to; He destroys only when there is no other option.

Your karma invokes His choice.

Prologue

I HAVE REHEARSED THESE LINES NUMEROUS TIMES SINCE THAT ill-fated night. The only question I'd ask God – if there is a God – when I see Him: why me?

If you asked me what one could change in a minute, I would say a whole life. Not even a minute. Just as a life can be created in less than a minute, so can it be taken. I understand that everyone who is born dies, but the time allotted between birth and death is your fate-determined tryst with life. Sadly, the fallout of annihilating a life prematurely is such that it alters the life of not only the one who dies but also the abandoned unfortunates', imprisoning them in a catchall of lifelong hurt – a pain that does not fade. In my case, kismet had cheated me. It deprived me of my expected predestined stretch with either of my parents on earth.

The day, which for most is the beginning of their lives, ended up being the gloomiest one for me. But it hadn't started out that way. The beginning and end of that Friday evening were as different as black from white. That evening – electrifying in more ways than one – gave way to a sordid denouement that, until a few hours ago, was absolutely inconceivable. And though it was a celebratory night for all of us who had taken the final undergrad paper, it was a forlorn finish for just one of us. Me.

I have rehearsed these lines countless times since that ill-fated night. The only thing I'd ask God – if there is a God – when I see Him: why me?

Why did it have to be my father who got murdered that night? And if that wasn't enough, why did it have to be my mother who was accused and convicted of the heinous crime?

My dad – I loathed him more than I loved him – was a successful real estate agent who had also invested in many other real estate developers' properties. And though he was the sole provider for our family of three, he was a heavy drinker – an obstinate man who had, of late, become a wife-beater. Brawls between my parents over trivial matters had become a regular occurrence. During the Emergency declared by Mrs Gandhi in the late seventies, the uncertainty in the country and the capital city Delhi led the property market to crash. At any given point in time, my father had millions invested in a multitude of building projects, so when the market nosedived, the money became inaccessible. Worse, no one knew how long it would take for the situation to change. The succeeding government formed by the Janata Party could not stay in power long enough to improve matters. Cash became scarce and alcohol proliferated in our household like a virus. The fights became fiercer, more frequent and filthier. Beatings became more unruly. It was almost every day that I saw my mother bruised, beaten black and blue when I returned from college. Now that I had grown up, I warned my dad, but he, still the sole provider, couldn't care less.

I remember the day vividly. I had returned from the college revelries, drunk and spaced out, maybe even drugged – who knew what we all smoked and drank back then. Walking through the front door, I saw my father leaning over my cowering mother as she lay wailing on the sofa. I rushed to help her, but seeing that my yelling didn't stop him, I ran into the kitchen, picked up the meat knife and returned to show him its gleaming blade. I told him in as many words that I wouldn't stop myself from slashing his throat if he didn't leave my mother alone that minute.

Retracing his steps, his bloodshot eyes staring at me, my father muttered something incoherent.

'Just get away from her,' I yelled again, the knife still in my hand.

'Ungrateful bastard, get out of my *house,' he slurred. Too drunk to argue or confront me any further, he stormed out of the living room and went straight to his bedroom. My mother gave me a vexed look first, then hugged me and followed my father into their room. I was too intoxicated to move, to go to my room or change my clothes, and the last thing I remember was plummeting onto the beige sofa where my parents' fight had played out only minutes ago. You could have had Kenny G play his soprano sax in my ears and I still wouldn't have stirred – until I heard my mother's scream in the early hours of Saturday morning.*

I have no recollection of anything except this image, burnt into my mind in 4D – I can still smell the blood, warm and flowing, my mother standing in shock over my father's body, holding the very meat knife with which I had threatened my dad, her prints all over the long black grip of the blade, her right eye still black.

Although I was wasted the whole time, I carry a faint memory of someone else being in our home that night. It only occurred to me later, much later, who *it was, but it was merely my deduction – nothing evidential. However, I never mentioned this to anyone, partly because I myself was never certain whether I had actually seen and heard or simply imagined this person. More importantly, who would have believed anything I said, considering the state I had been in?*

And then, the lights went out. I was groping in the darkness, the nothingness. There were flashes in my brain, but they vanished just as instantaneously. I remember tousling my hair in frustration, in shock and horror. Then I passed out again.

With my father dead and my mother arrested – and soon to be incarcerated for the rest of her life – I, Jay Singh, became an orphan that very day. The wheels of my life came off the rails. Clichéd dystopia followed. I was dropped into the real world without warning, like a rookie swimmer pushed into the deep end without a warm-up.

The luxury of dreaming was over.

1

THE BLACK AUDI SLOWED DOWN.

The chauffeur, Bhīma, certainly wasn't comfortable driving through this sea of traffic with chaotic waves of pedestrians, cycles, rickshaws, two-wheelers and various makes of cheap, derelict cars. Despite being in his air-conditioned enclosure, the sounds from the street were loud and thc stench from the open sewage overpowered the expensive deodorant in the car's ventilation system. The shops on either side of the road were completely rundown – broken signages, shattered windows; gaudy lighting and glaring displays put up to conceal the dilapidated exteriors. Some were even boarded up, and the homeless day labourers were settling in on those storefronts for an early night. An unbroken string of hawkers on trolleys and carts stood outside the shops, blocking access to them, but no one here sold anything of interest to the passenger, or even the chauffeur for that matter. The Audi, in these surroundings, was itself as out of place as a camel marching in a zebra suit. People turned to see if the car accommodated some celebrity – a film star, a singer, a cricketer – but the darkened windows disallowed it. They assumed it would be some VIP and moved on.

'Stop anywhere after that white building on the left,' said the *sahib* from the back seat, pointing at the building in the next block.

'*Jee, hukum,*' Bhīma replied.

The car turned left into a side road and stopped. Bhīma got out. He was wearing a suit. Summer, winter, autumn, spring, morning, noon, evening or night, Bhīma always wore a suit; it was part of his uniform. More importantly, in deference to his boss's safety, he kept a licenced handgun – a Colt Anaconda .44 Magnum – concealed inside his suit jacket. As with others like him, there were more firearms that Jay Singh owned, but this handgun was the only one that the authorities knew of. Bhīma looked around, his sharp eyes darting like a fox's to canvass the area around the car. Built like a small mountain, he could well have been a reincarnation of the legendary Bhīma from the Mahabharata or a cousin of the modern-day Khali of WWE fame. At six feet eleven inches and weighing over 170 kilos, he towered over everyone and everything, especially his boss, who stood at a mere five-foot-seven. He was Jay Singh's chauffeur-cum-bodyguard-cum-valet-cum-man Friday, and as loyal to his 'hukum' as a thoroughbred St Bernard. Truth is, no one makes such devoted friends in life without eliciting fierce animosity in others. Sometimes you create enemies that stay enemies till they croak. Or you do. An armistice is simply out of the question. Of course, some of Jay's arch enemies had attempted to do what they themselves couldn't achieve with Bhīma around: persuade and bribe him, but it wasn't money that got his loyalty. It was a deep-rooted debt of gratitude that – despite Jay treating him as a close friend – led the latter to revere his master as no lesser than a god. The alliance, the bond was simply unfaltering, and the fidelity absolute and indefatigable.

Once sure of the security details, Bhīma got out to open the rear door for the sahib, who offered an almost imperceptible nod of approval and walked towards the white building – a hospital. Just before entering, Jay put a hand in his jacket's inner pocket and speed-dialled Bhīma's cell from his spare phone. This covert call would continue till he returned within Bhīma's field of sight. This was standard operating procedure. Bhīma would attentively listen to all communication on his car radio – a passer-by could be forgiven for thinking that he was listening to the audio version of George Orwell's *Animal Farm* – and would react within seconds, in case his boss was in trouble of any sort.

The hospital – if one could call it that – was more of a general practitioner's clinic, with basic facilities and seven rooms for private patients. If one were to look at the official hospital listings in Gurgaon – the existence of which was a mystery in itself – BK Memorial Hospital wouldn't even feature. Jay's research had revealed that it was run by its owner–proprietor, one Dr K. K. Mehta, who was a plain MBBS with no specialization. Yet, business was brisk, with a never-ending queue of patients from eight in the morning until eight in the evening. In fairness, Mehta worked relentlessly and even took on apprentices to help out with the patients; he had ten nurses working in shifts to provide services to private beds 24x7.

'What can I do for you?' asked the receptionist with henna-streaked hair, looking up from the computer screen she might have been staring at for the last ten or so hours.

Jay could see the bewilderment on her pretty face. He knew that by no stretch of the imagination did he look or dress like the patients who consulted Dr Mehta on a regular basis, but he didn't care. Wasn't that the sole reason he was here? Moreover, she had no business judging him.

'I have an appointment with Dr Mehta at 7:45.'

'Your name, please?'

'Singh, Jay Singh.'

The girl quickly browsed through the diary on the screen in front of her.

'Take a seat, Mr Singh. Dr Mehta is with a patient. He'll call you as soon as he's done.'

Jay lifted the sleeve of his expensive olive green linen jacket and glanced at the Hublot on his wrist: 7:38. He was indeed early, despite the traffic. Looking around, Jay found the reception area to be completely unoccupied, exactly as he had expected. He had booked the last available appointment of the day as he didn't want Dr Mehta to be in any kind of haste to see a subsequent patient. One needed time to build comradeship.

Jay sat there, taking in the clinic: basic yet clean, professional yet unsophisticated – several past issues of the ubiquitous health and vigour magazines, found only in waiting areas of doctors, dentists and vets, were scattered on the only table in the room. Dr Mehta could do so much better.

'Mr Singh,' the girl's voice broke Jay's trance. 'Sir will see you now.'

Jay looked at his watch again. 7:53. The doctor had made him wait eight minutes. He got up and elegantly walked to the receptionist. 'Thank you,' he said with a charming smile that left the girl's knees a bit wobbly, and moseyed into the doctor's room. *What was the rush?*

'Good evening, Mr …' Dr Mehta uttered, looking up from his screen and standing up to receive his last patient for the day. His countenance also communicated that his clients didn't look anything like the swish client who had just walked in. '… Singh.'

'Good evening, Doctor.'

'How may I help you, Mr Singh?'

'You can call me Jay,' he said, skimming the room in one glance. Certificates of his practice, his medical school diplomas, a photograph of his hospital being inaugurated by somebody – even if the *somebody* wasn't influential enough to be a known face – and an overabundance of inconsequential freebies most obviously gifted by some pharma reps.

'I want to invest in your hospital, doc.' Jay pulled up a chair and sat down without invitation. He looked around to check if there were any cameras or recording devices. *None.*

'Excuse me?' Dr Mehta looked confounded. He almost fell into his chair and his eyebrows rose a few centimetres.

'You heard it right, Dr Mehta. I am here to make a deal.'

'Have me met before, Jai?'

'Jay, like the alphabet J.'

'Have we ever met before, *Jay*?' the doctor repeated.

'I don't think so.'

'So, would you mind if I asked who *are* you?'

'Jay Singh. I am a straight-talking defence advocate who wants to invest in your hospital—'

'I am a doctor and you, a defence advocate. Why would you want to invest in a hospital? More importantly, why would I let you invest in *my* hospital?' Dr Mehta interjected impatiently.

'Because, Dr Mehta, it will be mutually beneficial.' Jay smiled.

'I am not sure I understand you, Mr Jay Singh.'

'I have a very important client, of incredibly high net worth, Dr Mehta, who is also a prominent member of society. A scumbag annoyed him on New Year's Eve when my client was with a friend, *a lady friend*, and in the ensuing clamour my client shot the lowlife in the knee. You see, my client is a little hot-headed, but that is another story.'

'I am still not sure I understand what you're trying to say, Jay. Is there a real purpose to this meeting?' Dr Mehta looked at the Novatel clock on his desk. *Definitely a freebie.*

'Would you want to attend to something else before we continued with our meeting, Dr Mehta?'

'No. I need to visit the private rooms before I leave the hospital, but I'd like to hear about this strange and loony client of yours first, so please keep it short.'

'My client, Dr Mehta, as I said, is a prominent member of society who shouldn't have been involved in this brawl in the first place. To make matters worse, his 'girlfriend' that evening was an escort – you see, this information, and the unlicenced firearm my client used, could land him in a difficult position—'

'Please stop.' Dr Mehta put his hand up. 'I am not at all interested in your client, his extracurricular activities, his high net worth, or any of that nonsense. Why am I supposed to know all this? Please come to the point; I need to leave.'

'Oh yes, I forgot … you might have another appointment.'

'No, as I said, I need to wind up and go home.'

'Sure.' Jay passed a wicked, knowing smile. 'Dr Mehta, my client could not have shot this miscreant because he wasn't at the said location at the time. He was at your hospital undergoing treatment, under your observation.'

'Who is it? I don't remember any patient of mine who is a "prominent"' – Dr Mehta used his fingers as quote marks to emphasize the word – 'member of society. What treatment was he undergoing?'

'That's the catch, Dr Mehta, he wasn't. But I'd like you to work your records to provide him with an airtight alibi.'

'Oh, I see. So you want me to give a false statement in court?'

'You're a remarkably smart man, Dr Mehta.'

'Get out.' Mehta released a loud breath and pointed towards the door.

'You must be joking.' Jay did not even as much as shift in his seat. He had been in such situations before and some insolence was expected.

'I don't want any money, any offer of partnership, any more of your garbage. Please leave.'

Dr Mehta almost spat out and pointed towards the door.

'Dr Mehta—'

'I have ethics.'

'Ethics. Morals. Scruples. Before you realize, you'll pull your conscience into the conversation. Why get into all that rubbish, Dr Mehta? My client can build another hospital for you, renovate this one; he'll do whatever you ask for.'

'I cannot imagine that you, a protector of legal rights and a supposed upholder of ethics, are attempting to entice me, a doctor, to save a criminal's life. Is that why you studied law? To break it, to support criminals?' Mehta picked up his phone and fumbled with the numbers without taking his gaze away from the gutsy intruder. Jay's countenance still did not change one bit. It was water off a duck's back. He sat there, listening judiciously to the doctor – who, in his early fifties, was probably a decade older than him – as though some priest was admonishing him, an infidel, after a grave misconduct. Mehta, on the other side of the desk, sounded exasperated by Jay's lack of principles.

'Will you please leave, or do you want me to call the police?'

'I'm sorry to have bothered you, Dr Mehta. It's my mistake, totally, to have underestimated your integrity. I'll leave. But before I go, could I show you something, please?'

'It better be something worthwhile.'

'It sure is.' He pulled a white envelope out of the inside pocket of his jacket. Carefully – taking his time so as to irk the doctor – Jay drew out a couple of photographs from the envelope and handed them to Mehta. The doctor looked like a corpse; the blood drained from his face like someone had thwarted the supply. He turned the shade of cheap limestone. Jay noticed a discernible sigh and thought he even heard the doctor's stomach grumble.

'Where—?'

'Where did I get these from? Oh, Dr Mehta, I have sources. A middle-aged, respectable married man like you, with grown-up daughters, shouldn't be jazzing around with a girl your daughter's age. Truth is such a bastard. It always gets out at the most inappropriate time and place, without any warning. I would be devastated to send these to your wife. Think about your family, and if your patients – the people who respect you – came to know of this, what implications would it have on your practice?'

'What do you want?'

'Dr Mehta, I believe that our ancestors – the monkeys – had established a fair and simple exchange mechanism when it came to services. They scratched each other's backs. You must have heard the phrase: You scratch my back, and I scratch yours. Simple reciprocity.'

'And how do you intend to scratch my back?'

'First, I won't ask you for yet another favour. Well, not using the same photographs again, at least. Plus, I could arrange for a generous donation – from abroad, of course, which can never be traced back – to your hospital.'

'I guess I don't have a choice.'

'Not anymore. You made your choice when you agreed to have an extramarital relationship. So, do we have a deal?'

'Wouldn't someone ask why this prominent member of society was admitted into my care in this hospital?' Mehta looked around to convey that this wasn't the hospital where the high and mighty came for treatment. A smile appeared on Jay's face. Mehta's question suggested that his initial aversion to the offer was fading. Anyone with an above-average IQ knows that they have got to, at some point, pay the price for the derby they've lost. The doctor's payback time had come.

'Because, by the time this case comes to court, you, Dr Mehta, will be a big name. Your hospital will have been inaugurated and endorsed by powerful people.'

'How?'

'I bury such bodies every day. Leave the behind-the-scenes arrangements to yours truly. Don't worry.'

Dr Mehta looked crestfallen; he simply nodded. Just in case Dr Mehta didn't agree to Jay's proposal, he had an appointment with another equally unknown doctor, but he was confident Mehta would relent when his testes were put in a nutcracker. It was naive to argue with reality. Mehta's family and his practice would all be in jeopardy if these pictures of him straying were exposed.

'Someone from my office shall contact you with details of how, what and when, Dr Mehta. All I need is half a day of your time to testify in court when the time comes.'

The doctor nodded again. Trepidation showed in his eyes; he was reluctant but pragmatic. He couldn't picture a way out. What a fool he had been for pure carnal pleasure. His impiety had brought him to this. Jay got up, straightened and buttoned up his jacket and stretched out his hand. A startled Mehta offered his limp hand.

'Could I drop you somewhere? I'll be discreet,' Jay added earnestly.

'No, thanks.'

'Have a good day, Dr Mehta, whatever is left of it.'

Jay Singh was out of his room before Mehta could blink. He was gone, and he didn't leave any details behind.

♝

'We never came here,' Jay carefully articulated to Bhīma. It wasn't so much a directive for him, as an aside for the number-crunching bookkeepers that kept the taxman at bay. Unlike Grisham's novels set in the US, Jay didn't bill hours; he was retained for defence cases. Most defence advocates in India are put on a comprehensive retainer. In any event, you only came to Jay Singh if you had incredibly deep pockets and when you were book-ended by law enforcement. Politely put: when you were knee-deep in shit. The guilty – or the not-so-innocent – clients didn't challenge his exorbitant fee. Jay was paid for every waking minute of his time: his fuel, travel, meals, security and an unquestionable and generous expense account and whatnot by the clients that he signed up to represent.

'Where, hukum?'

Jay knew Bhīma would make something up if quizzed by accountants.

'Attaboy! It's been a long day. Let's go home now.'

'Jee, hukum.' Bhīma put the long-wheelbase A8 into drive.

Jay reclined into the comfort of the fawn leather in the rear cabin of the car, thinking about the case at hand as the vehicle negotiated this repulsive semi-urban part of Gurgaon. He knew that all courtroom trials followed the same routine. A good criminal defence advocate – the autodidactic Jay Singh reiterated to himself from time to time – needed to have a credible story and must know the art of telling it skilfully. The practised art of storytelling dictated that a proficient advocate discoursed a major part of the plot, allowing his client and witnesses to speak less. There was, of course, a very narrow latitude here, a fine line across which it could be deemed as leading the client and/or witnesses, and a good storyteller recognized exactly where it was and never crossed it – precisely, where the opponent could cry 'objection'. Jay was well versed in that. The prosecution and defence would present their respective narratives, using the same characters – not one less, not one more – and since there were no juries in India, the judge had the unconditional power to discard one account and accept the other. But here lay the catch:

It was almost a prerequisite that the preparation of the story began much earlier.

Jay had just started laying the groundwork. With an alibi from a soon-to-be highly reputable doctor, detailing the whereabouts of the accused on the night of the said incident, the prosecution wouldn't be left with much premise. No judge in any courthouse could argue with that. End of story. O. J. Simpson's case in the US was a lesson to everyone across the world – and maybe even on Mars, if the aliens were clued in – that there is a big difference between being *innocent* and being *not guilty*. That difference, in legal parlance, is called evidence. Not being guilty sets you free; the world can only point fingers.

The only golden rule a good defence advocate follows is that there is no rule. That accepted, everything is possible. Right, wrong, true, false were good for textbooks. The tyros believe in those principles, the naive philosophize about them, the religious get their consciences involved. Not Jay Singh; in fact, he found it intolerably difficult to comprehend the senseless morality bug. He believed that honesty was overrated and that the whole morality thing was hyped; he hadn't started out with that belief, but you couldn't argue with him on that. Not now. He bent witnesses, bought out the prosecution's testifiers to turn them hostile, blackmailed people into providing alibis. And was it finagling if the witnesses declined to come forth? Although it could never be proved, the word in some circles was that some of the mafia guys were paid protection money – *hafta* – by Jay Singh. He kept some VIPs on his side too, by being a bagman for them and thus, he was wired into the legal, political, medical and underworld communities, all while enjoying a kind of immunity. Nevertheless, he knew there was always danger lurking in the margins.

Jay hadn't always been like this. But the Devil is a bullish buyer and a fierce negotiator. How much you sell your soul for the first time depends on – and only on – how hungry you are. Jay Singh sold his soul for the proverbial song years ago, when he was starving.

Excused?

But once he traded it, he repeatedly peddled it like an aging hooker who craved to cash in as much as she could before her expiry date. If there indeed was a heaven, Jay Singh didn't aspire to witness it. He looked out of the window as the car crossed over to the newer face of the city. Droves of cars – moving slow like a cortège of snails – were almost parked in traffic in the city that provided no parking space otherwise. The irony made him smile. Gurgaon was a rabbit warren now. The veneer of civilization barely covered the piqued passions of the people honking a variety of horns from all sorts of automobiles. Somehow the bright brains responsible for the city's planning thought that the solution to all traffic problems was to build a flyover. No other way was even considered to ease the traffic. No bylanes, no channelling traffic, nothing. The city had nastily spread far beyond everyone's expectations, but the sameness of the malls, the concrete high-rises, the ostentatious display of wealth was now beyond vulgar. As they say, whenever prosaic life has threatened, man has gone to the moon or Mars or built yet another dick-compensating tower. The once small village – *Guru Dronacharya's Gaon,* hence the portmanteau '*Guru-Gaon*' – was now a sprawling and uncontainable city. Just then, the car ascended onto yet another flyover. Jay neither liked the grim nor the glitzy side of the city.

He got down when Bhīma passed the security gates and stopped by the front porch of his farmhouse in Chhatarpur. Security being paramount, Jay had decided to buy this place over any apartment or bungalow in New Delhi. A swimming pool and tennis court filled the large space between the main gate and the actual house, unlike the quintessential Delhi properties which, despite being exorbitantly priced, had very big houses packed into very small plots, with balconies sometimes jutting out over the main boundary wall.

Jay looked up to the heavens. The night sky was scattered with cumulus clouds, like faint white cotton wool floating across. Nothing major, they weren't rain clouds. The white bubbles looked more like a painter's afterthought: it might have been all inky blue; white was only to add another colour. Another irony, he smiled, knowing white was technically not a colour.

Sheeba, the faithful German Shepherd, came running to greet her master; her big bushy tail took it upon itself to shame a small windmill. Jay bent down to caress his best friend. Satisfied after a few strokes under her chin, Sheeba's enthusiasm waned; the tail moving listlessly, she lay on the floor with her eyes open, seeking belly rubs.

The Pharaonic house had a living area only on the ground floor, 4,000-square feet of open space with just four floor-to-ceiling red-brick pillars breaking the expanse of the room. No walls. The main door opened into this area and not a separate foyer. To the right of the entrance was the formal sitting room – a proper *drawing* room – that had black leather sofas, a coffee table and some Persian rugs. Champlevé lamps adorned the console table behind the three-seater sofa, red silk jacquard curtains draped the ceiling-high French windows – red, in Jay's mind, wasn't a fashion statement, it was an attitude, a passion for life. People who sported deep colours were, by nature, intense. As such, this expensively ornate part wasn't much visited unless formal guests, or sometimes clients, were being entertained. Despite it having no door or walls to prevent her, Sheeba was aware her fur was not welcome in the area. The left side of the living quarter was the informal entertainment zone with comfy fabric sofas and chairs with ottomans, a television, music system and a well-stocked bar. This area, too, had its set of French windows overlooking the swimming pool, and the sheer organza curtains allowed light to penetrate and permit visibility. The side being east-facing, the morning sun crept into the ground floor here. The back of the room housed a dining table; a door on the left led to the kitchen. A peep into the residence could never reveal the lack of a woman's touch.

The entire house and the surrounding area were covered by ANG 2000, a powerful counter-surveillance device designed to beat all wired microphones inside the walls and floor. The formidable audio-masking system could defeat any eavesdropping devices that banked on acoustic leakage. And before you think this was the only place protected, his car and office were equally well-secured too. The hunter who sets traps for others always ensures he guards himself against those very traps.

Jay got up after petting Sheeba for a while and headed straight for the bar. The evening had just begun. The caretaker of his house, a short and frail Nepalese man, Bahadur, must've heard him return. He entered the room with other bar accoutrements – an ice bucket, soda water, thinly sliced cheddar.

'Salaam, sahib.'

Jay smiled. 'Salaam, Bahadur. I'll dine late. Please give Sheeba her food, and you and Bhīma have your dinner whenever you're hungry. Don't wait up for me.'

Sheeba's ears twitched on hearing her name. Bahadur left the sahib in the living room and returned to the kitchen. Jay heard the front door open and, catching Sheeba's newfound excitement, guessed it would be Bhīma. Looking through his vinyls, he landed on *Symphony of Destruction*; some thrash metal was required to let the aggression out. He turned up the amplifier to a deafening level and Megadeth started dispensing the drums as Jay poured four fingers of Chivas into his tumbler.

'You take a mortal man and put him in control … watch him become a God.'

Jay smirked at the lyrics; a reptilian smile crossed his lips as he thought about how he had tilted the game for the prosecution and the plaintiff. They would be ambushed. There was little chance that they could survive the devious trap. Game over, job done. The sight of victory, no matter how small or disingenuously achieved, was always attractive.

2

THE LAW FIRM OF COOPER & SINGH OCCUPIED 20,000 SQUARE feet in Gurgaon's Unitech Cyber Centre. The plaque called out Sam Cooper and Jay Singh as the two partners. They had in their employ salaried advocates, associates, interns, notaries, secretaries and other support staff. No one had ever met Sam Cooper; he didn't operate from the Gurgaon office. He apparently worked in London and handled the firm's UK business. The truth was that Sam did not operate from any office, because he was not a qualified advocate. He was Jay Singh's friend from college, who only graced the advocate's residence infrequently and proffered advice, sometimes even unsolicited. However, having a fictitious consulting advocate and a spurious partner at Cooper & Singh was like gold dust icing on the proverbial cake.

When success had come calling without warning, Jay decided that a Western-sounding name lent more credence to his legal firm. That aside, it was fiscally beneficial too. As the senior partner of the firm, Sam Cooper had to be supposedly conferred with on critical cases, which involved an additional fee to be deposited in foreign currency into an offshore account. If the client wished to avail legitimate channels, they could pay Jay, who would then transfer the money to his partner. Alternatively, the client could pay directly into a numbered account in Switzerland that belonged to Mr Sam Cooper.

No one knew of this con. No one except Jay Singh, and he, too – after having repeated the story numerous times to all and sundry, including the lift operator in the office towers – had almost convinced himself that Sam Cooper was a partner. His partner. Cooper & Singh – now that was an act of genius.

Jay had two seasonal wardrobes. Sartorial elegance. The summer wardrobe featured linen suits in every distinguishable shade, from olive to khaki to white. The winter wardrobe consisted of pure wool suits, from ash to blues; no blacks, as that was the courthouse uniform. His mood dictated his choice of shirt for the day – plain white cotton or printed. A set of his clothes remained in the annexe of his office, and some spare clothes were even kept in the Audi. The court uniform – the black suits – were equally spread over his home, the office and the car.

Jay's head spun when he walked out of the elevator wearing a linen suit; he had wantonly consumed a bottle of Chivas, almost in its entirety, after his successful meeting with Dr Mehta the previous evening. Alcohol, for him, was both a propellant and a companion to his chronic insomnia. Still groggy, he had switched between hot and cold water in the shower to inoculate himself against the hangover, but it didn't seem to have worked much. As he walked past the 'good mornings', he asked his secretary Julie for a strong cup of coffee before pacing into his office and shutting the door behind him.

Julie brought in the coffee. 'Everything okay with you, Jay?'

'Oh yes, just a bit of a headache. I was working late last night. Thanks.'

He knew Julie could tell he was lying. He also knew she wouldn't probe or challenge him. And he was right. Jay took the first sip of the hot brew after Julie left his office and opened his daily folder. It was brimming with news clippings, political updates, judicial shuffles, murders, reports on current cases, dates for court appearances, personal appointments, internal office operations – the list was unending. Snafu, business as usual. He struggled to smile; his body hadn't recovered. He glanced at the plasma screen that hung from the wall on the right, a news bulletin running in the background. Besides the big screen, an iMac, the two phones at his desk and his mobiles, the office conspicuously lacked any display of technology. There was a large ebony desk with green leather inlay, and the walls were covered with mahogany racks filled with legal volumes. Jay held strong, unshakable opinions about most things; he believed that making an office too high-tech gave it an unfriendly touch, like the occupant was ostentatious. After all, the clients who visited him needed greater reassurance from him than his gadgets.

Jay had never experienced ataraxia; the past had hounded him when his career was flagging. The pain never subsided. He had been – for whatever inexplicable reasons – confident that all would be set right once his career took off. Now, even as his career flourished and he immersed himself in work, work and more work – and everything else stood a distant second in importance, including his son – his anxieties returned. Or maybe anxiety was his second nature. With his professional success failing to banish the constant anxiety, even hope had stopped visiting him. Images from the past scared him.

His mother had been accused, and convicted, of killing his father. Her own husband. That ugly truth had reverberated in his conscience for over two decades now. Even the thought of that black day tormented him; its memory had crucified him a million times over. Was there an escape from this? Would he ever be normal? His anxieties rose with the moon, not that they were tidally connected, but because he was usually drinking by himself until late into the night. Irrespective of how much he tried, misery remained loyal to him. Pushing back those awful feelings throughout the day and maintaining the façade of a successful vakil sahib was, well, part of the reason why the nights were so unforgiving.

He had tried to quit alcohol many times, but each time he had fallen through the cracks and gone foraging in the middle of the night, when some nightmare from his fractured past had woken him, shaking and sweating. He always came back to drinking even more excessively after such attempts. Then he stopped. Stopped attempting to quit, that is. A thriving career meant he could afford expensive scotch every night. And, if he required, vodka during the day – after someone had divulged to him that vodka didn't reek, at least not as much as whisky.

Fortunately, there was only one appointment on his schedule that day. No court appearances. It wasn't that he hadn't attended court while inebriated before, but it didn't help being so terribly hungover. Justice Chowdhary of the Delhi High Court had even issued him a warning upon noticing his befuddled state – Jay had pleaded it was from what he had drunk the previous night, but he, of all people, knew he had lied. Justice Chowdhary had put it in writing that he seek professional help and report back. Of course, he had appeared in court under the influence even after that initial warning, though only when it was unavoidable; luckily, he hadn't been caught out. The next time that he was ever caught in a similar state, Jay knew all too well, he could face suspension or even be barred from the bar altogether, depending on the judge and his mood on the day.

Jay understood the risk. He wanted to avoid it, but he knew

his drinking habits had spiralled out of control. His appointment with the therapist was today, yet he wasn't convinced they could say or do anything, unless it was magical, could make him quit alcohol. However, he acknowledged there was no way he could cancel or postpone.

A knock on his office door brought him out of his reverie. Bhīma brought in his bag from the car. For a man his size, Bhīma moved like a feather – swift and soundless: a butterfly in elephant's hide. A few times a week when Jay got intoxicated at home and fell, it was Bhīma who, like a ghost, silently picked him up and deposited him in his bed. Jay appreciated Bhīma's benevolence, but the two never spoke about it: No-ask-no-tell-no-discuss. Bhīma knew the boss had been hurt by something in the past, but he never questioned.

♝

Still recovering from the stupor, disinclined to start on anything, Jay heard the desk phone buzz and answered. It was Julie. Must be a call from a client, he reckoned.

'A Mr Vinay Kumar is on the line.'

'Who?'

'Mr Vinay Kumar – he sounds desperate and wants to speak to you. Only Mr Jay Singh, he says.'

It appeared as if Mr Kumar was in some kind of trouble. People didn't come rushing to a criminal advocate if their wife was in labour or if they won a fucking lottery. It was a professional minus – no one called up a criminal defence advocate in a happy situation, but a client in trouble always paid double.

'Put him through after two minutes.'

Let the desperation get to the brim.

Jay placed the receiver down and gazed at the blinking red

light, indicating a waiting call. He picked up the line only when he was certain that the casualness in his voice would sound natural, unpremeditated. 'Jay Singh here, how may I help you, Mr Kumar?' he asked in an unruffled tone, dropping no hints that he was aware of his fretfulness.

'Hello Mr Singh, I'm Vinay Kumar. You don't know me personally, but you might know my father, G. D. Kumar, an MLA from UP in the nineties. He's retired now.'

He isn't exactly on my speed dial, Jay fancied saying, but instead pursed his lips and closed his eyes, like he was in some meditational trance. It didn't take long for him to comprehend who Vinay Kumar's father was: a corrupt son-of-a-bitch state-minister who had pocketed millions. Sensing the fear and dismay in Vinay Kumar's voice, however, he quickly grasped it was probably good for *his* business.

'Oh yes, I do.' Jay maintained the gentle magnanimity in the tone. 'Very nice guy.'

'I'm in trouble, Mr Singh.'

Don't insult my fucking intelligence, I already gathered as much.

'I kind of guessed that. What kind of trouble?'

'I have been arrested this morning for the murder of my girlfriend.'

'Go on ...'

'Someone shot her point-blank last night. I was picked up by the local police and brought into the police station for questioning. I want to hire you to defend me and get me released. Would you please do that for me?'

'Okay, I get it. Do not, I repeat, do not speak to the police under any circumstances until I get there. What have you told the police so far?'

'Just what I've told you.'

'Have they charged you with anything?'

'They wouldn't tell me, I've been asking. Please come right away, Mr Singh.'

'Which police station are you in?'

'Saket. Please don't worry about the fees; I will pay anything you ask for.'

Oh, you definitely will.

'That's not important at the moment; we can always discuss it later.'

'Thank you, sir. And please don't tell my dad anything at this moment. I'll explain it to him when I see him.'

'Don't worry on that account. I'll be there as soon as I can. And remember, not another word to the police until I arrive.'

'I won't.'

'Good. See you in a bit.'

The phone clicked. What was this lamb worth? Probably millions, and in this situation he would pay with his skin if required. Was he the only heir to his rich and corrupt father? A good thing for billings. Whoever said earning money wasn't simple? Jay pressed the buzzer on his desk and a moment later Julie appeared.

'Send for Bhīma, please. And I am going out for a few hours to see a new client. Only redirect urgent calls to my mobile.'

Julie nodded and left the office as Jay slurped the last dregs of his coffee. It tasted disgusting, but it didn't matter. He was on a high now.

The drive from Gurgaon to Saket is long – whatever the time of the day, the cracked tarmac is never enough for the number of cars in the National Capital Region. The cars drive close to one another, like dogs sniffing each other's backsides. The Saket police station is nestled behind PVR, between the hip J Block market and the not-so-trendy K Block. With India's first Multiplex –

PVR – opening in the late nineties, the J Block transformed into a hangout joint for the young crowd. Then, with the arrival of Citywalk mall, the cafés, designer shops, fancy restaurants and the pretentious art scene drew people from other locations. The crowd had increased manifold and the state of the infrastructure – like that of many other places in Delhi – wasn't able to cope with the growing population. Bhīma knew where he was taking Jay, and he quietly slalomed around the stalled vehicles with dexterity to keep moving in the traffic until they got there. He cut the engine outside the police station.

Stepping into the building was like walking into a time machine. The place looked like it had been last refurbished when the Berlin Wall fell – or more like when the Berlin Wall went up; cheap vinyl pretending to be leather, paint peeling off the walls and the furnishings that were at least a decade past their expiry date. The Station House Officer recognized Jay Singh and smiled.

'Welcome, Mr Singh, welcome,' he said in a friendly tone.

Well-nigh-legendary, Jay knew that his mighty reputation always preceded him. After all, he was a known figure, a near-celebrity, a well-connected vakil sahib, and such courtesy was expected, for the police in Delhi knew too well who they needed to be respectful towards and who they could sink their fangs into.

'Thank you, Inspector,' Jay responded with his signature authority and charm, holding his hand out for a firm handshake. If you're five feet seven, you are considered short and inadvertently develop the Napoleon complex – an inherent defence mechanism to guard yourself from those who are bigger or taller. It isn't something you work towards; it's just a subconscious reflex. Of course, as you grow up you learn to cite examples of great personalities – Gandhi, Alexander – who were short but stood tall. You extravagantly claim you are glad to be short; there are far too many disadvantages of being tall; economy seats in airlines being one of most quoted of all examples. Jay Singh was no different. Building a large personality wasn't an option for him. It was a question of survival for the shorty: in school, to not be bullied; in a large crowd, to be heard; in parties, to shine. And in courtrooms and police stations, too, his personality overcame his physical stature.

Fortunately, for lack of evidence and/or witnesses, Vinay Kumar hadn't been charged for the murder. He was a suspect all right, but the police couldn't retain him. Ergo, no bail was required at this point. Jay signed all the necessary release documents and walked out with Kumar within an hour – by bureaucratic standards, no small achievement that.

Bhīma appeared immediately as he saw the two men come out of the building. Besides other features, Jay's right-hand man had an enviable quality: irrespective of where he was parked, and regardless of the fact that Jay could miss the conspicuous Audi and the even more noticeable man who drove it, Bhīma could always spot his hukum before the latter went looking for him.

'Can you guarantee that you can get me out of this mess?' Kumar asked the moment Bhīma put the car in gear.

'Unfortunately, there are no guarantees in this business. This is not a car repair shop, and we're not replacing a head gasket. If I agree to represent you in court, I sign on to save your head.'

'But I didn't do it.'

'Then you don't need to worry at all. Are you ready to come to my office to talk about it now?'

'I don't want to bog you down with details ...'

'Thanks for being considerate, but I love the details. If you were in my shoes, you'd appreciate details too. So, if you aren't ready now, call my secretary and fix an appointment when you are, Mr Kumar. Where can we drop you?' It was hard to fathom if this guy was still in shock or a complete idiot to think his own defence advocate didn't require every minute detail.

♝

Three hours later, Kumar and Jay sat in the latter's office to discuss the case.

Burly with a curly coiffure, and wearing a white button-down shirt with denims, even a seated Vinay Kumar seemed taller than Jay. That's the first thing the defence advocate noticed. Kumar's eyes were red, which was hardly a surprise since he hadn't slept much the night before, and the stress of being pulled up by the police must have only added to that. The coffee had been served and downed, the chinaware removed from the table and Julie had been instructed to hold back all calls unless there was an emergency. Jay had already received some details of the case from his inside sources at the Saket police station. Kumar's girlfriend, Gina Pinto, had been shot dead between 00:00 and 01:00 hours in the morning. A retiree who lived on a floor above in the building opposite to Gina had made the call to the police around 3 a.m. and reported the death. He had, supposedly, got up in the night for some cold water, walked into his kitchen and, as was his habit, looked out of his kitchen window. The voyeur could peep into Gina's living room and bedroom from his kitchen – and it seemed he got up several times most nights to 'check' if she'd indeed forgotten to pull down the blinds. How perversely convenient. But on this particular night, he had seen her lying in a pool of blood on her living room floor with the lights on.

Kumar, a married man, visited Gina on most evenings and dined with her. Kumar's wife had known about the illicit relationship and complained about it to her father-in-law, but nothing had changed. Kumar didn't bother to alter his ways.

Nothing suggested that his corrupt dad intervened to end the association. The apple, as they say, does not fall very far from the tree: debauched pig, crooked bacon. Rumour had it that Gina was now demanding more of Kumar's time and money, which wasn't good for this rich pervert's image and political ambitions. Thankfully, the news of her death hadn't made it to the afternoon bulletins. At least not yet.

'Care to give me the details now?' Jay started once Kumar looked a bit settled in his chair.

'I didn't kill her.'

'I got that part. What exactly happened?'

'I was with Gina – my girlfriend – last night, like most nights. She had cooked dinner, which we had with a bottle of wine. I left for my place around midnight ...'

'Could you please start from the beginning? Who was Gina Pinto, where did you meet her and how?'

'I met Gina at a party a few years ago ...'

'No ambiguities, please, Mr Kumar. When and at which party?'

'I met her in June 2007, at a common friend's party and we became friends almost immediately.'

Kumar provided details of said party. Some of the information was uncalled for, but Jay decided not to interrupt. He could always comb through the material later and skip the unnecessary bits. When asked about Gina Pinto's next of kin, Kumar informed him that she always insisted that both her parents were long dead, and she had no siblings. Kumar needlessly went on to explain that she had always avoided discussing her past and family. She was from somewhere in Bandra in Mumbai. Jay put in a note to check with the Bandra police station, if required.

'Was she single?' Jay asked after Kumar seemed to have concluded his loquacious yarn.

'Yep.'

'And you?' the advocate asked as he scribbled notes on his yellow legal pad without looking up. Jay was simultaneously making a task list of investigations he'd need carried out before deciding whether he was willing to represent Kumar in court.

'No, but we were just friends to begin with.'

'So you were already married when you met her?'

A nod.

'And how did you come to know her intimately?' Jay looked up to check Kumar's countenance. A bit of love or passion or whatever his face betrayed.

'Friendship turned into liking each other, I mean … I don't have a great relationship with my wife, so there was a natural attraction towards …'

How many women fell for the same ridiculous excuse men gave them – 'I don't get along with my wife'?

'… we occasionally met at random cafés before the companionship graduated to the next level.'

Tryst is the word you're looking for.

'What did Gina do for a living?'

'She was an event manager when I met her, but she quit shortly afterwards. She wasn't working.'

'So it is fair to assume you supported her financially. Correct?'

'Yes.'

'And you visited her regularly?'

'Most evenings.'

Kumar gave a maudlin account of how much he loved Gina. So much so that at one point even Jay wanted to offer him a shoulder to cry on or at least pass him a tissue. But the vakil had experienced all this nonsense first-hand numerous times before: actual murderers who grew mawkish in penitence or to convince others of their innocence. Having said that, this was no yardstick by which to measure someone's guilt.

'Let's start with last evening, shall we? What time did you two have dinner?' Jay intervened the moment Kumar paused to breathe.

'Around nine.'

'What happened between 9 p.m. and midnight?'

'We talked, listened to music, made love …'

'Did you use any protection?'

'How does that affect the case, Mr Singh?'

'Trust me, every detail counts. And please call me Jay. Mr Singh makes it sound like you're talking to my dad,' Jay wisecracked to lighten the mood. Talking about death invariably invites solemnity into the conversation. Talking about murder only raises the bar. Talking about murder to the accused usually takes the gravity to another level. Jay had, with experience, learnt to jest to keep his clients relaxed. When people were stressed, they were also restrained. He wanted Vinay Kumar to talk freely, chirp even.

'No.'

'No what? You won't call me Jay?'

'No, I meant I did not use any protection.'

'So I wouldn't be counted among the highly intelligent to pre-empt that your semen might still have been in her body when the police got to it.'

'Unless—'

'Unless?' Jay's eyebrows rose involuntarily. *Unless?*

'The killer raped her before he murdered her.'

'Now that's an interesting hypothesis. What makes you think the killer might have raped her?'

'What other reason would he have to kill Gina? As far as I know, nothing has been reported missing or stolen.'

'And you believe that the killer came with the intention of robbery or rape or both, and did neither, but shot Gina.'

Kumar nodded.

'Why would anyone do that?'

'Maybe because she woke up or something?'

'Another interesting theory,' Jay remarked.

'Possible, isn't it?'

'Everything is possible in this world. Why do you think the police took you in for questioning?'

'Well, the neighbours knew I frequently visited the place. Some might have even spotted my car outside Gina's flat last night like every other night of the week. Obviously, in the absence of any other suspect, perhaps the police presumed I should be the first one brought in for questioning.'

Jay sat in silence for a few moments, evaluating what he had heard so far. Kumar's expression was a poker tell – he wasn't telling the whole truth. But then again, most of Jay's clients were liars and predators. No one would pay top dollar if they weren't a bit guilty on some account, though not necessarily for the crime they were charged with.

'Did you two have any altercation yesterday?'

'Not at all. In fact, as I told you earlier, she had cooked a meal for me, and we wined and dined before going to bed.'

'Any disagreements or arguments that you two had in the past few weeks?'

Kumar energetically shook his head. *No.*

'Any unreasonable demands made by Gina?'

'What kind of demands?'

'Mr Kumar, you're a married man with kids. Gina was your illegitimate lover who you provided for. In the world we live in, such lovers or partners are termed mistresses. You don't want me to believe that your mistress was happy just being your mistress for the rest of her life, without any assurances of money or some form of legal status?'

'You mean if she ever asked me to divorce my wife and take her in?'

'Yes. Or asked you to pay a large sum of money to convince her that in the event that you, for some reason, lost interest in her, she had ample stash to live her life independently.'

Kumar stayed silent for a while. Jay tried reading his mind. He either felt guilty disclosing the details of conversations he'd had with his now-dead lover or uncomfortable telling it to the lawyer who he'd signed up to defend him. Either way, Jay expected some lies and omission.

'No, she never wanted that.'

'Mr Kumar—'

'Call me Vinay.'

'Vinay, in the face of circumstantial evidence, that is contrary to what I'm hearing from you. I am not yet totally convinced that you're innocent, but there is a strong possibility that one of your political rivals found an opportunity to frame you. In which case, you could well be on the periphery of a trap—'

'Why do you think I am not innocent?' Kumar almost sprung up from his chair.

'Convince me.'

'Uh?'

'Can you convince me you didn't kill Miss Gina Pinto, accidentally or otherwise?'

'God knows I have a clear conscience.'

Jay had seen enough Tartuffe to be wary of trusting someone whose only witness was God. Every accused knew that God wouldn't come down to the witness box. He kept quiet, waiting for Kumar to come up with a better testimony or alibi or a witness or some kind of contrary evidence.

'You think I killed her?' Kumar's tone was guarded now.

'You tell me.'

'What's that supposed to mean?'

'Can you convince me that you didn't kill your mistress?' Jay repeated.

'Why would I kill my own girlfriend?'

'How about money to start with?'

'You think I killed her for money?'

'Maybe, maybe not. You asked me to give you a reason why you would possibly kill your girlfriend, and I gave you one …'

'Wait a minute, do *you* think I did it?'

'The police surely think so.'

'And you?' Kumar asked in almost cracking, timorous voice.

'Doesn't matter what I think, but then again, I'm neither a police officer nor a judge, am I?

'It matters to me.'

'Then convince me. I don't give a rat's ass whether you killed Gina Pinto or not, but before I take you on as a client, I need to know the truth.'

'How does that matter?'

'It matters to me.' Jay smiled as he repeated Kumar's words. 'Look, you asked me to get you out of the police station and I walked you out, so you're free now. You're free to hire another advocate and I'll forget about all this. You don't owe me a penny. Just send me a "Thank-you" card and I'll be fine. Or you can decide to tell me the truth and I will defend you. However, if you decide to stay with me and somehow, at any point, I find out that you have lied to me, I will walk out on you. And if that happens, I can guarantee that there isn't a single advocate in this city who would sign you on. These are my terms.'

Incredulous? Yes. Overconfident? Yes, but that was the truth. If Jay Singh abandoned a murder suspect, who would agree to defend them?

'I trust you, Mr Singh.'

That was quick.

'Do you have any siblings?' Jay continued.

'No.'

'Where is your mother?'

'She passed away six years ago.'

'So it's just your dad and you?'

Nod.

'On an altogether different note, you specifically asked me not to speak to your father regarding this. Have you spoken to him now? Because it will be in the news, surely – someone as high-profile as you – it's hardly a matter of time.'

'I mentioned it to him, but I am planning to go see him directly after this meeting to give him the details. Thing is—' Kumar stopped mid-sentence. There was some hesitation, an iota of indecision.

Jay stopped scribbling and looked up. He could visualize Kumar's mind churning.

'Could I say something off the record?' he asked.

'Depends on what you say. I can tell you if I can keep that off the record only after I hear it.' Jay smiled charmingly.

'My dad wanted me to stop seeing her.'

'Why am I not surprised, Vinay? Given your political aspirations and the fact that you are presently being groomed for the next elections, a mistress would hardly score points for you. But how did you know what your father wanted?'

'He expressed it often. We even had a row every now and then.' Kumar's face had turned grey. 'He advised me to dump her several times. You see, he was old school and hence he was against the fact that she wasn't a Hindu.'

Would a Hindu mistress be legitimate?

'What about your wife? Did she never complain or try to stop you from meeting Gina?'

'What if I told you she didn't care?'

'She didn't care that you were sleeping with another woman?'

'It's not how you put it. Our relationship has been platonic for quite some time.'

After the two children, I suppose.

Jay probed for another hour. He made Kumar go through the previous night once more, up to the time he left Gina's place, to see if Kumar could furnish any more details. Maybe Jay could pick something up – was there anything out of the ordinary about the surroundings when he drove off? Any car parked with someone sitting in it? For someone to have got into Gina's apartment immediately after Kumar's departure, their paths would have crossed. But, Kumar couldn't remember seeing anything unusual.

Suddenly, Jay remembered he had an appointment at 7 p.m. Convinced that he wouldn't get any more information from Kumar at this point, he closed his pad. There wasn't enough comradeship to talk about anything else, so they exchanged a bit of malarkey around the weather and Delhi traffic and the rising cost of living until Kumar's driver called back, after being paged, to confirm that he had brought the car around to pick him up.

'I'm okay for now.' Jay looked up. 'You can leave, but I'll need to speak to your wife, and maybe your father, at some point.'

'Why would you need to speak to them? What about?'

'I need to investigate the case to be able to defend you. It is all in your interest. The police will certainly speak to them before me, so feel free to let them know.'

'Thanks, Jay.'

Vinay Kumar stood up to shake Jay's hand. Jay figured that Kumar was a good six inches taller than him.

Bastard. That was the only thing that disturbed Jay now. *Son of a bitch.*

'Just one more thing before you leave, Vinay,' Jay asked

abruptly when Kumar turned to leave. 'Do you own a licenced firearm by any chance?'

'Yes, I've got a Colt Defender, .45 calibre.'

'I'd like to see the gun when we meet next time. Could you bring it along, please?'

'Of course, but I swear upon my dead mom that I have never fired it … ever.'

Obviously, no murderer would fire from a licenced firearm. Do I look that fucking stupid?

Jay was quiet after Kumar left, assiduously reflecting on what his new client had just told him. He didn't dwell on it for too long. This was only the first meeting. If Kumar had lied, it was to be expected, wasn't it? Jay knew he would push him a bit harder next time. In time he would open up or he'd lose Jay. If Kumar thought Jay wouldn't confirm every minutia of whatever he uttered, he couldn't be any further from the truth. Snitches in the autopsy suite would ring Jay before the investigating police officer relayed the formal report in writing. It was Jay's standard operating procedure before he took the case to court. All advocates, he unashamedly acknowledged, were legal liars. The first thing any half-successful advocate worth his price tag learnt on the job was that truth and *evidenced truth* were two distinct entities. There was no room for questioning that axiom; bizarrely, all advocates he knew agreed on this one. No mumpsimus contradicted it. With that simple truism understood, life was simpler. However, all evidence was malleable witnesses could be influenced or coerced or bribed, experts could misjudge or misinterpret or be rewarded to misunderstand, technology could fail to provide any coherent or convincing evidence, and in the absence of any substantiation, confutation becomes simple. It wasn't within a defending advocate's province to suggest or prove who committed the crime; all he had to do was establish that his client did not do it. Defence advocates used the damned cliché the other way around: *Corrupt* the witnesses or evidence first. If you don't succeed, *confuse* the prosecutor to *convince* the judge that there were far bigger motives and opportunities for others to commit the crime.

But you had to know the truth before twisting it.

Bhīma arrived forthwith without being called.

'We'll leave in thirty minutes or so, Bhīma.'

'Jee, hukum.'

♝

Bhīma knew his new assignment began straightaway after Jay took on a new client. Investigation. There were, undoubtedly, far better investigators Jay could hire, but none he could blindly trust. And his in-house investigator had time in the day and night. Most days, Bhīma twiddled his thumbs in his assigned cabin or surfed the internet, after driving Jay to the office – he didn't mix with other drivers in the office building. He also had time in the evenings after bringing Jay home and depositing him safely in the farmhouse. Moreover, Bhīma could buy local help without Jay getting involved in the mess. Most snitches opened up to him like they would never to the sahib. Jay updated him on Kumar. Bhīma nodded and took the yellow pad Jay had scribbled upon during the whole meeting.

He then retreated to his unlisted (for the sake of security), sizeable office that was two floors below Cooper & Singh's main one. The office was secured with two impregnable EVVA MCS locks. Equipped with advanced software for tracking vehicles, even surveillance cameras sent regular feeds to Bhīma's Mac. The state-of-the-art voice decoders and listening devices that he used for tapping conversations could put the CBI to shame. Besides investigating cases like Kumar's, the placing of bugs also facilitated the accumulation of intelligence on any threats to Jay Singh. Of course, none of the information gathered through bugs would be admissible in any court of law, but at least Jay knew what he was dealing with. All proscribed information, papers, notes and communiqués stayed secured here – digitally backed up on a tier-4 data centre in Mumbai, and put on microfilm, too, to be taken home and deposited in the safe – just in case … He locked up the notes. No one would see them till he extricated what he thought was only for his consumption, then he would pass over the rest to paralegals and other staff who in turn would add ample calories to the file with legitimate investigations, interviews, court dates, etc.

3

THE TIME HAD COME FOR JAY SINGH'S ONLY APPOINTMENT FOR the day – with a therapist at seven in the evening. Isn't it entrapment when a law enforcement officer tricks you into doing something? Well, coming from a judge, this was the mother of all entrapments. Justice Chowdhary had knavishly set him up. A week before, Jay had seen a psychiatrist who determined that his dependence on alcohol was merely psychological and not physical at this stage, but it still required addressing. Ergo, the dipsomaniac advocate was referred to a practising therapist. Jay was pleased that he wasn't prescribed some mind-altering medication. He hated medicines, any drugs actually. Past images scared him – he had been drugged that night – the night of his father's murder. He relied on endorphins to relieve himself of most aches and pains, excluding hangovers, for which he only trusted mild analgesics. His body had long lost the battle with his brain – to be terribly hungover and still function in that state – so even analgesics were only popped as a last resort. He assumed it would be a one-off session with the therapist. *It was best to get it over and done with*, he naively reckoned.

The therapist's receptionist was pretty. Correction. She wasn't just pretty, she was the kind of seriously striking beauty that could be classified as misdemeanour. His trained eye helped him take in whatever he could in the first glance. Twenty-five, maybe twenty-six? Dark, straight, shoulder-length hair, dark brown eyes, barely there make-up, infectious smile, slim body, well-endowed. No trace of any rings, though she could be dating someone. In any event, he was over forty. She wasn't eyeing him as a prospect; she was only being hospitable to him because he was a client. Or thinking of him as a patient; worse still: a mental patient. Standing on the side of the desk, he saw that she wore a black skirt – not too short, the hem just above her knees. Bare legs. In shape. Très chic.

Nice legs.

'Anita will see you in a few minutes, sir,' she politely said.

Great voice too.

'Thanks … err …' He hung on for a wee bit longer, expectantly looking at her until she was discomforted enough to blurt out her name.

'Manavi.'

'Hi Manavi, I am Jay.' Before he could utter anything else, the phone on her desk buzzed.

He could smell her hair, some *L'Oréal* scent. *God, she was well worth it!*

'You can go in now, Mr Jay Singh.'

Is she not getting the hint or is she avoiding me?

Before fixing up the appointment with Anita, Jay had done some digging on her. She saw far less patients in a year than her competitors, but her reputation was unparalleled. She believed in curative therapy, and her record was a near hundred per cent in mitigating, if not remedying, mild psychotic disorders. Some of her interviews and press articles summarized her robust belief of how most disorders were rooted deep in the past, inadvertently entrenched in the personality. To get to the past, as unashamedly outlined in one of her interviews, she used various techniques: from interviewing the clients, their close friends and family members to gathering information on them from a multitude of sources, all to help the client. That had bothered Jay for a long time: *what all will she ask me? And what all will she dig up?*

But he was here now.

Anita was much younger than Jay had expected or imagined. *She must be in her early thirties*, he guessed. She had quick eyes, trained to discern more than a normal person, possibly even more than he could at first glance. Skilled and thorough, add to it a comely face – and that made her smart and sexually attractive. And in shape.

Wow! Everyone here was so young and fit.

'Welcome, Mr Singh.' She got up from her desk and walked towards him to shake hands.

'Jay.'

'Nice to see you.'

Jay didn't respond. It would be a blatant lie to say that he was happy to be here or to see her. Unsurprisingly, Jay wasn't amused. Psychiatry – wasn't it the branch of medical science that dealt with mental disorders? It's different when you realize that a part of the body needs attention, but when that part happens to be your brain it implies *you* need attention. Ironically, despite all the love songs written about the heart, it is the brain that guides humans. To say Jay wasn't happy would be an understatement. He had decided to make it difficult for the flipping shrink; he'd be sarcastic, he'd be evasive, he'd be annoying. Maybe, she'd just pack him off with a clean chit. A few niceties about the weather, and Anita called Manavi to bring in two coffees.

'So, Jay,' she began, once the coffees had arrived and they both settled in; he on the sofa and she on the armchair next to him, notebook in hand. 'What happened?'

'Nothing *happened.*'

'Nothing?'

'What part of 'nothing' is hard to follow, Doctor? Let's get this over and done with, please.'

'So you aren't interested in curative therapy, you simply want to pay and get away?'

'Oh please, I'm in no mood for lectures.'

'What do you do, Jay?' she segued into banal stuff. Perhaps she gathered she'd taken the wrong approach with him. With the appointment scheduled by the court, she would have already known about Jay's near-inebriated state that day in court, and that he shouldn't have lied to the judge. If she expected him to accept that, she had grossly underestimated the challenge. Her doing. Jay couldn't care any more than a butcher cares for the lamb.

'I am a defence advocate.'

'Do you like what you do?'

'Now, what kind of question is that? I am an advocate, a criminal defence advocate. I love what I do, this is my calling, and it is the very quintessence of my being. I don't care if the world sees this as my greed to make money, but this isn't just another job for me. I defend the innocents.'

'Who decides who is innocent?'

'The judge, of course. I merely present the facts.'

'You support capital punishment then?'

'What's not to support? You kill, you pay.'

'Don't you think life is sacred, that humans have no right to decide who lives and who dies irrespective of whether you're on the right side of the law or otherwise. I'm sure you know capital punishment is banned in Europe.'

'So people can kill and live happily ever after?' Jay made a face.

'I didn't say they should not be penalized or corrected. Only God has the right to decide about life and death ...'

'Who?'

'God.'

'I heard that. God who?'

'You need a smoke?'

'Do I get to see God if I smoke?'

'I asked because you looked annoyed.'

'Is smoking a doctor's prescription to calm people then?'

She didn't say anything, just beheld him.

'For the record, I do not smoke.' He was civil again.

'I think we should come to the point, Jay. You have been referred to me by a doctor, a psychiatrist, no less. All I'm trying to do here is figure out a way to help you.'

'I have no problems or issues as you might think. I was poor once, but poverty does not qualify as illness.' He could fathom that the sarcasm in his voice wasn't wasted on her. 'However, I get a feeling that this discussion doesn't seem to be getting anywhere.'

'How can you know that before getting there, and' – she raised her palm to gesture him to stay silent as his lips twitched to speak – 'if you keep cutting me off mid-sentence every time, this conversation isn't really going anywhere, just as you said.'

Silence.

'Your silence wouldn't help, Mr Singh.'

'I thought this was the Republic of India and we all had a right to freedom of speech or silence.'

'Try telling that to Justice Chowdhary, and that is not a threat.'

'Warning?'

'You're smart.'

'Smarter than I look?'

'Certainly, Mr Singh.'

'Thanks. Please call me Jay.' He let out a wry smile.

'There is no such thing as being a bit pregnant. You either take the entire treatment or you don't, Jay.' Anita flashed a disarming smile.

'And if I don't take your advice, you report it to my doctor and he reports it to the judge?'

'You've captured the right sequence, that is how the news will travel. As I said, you have sound logic.'

'Thanks, again. Could we skip the foreplay please?'

'You in a rush?'

'No, not in the mood.'

'Okay, so let me start again, and this time without the meandering questions. You have been referred to me because of your problem with alcohol. Correct?'

Jay nodded in acceptance.

'When did you start drinking?'

'A long time ago, way back in college.'

'How much do you drink?'

'Half a litre, sometimes more.'

'In a day?' Anita appeared surprised. Or feigned it brilliantly, Jay couldn't gauge.

'More like in the night.'

She scribbled something on her pad. He still insisted that the judge had caught him when he was nursing a hangover, that he hadn't appeared tanked-up in the courthouse. Jay slowed down at times to ensure she comprehended his perspective on the incident. From his background read on her, he knew she could, and would, get under his skin without being too apparent. She would – without letting him be aware – 'analyse each word' he spoke and then 'scrutinize the symptoms and demythologize' – whatever that meant – 'the angst and the accompanying fears and anxiety'. Only God knew how because he wouldn't be forthcoming with information about himself to a shrink. Thank you very much. He would respond to her questions with as little detail as he could possibly get away with, but he wouldn't reveal his inner self. As an advocate, he had enough experience in questioning clients and witnesses to discern that there were no innocent questions, and that, he reasoned, would made Anita's task trickier anyway; he needn't be rude or sarcastic.

After a few more questions, it felt to him like she was asking inane, hackneyed questions mainly for fiscal interests. Keep him talking, spend the time and bill him by the hour. Finally, Anita got up from the armchair and walked back to her desk and sat behind it.

'If you want me to treat you, Jay, you have to trust me,'

'I trust your words, not so sure about accepting the point that you are judging me though.'

Remember, no sarcasm, no impoliteness. This was bordering on rudeness.

'Your misjudgement regarding my judgement of you might get revised after a few sessions.'

'Few sessions? You mean I need to come here again? Why?'

Anita simply nodded, saying nothing.

'Why do I need to come again?'

'For another session?'

'But why?' Jay was annoyed.

'I absorb what you tell me now, I process it after you're gone from here.'

Jay sat mutely for a minute, taking in what Anita had just stated. She was being factual. *Didn't he do the same with his clients – reflect on what they said in their absence? She was no different. Why wasn't he forthcoming? Why was he being an ass when all she was endeavouring to do was help* him*?*

'I took some wrong decisions in my life when I was down—' he started but halted, looking at her for some sort of acknowledgement.

'Jay, there isn't a creature I've met yet that, at some point in life, does not think that she or he made a wrong decision at some crucial juncture in life. And what if, of the choices presented, they had taken the road they did not take? It's life, not mathematics, and there isn't just one way of reacting to situations. The good news is that there's always a way out of the wrong path taken, *if* that indeed was the mistaken path.'

Resplendent reassurance.

'You know, sometimes I wish I did not have a good memory. Then I could have forgotten it all.'

'Sometimes not forgetting something could be a good thing.'

'That's an interesting viewpoint. How, if I may ask?'

'Because memories need to surface before they can be exorcized. It's the latent ones that do more harm.'

'You sound like you're reading from a textbook.' Jay beamed.

'Believe me, I've seen more cases than the number of books I've read.' Her attractive smile reappeared, and Jay believed her. Maybe, just maybe, that was a tactic she used to beguile hostile clients like him. She looked sharp, which, in her case, was an honest reflection of her mental capability. She was elegant, not flamboyant or superficial. After being a tenacious ass for quite some time, Jay was beginning to realize that it was all for his benefit. He stared at his shoes for a long time, as if there was some absorbing piece of abstract modern art painted on them. The silence was totally non-buoyant; they both sank into it for a whole minute.

Then Jay began:

'I might sound pathetic, but I've had two lives; one before my father's death ... err ... murder, and one after it. And it wasn't about the money, it wasn't that I became the proverbial pauper overnight after being a prince, but it's the hurt … the feeling ... I've become vulnerable to, well, almost everything …'

Jay went on to give a detailed account of his father's murder, his mother's conviction and her subsequent cognitive decline. She had been in a mental asylum in Jaipur for over two decades now. All that, according to him, had coalesced to make him what he had become: an alcoholic. Not that he shifted the blame, but he narrated his perspective.

Anita listened to him without interrupting. Somehow, his initial fears of being probed by her had dispersed; he could see himself divulging more in further sessions if she could indeed get him off the alcohol wagon. He could perceive the happiness in her countenance, seeming pleased that he was opening and confiding in her.

'You know, I could never face the world after that night. Shame is one of the hardest emotions to come to terms with and to accept. It's noisome, it's revolting and it's ridden with guilt, despite the fact that *I* did nothing wrong. I somehow feel I, too, am guilty, as I was there, like maybe I could have stopped it from happening.'

Memories are like 5.1 surround sound – when switched on, they come in from all directions. The phantasmagoria ran through Jay's head like faded Polaroid shots. Jay tried to pluck out some pleasant memories but failed; only the ugly ones flooded back. Nevertheless, he kept talking.

'Thanks for the session, Jay. From what I can assess at this moment, I don't think there's anything sequelae – by that I mean there's no pathological abnormality, it's just that given the circumstances, you reacted a bit negatively, a bit harshly on yourself. But as I mentioned earlier, we'll need a few sessions to establish that and maybe further sessions to reverse it. Would you like to have another coffee?'

'Thanks. Why not?'

Coffee meant Manavi coming into the room. Anita hit the buzzer And Manavi entered.

Was she for real? To quote the rocker Prince, 'she was the reason why God made a girl'. He tousled his hair like a teenager, admiring her.

Anita requested coffees and observed Jay watching Manavi with excessive interest.

'Any woman in your life?' she asked after Manavi left.

'No.'

'No family, then?'

'I have a son.'

'You have a son?'

Nod.

'But you aren't married.'

'Since when has being married been a prerequisite to have a child?'

'So you have a son out of wedlock?'

'Out of humanity.'

'Does he live with you?'

'No. He's in a hostel.'

'Do you not want to talk about him?'

'Not at the moment, unless it's absolutely necessary.'

'We can always discuss him later, no worries. Any close friends?'

'Not many.'

'What do you do on weekends, Jay?'

'What do I need weekends for?'

'Rest, for one.'

'I rest every night.'

'Recreation?'

'I party most evenings.'

'With whom?'

'Are you applying for my social secretary position?' Now confident that his humour would not be taken otherwise, he started bantering. 'I can party on my own.'

'You mean drink.' She smiled.

'And music.'

'No friends come over?'

'Cooper does, sometimes.'

'Cooper is also your business partner, right?'

Nod.

'That means you're with a work colleague, doesn't it?'

'We never talk business at home.'

'Anyone else you meet socially?'

'I have another close friend, Akbar Ali. I go to his place every now and then, say once a week at least if not more.'

'Do you three not get together?'

'Never.'

'Why?'

'Akbar won't come to my place and Cooper won't go to his.'

'Quite a strange set-up, don't you think? Two of your closest friends don't want to meet each other.' She jotted something down on her pad. 'Why wouldn't Akbar come to your place?'

'He hates wealth, ostentation. Finds it vulgar and says it's against his conscience, blah, blah …'

'And why wouldn't Cooper meet you at Akbar's place?'

'He's too posh to go to Akbar's shabby hut. Now if you think both these guys also need therapy, I can bring them here and you can connect the dots.'

'Why don't you connect the dots for me, Jay, so that I can analyse?'

'What would be left to analyse after that?'

'I shall analyse the pattern of the line you draw to connect the dots. There can be several ways one could connect two dots, right?

'I follow,' Jay said, but it had never occurred to him before this point that it was odd that the three of them hardly ever got together. As a rule, the privileged and the unfortunates didn't intermingle, but with him in between, there was no reason why Sam Cooper and Akbar Ali couldn't get together. He was already connecting the dots, it seemed.

'See, these sessions could be fun and meaningful. You are virtually practising like you were in a courtroom, Jay. I'm sure you will be more at ease in future sessions.'

Coffees over, Anita, in the true manner of a therapist, prescribed a regimen: sessions twice weekly for three weeks, then as and when required. 'Please book your time with Manavi on the way out, Jay. Thanks for coming in today.'

'Thank you, Anita.'

Out at the reception, Jay blushed – for reasons he couldn't fathom. *Childish*? – as he approached Manavi. He was old enough to be her father. Well, not literally, unless he procreated in his early teens, but still. Didn't someone say that the generation gap was getting shorter? There was surely a generation gap between Manavi and him. He saw her looking at him and his heart – he thought – skipped more than one beat.

Old mug, she must think.

He gathered himself and, like a true gentleman, booked his next appointment, thanked her and exited the office without looking back.

4

SOMEHOW, THE MEETING WITH ANITA LEFT JAY FEELING AGITATED. Even though he had expected the therapist to get under his skin to scratch his unpleasant past, it nevertheless left him in a foul mood. The vile past he had kept buried had now been revealed to a total stranger. And the stranger being a professionally trained therapist would probe it in bits and bytes. Would she be able to help him after knowing all that he had told her today? Up until now, he had shared his past with just two of his closest friends. And he thought he'd better visit one of them now.

'Take me to Akbar's place, Bhīma, and stop at a liquor store on the way. We'll pick up a bottle of Chivas,' he instructed.

'Jee, hukum.'

'You can drop me and go back. I'll call a cab.'

'I'll wait for you, hukum.'

Jay appreciated that Bhīma wouldn't sleep till his hukum got home. He was dedicated to Jay's security and he would not budge.

'Okay, why don't you go home, have dinner and come back after midnight?'

The compromise was acceptable.

Jay Singh was once upon a time Jpeg Singh. Jayakumar Prankumar Girjashankar Singh. Jayakumar was the name they gave him at birth. Prankumar was his father's name, and Girjashankar, his grandfather's. In keeping with convention, his family name, Singh, was also added. After being ridiculed in school for his unusually protracted name, he introduced himself as JPG when he went to college. In the late eighties, what with the Internet and the standardization of the picture format, a cooller alias was used: JPEG. Jpeg Singh became a man of a thousand words when he went to study law at Delhi University. By the time he finished his law degree, Jpeg had spent his entire inheritance on his education.

The *coolness* evaporated once the law degree was earned and he struggled to find employment in any half-decent law firm. For more than a decade, his daily regime comprised cycling to the Tis Hazari Court where he had – like many other qualified advocates looking for daily work to subsist – set up a table under the shade of a banyan tree. He was one among the dozens of qualified advocates, trapped in the vocation of notaries, who sat verifying worthless documents, writing pointless appeals, certifying uncountable power of attorneys. Nobody did this dogsbody work willingly, not the least after being through the grind of legal college. But hey, whoever said life was fair should have his degree in writing bumper stickers revoked with immediate effect. Padlocked metal trunks containing important papers were piled along the desk-lined avenue, come wind, rain or floods. Talk about security and confidentiality. Across from the advocates, more tables were put up where rusted typewriters played Mozart all day long; they still used – and reused – the antediluvian carbon papers until they could transmit only inky smudges on the copy. A little way from these legal eagles, someone had set up an illegal stall on wheels to serve tea and refreshments to the hard-at-work advocates. On credit, in lieu of credit cards. Given the financial status of the tea stall's clients, the owner was paid on a monthly basis by the strugglers.

Though Jpeg Singh religiously sat throughout the day in the humid and sudorific Delhi heat – under a lean-to tent tied to a five-hundred-year-old tree's thick branch – some days didn't afford a single paying client, which left him to survive on water. In short, he was living a life he had never imagined, much less aspired to, his dreams vanishing quicker than fizz on a fountain. He despised his failure, but there seemed no way out of the living hell he was in – utterly and completely screwed by life.

Having suffered a traumatic childhood, for many years, he frequently withdrew into his shell, avoided company and even underwent therapy. But as money became scarce, so did the psychological treatments. Everything seemed fine when he was on a high; a moment of down and he became despondent and the depression returned.

All rookies in all professions have a fallow period, but a decade could break anyone. Jpeg drowned in alcohol. Every penny he earned went towards buying cheap alcohol, local rotgut on days he couldn't buy whisky, and bought food only if he had any money left. He had no friends and his peers – fellow advocates sitting under the trees – were not the people he wanted to socialize with. Despite bearing a striking resemblance to one of the Khans of Bollywood – he had no woman in his life. No woman wanted to date or walk down the aisle with an indigent lawyer with no future. Arranged marriage, though big in India, required parents or relatives fixing alliances. Being an orphan and that too with a tainted family background, all relatives eschewed meeting him, let alone finding him a wife.

And Jpeg was getting on the wrong side of thirty. The good looks were fast fading. He hadn't the time, money or inclination to take care of himself. When food was difficult to come by, how could anyone upkeep charm?

Life was tough. God was looking elsewhere. For years, Jpeg Singh thought life would take a turn, some fucking turn, but the bitch didn't move. It whipsawed him from all sides. Then one day the boat came in. Jpeg finally found a ticket. A deplorable one, but a ticket nevertheless.

The case that made Jpeg Singh was the rape of a poor woman by one Dickey Yadav, an affluent VIP's son. He was also the nephew of a Member of Parliament and had caused an unwanted pregnancy.

Apparently, uncontrolled avarice and debauchery had spoilt the twenty-two-year-old Dickey rotten; he had been molesting the servant girl, Sheila – a year younger to him – for over five years. A maidservant in the house was another object, merely a toy he could play with. What could Sheila do? Fight him – the powerful family's only male child? The poor girl had endured the pain for years. Having illegally emigrated from Bangladesh, the little money she saved from her meagre earnings doing domestic chores at the Yadav residence, she sent back to her ailing mother. And the obdurate Chhota sahib had carried on with his exploit. However, when she became pregnant, the truth was exposed. Clearly, the Yadav family wanted no part in the maidservant's or the illegitimate child's affairs, and they threw the six-month pregnant Sheila out on the streets. Dickey was asked to prepare for exams to go for further education to the US. Leave this place, leave this country. Get away.

The expectant mother – with no food, money or shelter and despite death threats from the Yadav clan – obstinate enough not to let go, came to the assemblage of advocates sitting under the trees at Tis Hazari Courts. Most advocates there had never prosecuted a criminal case and they weren't going to start now – when the defendant's family would bring in the best defence money could buy. Besides, none wanted to face the wrath of 'muscle'. Jpeg Singh took the case out of compassion. Pro bono, of course.

Yadav's defence unashamedly claimed consensual sex. The girl enticed the rich boy, encouraged him by making advances. She had engaged in sex with Dickey for years, with a predetermined intention to become pregnant so she could extort money from the respectful family by becoming a part of it. Dickey, in a weak moment, lost control. Plausible. The family were willing to pay for the mother and child to return to Bangladesh and provide for their upkeep. What more could anyone ask for?

Jpeg Singh attacked on another level. The criminal law in India, under Article 375 of the Indian Penal Code, defined any sexual relations with girls below sixteen years of age as statutory rape, notwithstanding the fact that the girl may have agreed to engage in the sexual activity. As Dickey was a few months older than Sheila, there was a three-month window – the slapdash defence advocate had left himself exposed by stating the couple had engaged in sexual intercourse for over five years – where the accused was over sixteen and the plaintiff was a minor. That settled it. The rest was easy. The opulence and influence of the accused were enough to convince the judge of his misdemeanour.

Winning the case didn't bring money, but it unlocked doors. Jpeg Singh became *Perry Mason,* and the hero couldn't turn back when another case, just as challenging, showed up. Winning the second case against another influential family placed him on *terra firma*.

If you win cases that everyone else believes you'll lose, you get recognized. The politicians and those in power have little interest in punishing the guilty; their prime interest is to be seen as sympathizing with the victims and to be perceived as doing the necessary to apprehend the guilty. In other words, earning their brownie points for the next elections. One of the ministers applauded Jpeg Singh on national television. Jpeg, who wasn't even on the fringe a few months previously, suddenly became the torque. Funny how an outcast becomes a king. Everything had coalesced to work for him. The sardine had morphed into a shark, and the shark hocked its soul to the devil willingly, which is a usual ramification when winning, and winning alone became your life's guiding value.

The second case bequeathed him a six-foot-eleven-inch teratoid of a man – Bhīma, an ex-Army guy – whose cousin sister's murder case Jpeg Singh had taken on and won. With each defence case that Jpeg Singh triumphed, the need for Bhīma to be by his side snowballed. The threats were no longer innocuous; their credibility went up and – after an unsuccessful shot at his car – he had unsurprisingly applied for a licenced firearm.

Bhīma had a past. He wasn't just another ex-army personnel; he had been hit in the leg at Kargil and was hence attached to an army surveillance group that used technology for intelligence gathering. He loved the whole spying business and mastered it. Working for Jpeg, he had wired more people than Reliance Telecom and Airtel put together in the NCR.

Jpeg had been in the trenches, knew the roots and had been an elite advocate long enough now. Having seen both sides from close quarters, no one could read the terrain like him. With Bhīma by his side and friends on every possible side of the fence, he was arsenic, or he was the elixir, depending on which side you were.

The two publicized cases brought fame. Fame started bringing in defence cases. Defence cases meant more money. Money brought its typical indulgences: Scotch replaced rotgut, Audi replaced the rusted bicycle and the farmhouse replaced the shanty. Good-looking he was, but what with the fashion and beauty therapists, vanity too became an overriding quality.

He didn't know what was more elite or acceptable: him or his American Express.

He'd had to fight and stick his neck out for everything that most other advocates took for granted after completing their degrees. But the days of destitution seemed to be over. Things changed. Those guilty or accused wanted Jpeg defending them. Once a penniless lawyer under a tree, he now operated a law practice with numerous people working for him. When he was a nobody, the name wasn't important, but Jpeg now sounded a bit juvenile; Jay Singh suited him better. However, the two cases he had won prosecuting pro bono had left him with legacies.

Sheila, the Bangladeshi girl, died shortly after giving birth to a boy leaving her son in Jay Singh's guardianship – after all, in this uncaring, apathetic world, he was the only good soul she had known towards the end of her short life. Jay legally adopted Yuvraj.

Jay had met Akbar Ali during those impecunious days when both of them sat under the same banyan tree, practising law. Despite Jay's success and his insistence that Ali join the flourishing Cooper & Singh to make it Ali, Cooper & Singh, the latter had declined the offer umpteen times citing issues of morality, conflict of interest and all that crap. Ali believed that money earned by defending those accused would bring material comforts at the cost of mental peace, which his ethics didn't permit. He was in his late forties, but looked a decade older. Being unkempt, malnourished and living on cheap alcohol had taken its toll. He was the only person, besides Cooper, with whom Jay had shared his past and all his secrets. Though both Ali and Cooper had known about the existence of the other, neither had made any attempt to meet, perhaps because of the cosmic differences in their outlook towards life. The reason of everlasting friendship with Ali was simple: he didn't judge Jay's self-destructive lifestyle, didn't ask questions; just accepted him as he was. Neither man questioned the other's warped logic of illogical principles or their lack thereof.

'What a surprise. How nice to see you, Jay. You should have let me know. I'd have got some good Scotch.'

'I already have it here.' Jay flashed the bottle of Chivas.

'You're always a step ahead, my friend, always a step ahead. Water or ice?'

'Ice, please.'

Ali lived in a dilapidated one-room *kholi*, rented out to him by a family who owned the shanty; he had limited material inventory but it included a refrigerator. He pulled out a decrepit ice tray and brought two glasses.

'Does this mean you will stop drinking soon?' he asked, after Jay told him about seeing a therapist earlier in the evening.

Jay didn't respond. He simply smiled and raised his glass in celebration. 'Cheers.'

'Cheers. You look disturbed, Jay. Are you okay?'

'Who is?' After recounting the past to Anita, the gloom was still fresh in his mind.

Ali let out an audible chuckle. 'I am. Contented, at least, if not utterly happy. Happiness isn't about looking back, Jay; I've explained this to you a million times. Bury the past, the more you dwell on it, the more it will hurt, but you don't ever listen to me, do you? Whatever happened is done with; you have no control over it, but you constantly allow your mind to ruminate over hopeless things and hurt yourself in the bargain. What's the point?'

'I understand what you're saying, Akbar. It's just that sometimes I have no control over my own feelings. I keep going back to recreate the moment to see if I can spot something I missed back then.'

'You won't.'

'Why?'

'Because you are going around in circles and going around in circles never got anyone out of them. So, unless you have a new piece of info or some fresh evidence, it is a futile exercise and you as an advocate should know that.'

'So where do I get more information?'

'Forget it. They say even a few hours' delay in starting a murder investigation is late. Twenty plus years late? Not a fucking chance. What new evidence can you find now?'

Ali's words resonated in the quiet of the room. He wasn't wrong one bit.

'What else is news in your world, Jay?' Akbar could see Jay internalizing his statement and supplanted the glum rhetoric with pointless chitchat.

'What if I tell you I met a girl?'

'Wait … hold that thought for a sec. Let me make another drink before you start.'

'It's nothing like what—'

'Shhh … shut up.'

Even in the world where Jay was now king, some old friends had the right to shut him up. Ali poured the drinks, rummaged in his rundown refrigerator for some shards of ice and brought the tumblers back.

'Now tell me everything from the beginning!'

'Like I was saying, there's nothing much to tell.'

'Then why did you say you met this girl, whoever she is. Come on, out with it now.'

'Well, she's the receptionist of this therapist I saw in the evening.'

'Name?'

'Manavi.'

'Age?'

'Late-twenties, maybe.'

'Hottie?'

'What is this, some kind of Mossad interrogation?'

'Poverty is a wretched thing, Jay. Not because you can't buy a new car or a new gadget – no, I don't mean that. I hate poverty because it robs people of the basic human emotions too. You and I lost out on more than the material belongings. We leapfrogged our youths in those struggling years. Even love didn't happen. It couldn't. We neither had the time nor the money – who would have fallen for us or reciprocated if we had shown interest?'

'So you mean—?'

'Yes, so regardless of my age, I am as curious as I would have been if my friend had told me this twenty years ago. Like teenagers talk about girls.'

Jay gave him a tight smile and continued. 'She's pretty.'

'Pretty or pretty-pretty?'

'The latter.'

'Did you tell her?'

'Did I tell her what?'

'That she is pretty?'

'What, at the first meeting in the formal setting?'

'So when is the first meeting in an *informal* setting happening?'

'I don't know.' Jay figured that he was blushing. *Why?*

'So, who knows?'

'I am not sure if I am ready for this.'

'Are you a moron?' Ali let out a laugh. 'If you're not ready *now*, when will you be?'

'I actually meant I'm too old for her—'

'You are not some doddery, senile old man who's halfway into the grave. You're still in your early forties, single, reputable and conspicuously successful. Why should she have any problems if she's single? What do you mean you're too old for her?'

'I've never been involved with a "girl", you know that.'

'There's always a first time, as they say.'

'I don't know if she's single, if she's even interested in an old dog like me. She might think I am an old fart with mental problems and that's why I see the therapist. Just because I found her pretty does not mean anything.'

'Now, now, now … if it did not mean anything to you, I don't think you would have mentioned it to me, Jay.'

'I never said I didn't find her attractive.'

'Then ask her out. Asking someone out for dinner is no crime. She can decline if she's involved with someone, and you'd figure out if she's not interested in you during the dinner.'

'I don't have the nerves for that.'

'When are you meeting her next?'

'When I see my therapist next, which is on Monday, so four days from now, why?'

'Okay.' Ali kept quiet for a while. Anyone watching him might have thought that he was working on the next foreign strategy for the country. 'I have an idea. When you go in next, do not book the following appointment … say that you need to consult your diary, and that you'll call back—'

'How does that help?'

'Hang on a minute, Mr Hotshot Advocate. Asking Manavi out for dinner would be a lot easier on the phone. Should she decline, you don't have to face the embarrassment.'

'I'll still have to face her eventually.'

'Come on now, we'll figure that out later. And if you can't find the balls to call, come to me and I'll call her.'

'Won't she figure out it's not me?'

'Won't she figure out it's not me?' Akbar mimicked Jay's words in

a shrill female voice. 'Don't be a jerk. Voices can sound different on a phone.'

'Okay.' Jay flushed like a teenager again.

It was past one in the morning when Jay sauntered out of Ali's place. His car was parked away, but Bhīma flashed the headlights once and gently steered the car towards him.

'Have you had dinner?' Jay asked as he jumped into the front seat; something Bhīma wouldn't have allowed in the day.

'Jee, hukum.'

'How many times do I have to tell that you should call me Jay?'

'You know I can't do that, hukum.' Bhīma politely replied and, with his eyes fixed on the road and surroundings, U-turned the car in a single motion and zipped. This was the only real time of the day when the lack of traffic let him enjoy driving the Audi.

Before Jay could counter Bhīma's response, his mobile rang. He looked at the display; it was the call he had always dreaded. A call at this hour from the nursing home that his mother had been in for over two decades couldn't be for a casual update or one to notify that the month's bill hadn't been paid on time. They almost never called. Something was wrong. Seriously wrong. He could calculate what it might be, but he opted not to, he decided not to unlock the painful chasm before he was certain. Not wanting to hazard a guess, he took the call.

'Jay Singh.' His voice sounded surprisingly stable to him, not drunk.

5

SWAMIJI.

Yes, that's what I have called him since I was six or seven. Or perhaps even eight. It's been such a long while that I don't exactly remember. I didn't know his name; I still don't know his name. He visited our home sometimes, but, predominantly, it was my mother who travelled to him during the daytime. As I was too young to be left alone at home, I tagged along. He lived in a decrepit, jerry-built house made of baked clay with cow dung slapped on the walls and a corrugated tin roof that I feared would fall anytime. It was always dimly lit. The temperature inside used to be baking hot and, if that wasn't enough to endure, there were a dozen or more cheap lit incense sticks that let out a profusion of smoke, and the resulting stench – a fusion of cow shit and synthetic sandalwood – was nauseating, to say the least. The incense sticks were supposed to cleanse and give the place a religious feel, which only the Swamiji might have found purifying and fragrant. On the flip side, it taught me to hold my breath for longer intervals to avoid filling my nostrils with the sickening odour.

Swamiji always wore a saffron loincloth. That's all. He was, at all times – summer or winter – bare-chested and barefoot; grey hair covered his entire body like pelage. And he had probably never heard of deodorant. He must have been in his fifties. The face a permanent red and sunburnt, and his long, unkempt hair was tussled into a tail. He sometimes carried a small trident in his right hand to remind people that he was a holy follower of Shiva, and as such had more powers than other mortals that visited him, though I never saw any other soul, besides us, at his house when we visited him.

Our visits had a distinctive routine. We started late in the mornings, usually after my father left for office. My mother drove our old grey Premier Padmini from Vasant Vihar to Patparganj – a distance of less than twenty kilometres, but it took over an hour in the traffic, and as we crossed the river Yamuna the pot-holed, crowded lanes took their toll on travel. The stench was a precursor to one I'd experience only a while later at Swamiji's place. It was for me, or anyone else who lived in posh New Delhi, another world: the topography, the housing, the edifices, the people, their minimalistic and tattered clothing, all looked alien. Blatant poverty was on display everywhere; even the few cars on the roads – the place was flooded with scooters, motorcycles, cycles, auto rickshaws and cycle-rickshaws – were rundown.

We parked quite a distance away from his hovel, as the dirt road that led to the holy shanty didn't allow cars. I sprinted along with my mother, holding her hand, as she walked swiftly to Swamiji's hut. She never looked up or acknowledged anyone around, not that anyone there would have known her. Swamiji never came out of his hut to greet anyone, and you only met him once you were cleansed. There was a municipal hand pump to dispense water right outside his dwelling, and mere mortals were supposed to wash their limbs before entering his sacred shithole. Admittance into his abode was solely bare-footed, like any footwear would soil his muddy, tile-less floor any further. And the stench, oh lord, the stench. I sometimes still feel queasy when I think of that malodour. Anyway, once we were in the shack we separated, my mother and I. For the next two hours or so – that obviously seemed like a lifetime to me, every time – I was expected to wait in the outer section of the hut and read the Archie comic digests I carried. Two hours. Sometimes, I wondered if my father had any inkling about my mother's clandestine meetings with the swami, though everything conveyed to me it wasn't.

If I needed water, well, there was the hand pump right outside the door, and if I needed to relieve myself, I could go behind the hut and do the job outdoors. Unsurprisingly, I was curious about the mystical adventure that transpired in the adjoining room, with my mother and Swamiji alone in the dark, but I never dared to even peep in. And though at the time my puerile mind was inept at comprehending what happened in the adjacent room, as I came of age my mind drew obvious inferences; whether they were right or if I misconstrued I would never know and never challenge or probe. But it sickened me for a long time. It even bothers me to no end now sometimes. Swamiji – a man of God – and my own mother? Sheesh! An apparently palpable truth I did not want to believe. The whole ritual seemed more Mephistophelean than religious to me. But what did I know?

When my mother eventually emerged from the dark chamber, I always felt her face carried a guilty expression. Swamiji didn't come out to see us off after the 'spiritual' two-hour sessions. The return journey from Patparganj to home was equally uninteresting too, with an added discomfort, as neither of us spoke on the one-hour drive home.

The most remarkable part is that Swamiji vanished from our lives the night my father was murdered. He did not come even once to console his earnest devotee – my mother – when she might have required the spiritual strength most. But as I've said before, I have faint reflections that someone else was present in our house the night my father got killed. And if Swamiji, indeed, had any part in murdering my dad – or helping my mother in the hideous act – and had got away with it successfully, why would he even hang around in the city, forget coming to see my mother?

In my mind, Swamiji was the most logical suspect.

But, of course, that Swamiji was even involved was only conjecture on my part. My mother never uttered a word or gave anyone any indication that he was.

And I never saw Swamiji again.

6

'BHĪMA, DID YOU MANAGE TO TAKE A NAP EARLIER TODAY?' JAY asked after he ended the call.

'A couple of hours, hukum.'

'Can you drive all night?'

'Jee, hukum.'

'Drive me to Jaipur then, please.'

Bhīma didn't flinch, didn't question, just as Jay had expected; Bhīma never questioned his boss. His immediate reflex was to glance at the instrument panel to see how much petrol they had left. Enough fuel. Jay could see that he was perturbed by the odd request at this unusual hour – after all the big man wasn't a yokel – and he decided it wasn't prudent to keep his friend in the dark for the unplanned travel.

'My mother died.'

'Sorry to hear that, hukum,' Bhīma uttered, his words perhaps attempting to belie the lump in his throat. 'Are you okay?'

If the urgency to get to Jaipur seemed bizarre to Bhīma – for Jay had never even bothered to visit the old lady in all the years – he did not ask or show.

'I've dropped a bug in Vinay Kumar's car,' Bhīma mentioned after a few kilometres of muteness.

'Already?' Jay couldn't care less for Kumar at this moment, but at least the distraction helped in taking his mind away from the pain.

'I did it when he was in the meeting with you. His driver isn't a very diligent man; he left the car unattended in the parking area below. I bugged it on the inside, so we'll know where Vinay Kumar travels and who he speaks to when he's in the car.'

'Let me know if you hear anything.'

'Jee, hukum.'

Silence again. The two were now on NH 8, the vein that connected New Delhi to Mumbai.

'Could you stop for a refill, please?' Jay asked, looking out of the car's window as the trees rushed past.

'The petrol tank's full, hukum.' Bhīma glanced at the instrument panel again to confirm.

'I need a refill, Bhīma.' Jay attempted to feign a smile.

'Sorry, I didn't grasp.'

'No worries.'

Bhīma switched on the fog lights and their brightness pierced through the smog. Minutes later, he put the headlights on high and pressed down on the pedal. The car's V6 engine did not hesitate. They crossed over into Haryana and stopped as close as physically possible to the first roadside alcohol booth that apparently sold '*Angrezi Sharaab*'. Not bothering to check what Jay wanted – knowing fully well that choice was not a luxury at this hour and place – Bhīma cut the engine, stepped out and looked around for any unwanted elements. Once satisfied that there was no one around except a stray dog who didn't even bother to raise its neck to acknowledge him, he walked to the stall.

His eyes raced across the small display to catch anything Jay could digest. Luckily, there was one bottle of Jack Daniels gathering dust in a corner. He bought it, along with half a dozen assorted cans of ice-cold colas available – Pepsi, Coke and Thums Up. Quickly paying the guy, Bhīma returned to the car, opened the boot and dumped five of the cans into the little cooler he had there for precisely such occasions.

Jay was happy to see the bottle of Jack and a chilled can of cola. The journey would be a lot easier now, he knew. And a lot faster!

'Have you eaten anything, hukum?'

'We'll pick up something at the next stop.'

Bhīma nodded.

Jay drank through whatever was left of the night. Fortunately, there wasn't much traffic, save the truckers and some buses that plied all through the night. Thankfully, there weren't many motorists at this hour. Despite Bhīma reminding Jay that he needed to eat, they only stopped for a short while when the vakil sahib needed a refill from the boot until they were at the outskirts of Jaipur. Bhīma, under the pretext of refuelling, drove into a petrol station that also had a café and bought an egg sandwich for Jay, which he savoured like a child.

Jaipur is one of the vertices of north Indian tourism's Golden Triangle: Delhi and Agra being the other two. Raja Man Singh built the Amber Fort in the sixteenth century. The ramparts underwent improvements and additions by successive rulers over the next two centuries. Since it was located on a hill, Jay, even in his torpor, spotted the artistic edifice built with sandstone. Dawn arrived as the car descended the hill into the old city. The rising sun, a shade of thick-cut marmalade, washed over the rose-hued Pink City to bring it to its full bloom. Every building was more beautiful than the one the car passed by. Commercial activities hadn't begun so early and all one could see were the striking pink exteriors – just how the city was visualized by its founders.

Jay's mind was, obviously, elsewhere. He had passed another night drinking and plunging into the dark nooks of his brain. The more he thought, the more it hurt but, as he had narrated to Ali, he had absolutely no control over that whatsoever.

As the car moved into the new part of the city, the haphazardness, the ugliness was more than evident. That the city would develop around this utter and complete *balagan* might have been the illusion of some minister who must have pocketed the money at the time and then gone out of power. It was never going to happen now. The lack of any semblance of order, that might have been promised to disguise this, exaggerated the visual chaos. Oh yes, you could even mess up something as beautiful as Jaipur if you tried.

The early-bird vendors were up, delivering milk and newspapers. The local city buses had started carting labourers across the city. Jay was awake, but only just. The nebulosity fuelled by Jack had taken him a million miles away. His eyes were open, but anyone observing him would surely have found them glazed like marbles in a taxidermy puppet.

'Where do we go, hukum?'

'What time is it?'

'Almost seven.'

'Let's check into Rambagh Palace. I need a few hours' sleep before we head to the hospital. You should get some rest too.'

'Jee, hukum.'

Bhīma stopped the car in the hotel's portico. Stepping out, he put Jay's arm across his massive shoulders and assisted his inebriated boss. Any onlooker would have thought he was helping an injured man; no one figured that he was sloshed.

Having rested and breakfasted, the duo was back in the car by eleven. Jay looked presentable again in the spare clothes that Bhīma had got out of the car and ironed at the hotel. Jay sat in the front as they silently drove to their destination.

The East India Company had established the Jaipur Mental Hospital in the early-nineteenth century as an asylum for the detention and care of, primarily, criminal lunatics. Legend has it that the patients then were detained with chains, but times had changed. It was now a mental hospital and rehabilitation centre – practising both curative and palliative therapies – within the catchment area of the whole of Rajasthan and adjacent states of UP, Madhya Pradesh, Haryana, Punjab, as well as Delhi. Rani Singh, Jay's mother, had lost her mental balance after her husband's murder. After being convicted, and when it was medically established that she wasn't mentally stable at the time of the crime, she was moved to this hospital for the balance of her sentence or until she passed away. The doctors had envisaged the death a lot sooner, but the angels of death didn't seem to be in any kind of rush, like they were bent upon making the woman atone for her sin.

The nurse at the reception seemed shocked at seeing the anomalous duo. With their identities established, they were sent to one Dr Mita Aggarwal who had been Rani Singh's doctor for the past three years.

Bhīma waited outside while Jay went in to see the doctor in her office. Dr Aggarwal explained that Mrs Rani Singh had suffered a stroke the previous afternoon and had been pronounced dead at nine last evening. She defended the hospital, stating that the patient had never complained of any chest pains before yesterday.

'Did she ever say anything?'

'She didn't speak a single word in the last three years.'

Jay had known that and regretted even asking the question. His mother hadn't uttered a word to him since the incident. Psychiatrists had adjudged that she had lost her mind and speech due to the shock, and they believed she would never get either back as there wasn't any effort or will on her part to come out of the condition. That was the principal reason he had stopped visiting her. Notwithstanding the shame of being the son of a murderer, he visited her in those early years to uncover if she would give some indication, some hint about the proceedings of that ignoble night, some sequence of events or the reason for the crime. When he didn't succeed in making her talk or reveal anything even after a few years of incessant probing, Jay simply gave up. Absolutely broke, he couldn't afford to follow a trail that wasn't there. In time, he gave up coming to see her physically. Call it good, bad, compassionate, conceited or maybe imperious, but he found it too painful to see someone he loved suffer in silence. But he was the only living family and hence, rightfully, he was the only one to be contacted when the time came. The truth, he gathered, was buried forever now. The pain he had so fervently wished to end would hurt him until *he* met his end. God's will.

'Would you like us to cremate her or would you like to take the body, Mr Singh?' Dr Aggarwal broke his agonizing reverie.

'Could I see her?'

'Of course. After we spoke to you, we decided to postpone the autopsy till you saw her one last time. Follow me.' She got up and walked out of her office to take Jay to his mother's room.

Jay followed her. Bhīma followed Jay. He had, of course, taken in the environment and checked the security. As they walked, Jay could feel Bhīma's eyes piercing his cranium. He wondered what the big man was making of it all? Did he understand the torment of seeing one's mother in a mental hospital? They walked along the corridor, took the elevator to the third floor and turned right when they got there. Dr Aggarwal stopped outside the fourth room on the right and pointed towards it.

'She's in there, Mr Singh. When you're through, please come back to my office.'

'Thank you, Doctor.'

Bhīma looked the other way to avoid the embarrassment of sighting tears form in Jay's eyes. He paused outside the door, which Jay appreciated: giving the son a final few moments with his mother.

Each time he had visited his mother in the hospital, Jay had only looked into her vacant eyes. He could tell she wasn't really there; she was living, but was hardly alive. But, today, a paroxysm of guilt hit him in the gut. Maybe he could have done more if he hadn't loathed her deliberate silence. Maybe ... Memories fused into one another, losing chronology as he saw her at peace finally. Yes, there had been some good times before his father lost money and sense, but that had been long before the incident even.

He looked at her lifeless body now. Her skin had calloused like leather. Dead.

'Why don't you speak to me, Ma? Why didn't you want to tell me who it was you tried to save?' Jay stared at her till his eyes welled up and he realized he was talking to the corpse that had once been his mother. Nevertheless, he continued to stare at her and make conversation like she might respond. He could never comprehend who abandoned whom? Did his mother abandon him for someone he only suspected? Or did he abandon her because she wouldn't divulge the truth? What if the truth wasn't what he had construed in his mind, after all? Too late, Jay Singh, useless navel-gazing never calmed the heart.

She had silently suffered and penanced for the crime for a decade more than she would have had to, had she been incarcerated for manslaughter or premeditated murder. All the psychiatrists, their therapies and the electric shocks could never even make her speak, leave alone make her sane again.

'Why?' Jay murmured again, then held her cold, bloodless hands in his and sank to his knees. An avalanche of memories struck in a flash; the college friends, the party, the booze, the drugs, his state of unusual inebriation, the altercation between his parents, his intervention, his mother's scream piercing the dawn, the body of his father in a pool of blood, the stranger in the house.

He finally broke down. The tears, like they had been waiting all along, ran down his face like a wild river that could never be staunched. He didn't wipe them. Perhaps it was good she didn't have to suffer anymore. Perhaps her soul could rest now. The contradicting emotions struck him concurrently. How could a single occasion cause pain and provide solace at the same time?

Jay decided to leave the cremation up to the hospital authorities. Not because he didn't want to fulfil his filial duty, but because, for him, his mother had died the same night his father had, this was only the passing away of the mortal remains. Moreover, taking her body back to Delhi would raise eyebrows and instigate questions that he didn't want to answer or entertain. No one knew about his mother, least of all that she was in a mental hospital. It was better this way; sleeping dogs were better left asleep. Next to his mother's bed, there lay a tiny wooden chest containing whatever little belonged to her. Bhīma lugged that from her room into the boot of the car. The formalities were complete by the evening, but Jay – conscious that Bhīma had driven all through the previous night – planned a brief stopover in Jaipur.

The bar at Rambagh Palace did not disappoint and neither did the service. Later at dinner, Jay took off his monogrammed cufflinks, rolled up his sleeves and wolfed down a big portion of rice and *laal maas*, using his hands and without a care in the fucking world. They might have known him by name, read about him in newspapers and magazines, but no one recognized him here. The mighty Jay Singh was a nobody this night and he was enjoying it. He should do this more often, he thought.

They started for Delhi at five in the morning. As they drove back from Jaipur, Jay felt he had aged ten years overnight. The chapter had finally come to a close. Not the kind of closure he would have liked though. The journey home – and beyond – would be full of questions. At least, for Jay, Bhīma drove without any complaints.

Memories had deliquesced – faded and dissolved. Everything was a dead end now, except for the hurt and the undisclosed shame. The ink would never dry. There wasn't even an illusion of cheer as they drove back. Bhīma cruised at ninety kilometres per hour. More than a kilometre per minute, but the traffic averaged the speed to less than fifty kmph. Motorists and truckers, tollbooths and jeep taxis – there was no escape from them. Jay always sat in the rear on the nearside for many reasons. First, it was impossible for anyone but an elf to sit behind Bhīma; second, even if you squeezed behind the giant, the whole view ahead was blocked and, third, Jay trusted Bhīma and his driving. Most often, in the case of an accident, the driver, by instinct, swerves his side to safety, thereby damaging the other side. It is a natural reaction. But Jay knew that Bhīma's natural reaction would be to save him irrespective of which side he sat in. He played the odds; playing odds did not utilize his brain in this case, it just used the other man's orientation.

The dark amber cloud of Jack Daniels was slowing Jay's thoughts, making him numb, the way he liked.

Seven hours, considering the traffic. They didn't exchange many words.

No radio. *iPod.* Jay had Led Zeppelin's entire discography on his playlist. He put it on shuffle and asked Bhīma to plug it into the music system.

The big engine barely whispered. The sound of tyres on tarmac was the only killjoy.

Road. Traffic. '*Stairway to Heaven.*'

Civilization. Manpura.

Road. Traffic. '*When the Levee Breaks.*'

Civilization. Shahpura.

Road. Traffic. '*Kashmir.*'

Civilization. Kotputli.

Road. Traffic. '*Dazed and Confused.*'

'We'll breakfast at Behror,' Jay said.

Bhīma glanced in the rear view. *No tail. All good.*

They drove into the midway hotel at Behror. Despite no tail in sight and the near-zilch probability of anyone looking for the vakil sahib here, Bhīma got out first and looked around to see if he could spot any trouble. None. He indicated it was safe for Jay to exit the car.

The two had coffees and sandwiches and were back on the road in twenty minutes.

Road. Traffic. '*I Got a Woman.*'

Neemrana Fort was visible from the highway. *Someday*, thought Jay, *if I have a woman in my life, I'll bring her here*. Manavi's face instantly flashed through his mind, taking the aching thoughts away. Maybe, just maybe, Ali was right. If it hadn't been for Ali's instigation, Manavi was just another pretty girl, but Ali had planted the thought of taking her out on a date in his mind and made him feel like he was in falling in ... love?

They were in Gurgaon, finally.

Delhi was now just around the corner.

It was traffic all around. '*Black Dog.*'

Sheeba was the happiest to see Jay and Bhīma. For her, the two were equals: a dog's unremitting love that wanted nothing in return. She didn't care who paid for the bread, but only who loved her and both men showered her with equal affection.

7

AS PREDICTED, THE MEDIA DIDN'T DISAPPOINT. THE DOCUDRAMA had begun. '*Ex-minister's son's girlfriend shot dead at her Saket residence.*' Most morning newspapers and news channels professed it to be another piece of 'news of the decade' – quite absurdly, the moniker was bestowed on something different every week in the naked hope that at least some story would stick to sell paper and increase TRPs. Nearly all newspapers had covered the investigation with drops of facts and oodles of insinuations: less news, more opinions. Sad, but true, that bad newsflash always got better coverage. Ergo, the media incessantly foraged for such incidents to feed the scavenging public. The case had the potential of being big; some local television channels had given it its own branding: tickers reading '*Ex-minister's son in the box*' scrolled at the bottom of the screen. Thankfully, the police had not released much information, as they hadn't received the forensic reports or postmortem results yet.

Jay had known from the start that Kumar's case would eat up his calendar like Pac-Man swallowed pellets, and that was agreeable to him. More media meant more limelight, which was good for business. The return to office wasn't ceremonial, with Bhīma having been briefed not to mention Jay's mother and her demise, the mental hospital or their surreptitious jaunt to Jaipur. If the office missed them for a day, it was because the boss was busy elsewhere on some case that might have been too private to discuss. Jay didn't need to explain. Bhīma had called Julie from Jaipur to notify her to reschedule all appointments. Vinay Kumar's file was being readied and all reports – permissible and proscribed ones – were catalogued at Jay's desk, just in time before Kumar's visit to the office again today.

But, first off, Bhīma was to run a search for the police officer in charge of the investigation of his father's murder. 'I'm fairly certain he must have retired by now; he looked old even back when I was a teen. But please track him down if you can. We resided in Vasant Vihar at the time, so finding the right police station in the precinct and the name of the person should not be a challenge. Sussing out where the old man is now – if he is still alive, that is – might be a little tricky.'

Bhīma acquiesced. Jay didn't require a verbal confirmation or the need to mention to Bhīma that this was personal business. His man Friday understood the significance and confidential nature of the task. No records of this search were to be maintained. Jay knew Bhīma would be on the job straightaway.

He spent the next hour speed-reading Vinay Kumar's dossier, his practiced eye discerning the imperative from the routine. He read the unofficial material he had received from the informants before going through what was collected by his office staff. Examining everything closely, he pulled out crime-scene photographs and looked at them through a magnifying glass. He studied the case, noting each name, drawing a character of witnesses. Then, he drew a flow-of-activities chart to put everything in a bead. It wasn't a day's job and, as such, there wasn't any rush to figure it all out.

'Waiting for me?' Kumar knocked, thrusting his head into Jay's office at eleven.

'Nope, I was on a call with the President of India, but I told him I'm busy as I'm at your service,' Jay quipped with a smile and got up to shake his client's hand.

Kumar flashed what appeared to be a genuine smile. Perhaps he understood the humour. He was dressed in Diesel jeans, a crisp powder blue Ralph Lauren button-down shirt and leather sneakers – although the brand wasn't visible, Jay knew they would be expensive too.

Diesel may adorn your ass, but is the denim strong enough to save it? The thought crossed Jay's mind, but he stopped himself, lest he be deemed inappropriate.

Like a computer that tracked cookies and identified if you logged on to the website the second time, Julie remembered from a client's prior visit what they preferred. Coffees arrived without being asked for.

'I've been reading your file, Vinay.' Jay raised his eyebrows to point towards the big docket that lay at his desk.

'And?'

'Do you have anything new to tell me?'

Kumar looked up, down and then sideways, indicating he didn't have anything fresh. Maybe he wasn't aware that Jay had got the details before the police.

'No fingerprints, not even partials. No witnesses, no weapon. And the only person, at least apparently, who seems to have had a motive and the opportunity, is you. It's a lot easier to send you to the cell than to save you. Obviously, it's your hide anyone would come after first. You're in so much shit even the world's best proctologist can't help you, Kumar. So I request you one last time: stop lying.'

'I am not.'

'Okay here's my proposal. Every time you perjure, my fee doubles. Agreed?'

'Of course, but you haven't told me your fee …'

'I will, after I add up all your lies. Was Gina pregnant?'

'How'd you know?'

'Doesn't matter how I know, what matters is, did you know?'

'Of course, I knew she was pregnant.'

'And you forgot to mention that to me?'

'I didn't think that was important.'

Do I really look like a fucking idiot?

'Drat.' Jay was fast losing confidence in his client now. 'May I request you once again to tell me *everything*; I don't want you to be economical with the truth here. Let me be the judge if I need that info or not.'

Nod.

'Vinay, I think the Chinese Triad wouldn't have had any interest in Gina's pregnancy, so I think it's safe to rule them out.' It was part anger, part frustration siring the sarcasm. No sooner had the words left his mouth, than Jay realized the impropriety of the caustic remark, but what the heck, Vinay Kumar could either drop all pretences or leave. He didn't need Kumar as much as Kumar needed him. Some verbal whipping was essential.

The client did not utter a word. He appeared dazed. Either because Jay had unearthed an important fact before the police came looking for him or that he had been caught dodging details by omission. The moron should have known Jay would be verifying every word he spoke and especially the ones he didn't: lying by omission could cost him.

'So do you see what I see? A pregnant mistress, maybe asking for rights, maybe asking for money, got killed? And interestingly, you had just left her residence, so you have no alibi, no witnesses, no contrary evidence, nothing? I could be wrong, but it looks like the rich, unbridled son of an ex-minister shot her. It's not looking propitious for you, whichever way you look at it, Vinay.'

'Are you saying that's possible?'

'Are you saying it is not?'

'I mean … I did not do it.'

'Vinay – let's look at the possible scenarios the prosecution might present in the court. Scenario one: Mr Vinay Kumar, a married man with kids, recognizing that his mistress was pregnant, could not take the risk that it could bring to his political destiny, so he thought it was sensible to finish her off …' Kumar attempted to interrupt the monologue, but Jay gestured him to hold it. 'Scenario two: Mr Vinay Kumar impregnated his mistress Miss Gina Pinto, a single woman. Nowhere to go, she rightfully asked her paramour to marry her. They had a fight and Mr Vinay Kumar was left with no choice but to get rid of her. Which scenario do you prefer?'

'Eh?'

'There could be a third and fourth scenario where you get her killed by someone else – contract killing. But that doesn't matter. If the first two scenarios are so similar that the difference is indiscernible – who actually pulled the trigger? – then the verdict would be the same in either case. Remember, if it walks like a fucking duck and talks like a fucking duck ...'

'Huh?'

'Then it has to be a fucking duck, doesn't it?'

'I did not kill her.' Kumar was literally in tears. The consummate actor could get nominated for a Filmfare award. Or he was shit-scared and not pretending. As an advocate you need to pick up the subtleties in a yarn, the untold, the slipped-up fragment of facts. It somehow seemed to Jay that Kumar's mien wanted to convince him that he was still in love with Gina. But it came across as insincere. How much could Jay trust a philandering client?

The why, who and how was something Jay had to figure out. Surprisingly, this was a city that never woke up, never opened its eyes; no one ever saw a crime being committed. Ergo, it was futile to expect someone would walk into the Saket police station to give a testimony. Vinay Kumar had the motive and Vinay Kumar had the opportunity. Just because the gun wasn't traced didn't mean Kumar could – or would – be deemed innocent. There were more than a thousand and one ways in the book to dispose of the bloody gun.

'My source tells me they suspect you,' Jay mentioned with blatant mendacity. He wanted to give Kumar one final chance.

'That isn't true. Who is your source?'

'I cannot tell you, and you should know that.'

'You have to believe me.'

'And I should believe you because …?'

'Because I'm telling you the truth … I loved her … I still love her.' Kumar's eyes started welling up with tears. Liars can bring up tears too; in fact they say liars can call upon tears much more quickly. With one swift motion, to preserve his self-respect, Kumar wiped his face and cleared his throat. 'Do you think anyone can kill the mother of their unborn child?' He put on what only he must have believed was a disarming smile. Jay could see through the façade.

Ouch, that last dialogue could do the noted Bollywood dialogue writer Kader Khan proud.

'Could you stop playing hypotheticals with me? Please? Tell me the truth. Let *me* hypothesize. That's my job – to make up the case,' Jay articulated pitilessly.

'Do you believe me?'

'Well, you haven't given me any reason to and, as I've told you before, it's not for me to believe. It's for the judge to be convinced. You haven't given me anything to build the case on yet and you should know that.'

'What do you want me to say?'

'Firstly, no lies, not even by omission.'

Nod.

'And certainly not by admission.'

Nod.

'Is there anything you could think of that might impact the case going forward?'

'Like?'

'Any other affairs, any insurances—?'

'Gina was insured, certainly.' He mentioned *certainly* like everyone in India was insured.

'Now, please don't tell me you are the beneficiary?'

'Of course I am. I am the one who insured her and paid the annual premiums.' There was a certain pride in his voice.

Jay's elbows were already on the desk, his hands in a steeple against his lips as he heard his client speak. Catching those last words from Kumar's mouth made his head drop into his hands. Kumar was a sitting duck: pregnant mistress shot dead, insured, with him as the sole beneficiary. It didn't require Einstein to solve this one.

Jay grilled Kumar for another two hours. Kumar had brought his handgun along, which he offered to surrender to Jay for tests. It was an altogether different make – Colt not Glock – and Jay didn't fancy keeping it. It would need a lot of paperwork to confiscate a firearm, even for the sake of investigation. He wasn't still entirely convinced Kumar hadn't killed Gina, but he didn't want to focus solely on him.

'Let me reiterate that if at any point I find out that you've lied to me, I *will* pull the carpet from under you and send you go to the gallows. On the other hand, if you admit – even if the truth is that you deliberately or accidentally killed Gina – I promise to stand by you until the very end.'

'I know, and I agree to your condition. I swear upon my dead mother that I did not kill Gina. If I had a choice, I'd walk away from my wife and kids, denounce politics and be with Gina for the rest of my life.'

How romantic!

'The police would most definitely take you for questioning. Do not, under any circumstances, agree to speak to them in my absence. Tell them you need your advocate present.'

'Of course.'

'I shall get a bail organized for you, if required.'

The police had already discovered semen in Gina's body. Soon, they would also know that she was pregnant. With Gina being Kumar's mistress, the doctrine suggested he was the main suspect. His DNA would substantiate that both the seed in her body and the bun in the oven were his. Naturally, they would incriminate him, given his motive. Knowing he was the son of a once powerful politician and was currently being groomed for the next general election, the police were taking it slowly. Where would he run to if he were guilty? Why would he run if he weren't? The police were known to stretch the charges, especially when they knew the accused was worth a lot, like Vinay Kumar. It would be a ripe time to mention the fees then; Jay ameliorated with each case. In the end, it was all for money, wasn't it?

'Thanks, Jay.'

Kumar left the offices of Cooper & Singh at three.

Jay kept thinking about the case for another hour. Why would Kumar lie when he had the the best advocate in the city fighting his case – however unsavoury the truth might have been for the advocate's consumption the first time he heard it. Jay had promised to represent him even if he was guilty and his reputation wasn't exactly Gandhian. He was known to represent those not innocent, but not evidently guilty. Why would Kumar take the risk? Additionally, Jay, knew humans well by now, and he had seen some strange confidence in Kumar's eyes. It was no exact science, but then what was?

In the car later that evening, as Bhīma drove his boss back, Jay was still a bit troubled. 'There's a conceptual problem, Bhīma.'

'What is that, hukum?' he asked, looking concerned.

'Vinay Kumar might not be the killer. Look elsewhere, too, spread the net; look in his near quarters: his wife, his father, his friends and his political opponents. If we suspect only Vinay Kumar at this moment, we're getting ahead of ourselves. We might need to do some reverse engineering here – it could be anyone who didn't want Gina to see our client. Ask your snitches where the handgun came from.'

Bhīma nodded.

A stray thought passed through Jay's mind. Kumar had voluntarily given out information about his father disliking his relationship with Gina. Why? No one offered a pawn for sacrifice in this game. There had to be a trap somewhere. He made a mental note of it.

'Thank you, Bhīma. Did you find out anything else today?'

'Hukum, the senior inspector who handled your father's case retired as Superintendent of Police in Pondicherry. Retired SP Amrit Saxena.'

'I remember the name, yes. It must have been him. Did they tell you where he is now?' There was excitement in Jay's voice, though he wasn't sure what he could find out from the police officer decades after the murder.

'I should find him too, hukum; it's only a question of time.'

8

CONNIVING AS HE MIGHT SOUND, BHĪMA WAS A CREATURE OF THE night. It was normal rota for him to drop Jay home, check if he needed to go out for something; if not, he took Sheeba for a run on the farmhouse grounds, have his dinner and slip out of the premises. He owned a Royal Enfield, which he cherished riding.

Bhīma's first stop this evening was his office. The guards and doormen knew he worked ridiculous hours, and so no one bothered about what time he arrived at and left the building. In any event, no one thought it was advisable to stop a man of Bhīma's bulk.

Bugging a car was the simplest thing, as the car's battery supplied a potent power source; the acoustics in his office cabin were unrivalled. All one needed was a small transmitter and an even smaller, albeit extremely powerful, magnet. Money not being a problem for Jay, Bhīma used adhesive neodymium magnets. All he needed to do was peel the cover, stick the tiny coin-sized magnet under the car's instrument panel and connect the wire to a micro-GSM listening device, which was as small as a coat button. It took a practiced hand like Bhīma's under five minutes once he got access to the car. One such bug had been travelling in Vinay Kumar's car. The bug helped him track the car and transmit the sound signals to long-range transmitters. These were connected to other transmitters that Bhīma had implanted on random electric poles across the city to create a loop of wired and wireless networks. Were someone to go around snooping, they would never reach the ultimate receiver. Also, if one of these devices ever malfunctioned or got pulled off, the data – till that second – would have already been logged on Bhīma's Mac; asynchronous transmissions from indicators like GPS or voice, were recorded 24x7 from various sources. Bhīma artfully analysed the voice signals and put them in a chronological string for his boss.

He made himself a coffee and sat down comfortably in front of his already switched-on computer. His computer was equipped with SecurID and required a memorized password for authentication. Unlawful establishments always require that additional level of security, don't they? As Bhīma logged on, the screen reflected a notification for incoming data and the red light on the connected listening device began blinking. But that was expected. It was foolish to assume Kumar wouldn't speak a word while he was in the car, even if it was only a few words or sentences to the driver to request where to go next. And the car, too, had started to move – the tracker now mapping its route. Bhīma put on the headphones to listen to the voices. There were some instructions for the driver: addresses for visits, a stopover for a pack of Gold Flake Kings. But the conversation that Bhīma really wanted to listen to started twenty minutes later when Kumar called one of his close friends. The transmitter was sensitive enough to even catch the ringtone emitted from the other end of the line while Kumar waited for the call to be picked up. Bhīma carefully listened to the entire twelve-minute conversation and a wry smile tugged at his lips as he sipped his coffee: Jay's instincts were appreciable.

He downloaded all the incoming data from Kumar's car. The only missing link now was any conversation he had outside of the car, which Bhīma swore to take care of shortly.

Maybe the next visit needs to be elsewhere. He beamed.

Then copying all significant data onto a pen drive, he deleted the balance from memory, reset the flashing device, logged out, exited his office, locked it with the utmost care and, taking the lift down to his parked motorbike, rode away into the dark night.

Bhīma was indeed a creature of the night.

9

THE NIGHT WAS STILL AND QUIET WHEN SEEN FROM THE LITTLE balcony that hung from my first-floor bedroom. The air was humid and the moon a sliver on the second day after its ascendance. I took a generous sip and gulped; the liquid lava burnt its tracks as it travelled down my throat into the gullet. Just another normal never-ending evening in my life filled with questions and restlessness and shame. Frustration at the end of it all. I kept twisting and turning the facts in my mind, like a Rubik's cube, but nothing fitted. Nothing fitted since I had no new nugget of information. This, as Ali had so rightly warned, was going around in circles. It annoyed me, nonetheless. Exasperation and exhaustion had schemed to get me down, but even together, they had failed to drive my fucking insomnia away.

I knew I was quite drunk now, yet I didn't want to lie in bed with my eyes closed, only to toss and turn for a few hours. My drink was over; I decided to tiptoe down to get another one – this would be the last one, I promised myself – knowing Bhīma was out and Bahadur would have been asleep by now. The old boy worked hard all day and needed the rest. So did I, but the ghosts of the damned past wouldn't let me.

It was dark in the living room.

Sam Cooper preferred it that way. Always. He sat on the sofa facing the windows, feet up on the ottoman, his hands laced behind his neck like they were supporting his head as he gazed out at the tranquil pool.

'How have you been, Jay?'

'Fine, thanks, buddy. How about you? When did you come?' Cooper and I went so far back that his visits didn't require a courtesy call to warn me. Sometimes, he'd just visit and leave without meeting me.

'I found out about Ma. I had to come.' Cooper didn't care to respond to my question or the pleasantries.

I liked the way he always made me feel the bond. He called Ma 'Ma', and not your mother, auntie or Mrs Singh. Ma.

'How did you know about her passing away?'

'You are a famous advocate, Jay. Whatever happens in your personal life does not remain personal for very long. As they say, if it doesn't travel fast enough, it probably isn't worth being news. You insult my intelligence if you think I wouldn't have figured out that you had left town.'

'Uh-uh.'

'She suffered a lot, didn't she?'

I didn't know how to respond, so I let the silence hang in the darkness.

'Penance,' he finally answered on my behalf. It was exactly what I had been thinking.

'What?'

'She atoned for what she didn't do.'

'Why did she punish herself then?'

'Who knows? The secret has gone with her. Death is only a word; the Gita *says it's a word to express the passing from earth to another place, supposedly better. Only the body dies, Jay.'*

'But she didn't even consider that by protecting some stranger, she abandoned me, her own child?'

'Are you still angry, Jay?'

'Wouldn't you be if she abandoned you, Cooper?'

Even back in their college days, no one called Cooper by his first name.

'Depends.'

'On?'

'Well, it depends on why she did it.'

'What or who could be dearer to her than her own child?'

'Maybe it wasn't 'someone'. Maybe it was just shame. Imagine the shame if she had come out with the truth, whatever that might have been. Or what if she had killed herself too. How would that have been any better for you?'

'It's difficult for me to imagine,' I sulked.

'There isn't much point in fostering grudges against the souls who've departed. And to top that – she was, after all, your mother, Jay.'

'You may have a point. Drink for you, Cooper?'

'I was waiting for you to ask. Yes, please.'

'What will you have?'

'What a rhetorical question, Jay; how long have we known each other?'

'Since college, why?'

'You know what we drink when we are together, don't you?'

'The strongest whisky in the bar ... would cask-strength Single Malt do?'

'Thanks. Make it a double for me, please.'

'I know. No water, no ice—'

'That's like the Jay I know. Do you mind putting on some music, too, please?

'What would you—' I stopped mid-sentence. I knew exactly what we listened to ever since I had known Cooper. He always said there was a connection between Jazz and whisky. I put on Nina Simone and 'Either Way I lose' *sprang to life.*

I poured two double fingers of Aberlour A'Bunadh for him – the only cask-strength whisky I currently had in my bar: 59.7% vv. I carried the glass to him and left it on the table beside him. He didn't even bother to look at the glass or me.

'Thanks, Jay,' he uttered when I returned to the bar.

I poured myself another drink and looked at him. He still sat motionless, looking out at the pool.

'Did you go through her belongings?' Cooper asked.

'Why should I?' I took a sip.

'Who knows what you may find?'

'Her lover's photo?' I was full of cynicism.

'Or possibly your father's killer's.'

'Ha, you know Ma didn't recover from her insanity, hence, in all probability, she perhaps never got any time to clear out her stuff. All I might expose is something that proves her guilt—'

'Or her innocence?'

'Cooper, I am worn-out. I think you should sleep too.' The big gulp of potent whisky rushed straight to my head. I swallowed the whole thing in one go and, I think, that did the trick. 'Are you leaving now or in the morning?'

'Haven't decided. Leave me here and I'll see myself out after I finish my drink. Leave the music on.'

'Can you drive? It's not a problem; Bhīma should be back soon, so he can drop you back.'

'Let the big man sleep. I have my driver waiting.'

'Good.'

'Goodnight, Jay.'

'Goodnight, Cooper.'

10

BHĪMA WAS IN THE GARDEN, PLAYING WITH SHEEBA, WHILE JAY ate his breakfast, watching the two through the glass doors. His brain was still numb. Bahadur had cleaned up the crystal and put everything back in the bar. *Or her innocence*, Cooper's words from the previous night still resonated in Jay's head. But he had no time. He was already late for the office. There was a court hearing in the afternoon, albeit trivial, but he had to get sober by then. Black coffee, as black it could be, as often as he could take.

'Do you have Ma's little trunk we carried back from Jaipur?' Jay queried as soon as he was on the road with Bhīma.

'Jee, hukum.'

'Good.'

'There are some recordings from Vinay Kumar's car that you may want to hear, hukum.'

'I must prepare for court the entire morning. Why don't you play it now in the car?'

Bhīma nodded, pulled the pen drive out of his pocket and plugged it into the USB drive.

Vinay Kumar's voice reverberated clearly through the speakers. It was a tête-à-tête with some close friend called Praveen, who apparently knew Kumar had a mistress who was now dead – murdered – and that Kumar was a possible suspect.

'I didn't do it, Praveen. I just got picked up in the night by the police, and it was then that I first came to know about it,' Kumar stressed.

'You've hired Jay Singh?'

'Yes.'

'Good. He's the best in the business.'

Did the idiot want to say there were other good ones that had gone out of business? Jay smiled.

'Thanks. He gives me confidence.'

'Do you suspect anyone?'

'I know my father and my wife were against my relationship with Gina, but none of them could stoop so low to kill … you know what I mean?'

'Of course I do, Vinay. I know both of them; they aren't that sort of people.'

'Praveen, I am too tensed.'

'That's why I called. Listen, why don't you come over? I have a guest coming, we'll have a few drinks and you can relax.'

'Who's this guest?'

'You'll love to meet this hot number, believe me.'

That was pretty much it. They required no furtherance to know that Kumar had changed course and gone over to Praveen's as the GPS revealed.

'Do we know where Praveen lives?' Jay asked when the recording concluded.

'His car was parked at a house in GK 2 all night.'

Bastard. His mistress's body hadn't even come out of postmortem and Kumar was spending a night with a friend and a guest, 'a hot number'.

Then again, people are wired differently. Some get maudlin for weeks, even years, while others move on faster than many can imagine. That aside, the conversation didn't absolve him of the crime. Even though Kumar spoke to a close friend, with whom he had a sleepover arranged, it did not mean he was foolish enough to own up to killing his mistress.

'Keep the recordings on, Bhīma.'

'Jee, hukum.'

'Get some more equipment ready and keep safe distance; nothing should ever be traced back to us. Do it utterly *sub rosa,* my friend.'

Bhīma nodded.

The day at office was usual snafu: preparing appeals, engaging with clients, overlooking files and one court appearance, which Jay delegated to one of his junior advocates after conferring with the concerned client. Without divulging the obvious reason, of course. He wasn't drunk, but he wasn't completely sober given the previous night's long drinking session. To cap it all, the hearing was, in the same court where Justice Chowdhary's office was and heaven forbid if the judge and Jay crossed paths. The risk of getting caught a second time was simply too high. He knew that the next time wouldn't involve an informal reprimand. It would be judicial. Why go near a shark when you have blood on you? Moreover, since the time he had got to the office, Jay was keen to get back home to look at his mother's belongings. He wondered why he hadn't done so before leaving his house in the morning. *Or her innocence.* Cooper's voice had been echoing in his ears, verbatim.

Back at home, Jay fixed himself a drink and went into his room. Bhīma had been instructed to leave the trunk that they had carried from Jaipur in Jay's bedroom. The trunk was sacrosanct, whether or not he found something of consequence in it. This was his mother's trunk, and he wanted to see everything personally without any intrusion. He sat on his bed and observed the unopened wooden chest for a while, as if some genie would rise from it. Then, collecting enough nerve to unlock it, he investigated it, without purpose; Jay wasn't sure what he was looking for.

The smell of mildew hit him. It seemed like even his mother hadn't opened the trunk for a while. Good – it might contain something she'd forgotten to hide – but then was there a need for her to cover up anything when she had already taken the blame? Jay's brain was needlessly yapping. There wasn't much in the chest anyway. Her clothes were obviously not here. He found her *mangalsutra*, which, Jay remembered, she wore only on occasions. Some tidbits of jewellery, a non-precious bracelet that simply disgusted Jay as he recalled seeing it on his mother's wrist the first time they had returned after seeing Swamiji. He'd probably given it to her. Out of sheer annoyance, he slammed the chest shut and went down to refill his glass; he didn't want Bahadur to bring him a drink and see this mess. Once down in the lobby, intermittent scenes from his childhood played in his head. Thoroughly defeated, Jay gulped down some whisky quicker than he should have. He wanted to go up and scrutinize what was in there, but also delay it all the same. The chest wasn't proving any of his mother's innocence. Or her guilt, for that matter.

An hour later, when he had cooled down a bit, he climbed up the stairs.

There has to be some clue in there.

But there was nothing.

A letter came in the post next morning. Bahudur had placed it at the bar counter for Jay to take a look when he returned from work in the evening. All post ordinarily went straight to his office, except for junk mail. Jay looked closely at the handwritten address on the white envelope. The scrawl seemed familiar, but not something he had seen in years and hence it was impossible to identify. As such there was no urgency to open it. It must be one of the many handwritten pleas for charity, he thought. It could wait. He made his drink first, a liberal *Patiala* peg of Chivas, no ice, and gulped it in one go before he tore off the envelope from the side to reveal a single sheet inside.

'*Dear Jayakumar.*'

The familiar handwriting and the reference to his given name startled him – it couldn't be. He observed the paper up close – this wasn't some decade-old crumpled yellowing paper; this was fresh. He finally recognized that it was his mother's handwriting. And only she would have addressed him by his full name. But she hadn't spoken a word in years. Could she have been in any mental disposition to write coherently? The suddenness of it all made him sweat. He picked up the bottle of Chivas on the counter, took a swig straight from it and started reading again.

Dear Jayakumar,

This letter will come as a surprise to you, I know, but I can't figure out how to tell you this in any other way. I hope you will forgive me for lying to you all these years, but I preferred being a lunatic in a mental hospital to being incarcerated as a criminal in police cells. Though I'd actually suffered a psychological concussion when your father died, I recovered soon after, only to understand what lay in store for me and for you had I been diagnosed as normal. It was in the best interests of everyone, including you, that I was declared mentally unsound when I was not. It immensely hurt me to remain silent all those times you came to see me, but I acknowledged that it was the only tactic to keep the story covered, to keep me from being labelled a convict; no one should know.

You might want to ask me why I wrote this letter, then? It's because I wanted you to know the truth: I did not kill your father. Despite our apparent differences, I loved and revered him. He generously provided for us and loved me too. His temperament was largely a result of his business failure, and I never despised him for it, although, as you know, things did get ugly at times.

I can discern that you despise me for robbing you of both your parents, but what good would I have been if I did not claim insanity? I would have been imprisoned for life, and that, according to me, would have been far more disgraceful for you. If it is any solace, I loved you, and I could feel the hurt in your eyes each time you came to see me. I am told that you are a very successful man now, which I secretly relish without displaying any emotions to anyone. I pray to God every day that you become even more successful and cherish your life.

I know I have lost the right to ask you for any favours, but, as your mother, I think I can still ask you for one: forget about that unpleasant night and please do not go digging to seek the truth after receiving this letter. The truth might be a hundred times more dreadful.

I don't have long to live now. I can feel it. I can't explain how, but I know my end is near. I will leave this letter with a nurse to be posted after my death. Hopefully, you will get it one day and forgive me.

Ma.

Drunk as he was, emotions rushed out, no holds barred. The tears just wouldn't stop. He had taken a few more gulps of the whisky while reading the letter. The truth, as he had suspected, was now on paper.

When did she write this? And if she wasn't the killer, as she had mentioned, why did she take the blame upon herself? Since she had never appealed 'not guilty', had he – following the court's verdict – assumed she was his father's murderer? Did he have no other choice or was it only too convenient? Jay cursed himself.

In the absence of any other suspect, the state prosecutor had an easy case. Maybe the defence advocate had been incompetent. It wasn't the idiot's job to provide another suspect; his job had been to prove his mother's innocence. His mother's posthumous admission put Jay in an emotional free fall. He felt dizzy; his mind descended into rage and grief. All these years, he had lived in anguish, having believed that his mother was guilty. The slight relief Jay felt at the thought of her purity was swiftly overtaken by grief. Could he reopen the case for a posthumous pardon? He knew he couldn't until he had some concrete evidence. A mere letter from his mother could convince *him*, but would it convince any judge? The letter would be unusable in court.

Everything else seemed vacuous.

'*Or her innocence*,' Cooper wouldn't stop.

The trouble with all tragedy is that it overtakes all objectivity; much later, when objectivity returns, the mind finds central pieces of the puzzle missing. But Jay knew he needed to go back in time – travel twenty years back – to establish the chronology of events. Reconstructing the day would be the key to figuring out what had gone down and what had not. Where did it all go so wrong? And how? More importantly, who had escaped? His intoxicated state that day was his prime regret, but he had consumed alcohol before that evening; the anomaly was that everything had been wiped totally from his memory. Or had it – if he remembered there was an extra individual in the house? The body needed rest, but the brain defied it; nightmares and ghosts always accompanied sleep anyway. Why bother with sleep when the truth was out there, so close yet not within his reach? The facts were accumulating but still adding up to nothing. He had focused long enough on what could have happened; it was time to turn that question on its head: what couldn't have happened?

11

NOT SURE WHAT THE BEST THING BEFORE SLICED BREAD WAS, BUT Bhīma was undoubtedly the best thing since. At least, according to his boss. Like his namesake in the *Mahabharata*, Bhīma could deal with anything. Given his sharpness and size, there were few things he couldn't accomplish and if that wasn't enough, his military training had prepared him well for multitasking. That left his boss to care about the more important and complex stuff, chiefly where His Advocateship's personal presence was absolutely required. Putting his inebriated boss to bed – despite the fact that Jay hadn't had dinner that evening – Bhīma ventured out on his nocturnal duty. Of course, he understood Jay wasn't helping himself with all the alcohol, but Bhīma was aware that his boss's life was personal and beyond his scope. He was willing to help whenever and wherever he was asked to. And tonight, he had a mission. He needed to get to his rats to ferret out if any Glock – the murder weapon – had changed hands recently.

His first stop, however, was Kumar's residence in New Friends Colony. With the headlight of his motorbike switched off, Bhīma went around the lane twice to spot the right address. Huge house. He'd also spotted one of his henchmen in that first round of the lane but circled the place again, just to be sure. The registration plate of the white Honda Accord stationed in the driveway confirmed it. This was Vinay Kumar's house. He rode past it, stopped at the corner and switched off the engine. The helper jumped pillion.

'I thought you wouldn't come, Bhīma *bhai.* You had said 11 p.m.'

'I got waylaid,' Bhīma uttered without apology. The guy could have left if he wanted to, but didn't because he knew there would be a hundred others to fill his spot as Bhīma paid handsomely. Having experienced poverty and hunger, and drudgery first hand, Jay had given Bhīma a freehand to disperse money for the best underhand dealings. Bhīma's current aide was actually a linesman from MTNL, who worked extra hours to pay for his children's education. A bad deed to pay for a good one; he wasn't siphoning millions like some ministers did, only tapping into the leftovers to ensure his children didn't have to do low-paying menial jobs or dishonest ones all over again. And he had been promised that were he to ever get caught, he'd have a saviour in one of the best advocates in town. Pro bono. This was chicken-shit for someone like Bhīma's boss. A telecom linesman caught on the telephone pole or having gone in to repair a line without approval from the authorities would hardly require more than a phone call from the Cooper & Singh offices.

No words were exchanged. Bhīma had already agreed on the task for the night. He handed the parcel and rode off.

The linesman climbed the pole and disconnected Vinay Kumar's telephone line. Tomorrow, he would go into the bungalow to restore the connection and bug the place. Kumar's house would be connected to Bhīma's powerhouse computer, illegitimately, of course.

Bhīma's next stop was Rajpath, the road leading to Rashtrapati Bhavan – the official residence of the President of India and the largest presidential estate for any Head of State in the world. It is more than five times bigger than the White House, bigger than

Buckingham Palace and is also one of the most well-guarded properties in the world, especially after the attack on the Indian Parliament House only a few years prior.

No one envisages risky activities could occur in the most conspicuous places. They do, they prosper and they go unnoticed for understandable reasons: who would dare?

Bhīma turned off the headlight, switched off the motorbike engine from a distance and let the wheels roll to their destination. Three men waited for their orders. All clad in white, they stood silently.

The Brobdingnagian man used his left leg to slide the side-stand into position, pulled out the key from the ignition and looked around before he got down from his bike. He then slowly walked towards the waiting men. Displayed urgency or panic can make even the smallest of jobs cost more.

'Good evening, Bhīma bhai.'

Bhīma nodded to greet them.

'What can we do for you?'

'A Glock changed hands a week ago, a month ago or maybe earlier. There can't be too many Glocks coming into Delhi. I want to find out who sold a piece recently, who bought it and when. And I want to know that quickly. Want to help?'

They nodded. No one bothered to ask what the remuneration would be. They knew they wouldn't be disappointed.

'Okay. Go ahead and spread the word, but be discreet. No one should know who's asking for the information, mind you. I need to know how a Glock got into Delhi. All understood? Any questions?'

None.

Bhīma repeated the sequence in two other areas: Barakhamba Road and Nehru Place. Same directions were given, same response. If anyone sold a Glock it wouldn't be long before Bhīma and Jay would know about it, no doubt about that. But if the killer had bought and got the Glock in from elsewhere, it was a different story altogether.

The motorbike returned to the farmhouse at two in the morning. Bhīma went to bed right away.

12

OVER A MONTH HAD PASSED SINCE JAY RETURNED FROM JAIPUR. The initial despair had been waning as expected, though the words from Cooper and the subsequent letter he had received from his mother after her death had steered him nowhere, really. The search for the police investigator, Saxena, who had been the lead in investigating his father's case, was still on. It was a cause for concern as the failure was being attributed to the era: too old to dig out.

Jay's son, Yuvraj, was over for the Diwali break. He was eleven, an adolescent going on to become a man. The circumstances and hostel life had made him far more mature than his other classmates. He had once asked Jay about his mother, but a few sob stories later comprehended that Ma was no longer alive. He had no knowledge that he was adopted. He loved his dad and Uncle Bhīma who untiringly taught him how to ride a bicycle and took him on endless rides on his motorbike within the premises of the farmhouse. Sometimes amusing, at other times inspiring and occasionally extremely annoying but, as they say, the heartache from the passing of a family member can only be relieved by the mirth of the next generation. For the ten days that Yuvraj was in town, the funk deserted Jay. Yuvraj's incessant demands on Jay's time came as a desirable break. He had taken time off work. The courts were closed so there wasn't anything he needed to step out of his house for. Father and son watched boy-flicks: Vin Diesel, James Bond, the Bourne series.

Sheeba was over the moon and back, a few times; the attention she got from Yuvraj always pampered her rotten. She had been taught that all feral behaviour would have to be abandoned the moment Yuvraj went back to school, but dogs, unlike humans, live in the moment.

A lot of whisky was relocated from the bar to Jay's room on the first floor. The last thing Jay wanted was his son to see that his father was an alcoholic. He had enough other problems in life to add any new ones. And he *was* getting treatment from the shrink, wasn't he?

One of Yuvraj's friends from school, Raaj Rohatgi, was the son of Jay's own school-time friend. While socializing with Raaj's parents, Jay passed his mother's autopsy file to Raaj's dad, who was a clinical pathologist. Dr Rohatgi agreed to look at it, though neither expected anything seismic from it. If anything, it would support putting the whole thing to bed.

Diwali break was short. As always, Yuvraj had to be mollycoddled to return to the hostel. However, he knew it was a short term, as he would be back for a longer break at Christmas.

Bhīma's search was proving to be more exacting than initially anticipated. So far, all his snitches had failed to unearth where the Glock had come from, which could only mean one of two things: either the gun had changed hands in some other geography or the deal had taken place in ancient history, long before Gina's murder. His snitches had also been unsuccessful in locating where the weapon was discarded after the deed, which was anyway more Herculean to work out than its origin. With a myriad of khakis looking for the same, the snitches had to stay away. However, they looked at places the police had ignored and scavenged those that the police had already rummaged through when the moon took over its daily duties from the sun. But nothing turned up. The best guesstimate was that it was thrown into the river Yamuna, and if that was actually the case, the police weren't going to spend precious resources on a deep-dive search for someone like Gina. Of course, it would be an altogether different matter if Vinay Kumar had been shot. A politician was first among equals.

Kumar had been called in for questioning at the police station. As previously agreed, Jay had accompanied him to the investigation. With his advocate present there wasn't much the police could get from Kumar, which was the whole idea. The police had done their homework; after the FIR and initial enquiry, they had investigated the circumstances of the crime, ascertained the facts – one of Gina's neighbours was all too eager to oblige the police about Vinay Kumar's surreptitious visits. And if that wasn't enough, the autopsy revealed the moron's seeds in her body along with his unborn child. And though the police didn't discover or collect any real incriminating evidence to suggest that Kumar was the perpetrator, it being a cognizable offence, they needed no warrant to arrest him on grounds of homicide. The chargesheet was filed under Section 173 of the Criminal Procedure Code and sent to the Magistrate, who was convinced that the crime, if proven, attracted more than a seven-year sentence, and hence, he was legally obligated to forward the case to the Sessions Court.

Murder is a severe crime anywhere in the world; in India it is a non-bailable offence and, as such, an accused is not entitled to bail as a matter of right. However, citing Article 21 of the Indian Constitution – a provision that protects every citizen of India from illegal arrest and governs the concepts of bail – Jay Singh filed an application to convince the magistrate that the allegations levelled against Vinay Kumar were, prima facie, in no way established by the police or any other investigating body. The court appreciated that someone as recognizable as Vinay Kumar would neither hamper the evidence nor tamper with the witnesses. Furthermore, Jay Singh assured that the accused would, at all times, cooperate with the investigations and appear before the court whenever required. The court asked Kumar to surrender his passport, but that was hardly a price. Thankfully, as it is the discretion at the Session Court judge's level to either grant or refuse the bail, the issue wasn't flagged to higher authorities or the media, lest the result be entirely different. With all those conditions in place and thanks to an undisclosed amount, *zamanat* was granted. There was a huge relief in the defence camp. Whether Kumar was guilty or not was a question for another day, in another courtroom. For now he was free; he only had to report to the Saket police station once a week.

Even criminal cases in India can be protracted. One can take unnecessary adjournments on the flimsiest of grounds, but Kumar was adamant that he wanted a quick trial to clear him of the charges. With elections looming, the last thing he wanted was a pending criminal case against him.

'*I know I am innocent, what do I have to worry about? This is all a set-up*,' he had been adamant.

No one from Gina's family came forward and, hence, the state had to provide a public prosecutor who wasn't named yet. As such, the first trial date would easily be four to six months away.

Jay had repeatedly postponed his appointment with Anita, pretending to be overloaded with work, citing the infamous murder case he was working on. And though a mere thought of Manavi always made his blue funk disappear, it furthered his insomnia. In more rational moments he knew it was a fantasy, but he had started having more irrational moments since he had met her. The acorn of love that Ali had sown for Manavi had been blossoming in his fertile mind. Quite often, it is said, though at first reasoning lapses gradually when you are toying with love, rabidity accelerates without forewarning and, before you know it, you find yourself on the periphery of a trap called love. Incessantly denying himself that he was besotted, partly because he found it crazy to accept the pining – he was convinced that he only wanted company – and partly because he had never been in love before this to discern the feeling itself. Nevertheless, love is very much like law: simply not knowing the law does not mean you aren't reined in by it, but it wasn't something of which Jay Singh was aware.

Bureaucracy has its own pace; at most times it can put a snail to shame. The autopsy files of his mother had taken over seven weeks to travel from the hospital in Jaipur to Dr Rohatgi in New Delhi, the doctor nominated by Jay. He wasn't expecting anything, but he knew it would cost nothing either. Why leave any little stone unturned?

Hence, it was a surprise when Dr Rohatgi called Jay one evening. Sounding solemn, the doctor asked Jay if he could visit him some time the following week. A slave of habit, Jay Singh had drained quite a bit of whisky when the doctor phoned and agreed to see him the coming Thursday.

'My watch was a bit slow,' Jay apologized as he walked in to see Dr Rohatgi the next week.

'It happens sometimes.' Rohatgi smiled. Not like a saturnine smile; nevertheless, it had shades of sarcasm.

'What?'

'How about your calendar? Was that slow too or do you not have one? You were supposed to be here yesterday.'

'What?' Jay said, realizing he had really messed up. There

wasn't any coming back after being a day late for an appointment. It was Friday, a day and thirty minutes late. 'Guilty as charged, Doc,' he sheepishly apologized.

'Apology accepted. Hope all is okay.'

'Oh yes. I'm just stressed out because of a case.'

'Okay.'

'So?' Jay let the unspoken words hang, like he was expecting Rohatgi to disclose whatever he had called him over for.

'You know, Jay, sometimes death can tell us more than what a living person can,' began Dr Rohatgi.

'Last I heard, you were a doctor of medicine. Since when have you become a dialogue writer for B-grade Hindi films?'

'Well, Shilpa Shetty wanted me to write a film script and also, maybe, star opposite her, but I declined.'

'Why, if I may ask?'

'I prefer the dead. Moreover, I needed time to talk to you, my friend.'

'Huge sacrifice, I have to admit,' riposted Jay.

'Care for a drink?'

'Yes, vodka would be nice.'

Both laughed out loud, shook hands and sat down on the beige sofa in the doctor's office.

Dr Rohatgi and Jay Singh had attended the same Delhi Public School – DPS – for five years before Rohatgi's father, an army colonel, was transferred out of Delhi. Decades later, after Jay's legal practice flourished, he ran into Rohatgi at the Delhi Gymkhana. The childhood bond refurbished. While Jay had spent his entire life in Delhi, Rohatgi had moved around with his parents, completed schooling and gone to the US for a degree in medicine, worked in Los Angeles for five years before returning to his homeland. The Americanized tall, bald, gangling doctor wore a button-down white Oxford with suspenders and ash grey trousers. His navy blazer hung on the coat rack. He was married, and his son Raaj studied with Yuvraj at Lawrence School in Sanawar. Their bond had henceforth strengthened, with the friendship passing on to the second generation. As Rohatgi had known Jay's parents, he also knew about the family mishap, but only to an extent. He, along with his wife, saw Jay as one of the most successful men of his time with a flourishing law practice that flaunted a roster of clients who were the who's who of society. The bachelor was attractive – both physically and monetarily – and well-connected in the community. As expected, Rohatgi's wife, Bindu, had tried fixing alliances for Jay, but none of the women even remotely fascinated the advocate; most were interested in his money, which he figured out at the first coffee dates.

Dr Rohatgi ran one of the best pathology lab franchises across the NCR. He had become more of a corporate businessman than a doctor. On the day, he sat in his tenth-floor Nehru Place office with a blue-coloured box file on the coffee table between them, titled: Autopsy Report – Mrs Rani Singh.

'Is this it?' Jay gestured towards the file with raised eyebrows.

'Pretty much. As I said, a lot in this file could be so different from a living person—'

'Come on, you asshole, stop talking like Kader Khan, tell me what it is that you didn't want to tell me on the phone. I've had to cancel a client meeting; why couldn't this wait?' rejoined Jay. A few swear words were acceptable amongst school friends, though not when Bindu or the kids were present.

'Look, I'm your friend, but I am also a doctor—'

'Do you want to show me your certificates now?' Jay interrupted again, impatient to hear what Rohatgi had to divulge; the doctor's expression did not portray glee, which caused further concern. He felt the adrenaline rush. 'I know you're a doctor, and

I know you're my friend and I know whatever you tell me will be in good faith and true. What is it? Any foul play?'

'No. She died of increasing senescence. I'm sure the circumstances and the surroundings in which she spent the last two decades weren't conducive to a healthy life. Add all the stress she endured and you can imagine obvious acceleration of the ageing process. The report here says,' he pointed to the box-file, 'she suffered a stroke in the evening, fell into a coma and passed away within an hour. The stroke caused an intracranial haemorrhage that accumulated blood on her brain. It was a big one, and, it seems, she would have been permanently disabled had she lived. So, all I can say is that it was fortunate she didn't live to suffer.'

'Fortunate ...?'

The irony wasn't lost on Rohatgi.

'I know,' he feebly agreed. Despite being oblivious of the exact incident and utterly unaware of the recent letter that Jay had received, there was no arguing the fact that Rani Singh and good fortune did not fit into a single sentence. He bent forward and from the box on the coffee table pulled out a white A4 envelope that had a glassine window that boldly stated: 'Confidential.' He took out the one-sheet report from the envelope and looked at Jay.

'What's this now?'

'This is what I called you here for, Jay.'

'Is it bad news?'

'Good and bad are relative terms—'

'Cut out that shit before I throttle you. No more nonsense – come to the point.' Jay was back in his jovial mood. There hadn't been any unfairness in his mother's death. What could possibly be bad?

'Did you know that your mother had AIS?'

'Am I here to play Scrabble now? What's AIS?'

'Androgen Insensitivity Syndrome?'

'What *is* that?'

'That she had one X and one Y chromosome, does that mean anything to you?'

'No. I was, you could say, a little weak in biology.'

Rohatgi watched Jay for a minute, shook his head in disbelief and handed the paper to him.

'Your mother could not have conceived. Biologically, she couldn't have been your mother.'

'Are you fucking kidding me?' Jay briefly glanced at the paper and looked back at the doctor.

'I wish. When they found this in the autopsy, they ran further pelvic tests to establish that your mother never gave birth to a child. The physical evidence substantiated the pathological finding. It all ties in.'

Gloom descended – anger, abhorrence, annoyance, anxiety. There had been times in the past when he had wondered what could possibly be worse? Hadn't he been through everything? Orphaned by accident or treachery, lived in absolute drudgery, convicted mother in a mental asylum, alcoholism, but this was something else: to know that your mother wasn't even your mother. And yet she never uttered a word, not even in her last note. Did she think he would never find out? In fairness, he wouldn't if he hadn't asked the folks at Jaipur to send the file to Rohatgi. Is this what she had meant in her note when she said, '*Don't waste your life looking for the killer ... if this was devastating, the truth will destroy you.*' Bottom line: he wasn't orphaned the day his father died; he was an orphan already. Or was he? Where did he come from? To his knowledge his father had married his mother when they were both quite young, so there wasn't a chance of a previous marriage. Adopted? Picked up from some doorstep? The outcome of some lusty, one-night stand?

The truth has a wicked tradition of arriving naked at times and its nakedness, at this moment, wasn't pleasing. The trapped silence took longer than a few minutes to dissipate. Rohatgi didn't speak for a while; perhaps he thought it was wise for the initial shock, the angst, to recede, which had completely immobilized Jay, who couldn't fathom what to believe or what to expect next. Part of him that had unsuccessfully tried to forge ahead had received another hard knock-back. The emotional springs that had been locked down by the passage of time were rapidly becoming loose. Another single piece of news had driven home with a devastating jolt. It was like some invisible power relished whipping his soul. Tears sought to flow out, but he vowed to stay resilient. He held them back and clenched his teeth till his jaw hurt. There were too many unanswered questions racing through his mind; the primary one being, who had his mother tried to shield all along?

'I'll ask for some coffee.' Rohatgi finally broke the silence and stood up.

'Forget it.' Jay held his friend's hand as he moved across him. He took out a flask from the jacket pocket and looked at him for gestural approval to drink in his office.

Rohatgi nodded sympathetically.

Jay opened the flask and took a long swig, waited for the liquid to go down and then, upending the flask, he finished the drink in the second mouthful.

'Calm down, Jay—'

'I am calm, this is only an emollient. Don't worry, Doc, I won't pass out in your office.'

'You know that doesn't bother me one bit. Are you okay?'

'Yes. Is there anything more you want to tell me?' Jay smiled. A reluctant, sad smile.

'Isn't this enough for one day?'

'Fan-fucking-tastic. This is enough for one lifetime.'

Both men smiled. Both understood that a lightning had just struck Jay, but they wanted to lessen the impact.

'What do you intend doing with this info?' Rohatgi asked after a brief pause.

'Don't know, frankly.' Jay got up. The mental blow and then the quick shots made his feet waver. He saw Rohatgi rush to his aid. 'I'll be okay, my friend.'

'Why don't you call—?'

'Call whom?'

'Start with Rashtrapati Bhavan? Should I call Bhīma to pick you up?' Rohatgi kibitzed.

'Don't bother, my friend. I'll walk down on my own. I think I need some time alone.'

'Jay, please don't go so far out somewhere that you can never return,' Rohatgi almost pleaded as Jay held the door to his office.

'What makes you think I'd want to return?'

With that, Jay was out walking towards the elevator.

Bhīma was waiting right outside the elevator doors. The customary mobile phone that was always switched on whenever Jay was out of his sight had already conveyed the proceedings of his boss' meeting with the doctor. While Jay appeared unruffled, Bhīma – now having worked alongside Jay for years – recognized it was a façade. After all, he had driven Jay to Jaipur just a few weeks ago and grasped some of the reasons for his boss's errant behaviour and continued grief and love for alcohol. Devoted as he was, it disturbed him as the chips were now falling. There was very little he could have done. Bhīma was well aware of Jay's visit to the psychiatrist, however, he wasn't privy to the actual session.

Did he need to speak separately to Jay's psychotherapist? There was a mine of information that he could share with the therapist, information that she could never access anywhere else and if that meant it could take only some of his boss' miseries away, would that be a breach of faith? He pondered this as he walked Jay back to the car.

♝

Jay decided to go back home for the rest of the day. The police, meanwhile, had asked Vinay Kumar to come down to the Saket police station to answer a few more questions regarding Gina's homicide. For Jay, there had been no ambiguity. It was a clear homicide: circumstantially speaking, how could the weapon have disappeared after Gina's death if it was a suicide? To the best of his knowledge – and his client's – Vinay Kumar certainly was the accused, and with the facts that the police would now have received after the formal autopsy would have pointed robustly at Kumar, what with Gina's pregnancy and signs of recent sexual activity with Kumar. As agreed in their previous meetings, Kumar had informed Jay and the advocate was to accompany him the next morning. But that was tomorrow and as such there wasn't any pressing need for Jay to be in office on this day. No client engagements, no court appearances. He could well accomplish pretty much everything else on the phone. Not to forget the additional allure of alcohol, which he could really do with in this moment.

The mercury hadn't stopped pushing north even after forty. It was expected to break records, they had announced on local television in the morning after the news bulletin. Mercifully, it was a short walk to the car and its air-conditioned environs. As Bhīma steered the car through the daytime traffic, Jay couldn't help but look at the world around him. Everyone he saw, seemed happy. Not a worry on anyone's mind or at least it wasn't obvious. Why shouldn't they be happy? Their mothers hadn't lied to them or withheld any truth. He got increasingly restless, impatient. All along he had twisted the facts to fit his imaginary theory of some clandestine relationship between Swamiji and his mother. Now that it had dawned on him that even his mother wasn't his birth mother, maybe his entire theory had been bunkum; *bakwaas*. Anyway, didn't they always advocate that the theory should fit the available facts? And what facts did he have? None.

Sheeba was naturally excited to see the two men in her life return to the farmhouse earlier than usual. Jay was starving, he hadn't eaten anything in the last eighteen hours and the liquids he had consumed all this time had exited his body. Bahadur decided to cook a big lunch. Lamb curry, Jay's favourite. Jay quickly changed into his swimming gear and requested Bhīma to fix him a drink.

Ten minutes later, Sheeba and Jay were in the pool, playing with a ball, martini on the side. It had been ages since Jay had taken out time for some fun. Today, surprisingly, when his world had overturned again, he resolved to swim in the pool rather than drown in alcohol. He was deliberately pushing the unpleasant thoughts back, attempting to look forward. He got reminded of Manavi, though he wasn't sure if it was a good time to call in the middle of the afternoon, three drinks down.

Nothing more sinister could happen, he convinced himself.

'Bhīma, please get me my phone,' he said, coming to the edge of the pool. He climbed out, put on his robe and took a sip of the cool martini.

13

SURPRISINGLY, JAY WAS LOOKING FORWARD TO HIS SECOND SESSION with Anita.

Though Jay Singh was dazzling even on a bad day, today was unusual. He also dreaded it like a schoolboy who carried a bad report card. Akbar Ali had highlighted that this conversation could have happened later on the phone and as such – it wasn't like the aircraft had reached the end of the runway and it had to take off – Jay didn't have to broach the topic with Manavi today, but he wasn't the one to forsake an opportunity when he met her face to face.

Why should Akbar Ali call the shots? Was he in schoolboy competitive mode?

He was dressed in his usual summer linen suit in a neutral colour: powder blue button-down shirt, collar open with no tie; tan moccasins completed the attire. An extra fifteen minutes had been spent getting ready in the morning; he had asked Bahadur to iron his clothes all over again, as though Manavi would take any decision on the sharpness of his trousers' crease. In any event they were linen and by the time he sat in the car to get to Anita's office, they would crumple.

The otherwise busy Jay Singh arrived twenty minutes before the appointment. There was nothing more pressing for the busiest defence advocate in town than to squander time at a shrink's reception reading *Reader's Digest*, was there? Vinay Kumar would have to hold his horses for some time.

Manavi sat behind the bureau, only her attractive face visible when Jay arrived.

'Good morning, Mr Singh.'

'Good morning, and please call me Jay.'

First names generally engendered intimacy, which was always a good beginning.

'As you wish, Jay.' She beamed. 'You'll have to wait, as you're a bit early.'

My pleasure.

'Oh,' Jay said aloud, looking at his watch and raising his eyebrows in surprise, like he hadn't realized he was early for his appointment. 'No worries.'

As he stood at the reception desk, he glanced down at her outfit. Manavi wore a white shirt with a nice décolletage that offered quite a glimpse from the angle he stood. He could discern a grey skirt, but couldn't gauge the design or length. She'd have to stand up for that. With only the top half of her image in his mind, he walked to the sofa, picked up the previous month's issue of the digest and flipped through the pages. *Reader's Digest* – as a magazine – had long lost its appeal. It had a loyal readership amongst his father's generation that was fast depleting and the content wasn't fashionable enough to keep it running for long. But that wasn't his problem. As he ostensibly read it, he was convinced this might be his best break. There were no other clients waiting. With him being the first appointment of the day, maybe Anita wasn't yet in the office either.

What could possibly go wrong?

Maximum damage: loss of face.

Acceptable.

Ideas came in bursts. Then they battled amongst each other

and – Darwin was right, only the fittest survived. Sometimes one, sometimes twins. At this moment, the mêlée in Jay's mind was no different. From the profusion of ideas, Jay finally picked one and mustered enough courage to walk up to her to ask: 'Are you free this weekend, Manavi?'

'Sorry?'

Moment of embarrassment. Oh Lord! Now he'll have to repeat the question.

He could either change course to ask something irrelevant and save discomfiture or continue with his line of proposal. He chose the latter. 'I asked if you were free this Saturday for dinner?'

'Are you asking me out on a date?'

He was indeed a generation behind. This wasn't the eighties; they called it the '*Naughties*'.

'Dinner, date. Is there a difference?'

'Of course there is.' She may have wanted to add '*old fool*' but she gratefully didn't.

'In that case, dinner,' he meekly uttered.

'Not that I'm doing anything in particular, but may I ask the reason for this generosity?'

'Generosity? That's quite an exaggeration. I'm only asking you out for dinner.'

'Only if it's not too expensive a place and we split the bill.'

It sounded comforting that she wasn't after his money. He was almost certain she knew his financial standing.

'Why should that be of significance?'

'Because you asked me out for dinner, not a date.'

'Is that the difference between dinner and date?' No sooner had the words left his mouth than he realized he had actually put his foot in there by asking such a foolish question.

She smiled. But before she could respond, her desk phone buzzed.

'Yes, Anita, he's here,' she said, looking up at him. 'I'll send him in now.'

'I thought Anita wasn't in yet.'

'She is. She usually spends the first half hour of the day on things other than seeing clients, organizing stuff, you see. You may go in now.'

'Thanks. I'll speak to you when I come out.'

She gave him a wink.

God, she winked. Doesn't controlled coquetry come with practice? It wasn't something Manavi could attempt without years of rehearsal. That or she had expected him to invite her out. That again, needed experience to estimate.

Dazed at her move, he walked into Anita's office.

'Good morning, Jay.' Like in a black-and-white film of yesteryears, the professional countenance of Anita superimposed on the kittenish image of Manavi.

'Good morning, Anita.'

'You sound cheerful today. Please sit.' She pointed towards the sofa.

A dinner with Manavi three days later, almost finalized. I'm not just cheerful, I'm fucking ecstatic.

Anita poured two coffees from her cafetière into expensive China cups, which were as thin as rice paper, and brought them along to the coffee table that was between Jay and her.

'How have the past few weeks been, since you saw me?'

'Hectic. But first, I owe you an apology—'

'For?'

'For being such a prick last time.' He gave an appealing smile.

'I thought we had gone past that stage. No worries, apology accepted. So, why was your time hectic?'

'My mother passed away.'

'I'm so sorry. My condolences.'

'Thanks.'

'How do you feel about that?'

'I wasn't surprised, but I am disappointed, nevertheless. In one sense she is past all suffering now, which is the only silver lining. But if there was even one per cent of hope lingering somewhere, it is now gone. It's over.'

'What hope? I don't think we discussed anything like that?' She flipped through the pages of her pad to go through her notes.

'I'm sorry. Did I not tell you that I don't believe my mother killed my father?'

Anita closed her pad and crossed her legs – she was wearing navy trousers this time. She let out a loud whoosh. Perhaps she was only now gathering that there were more complications in his life, more issues bothering him than she had known hitherto.

'Tell me, why is that?' she began.

'Sorry, why is what?'

'Why do you think your mother did not do what the courts convicted her of?'

'I think it was a cover-up.'

'As far as you told me it was only you and your parents in the house that night, so ... who was she covering up for?'

Jay Singh took a sip of the coffee and exhaled hard before he started talking about Swamiji, the visits, his interpretation of the godman's surreptitious relationship with his mother and the letter he had received in the post from his mother only after her death. He pulled out the letter and handed it over to Anita. It took him twenty-five minutes to provide the balance details and arrive at the climax: that his mother was not his biological mother.

'So, if I understand this correctly, there was a fourth person in the house that night who, in your opinion, did the hideous deed and your own mother sought to protect him rather than tell the police?' Anita asked after a few minutes of contemplation.

Jay nodded. The last dregs of coffee were in his mouth now.

'Is that what bothers you?'

He nodded again.

'Does it bother you more than your father's murder and your mother's plight?'

'Yes. While I know nothing I do now can bring back my parents or my lost years, it would still be a relief to know the truth. Don't you think?'

Anita revealed no signs of agreement or disagreement. Talk about professionalism.

'But how would you find anything now? It was a lifetime ago.'

'I've always had an inkling that she didn't kill him. Her letter states that she didn't—'

'She also advised you not to go looking for the killer,' Anita interrupted.

'I know, but the buried truth wouldn't let me live in peace. It was okay when I'd assumed she didn't kill him; it's quite different when I *know* that she didn't. And if she didn't, who did? And why should he get away?'

'Why do you think it was a 'he'?

'Just a figure of speech, though I won't lie, everything points towards that Swamiji.'

'The truth can devastate you, she's told you in her letter.'

'If she thought I'd was too young to remember or know about her and Swamiji, she was clearly mistaken. If the rascal has got away with my family's ruin, I swear I will bring him to justice.'

'I appreciate that, Jay, but as a successful lawyer, why wouldn't you concentrate on other positive things rather than go digging for dirt on something that happened a lifetime ago?'

'Sorry, Anita. Success isn't always about career or money. I can expand my practice, but I already have more money than I could ever spend. There aren't many more toys that I want. What would I do with more money and a bigger law practice if they cannot even buy me sleep? Maybe I should have a second bite at the cherry …'

'You mean, reopen the case?'

'If required, yes.'

'How do you even start?'

'Bhīma is already looking for the police officer who conducted the enquiry, that would be my first call.'

'Bhīma? I thought he was your driver.'

Jay gave a succinct account of Bhīma's cousin and how the ever-dependable man came into his life. He spoke of his loyalty, his dedication, his secrecy and his technical and investigative skills without giving away the illegal methods employed. Jay concluded by admiring how Bhīma quadruplicated a friend, chauffeur, security and valet.

'So you trust him?'

'With my life.'

'Amazing, isn't it … that you can trust someone with your life, someone who you met by a quirk of destiny?'

'It is. He takes care of me like my dad should have,' he said, smiling softly to cover up an old hurt.

Jay waited until Anita absorbed what he had just revealed. The discussion ahead wasn't going to be cheerful, but it was good that he talked about his father and the past. There was a long pause.

Anita leaned back expansively.

Is she waiting for me to divulge more?

'More coffee?'

'That would be lovely, thanks.'

'Did you witness a lot of altercations as a child?' Anita began after refilling the coffees.

'Frequently.'

'Would it be too far-fetched to assume that, in some perverse sort of way, you were glad that your father's death ended those fights?'

'I wasn't glad. Relieved? Perhaps. But that was not how I had anticipated they would end.'

'Of course not.'

Neither of them spoke for another full minute.

'Have you met any of your friends since your mother's death?' Anita glanced at her pad for the names. 'Akbar Ali or Sam Cooper?'

'I didn't get a chance to see Akbar.'

'And Sam Cooper?'

'He came to see me when he found out about it.'

'How? I thought you said you didn't tell anyone.'

'I didn't. But Cooper has sources, more sources than I have. He knows everything about everyone, especially me.'

'Interesting,' she muttered. 'How?'

'We have been close friends since college.'

'But that should reveal all your past – how does he know what happened now?' she probed.

'Told you, he has sources.'

'I'd like to meet him.'

'Why? He's sane,' Jay chuckled.

'For the record, I don't see insane people and you aren't insane either. The reason I want to see him is to know more about you, that's all. A close outsider's view might give me a better insight or, at least, a different perspective,' she answered sagely. 'As a matter of fact, I want to see Akbar Ali too … if you permit me to.'

'I can ask, but I'm not sure it they'll come.'

'If they want to help you—'

'I'll ask them, no promises, though.'

'Of course.'

It had been more than an hour now, but Anita hadn't bothered to conclude the session till it reached a natural pause. There wasn't much else to talk about at the moment. Anita, Jay was aware, would need to analyse all that he had articulated today. He had given her lots to digest: the revelation about his trust in Bhīma, Swamiji, his mother's letter and that she wasn't his real mother. And the poor therapist would also have to work out how to bring him back to normalcy, to a life without alcohol.

Now out of her office, Jay stopped at the reception desk. There was a middle-aged lady waiting for her turn. Manavi smiled when she saw him.

'Good session?' she asked, looking at her desk clock, indicating it had taken longer than the usual hour slot Anita dispersed.

Overrun by twenty minutes. Did that mean she was engrossed in his conversation? Or had she figured out some answer to his problem?

'Oh yes.'

Disinclined to speak in the presence of another client in the reception area, Manavi passed him a slip with her number on it and mouthed, 'Call me later.' She shot him a playful grin.

Jay folded the piece of paper, thanked her and walked out happy. She waited for him to go out of sight before rushing to Anita's office.

'I'll only take a minute, Anita,' she gently said.

'What is it?'

'I've been invited to dinner by one of your clients.'

'Let me guess. Jay Singh?'

She nodded.

'Manavi, I am bound by an ethical code, but you are not governed by it at all, especially if he's the one who initiated it. I know he's single, and it is entirely up to you to make that choice. I won't discourage you, though I want you to understand that you should not be doing this for our clinical practice. Personally, if you want to, please go ahead. If anything untowardly happens, anything you're not comfortable with, walk away. I hope you're meeting in a public place.' Anita saw a grave expression emerge on Manavi's face. 'Don't get me wrong, I'm not saying he has any wrong malintent, but it doesn't harm to play safe. And, of course, if you see, hear or observe something that you think might be important to report back for his own benefit in any way, please tell me.'

Manavi felt like the hostel warden had just granted her late-night permission. Feeling excited, the only thought that crossed her mind was: what was she going to wear?

Jay had a lot of work at the office and realized that, despite his desire, he wouldn't be able to see Akbar Ali immediately. Moreover, Akbar, too, would be sitting under a banyan tree somewhere, toiling hard for his bread. Back at the office around eleven-thirty, he first visited the discreet windowless room set up for Kumar's case. It was usual practice to set one up whenever they signed on a potential big case: the Case Room – Jay colloquially referred to it as the War Room at times – was festooned with crime scene photos, medical and police summaries, witness lists and statements, police investigations, results of clandestine private investigations conducted so far, a detailed client profile and various other exhibits. The white walls were completely covered in charts with information and then some.

Walking into his own cabin, Jay flung his jacket on the coat hanger from a distance and winked at Julie when it wedged on the hook.

Double-O-Seven style.

He could bet Julie noticed the jubilance in his demeanour.

'Coffee, please.'

Amazed, she nodded and smiled back.

'Actually, bring in two coffees, Julie. I haven't had a coffee with you for quite some time now. Also, convey to the team working on Kumar's case to gather for a briefing at 2 p.m., please.'

'See you in a minute, Jay.'

♝

Kumar's defence case file was growing thicker by the day. Though he had had a chequered past, what with all the drinking and womanizing, nothing indicated violence or any conviction. That Vinay Kumar was Gina's paramour and her unborn child's father was something Jay had decided to present in his opening statement at the court rather than letting the prosecution checkmate them. Concealing that bit of information would indicate guilt, and if found guilty on one count, it could create a hole in the defence strategy left open for the prosecution to exploit. On the contrary, if Vinay Kumar openly confirmed the nature of their relationship, the defence could argue that why would he resort to anything as violent as murder? However, that meant the now politically ambitious Kumar had to accept having a mistress in public life. But that could be cloaked as an isolated mistake. There wasn't much choice in that matter.

The basic structure, the bare bones, of the case was ready. Truth was that Jay prepared much of such a case – one with no alibi or any other suspect to build a real defence strategy – only as the prosecution commenced calling the witnesses. It was the best time to create holes in their strategy, not giving them time to recover. As they say, things don't just fall into place, a good advocate fits them into place and that was what Jay Singh was very proficient at. The only element that could spoil the party was if the missing gun turned up. However, with Kumar incessantly insisting that he was innocent, even if the gun turned up, there was no reason to fret that it could be traced back to him. Ironically, it was Kumar's persistence of his innocence that bothered Jay. You don't hire the country's best and most expensive defence advocate if you're not guilty. Then again, if Kumar was the murderer why wasn't he answering the door when Jay was loudly knocking, promising to represent him even if he was guilty? In fact, if he pleaded guilty to his own defence advocate then Jay could never call that out in court.

The day in the office ended with success in another ongoing case. Bhīma's pigeons had finally located the retired Superintendent of Police.

Better still, the retired SP Amrit Saxena was in Delhi.

14

JAY HAD GARNERED ENOUGH CONFIDENCE TO MAKE THAT all-important call to Manavi after she had slipped him her number. He had never actually dated anyone before, although he had experienced a romantic liaison back in college, but it had all evaporated post that dreadful evening. Then suddenly, there was no time, no inclination and no one to date.

He was casually attired in jeans and a linen shirt. Jay deliberated leaving Bhīma behind and to drive alone, but his overprotective sidekick wouldn't let that happen, not in a public place. When he had hired Bhīma for his security, Jay had wholeheartedly agreed never to jump the latter's advice. And rightly so. Just because there hadn't been any untoward incident in the recent past didn't mean that all the adversaries had renounced the very idea. To avoid letting his date see he was chauffeur-driven for the dinner, Jay arrived a good twenty minutes before seven. However, he knew that Bhīma would follow him like a shadow, watch him from a distance and it might be difficult, if not impossible, for anyone to miss King Kong in the Claridges' lobby. Like a teen, Jay disappeared into the washroom. Then he briskly walked into the restaurant to check if the table he had booked was in the less crowded corner.

As he walked back into the lobby, he saw her.

Manavi had put on a little black dress that would have done Coco Chanel proud. The pencil dress was crafted from stretch fabric with a lace sweetheart neckline – chic, not revealing. Bare legs – no stockings – in patent croc black leather stiletto shoes. She looked a lot taller than he had imagined. Almost as tall as him, but that, for once, did not bother him.

Manavi wasn't merely another slim, petite lass. She was a hard-bodied hottie, who looked like she visited the gym and spent a few hours there. The muscles well-toned, like she worked out regularly. Her diminutive triceps were well formed to show them off, along with miles of alabaster skin. Her stride oozed confidence, what with a body and face like that; her style exuded élan and raw sexuality. She looked anything but a shrink's receptionist. She could walk the ramp, but for her height.

Was that one of the attractions for the short advocate?

'*Mesmerizing*' was the only thought that crossed Jay's mind. She was so well dressed – her sensuality was extreme – and for an instant he wondered if he was too casually attired, but she was already walking towards him. Her perfume hit him before she came close and pecked him on both cheeks.

'Hi Jay.'

'You look ravishing, Manavi,' Jay murmured as she withdrew herself from his arms.

Despite having been counselled by none other than Mr Akbar Ali, Jay hadn't coloured his hair, though he had toyed with the idea. Now, looking at her, the panic that he might appear old enough to be her dad hit him in the gut.

What would people who saw them together think?

Who the fuck cared?

'Should we have a drink first?' he asked.

'Yes, thanks. I love their bar.'

He turned towards the bar. She put her arm through his. Arms linked like a couple in love, the two walked towards *Aura*. Thankfully, it was softly lit and sparsely populated.

It was essentially a vodka bar and when she ordered her drink, he realized why Manavi liked the place. The server took their orders and retreated.

For Jay, and maybe Manavi, too, it was the moment of truth. *What would they talk about all evening?*

'Do you come here often?' Jay asked.

How's that for an icebreaker?

'No. Not because I don't want to, but because I can't.'

Jay narrowed his eyes to ask why, but the server had arrived with their drinks.

'Because … I cannot afford to come here as often as I would like to on my meagre salary. Cheers, Jay.' She raised her glass to toast.

'Cheers.' He clinked his glass against hers.

'Why did you ask me out?'

'Because you're a *hottie.*' The truth had already left his lips before he realized that his choice of words might not have been the most elegant.

'Thanks. I know you said it in the right spirit, but that isn't the best way to compliment a lady,' she said.

'I'm sorry, I know …'

'It's okay.'

She was being nice to him. Did she see him struggling?

'But—'

'You are wondering why someone would mind being called a "hottie"?' she intervened.

'Kind of … yes.'

For God's sake, shut up, Jay. This acceptance of your foolishness might not go down well either.

'I guess you have a point, but while a subtle appreciation is desirable, your word choice takes it to another level. No one likes being treated as an object.'

'I said I'm sorry, I meant to be appreciative, not offensive.'

'No offence taken, my lord.' She smiled disarmingly. 'I'm glad you noticed.'

Just when her smile eased Jay, Bhīma entered the bar. Thankfully, Manavi was seated with her back towards the entrance or missing the colossal man would have been near impossible.

Another of Bhīma's virtues was he did not drink alcohol. The joke he always shared with Jay was that the latter more than consumed his share too.

What would he order in a bar? Milk?

Jay brought his wandering thoughts back lest he offend Manavi twice on the first date if she thought he was interested elsewhere. In another man? He saw she was pensive, preoccupied. He wanted to ask her if something was bothering her, but decided he didn't want to get involved in any more problems.

'What's bothering you?' he heard himself say.

'How old are you?'

She surprised him. He hadn't expected this question.

Was he supposed to lie? Evade the subject? What was the point? If his age bothered her it was best that they had dinner and forgot about this meeting.

'Forty-three. Too old?'

'For?'

'Dining with you?'

'How old do you think I am?'

'I shouldn't be guessing.'

Liar.

He had made a part-timer in his office do the research, not Bhīma. Jay knew where his date lived, that she had broken up with her long-term boyfriend a year ago and hadn't dated anyone since.

'Somewhere between twenty-seven and twenty-nine years old?'

'Wow, that's too wide a range.'

'Good guess?'

'On the dot.'

They sipped their drinks for a few silent seconds.

'So, how come you are single …' she started.

'At my age?'

She nodded, sipping her drink.

Jay walked her through his uninteresting life – carefully avoiding his murky past – the way his life had run its course, with him being the spectator at times, with no time to interpose, none for a woman, for anything, really. Life had been work, work and more work. And now, he had a son – adopted – who was in a hostel. So that's it. You could say I never had time to find someone suitable.'

'You're a great man to have adopted a kid, to have taken responsibility of someone without being forewarned. Most men I know would shy away from that.'

Jay smiled. He sneaked a glance behind her to see Bhīma sitting with a glass of water; also kept on the big man's table was a tankard of lager that he was nursing to keep prying eyes away.

'So you live alone?'

Should he tell her about Bhīma and Sheeba?

'You could say that,' he heard himself say. As an advocate he often surprised himself. Some of the responses left his mouth faster than his mind could process. Or, occasionally, as if his tongue disconnected from his brain, he responded with something else rather than what was on his mind. It hadn't got him into any trouble professionally, yet. 'What about you? You are so gorgeous; how come you are single?'

'Thanks. I wasn't single until a year back.'

'What happened? I mean I don't want to be intrusive …'

'Nah.' She took a large sip.

Jay saw that she was almost finished with her drink, while he had a large portion left. He took a generous sip to catch up. The waiter, also eyeing her glass, came right on time and they ordered a repeat.

'I broke off with a guy a year back.'

'I got that part.'

'We were together for four years.'

Jay kept listening. His couldn't help but appreciate how beautiful she was. Perfect set of teeth, lovely dark shoulder-length hair surrounding her youthful face, enthralling chocolate-coloured eyes, painted nails, impeccably dressed. Had all his lucky stars finally aligned?

'We had a great time. I have some good memories. We even travelled to Goa once.'

Jay flashbacked to his college days when your girlfriend letting you kiss her was a big deal in the eighties. How times had changed. Here, he sat with Manavi telling him she had travelled and lived with her ex. He had stayed in a time warp. His memories and understanding of the dating game still stuck in a time when he was single and making the most of his youth.

'Are you listening to me?'

'Oh yes. I love Goa. What happened? I mean, you seemed to have had a great relationship going.'

'He wanted to go abroad to study.'

'And you didn't?'

'I wanted to, but couldn't afford it, and he couldn't pay for both of us, so ... we split up. Nothing acrimonious. It couldn't work long-distance, and I don't suppose he'll come back.'

'What about you joining him?'

'In my dreams. Jay, I work as a receptionist. On a salary that allows me to live comfortably, not luxuriously. How can I ever afford to study in the US?' She rolled her eyes.

'But if you had a choice?'

'Choice of what?'

'Hypothetically speaking, if you had the money to go abroad, what would you study?'

'Interior designing. I have done up a few of my friends' homes, and they look great. Or so I'm told.'

'Wow. I've never had a designer look at my house.'

'Now you can.' She giggled coyly.

'Of course. My pleasure.'

♝

The Dhaba in Claridges supposedly serves highway cuisine, hence the name. The décor is complete with a truck mural and countryside interiors resembling a typical north Indian roadside eatery. The furniture is rustic, the walls rough, all done to replicate that ambience. The food is exceptional and exceptionally expensive. Jay escorted Manavi into the restaurant. They discussed food most of the time as they ordered and ate it. The bill was served – chauvinistically – to Jay, which he pulled close until Manavi reminded him of the promise.

'What if it's a date?' he quizzed.

'Is it?'

'Okay, let me ask you, what will make it a date?'

'Take me for a drive after this?'

And what do I do with Bhīma?

'My pleasure.' He knew he'd have to go to the men's, explain the situation to Bhīma and agree on a win-win situation. Bhīma could call a cab and follow them at a distance.

After dining and freshening up, they walked to the door. Manavi came close and slipped her hand into Jay's. Love birds from diverse eras. They drove around Connaught Place and stopped for coffee.

'Where do you live?'

'I am a country boy; I live at a farmhouse in Chhatarpur, away from the city.'

'Probably plush.'

'You should visit sometime to tell me what we could do with the interiors.'

'How about we plan for some weekend?' She looked at him. 'It takes time to look into such things.'

'How about this weekend? We could listen to music, barbeque something for dinner, have a drink, have a swim, after you finish—'

'You've got a swimming pool?'

Jay nodded. 'A small one.'

'Wow! I am impressed. And how do I get back from your place after you get me drunk?'

'I'll get you dropped, that should the least of your worries. Or I have a guest room if you want.'

That was brave, mentioning the guest room to stay over, Mr Gatsby.

'Could I confirm later, sometime during the week?' She gave him a peck on the cheek before getting down from the car, outside her DDA flat in Munirka.

Jay must have driven a couple hundred metres until a white cab overtook and stopped him. Bhīma got down, paid the driver and opened the door to Jay's side. Gently, he told Jay that this was a one-off. There was no way he was allowing the vakil sahib to drive out on his own in the night. Jay was in a great mood and didn't want to start thinking about how he would handle Bhīma or explain his presence to Manavi.

Jay stepped into his farmhouse after eleven, exultant like

a kid who had eventually spotted Santa Claus. He could have hung up the socks tonight. It had been a long day, but he wasn't tired. Manavi had given him enough hope that a relationship between them could be cultivated. She had been lively, entertaining and hung around regardless of his blathering at times. Bahadur had crashed, and Bhīma came inside only briefly to inspect if everything was in order. Once he left, Jay fixed himself a drink, put on a Gilberto vinyl, kicked off his shoes and placed his feet on the table. Within moments, the music came to life with his feelings '*about some tall and tan and young and lovely girl from Ipanema who went walking …*'

Manavi had looked young and so pretty, so sexy. It was like spring had sprung. Some clichés were so wrong: one swallow *could* make a spring. He had a childlike smile on his lips as he drifted off to sleep.

15

I WOKE UP WITH A START AT THREE. THE ONLY THING I remembered was that I was having a beautiful dream, but in those waking moments, the poor dream had got pushed down like a castle into a quagmire, so far deep and so out of my reach that I couldn't even fucking remember what it was. Mere strobe lighting flashed in my sleepy brain. Nevertheless, the leftover smile of the happy dream still adorned my dry lips. Sheeba lay on her back on the carpet next to me, her feet twitching in the air, like she was in the middle of a happy dream too. As always, she hadn't left my side. Bless her!

My subconscious told me that the music around me had somehow changed. And it, in fact, had. The music had changed to Zakir Hussain drumming away 'Rhythm Sonata in E Major'. *His fingers on the tabla sounded like pure bliss in the silence of the night and I realized I had dozed off on the comfortable sofas in the living room on the ground floor itself. I looked around to find that someone had even refilled my drink, kept the bottle of whisky next to it on the side stool: all tell-tale signs of someone having visited me while I was asleep. In the past, in very early years, I didn't realize that, or maybe my visitor was a little more discreet, never leaving any discernible signs. But with years of experience, I knew it had to be Cooper, who had visited me and was now gone. He must have wanted to have a drink, made me a fresh one too and changed the music. I looked carefully. The Gilberto vinyl that I had been listening to was now back in its jewel case, rearranged alphabetically, just as I liked.*

I finished the drink my friend had so kindly dispensed in my glass, but decided against pouring another one, as I had work in the morning. For a fleeting moment I felt miserable that I didn't wake up to speak to Cooper, to update him on the case and seek his advice. Although, if I were to be honest, I wanted to talk to him about Manavi more than the case. I had no misapprehension that given the way he so fascinatingly conducted his business – with a million eyes and ears – he'd already have known about my meeting with her last evening. Perhaps that was why he had come tonight – to raise a toast?

I elected not to go up to my bedroom to change for I had, in the past, made the mistake of walking up the stairs and changing into nightwear but by the time I was finished doing all that, sleep had given me a wide berth. I switched off the table lamp, covered myself with a throw and settled in for the remainder of the night. My brain was exhausted, drowsy and tipsy, what with the mishmash of events happening around: visions of my mother splashed in front of my eyes as moments marched on. Thoughts of Swamiji, then of my mum's letter, segued to Manavi and were alleviating. The moonlight showering on the swimming pool was visible from the French doors; the wind gently whispered something into the oak tree's ears outside; it hissed a smile in spurts. It sounded like the crickets were in mating season. Was it their version of howling at the moon? The pool looked all blue and beautiful. Everything was serene. I didn't want peace to leave and my mind to engage in unbidden thoughts. And so, before the ghosts of yesteryears could pop up or my mind actively engrossed itself in the current case, I vehemently shut my eyes and forced myself back to sleep.

16

'SO, DO YOU WANT TO TELL ME ANYTHING?' ANITA ASKED MANAVI when she saw her in office the next day.

'What about, Anita?' Manavi was stunned.

'Jay and you?'

Why would Anita be interested in knowing the intimacy she shared with Jay? Hadn't her employer made it clear that she could do as she pleased?

'Forgive my confusion, but I'm still not sure I understand what you mean, Anita.'

'Ah, it's not what you think; it's not that at all, silly girl. I have no interest in your personal life. I was only worried if anything untoward happened, which you might want to discuss.'

'Oh ...' Manavi let out a sharp breath. 'I wondered why you were curious about Jay and me.'

'I only have a clinical interest. Unless, of course, you want to share some other stuff. I'm here for you.'

'There's nothing like that, I promise.' She was aware that she was blushing. Would Anita catch her fib? The memories of the previous night's dinner and drive and the plan for the upcoming weekend started playing in her mind. They were so surreal that she almost grinned but stopped herself in time. *God, that was close!*

Was there any point in letting Anita know if she went over to Jay's place?

No.

Anita looked embarrassed. 'Coffee?'

'That'll be great. Thanks.'

'Take a seat. Let's have a chat. I don't have any appointments this morning.'

♝

'I called up Mr Saxena to fix an appointment for tomorrow afternoon at two, hukum. I've also informed Julie that you will not be in the office after lunchtime tomorrow, so she will reschedule all your appointments. There is only one court hearing tomorrow, which isn't important enough that you personally need to attend. She will ask someone else to be present on your behalf.'

That was Bhīma: loyal and dependable, caring and persistent.

Jay did ponder what new information a meeting with the man responsible for his father's homicide investigation over two decades ago could bring. For him, it was the murder of his father; for a police officer, the case would have been just another criminal investigation. What could the old man even remember? But curiosity was biting into whatever little patience he had left, and it was best to check, to turn this last stone too.

Bhīma had checked with the retired SP if he was okay to see them regarding the case. So, maybe, just maybe, the old man remembered something.

Didn't everyone live on wisps of hope?

♝

Vasant Kunj is a colossal complex. Located in southwest Delhi, the area was originally farmland spread across four villages. Post-Independence, with a young India waking up to its population demands, the villages were acquired by the Delhi Development Authority, under the leadership of the then Prime Minister Nehru, to build apartments for the city's residents. However, the construction only started in the eighties. It now housed over a hundred thousand people, most of them affluent, as expected anywhere in South Delhi: retired cricketers, golfers, bureaucrats, intellectuals, prominent businessmen.

Retired SP Amrit Saxena lived in the oldest part: Sector A, in Pocket C. It seemed like Saxena was waiting for his guests. When Jay rang the doorbell, the retired SP was immediately at the door with a smile wider than the Suez Canal, a universal sign of loneliness – you crave company to such an extent that you feel excited to see anyone at the door. His small apartment was spartanly furnished: an old two-seater sofa, a matching single one, a few chairs pulled from the dining table and a round glass coffee table with more scratches than the old man's age in months. The curtains didn't appear to have been taken down for a wash since his wife had passed away in the nineties. There was an old television, a CRT, in one corner and a collection of VHS tapes. Modest and time-warped existence, waiting for the eventuality every mortal is aware of but doesn't look forward to. The policeman was now a shadow of the powerful man Jay remembered him as. Bent, slim, hair – whatever was left – unkempt and white and, hence, the only trace of dandruff Jay could see was on his crumpled powder-blue shirt. Despite his advancing age and waning health, the SP had bathed and shaved to meet his guests.

After a few minutes of polite conversation about retired life, rising prices, increasing traffic and crime, the SP asked without warning, 'Why now?'

'Why now what, sir?' Jay repeated the sentence to comprehend what the old man was talking about.

'Why do you want to know about that incident after all these years?'

'Who knows? Sometimes the chips come together only when they do. The Kumbh Mela can happen every year, yet it doesn't. You see what I mean?' Jay wanted to add: 'I might not be smarter than you in my search, but I do have an emotional involvement', Avoiding any such words, instead. Instead he said, 'I am not here to solve the case, sir. I'm here to do whatever it takes to get to the truth, with or without evidence. How much do you remember of the case?'

'It was one of the most publicized cases in my career. A big-time real estate developer killed by his wife in his own home. The media had a field day. Oh, I remember everything. Does that make sense?'

'It does, but it prompts another question, if I may?'

'Of course, I'm retired and live alone, so any company can keep me talking for hours. Care for a drink?' Saxena asked in mirth.

Jay smiled. How fortuitous. He nodded acquiescently.

The old man got up and walked slowly towards his kitchen. He came out a full five minutes later with two glasses of orange juice.

'Isn't there a possibility that there was someone else in our house that night?' Jay started after the old man had settled back into his seat and taken his first sip.

'That's a bit of a stretch. We never found any evidence of that, but …' the old man hesitated, stopping mid-sentence.

Jay waited for a while. The old man shook his head in disgust.

'But …?' he asked when the old man did not speak for a while.

'Jay, trust me, every police officer retires with one or two cases that scorch his soul till the grave accepts us. An unsolved case is a failure.'

'Why do you think it was a failure when my mother was convicted for it? For the police it was solved, closed. Isn't it?'

'Don't forget we're talking about a time when a murder accused or suspect was already deemed guilty even before they were brought for trial before a judge. Then in your mother's case, there were no other suspects, no one found with a tangible motive. There was one thing, however, that intrigued me then and bothered me for a long time and probably even now as I speak—' the old man took a sip of the orange juice and slurped – 'when the knife was analysed by the forensic experts, there was only one set of fingerprints on it. No partials, no smudges, just one set – your mother's. She seemed to have wiped off the knife right before she used it to stab your father, or so it appeared. Therefore, I looked elsewhere. I wasn't a hundred per cent convinced she killed him, but please appreciate that there was a lot of pressure from the top to bring the case to a closure. And, as though that wasn't enough, she pleaded guilty. What could one expect?'

Again, Jay waited for the old man to continue.

'It's one thing to find partial or unrecognizable fingerprints, it's a totally different situation when they've been wiped off the murder weapon. You see what I mean? It was like no one had ever held that knife before.'

Which was untrue. Jay knew that he had held that knife to his father's neck only a few hours before his murder, so the forensic team should have recovered his partials, but they hadn't. His theory was finding some roots again. He racked his brain, his eyebrows arched; his eyes widened and narrowed a few times. Disbelief? Shock? Was his mind playing with him? Was he in some trance or had the old SP lost his marbles? Could he be trusted? Then again, what was in it for a retired police officer to prevaricate?

'Your best guess?' Jay softly asked.

'Faugh!' the old man exhaled. 'I've always believed she covered up for someone, protected someone. We found out that some people owed your father money, lots of money, which was not in the books. Hence, the debts died with him. But there wasn't even a remote piece of evidence of someone being near your house that night. Everyone we checked had an ironclad alibi. So you can say that though some other people might have had the motive, they certainly did not have the opportunity, which saved them from any further stringent investigation.'

It all sounded egregious, but Jay sat silently.

'The case was closed years ago. She never said anything except admitting to the crime. You won't find much now, Jay.'

'The case might have closed for the world. For me it will remain open till I find the truth.'

'And that is ...?'

'I wish I knew, but I will.'

'So you think the police of this city apprehended the wrong person and the courts convicted that wrong person?'

'I don't know.'

'Then, why?

'Why, what?'

'Why bother with the past?'

'Because the past is waving at me, looking at me for an answer.'

'That sounds philosophical.'

'I know it does, but it's the truth. If the past wanted to stay buried it needn't have called me.'

'You're not making any sense to me.'

'Don't bother, sir.'

The two sat looking at each other for a while, sipping their drinks. The silence was heavy – like bumping into your ex in a lift on a journey up to the seventy-first floor with nothing to say. Or more like, struggling to find the right words to re-break the ice or wondering if it's worthwhile to even attempt rehashing the past. A total impasse.

'Imagination is useful if you are an inventor or a creative person, not when you are a police officer. It's a strict no-no. We work with facts and facts alone. I'm sure it's the same for you advocates too.'

'I am not imagining it. My mother died recently and left a note that she hadn't committed the crime.' Jay enlightened Saxena about the letter.

The policeman looked hurt. Since time immemorial, it has been observed that people generally don't lie right before their deaths. With his mother having repudiated her guilt before her death, Jay knew it was something that would bother the old man's conscience till his own end. He looked crestfallen.

Jay left Vasant Kunj a little before four. He hadn't got anything new from Saxena, but sometimes things just topple into alignment. The epiphany had brought a new spin on his theories. Mulling over the information he had just received made him livid. Hitherto unknown and therefore impossible scenarios now performed zumba in his head. Someone had killed his father and escaped. And his mother had borne the brunt.

Saxena had rightly said that an unsolved crime is a failure: failure for the investigating officer leading the enquiry, failure for the trial judge sentencing the innocent, failure for the victim, failure for the accused and failure for the family of the accused innocent. The whole thing had flunked on so many levels. There were far too many coincidences for someone like Jay, who did not believe in them. The forensics should have found an overlap of fingerprints, some latent prints, partials. But they didn't. The latest discovery led the questions that had long bothered Jay to return. Had his mother accidentally cleaned all prints? Or did she scrub the knife after the murder and planted her prints firmly on the weapon – in the process wiping off any back-story. Did she not realize that by doing so she would become the prime suspect? Or was she shielding someone?

The obvious question was who. Who had she done it for?

The obvious answer had to be Swamiji.

The next obvious question was: what to do next?

Finding that damn godman was of utmost importance now. No one can cover all their tracks; it was altogether a different matter if Jay couldn't uncover the swami's tracks, though he was confident that Bhīma, who was proficient in finding the proverbial needles, would find the swami too. However, given the isolato's age, the only problem was digging him out before he turned to ashes.

On the drive back, Jay updated Bhīma on other possibilities that the SP had mentioned. He remembered some – not all – of his father's alleged close friends who owed him money and had disappeared from Jay's life when tragedy struck and when he needed them the most. Jay was so consumed by the calamity that he had held no prisoners then. But it was time, now, to look for those gentlemen too. He gave some names to Bhīma.

'Don't worry, hukum, if the swami is alive, I will find him,' was Bhīma's reticent yet confident response. 'And I'll find the others too.'

One of the key factors behind the success of Jay Singh's legal practice was Bhīma. While most other defence advocates were just that: defence advocates, Jay's investigative arm – in the form of Bhīma – got great results, which helped him twist cases. And although he worked on investigation results provided by law enforcement officers and the discovery file handed over by the plaintiff's advocate, he was cognizant that the police weren't inclined to help the defence. If anything, it set barriers for the defence to get to anything that could marginalize the evidence they gathered to prosecute. He primarily relied on his in-house Sherlock, Bhīma.

Jay skipped work for the balance of the day. It was communicated to Julie that Jay was out on personal business. Put impolitely, for anyone in the office, it was none of their business to ask or know. Julie understood this.

On the drive back home, they were bubbled into the evening rush hour. The silver lining in the slow traffic of this forever-growing metropolis was that it gave travellers a lot of time to deliberate. Jay thought about his latest hot topic: Manavi. But for some strange reason, his mind quickly wandered to Gina's life. Where was she headed in her relationship with Kumar? Was that love, lust or financial security that tied her to a married man? And what was in it for Kumar? He had money and he had a wife and kids. What place did Gina have in his life? Then he figured that extramarital affairs were never about love or lust; they were about ego. Thankfully, or sadly, he wasn't married and, although he could theorize, he'd have to make a giant leap of thought to comprehend. Kumar was either innocent or a consummate liar. There was nothing that Jay had noticed that gave any indication that his client had been paltering except for some omissions in the beginning: his voice never wavered, and his eyes didn't blink even once. All the usual signs of prevarication had been absent. Jay had a hunch that something wasn't right. It didn't fit. Was there a missing piece in the script that he had overlooked and that might come back to bite him later? He decided he should have one more meeting with Kumar and suggest a self-defence route to check for any inconsistencies in his story. However, if Kumar declined that, then Jay had no reason to think he was the perpetrator of the crime. He pulled out a bottle of whisky and tumbler from the armrest in the rear seat, opened the tray table fastened to the back of the front seat and fixed himself a drink. He took a sip, closed his eyes and drummed his fingers on the table.

'Bhīma,' he suddenly said.

'Yes, hukum?'

'I don't want to go home. Please take me to Akbar's place.'

Bhīma nodded. The Delhi Metro Rail Corporation had dug up a lot of land for the construction of a part of the overhead Blue Line extension, and being in the area they were entrenched in traffic of all sorts on all sides. They drove a further kilometre before Bhīma found the next U-turn.

Jay fixed himself another drink and promised himself it was his last one till he got to Ali. His excitement of telling his friend all about Manavi had waned a bit after this meeting with Saxena. Nevertheless, he knew, he would discuss both things. If he didn't bring up Manavi, he was certain Ali would.

There wasn't much point in asking Bhīma to return home without him; Bhīma wouldn't budge from his position. The next best thing was to send him for his dinner and to return to pick up Jay. That suited them both.

As expected, the initial jubilation at seeing his friend faded when Jay relayed what Saxena had told him. Added to the mix was the letter that Jay had received from his mother. In all the years that they had known each other, for the first time Ali was convinced Jay had a point: it was worth resurrecting the old case. Something had gone drastically wrong. Both men agreed that the investigation was botched and the consequent trial was erroneous: if the source of information is rotten everything else that follows cannot be trusted.

Both friends decided that finding the godman should be a priority. It was equally paramount to look for the few supposed friends who owed money to Jay's father. Those *friends* being from business families and their residences being in Delhi, the search wouldn't prove to be as problematic. That the police may have checked their alibis and cleared them did not mean they could not have hired someone for the task. But how did his mother fit into all this? Why would she let anyone walk away with the family money after getting rid of her husband? The more they deliberated the more they zeroed in on Swamiji.

Bhīma returned with *kathi rolls* packed for Jay and Ali, which were appreciated since the two had been drinking on empty stomachs. Thankfully, the dinner also changed the tack of their sombre conversation. Ali was ecstatic to know that not only had Jay made the call to Manavi, but he had already been out on their first dinner date too.

'See, didn't I tell you that she wouldn't have any objections to dating you?'

'It wasn't a date,' Jay corrected him.

'Oh, really? What is a date then, lover boy?'

'We merely went out for dinner. That's it.'

'That's a date as far as I am concerned. What did you think, she'd jump into bed with you on the first date?'

'I had no intention of getting her to do that.'

'Oh, really?'

Jay nodded, took a sip, but didn't say anything.

'Good, when are you meeting her next?'

'This weekend.'

'Where?'

'At my place.'

'Hmmm …'

The two friends looked at each other. Their eyes twinkled with joy and mischief. A strange happiness sprung in the air.

'Should I take it that you two would play bridge or chess?'

Both burst out laughing. Jay had to spit out the drink he had just sipped.

'We're more health conscious than you think. We'll swim.'

'Ooh-la-la, I can see someone is looking forward to it.'

Jay could feel his face flush. He just flashed a wide smile in response.

'Treat her well, my friend.'

On the drive back Jay realized that he didn't want any more to drink, which was unusual. He was occupied with beautiful thoughts of Manavi. If she came over this weekend as she had promised, seeing her at the pool (Would it be a swimsuit or a bikini? What colour?) would be divine and he refused to envisage the scene. The only apprehension he felt was how was he going to explain Bhīma to her? There was no way he could hide the big man for long. After the first dinner and the drive, Bhīma had categorically refused to leave Jay alone or to drive by himself. How would he break the news in such a manner that he didn't come across like a scared cat? It was only right to tell her that his life was fraught with danger, and that the danger could be contagious – and inadvertently traversable – if she linked up with him.

What if she wanted no part in it then?

17

THE FIRST TRIAL DATE FOR *STATE VERSUS VINAY KUMAR* WAS SET for four months later. The clock had finally started ticking. The public prosecutor was recorded as Ramesh Talwar. Jay had tangoed with Talwar before, thrice to be precise. Talwar, true to his name, had a tongue as sharp as a sword. Caustic and uncouth, he never minced his words. In fact, sometimes he temerariously used provocative vocabulary and histrionics to dramatize, to invoke anger and uneasiness in both the defendant and the advocate. It was a grandstanding tactic in his book and, though it had limited usage for the court, it provided great *masala* footage for the media. However, Talwar was bloody good at what he did. He had lost twice in the three times he had faced Jay in the past. The third case happened to be the only defence trial that Jay Singh had ever lost in his illustrious career. Talwar was *that* good. He was admirable but not when he was your opponent. For any other defence advocate Talwar could be intimidating, but for Jay only an opponent like Talwar could make the trial more difficult and interesting, and eking out a victory would be that much more pleasurable. The only silver lining was that Talwar, unlike Jay, was known to play fair. But then again, in most cases, the prosecution had to play fair, what with the burden of representing the state, and their investigation and discovery being run by the local police; they could, however, delay sending the discovery files to the defence. And they did, but they could not conceal evidence or witnesses. Unfair play, therefore, wasn't a conscious decision; it was thrust upon most prosecutors.

Jay knew that with any other advocate, he could have taken a shot at negotiating: bribed him, bought him or maybe threatened him. But with Ramesh Talwar, he couldn't attempt any of those manoeuvres. Talwar couldn't be bought and he had enough clout not to feel threatened even by someone like Jay Singh.

The case should ideally have been allocated to an additional district judge, but given the workload, it ended up getting escalated to a district judge. Like in all trials, an internal process that no one controlled randomly selected judges for criminal trials too.

When it was announced that Justice Alok Nair would chair the hearing, Jay Singh knew he was running against the odds. Judge Nair was known to be notoriously pro-prosecution; for the defence, a victory was well-nigh impossible. It would be like pissing in the gale. With no jury trials in India, the decision of the Vinay Kumar trial depended on the sole discretion of one man: Justice Alok Nair.

He had been a prosecutor for fifteen years before being appointed as the district judge. If rumours were to be believed, Nair was never good at his job as an advocate but highly efficient at brown-nosing. At all times, he maintained cordial relations with his superiors and peers. Ergo, after he cleared the test, there weren't any eyebrows raised when the Governor of the State, after consultation with the Chief Justice of the Delhi High Court, appointed him as District Judge. He ran his court like a high school class. Discipline and subservience were appreciated. No, not appreciated, expected. He worked extremely hard to be seen to be doing the right thing because the next level of ascendancy was clearly in sight. He had served as a district judge for enough years now, and the post of a High Court judge was a tangible possibility. Of course, if Judge Nair's ruling was not in favour of the defence, Jay could appeal in the High Court. But that could drag on for years, which wasn't what Vinay Kumar wanted; nor could Jay afford another defeat by Talwar.

Royally screwed, Mr Jay Singh.

♝

Bhīma's spy-force had bugged Vinay Kumar's home. Going through the initial recordings, Bhīma found one that he knew would be interesting to Jay. It was an altercation between Kumar and his wife, Rita.

Rita: 'Didn't I warn you to stay away from that bitch, you bastard?'

VK: 'She wasn't a bitch, you are a fucking bitch.'

Rita: 'You are the one who keeps dipping your dick in such dirty whores, and you have the balls to call me a bitch? Just wait till I speak to your dad.'

VK: 'You talk to him one more time, and I'll break your ugly pig face again.'

Rita: 'Try it. You think I'm scared? You are a fucking eunuch, who goes around hitting and dropping women …'

Smash …

The sound suggested a slap. Then, some crying and then howling.

Rita: 'I'll tell your dad. I'll tell the police. I'll tell them everything.*'*

VK: 'I'll kill you.'

The stomping sounds indicated the couple took some stairs to another floor.

Bhīma promptly edited this part out and took it to Jay, who was sitting in his office. He closed the door and plugged the USB drive into Jay's computer. Instinctively, Jay put on his headphones and listened to the conversation.

'What do you think, hukum?'

'It is time to meet Vinay Kumar again. And maybe his wife, whether he agrees to it or not.' Jay stopped to think for a minute. 'Perhaps he might want to change his version of the events.' He looked up at Bhīma.

Bhīma smiled, unplugged his USB and turned to go.

'One more thing, Bhīma, it might not be a bad idea to check Vinay Kumar's past. He may not have any cases pending, but ask your team to check again. His wife talked of *women,* not *a* woman. I have a feeling something is out of character here.'

'Jee, hukum.'

♝

Rita was a gorgeous woman. Jay wondered why someone married to her would even think of another woman. Men – and why blame men alone, the whole humankind is injudicious – always seem to want what isn't righteously theirs. That's how all the extramarital affairs start, don't they? Rita was a slender woman with long black straight hair one could fall in love with and a well-chiselled face. There was not an ounce of extra fat anywhere on the petite body. She had a lot of make-up on to cover what seemed a blue-black mark under her right eye. Jay wondered why she still stayed with Kumar. But that wasn't his problem. Thousands of abused women stuck with their husbands, despite being educated and knowing they could step out, get a job, take the swine to court and hang him out to dry. But they didn't.

She sat on the black leather sofa sipping a Diet Coke when

Jay walked in. She did not get up to receive him when the male servant showed him in. She did not offer him a drink either.

'Apologies for bothering you without notice, Mrs—'

'Rita. I prefer to be me, than being someone else's property.' She smiled a fuck-all-you-men smile.

Jay took in whatever he could about the woman who sat there. 'Sorry. Rita, I'm Jay Singh, hired to represent your husband, Vinay, in the murder case. I believe you are aware of—'

'Jay, is it?' Rita interrupted.

'Yes. Jay.'

'So Jay, tell me when is the bit where I should act like a devoted wife who covers her ears with her hands, closes her eyes and screams, 'Oh no!'

For a minute Jay thought she was rehearsing lines from a seventies Bollywood flick. Then she let out a laugh and took a big sip of the cola. He comprehended she wasn't someone who fancied meaningless pleasantries to drag on for more than a minute. But before he could say anything, she started talking again.

'Gina.'

'What about her?'

'My husband has been accused of murdering her and I know that. What I don't know is what you're looking to get from me. I know he was fucking her. She was a bitch who, despite knowing he was married and had kids, sought to take him away from the family.' Rita didn't mince her words. Nor was there any mellifluence in her tone.

As Jay settled in the room, he realized it was redolent with alcohol fumes. Rita wasn't having Coke; it was either a mixer or a camouflage.

'It's never one-sided. No one can clap with one hand, Rita—'

'Oh yeah,' she interjected again. 'She was younger, sweeter flesh, as all you men want. She was a whore if you ask me. A big-mouthed bitch that sucked my husband's cock and swindled cash out of him at the same time. You see, whoring might not be permitted, but it's tolerated in our country as long as it isn't too obvious to be made a fuss about. After all, the supposedly blessed ones also need to slake their despicable thirsts, don't you think?'

Jay looked around. Rita looked like someone who believed in what she spoke. And in reality, she wasn't very far from the truth. *What was Gina expecting? Money? Status? More?*

'And I bet she wanted more than he could give. That, or maybe he got bored with the bitch.' This was spoken with a tear forming in her eyes.

'What do you mean?'

'What do you expect from me, Mr Jay Singh?'

'Nothing, to be honest, and you don't even have to speak to me if you don't want to. Anyway, anything that you tell me won't be repeated in any court of law across the country. So you don't have to entertain any of my questions. I am just an advocate representing your husband and, as such, it's in your interest or at least, that's what I thought when I came here. The police are carrying out the investigations, but all I wanted to know is if there is anything you would like to tell me that could help his case.'

'Nothing.' She sipped her alcohol-infused Coke. But even her *nothing* carried a lot of weight. It seemed like she wanted to say things she didn't want anyone else to hear, much less an advocate who was representing her husband. But her demeanour said everything Jay wanted to know. The advocate, discerning that she couldn't care less about what happened – he could go fuck himself – stood up to leave.

'Is it okay if I get in touch with you again, Rita?'

'I can't possibly tell you anything important.'

'Everything's unimportant until it is important, Rita. I'd

rather you tell me everything you know than not tell me because you think it wasn't important.'

'Do you want to fuck me?'

Aghast at the words and stunned by the implication they carried, Jay felt his cheeks burn, as if he was the one who had uttered those unscrupulous words. Her icky and surprising remark piqued him. For a minute he didn't know what to say to her. He wanted to ask what she meant but turned to leave rather than engage in any further dialogue.

'I mean it, Jay.'

Jay couldn't just walk away with her speaking after him. Ergo, he turned around to face her.

'If he can fuck other women, why can't I fuck other men? Or are you a chauvinist too, who thinks men are on higher ground and only they can afford to jazz around, but women should be kept at home?

'Your point is ...?'

'Would it be very offensive if I screwed around?'

'Who am I to judge? It's your life, and you can do whatever you want. That's your choice or discretion, but why me? I am not here to be seduced.'

'I'm not wearing a bra and if I take off my top, what would you do?'

'This conversation is over. I am leaving, ma'am. Have a good day.'

'Cheeky, isn't it? Wouldn't you like to see what Vinay is missing? I was a model, now I'm a dump, dipso ...'

'No. Thanks. And bye, Mrs Kumar.'

He walked out.

♝

Driving back in the car, Jay thought about the whole unsavoury episode. Estranged wives were known to be dangerous, but this outlandish behaviour was utterly unheard of. What had prompted Rita to do such an outrageous thing? Why did she want to do what she said she was willing to? The spectacle wasn't for sex. A woman of her stature and gorgeousness could get her physical cravings satisfied by the scores of aides she had in the house. Who would know if she jazzed around with the cook or the cleaner or the driver or the security guy? Why suggest it to a first-time visitor, especially if he was over only to save your husband? Trying to fuck the advocate didn't make any sense. That her husband was a philanderer, Jay knew. But her trying to seduce him was something else. It was undoubtedly orchestrated to relay something she didn't speak.

What was it?

'I need Rita's CV, too,' Jay told Bhīma as he got into the car.

'She is from an extremely rich Marwari family in Calcutta,' Bhīma offered. His army of informants were as secretive and realistic as they showed them in detective shows. Probably better. They had already divulged to Bhīma about Rita. 'She had a roaring affair with a Muslim guy in her college, but her parents did not want her to be married outside the community. Vinay was chosen for his political pedigree so that the guy would have to forgo her and not follow or blackmail her in any way. If she had been married to anyone less than Vinay Kumar, the previous boyfriend might have chased her. But given Kumar's background and resources, the poor guy gracefully accepted defeat. That said, she has never strayed and has always been a good wife – bore kids and has never been known to do anything immoral or untowardly, hukum. She never even once – going by records and information received – tried to establish contact with her ex-boyfriend or her past.'

Bhīma could make Sherlock Holmes bite his tongue and cheek and …

But did his men know what to read between the lines?

'I need detailed intelligence on that guy and his whereabouts. Let's not rule him out from the investigation. He could have a vested interest in getting Kumar out of the way.'

'Jee, hukum.'

'Where would I be without your help, Bhīma?' Jay abruptly said.

'Hukum, you underestimate yourself. I am just a servant.'

'Stop the car. Now.'

Without questioning, Bhīma fought the traffic to get the Audi to the left-most lane. Bringing it to the unpaved area, he brought the car to a halt. He turned around and asked, 'Is everything okay, hukum?'

Jay, not waiting for Bhīma to step out and give a shufti, got out, slammed the door and walked out. He then opened the front door and slipped in shotgun.

'You're not a servant, Bhīma, and you know that.'

'I'm sorry, hukum, I did not mean it that way.'

'You're my friend, a brother that I never had. Heck, you've done for me what my dad should have done. I do not want to hear anything like this ever again.'

'Hukum.' Bhīma nodded in agreement.

'And there's one more thing, Bhīma ...' Jay shifted uneasily in his seat. 'How do I explain you to Manavi? I mean, she doesn't know I need you, but you and I both know we are inseparable.'

'Hukum, I won't let you drive alone ever again,' Bhīma stressed.

'I know that. And it is appreciated. But I don't want to look like a pansy, either.'

'Unless, *bhabhiji* knows the danger you carry, it will be difficult to explain, hukum.'

Bhabhiji? Jesus Christ. Bhabhiji? Sister-in-law?

Jay's heart couldn't help being amused, but he made an effort not to smile. To avoid any embarrassment by opening his mouth to accept or decline the bhabhiji status, he disregarded the word totally and carried on.

'Let's talk about it when we get home. Press on the paddle, Bhīma-*ji*.'

Bhīma smiled at the 'ji'.

Jay wanted to discuss the encounter he had at Vinay Kumar's residence with Bhīma but decided against it. Bhīma would have heard the whole nasty conversation on his mobile anyway. There wasn't any point in discussing the disgusting detail. Bhīma was instructed to find Rita's ex. That was his job.

As the car trundled through the tsunami of traffic, Jay wondered. What if he had stopped by to have a little nookie with Rita? If nothing else, it would have provided him with some carnal experience that might have come in handy in dealing with Manavi. When was the last time he had sex? *Never* was the only answer. Forget the film, he was the true over-forty-year-old virgin. An uncomfortable smile washed all over his face as he thought of times ahead.

Do I let her know I don't have any experience? was the question on his mind when he drifted off to sleep in the front seat of the car as it snailed through the traffic.

18

BHĪMA WORKED MORE RELENTLESSLY AND LONGER HOURS THAN his boss. His tasks were fraught with dangers, but that didn't worry him, not one bit. That was in Bhīma's DNA. He recognized this particular investigation was personal for Jay. After driving his boss back from Kumar's house, he had dinner with Bahadur and then left on his nocturnal prowl. He rode through the near empty Sri Aurobindo Marg, passing Yusuf Sarai, Hauz Khas, then took the Ring Road and was on the Nizamuddin Bridge in less than thirty minutes. He crossed the Yamuna and rode into East Delhi.

Patparganj was once a flourishing town and an important grain market for the Mughals. However, after the Battle of Patparganj in 1803, when the British took over Delhi, Patparganj's fortunes declined and it never regained its lustre. Even today, it was considered an area where the children of some lesser god resided. Bhīma's contact Raja was expecting him at Max Hospital's parking lot in Indraprastha Extension. As a rule, Bhīma never met his informants at seedy locations. He believed in robust surroundings, where no one ever suspected anything unlawful would happen. By the nature of its work, a hospital was a place that expected visitors even in the middle of the night. Raja was one of Bhīma's most trusted informers; he had served under Bhīma in the army and – both being Kargil War veterans – the camaraderie and trust had continued beyond the battlefield. The two could feel at ease with each other, they could discuss matters beyond those at hand and let the guards drop for a while. As Raja was an ex-colleague, Bhīma rarely engaged him in anything that was even remotely bent, but this was different. In any event, this search could in no way be classified as unlawful.

Raja was smoking a cigarette in the parking lot when Bhīma entered. He stubbed it out when he saw Bhīma's motorbike approaching and walked towards him. Bhīma parked his bike, took off his helmet and the two walked into the main hospital building like they were visitors or members of staff and were arriving for their night shift. Resourceful as he was, Raja had arranged, with the help of some distant relative in the hospital, keys to a generic consulting room for their clandestine meeting. They grabbed some coffee from the vending machine in the foyer and confidently sauntered to the elevators, without raising any eyebrows.

'Long time, Lieutenant sahib,' Raja uttered as he unlocked the door. 'Is vakil sahib keeping you busy?'

Bhīma let out an assenting chuckle.

Raja switched on the light and the two men sat down at the table, like a consultant-patient duo. The disinfectant smell prevailed, but that was hardly a bother considering that the alternative would be to stand in the shady car park or next to some open sewer. Not under any kind of time constraint, Bhīma started with a bit of chitchat about Raja's family and his only son's education, which was sponsored by Bhīma and intrinsically funded by Jay. The arrangement was totally exclusive of whether Raja agreed to help or not in this particular case and was something that Jay and Bhīma believed they did for their own redemption. The boy was doing fine and planning to take the National Defence Academy entrance examination, which was pure symphony to Bhīma's ears.

'So, what brings you to me, sir?' Raja still addressed Bhīma deferentially, camaraderie or not.

'I am looking for someone.' There was no ambiguity. Raja would carry out the task like an informant, but he wasn't the usual rogue snoop from whom Bhīma had to conceal any information. 'However, firstly what might make it a little difficult is the time lag. I'm looking for someone who resided in this part of Delhi in the eighties.'

'Eighties, that's like more than thirty years ago, really ancient.'

'I know.'

'Who is it?'

'That's the second hitch, I don't know the name.'

Raja rolled his eyes. 'Photograph?'

'No.'

'Male or female?'

'Male.'

'So, let me understand this correctly, sir. You want me to look for someone who resided here in the eighties without knowing his name or what he looked like? How would I even explain this to my boys?'

He was referring to the real informants who would go around snooping for intelligence. These infiltrators penetrated places that the police couldn't and spoke to people whom a person in uniform never would. These infiltrators were very localized and knew the neighbourhood inside-out, the residents and local folklores, and had an expansive network across the country. The whole thing worked on reciprocity: *If you do something for me that I can't do for myself, I will do something for you that you can't do for yourself* – that's how the entire underground snooping world worked and thrived. If they couldn't locate someone, you could rest assured that the target was not in the country. Either that or it was only a matter of time before a death certificate emanated.

'Well, I think you will need to find someone who resided here in Patparganj in the eighties or who knows of someone who inhabited this area at the time. Know anyone?'

Raja pursed his lips and looked upwards to think. 'Not off the top of my head, no.'

'There was a so-called Swamiji who lived in a hut before this area was developed. I've done some homework using old maps. The extent isn't wider than about a three- or four-kilometre radius around this hospital.' Bhīma provided more details about the location: it was near a municipal water hand pump, it was more than likely that the blueprint would be available in the town's records even if the pump no longer existed – and a little about the what the Swamiji looked like, based on a description provided by Jay. Nevertheless, how much could one trust the memory of a prepubescent boy?

'How old was he then?'

'Very old even then, probably in his late fifties.'

'So he could well be in the heavens now?'

'Probably.'

'Did he have any family or an assistant or helper, anyone he lived with?'

'Not that I know of.'

'That's great help, sir,' Raja cracked.

Bhīma smiled. He knew exactly what Raja meant. He was being commissioned to look for someone without any details. The first task would be to establish who it was that they were looking for.

'It's not very different from the old days in the army, Raja – you had to identify the enemy before you fired.'

'Yes, Lieutenant, I see what you mean, though the challenge is that none of the boys here are trained as well as our soldiers were in the army. But leave it to me, I'll do whatever I can to find this swami.'

'Raja, this search is personal,' Bhīma added solemnly.

'Personal?' If Raja wanted to probe any further, he didn't. 'It will be done, sir,' is all he uttered.

'Money will not—'

'Please don't slight me, sir. Money's never been an issue when dealing with you.'

Bhīma left Patparganj around midnight. He had yet another appointment regarding the other ongoing case to attend to in Connaught Place. Another guy – one of those he had instructed a few weeks back – were waiting for him. The business and tourist humdrum of Connaught Place were long over and the man stood in a dark corner in H Block just outside the closed offices of Cox & Kings. He looked like a tourist who had been locked out and was waiting to buy his ticket the next morning. The meeting had been set up by Bhīma to get an update on the Glock. A lot of time had passed and the machinery had been unsuccessful in finding where the damn handgun had changed hands in the capital. That had been never the case in the past, which was worrying. Jay's concern, and hence Bhīma's, was that the weapon – that could alter the case – had disappeared. It was imperative that they, at the very least, identified the origin or the possessor of the Glock to decide whether Jay should include or exclude it from the defence strategy. It wasn't sensible to remain ignorant till the prosecution pulled the rug from under them. To make his request more exigent, Bhīma upped the reward, which evidently translated into increasing the number of eyes and ears on the ground. He exerted pressure, highlighted it was important and asked that no effort be spared.

'Bhīma bhai, do you have contacts in Mumbai?'

'Yes, why do you ask?'

'I have a feeling the gun changed hands outside Delhi,' replied the guy.

Bhīma made a note. The guy had a point. And Bhīma instinctively knew that the information being relayed to him was a collective conclusion among several such informants. He nodded in agreement and then asked him to dig out further details on Mrs Rita Kumar's ex: where was he, what he did and when was he in Delhi last. He knew this part would be much easier than locating the murder weapon.

Back in the farmhouse, he heard Sheeba whimper. She quickly went back to sleep upon confirming Bhīma's presence, whose predictable nightly outings she had grown to become astutely aware of. Bhīma tiptoed into his room on the ground floor and switched on his computer. It was still only two in the morning, and he had some more work to finish before the day formally began. He decrypted his address book and rummaged through his Mumbai contacts in hopes of employing a robust partner on this one. The Glock, he reckoned, had most likely been brought from outside Delhi. That or he had missed something very significant. He fretted for a long time till sleep overtook his senses.

19

FROM THE LOOKS OF IT, THE FARMHOUSE SEEMED LIKE IT WAS being prepped for Diwali. It all began the day Manavi confirmed she would be coming over on Saturday to spend the day with Jay. Professional cleaners were called in to drain the swimming pool, give it a total scrub and get it ready. Fresh towels and bathrobes were ordered. The bar was replenished with vodka – Absolut, Smirnoff and Grey Goose. Bottles of Belvedere and Chopin – not easily accessible – were acquired at astronomical prices. The refrigerator was stocked with orange, cranberry and tomato juices and tonic water. Bahadur was asked to hire help to clean every nook and cranny of the house as if Manavi might kneel down and slide her finger in one corner and walk away on finding any traces of dust. Curtains and blinds were pulled down, vacuumed and rehung. Bhīma and Bahadur understood Jay's anxiety; the extra hands employed neither knew the reason nor wasted their time asking. The car was valeted. The garden was tended. Flower baskets were suspended all around, and any junk in sight was trashed or sent to out-quarters. The menu for the day was decided and everything was chopped and ready to cook fresh in the evening.

Sheeba, too, was given a shampoo and blow-dry by a professional.

Despite Jay's insistence, Manavi didn't agree to be picked

up from her place. She had some important work to do in the morning, she had informed him and would be at the farmhouse around four on Saturday afternoon. She had no plans to stay the night; they would see how the evening progressed. In all fairness, she was smart enough to keep the plan wide open. It was one thing to have a few drinks, dinner and a little chinwag with someone for the first time in a restaurant and go for a drive around town. It would be altogether different to commit to staying overnight at a man's place – someone she had met just once outside of her place of work.

Jay had a barber brought in for an extra close wet shave and a head massage at noon. He deliberated getting his hair coloured but decided against it in the end. Manavi had already seen his greys; there wasn't much point in concealing them now. A little bit of fur on his chest, too, had started to grey. If they actually got into the pool, as was the plan, the different colours would look bizarre. That reminded him that he hadn't reiterated that a swim was on the cards. Calling her again would look like he was too eager, so he dropped the idea. If she brought her swimsuit they'd take a dip, otherwise there may be other times.

Really? Would she come again?

Jay shampooed and blow-dried his hair and changed four sets of clothes before concluding that he should wear his usual white linen trousers with a white polo shirt. Nothing fancy. He was ready by three and then the fretting started. It didn't matter how old you were, first love always made one feel like an excited teen. He didn't want to start drinking before she arrived, so gawking at the clock was the only option. Picking out the only vinyl with romantic ballads that he had in his music collection, he rearranged the candles and instructed Bahadur not to light them. He would. How impressive. Jay was like forty-something going on fourteen, a butterfly trying to be a caterpillar again.

Bhīma and Bahadur were ready by 3:30 p.m. too. Bahadur giggled like a schoolgirl all through the day. That led to further fretting. Jay knew he had to introduce them to her today. Bahadur was justifiable, but Bhīma?

They were the longest seventeen minutes everyone in the living room had seen. Nothing moved. No one did anything; they just sat or stood as statues till the voice entry system from the main gate beeped.

4:17.

To Jay it jarred like the tectonic plates had shifted. He felt his heart sink deeper than the Mariana Trench. Bhīma buzzed the gate open but stayed put. Only Jay walked out to receive her. Bahadur couldn't help himself peeking out from the windows.

Manavi had decided to leave the cab at the gate and walk in. That's when he saw her. She had a handbag, not the clutch that she had carried for dinner. An off-white knee-length floral dress made of some kind of stretch material that gave it a porcelain feel and hugged her body; the cut-off shoulders flaunted her toned triceps. Very classy. She wasn't wearing any heels; her feet were in white and tan crisscross ankle-wrap sandals with open toes. Her nails were painted in pastel blue. *The girl had made the effort.*

Jay smiled. She returned the smile and almost ran to him, landing straight into his arms like a long-time friend.

Or lover?

'How was the journey?' he asked, releasing her.

'Fine. Something as big as this,' she looked around to emphasize, 'can't be hard to find.'

'You embarrass me.' He felt himself blush. 'To cut a long story short, I have a reason why I live here …'

'Oh, we have no lack of time today, why not let the long story be long?'

'Whatever you say, Manavi. I am so glad you came.'

Sheeba couldn't contain her excitement any longer. Her tail wagging, she escaped from the confines of the house and ran towards them.

'You didn't tell me you had a dog.'

'This is Sheeba.'

Manavi was already on her haunches to pat the lovelorn Sheeba. Then they walked toward the house trailing her. Bahadur, as enthusiastic as Jay and Sheeba, was already standing at the doorstep with a tray of cold water. If they had walked any slower, he would have surely stepped out to serve.

'Hello—' she smiled.

'Bahadur, *memsahib*,' he introduced himself in his Nepali accent.

'Bahadur is the caretaker of this place.'

'So, you two live here with Sheeba?'

'Three of us and Sheeba.'

'Who's the third person?' she quizzed.

'Don't worry, it's not a woman. Have some cold water.' Jay smiled.

She took the glass from Bahadur's tray, thanked him and looked expectantly towards Jay to explicate who the third person was.

'Bhīma – he does everything else.'

'Everything else?'

He gestured to her to sit, taking her towards the formal part of the house. She turned, looked around and saw the pool through the French doors.

'Shouldn't we sit outside?'

'Of course.'

As they walked to the pool, Jay explained he had received death threats a while ago – he did not mention the actual attempt on his life – and that Bhīma had been hired to be a twenty-four-seven valet-cum-security-cum-chauffeur-cum-man Friday.

She didn't seem to think of it as any threat to her, which was good. In time he would explain it to her that she, too, could become a target if she ever became his weakness. It would be premature to ask her to take a decision at the moment. Foolish even.

'I've got my swimwear,' she said as soon as they sat down.

'Great. Let's grab a drink first.'

'Good idea.'

Jay realized that someone had to enlighten Bahadur that he didn't need to follow the pair everywhere like Sheeba. It would not only give her the jitters but also invade their privacy. He put his arm around Bahadur's shoulder and accompanied him inside for the drinks, leaving Manavi by herself at the pool chair.

Bhīma brought the drinks out. Introductions were made and he retreated inside the house. After the drinks, Jay showed Manavi inside and led her to the guest room, which hadn't been used in years. Minutes later, Jay was at the pool, wearing his swimming shorts. Manavi came out in a bathrobe and, almost immediately, took it off. She wore an olive-coloured bikini that, at best, was modelled from just enough fabric to make a couple of eyewear cleaning cloths. Jay wondered if the angels were even worth dying for. He didn't know if they were going to close the sale today though and he didn't want to think about it. And he didn't care; window shopping felt exhilarating enough. Prurient thoughts, but what else was expected when sufficient blood – and adrenaline – had scurried to the wrong parts of the body?

Water glistened on her flawless skin as they sat down after the dip. She made no attempt to dry or cover herself. Bahadur brought over cheese and biscuits and took their glasses inside for a refill. The two chatted for a long time as the sun retired and dusk started to settle.

'What time do you have to leave?' Jay asked, conscious it was getting late for dinner.

'Do you want me to?' she whispered and leaned closer.

For someone kissing after a lifetime, infinite questions emerge. How does one angle the face? Should he close his eyes? How long should the kiss last? Was he supposed to do something or let her tongue do the exploration? Nevertheless, Jay and Manavi shared a long, deep and satisfying kiss. A passionate one, one that he felt deep down in his groin; if he pressed any closer, he knew she would feel it too.

But if he moved back, wouldn't she see the bulge?

Moment of embarrassment.

'Jay,' she uttered in a soft, mellifluent voice.

'Let's go inside, you'll catch a cold.'

Bummer!

Both of them donned their robes, went up to their rooms, showered, dried and came back for dinner, which was a quiet affair. Despite the instructions, the zealous Bahadur had already lit the candles. Both carried on with their drinks, albeit slowly. Neither wanted the night to end, or to waste it. The delicious lamb curry Bahadur had prepared was more than appreciated. Manavi even asked for the recipe. The evening seemed to be going well. They sat out on the poolside after dinner with Rémy Martin, sharing a Romeo y Julieta. Jay, in a candid moment, admitted to Manavi that she was the first woman he had brought home.

She laughed, thinking it was some kind of a joke.

'You don't have to make any such claims, Jay. You know I was living with my ex.'

'I've never been with a woman before.'

'Really?' she said, suddenly serious. 'Why?'

He took his time; her question was only completely answered by midnight. He told her all. Everything. For some strange reason, he trusted her. And what harm could she bring anyway? If she wanted to walk away because of his past, it was best she did it sooner rather than later. Why raise any hopes? If what they had couldn't survive the past, what prospects did it have for the future? They stood in each other's arms for what seemed like a lifetime. The oak had started whispering again, the pool had become a mirror to the moon. Jay could feel her tears.

'You're crying?'

'Tears of joy! Should we go inside?' she asked softly.

They kissed again. Jay was a bit more confident this time.

'Last drink?'

'One for the long road?' she bantered and stretched her arm forward. He took the glass from her hand and refilled it when they went in.

Thankfully, the well-spent evening had left no ambiguity about whether she would be sleeping in the guestroom or the master bedroom …

His explosion was delirious. A lifetime of unintended restraint of unquenched thirst, of unrealized fantasies. He was willing again before he knew it and went on to rock her universe. The second time took longer, but he worked all the way in. It was even more shattering an orgasm, like all the planets had aligned themselves to cheer and celebrate.

'Jay,' Manavi breathed out, throwing her neck and head back as the throes of passion hit her, like thunder followed by rain. Totally spent, she dug her nails into his back.

'Yeah?' he asked and realized later – *sheesh!* – he wasn't to answer to his name. They were soft mumblings of intimacy.

'Don't,' she said as he began to withdraw. 'Stay in me.'

A frisson of delight went down his spine.

20

I WOKE UP WHEN I HEARD SOMEONE MOVE AROUND ON THE ground floor. With one open eye, I glanced at the bedside clock. It was a few minutes past three. I turned to see if she was really in my bed. Had I been dreaming all this while? Manavi was sleeping peacefully like a baby with her back towards me. I could see her soft, smooth skin shimmering in the moonlight that peeped in from the sliver between the curtains. And it all came back in a flash. She hadn't carried any changeover and she didn't care. We had peeled each other out of the clothes and jumped into bed. She had, after a lot of caressing and smooching, guided me into her. My tutor. I smiled and got up as softly as I could, not wanting to wake her up.

Donning my robe kept near my bed, I trodded gently down the stairs. I knew it must be none other than Mr Sam Cooper, and I wasn't wrong. He sat in the dark, in his usual sofa facing the pool, his back towards me. He had a drink on the table next to him.

'Where is this going, Jay?'

He must have heard me coming down the stairs as he intoned without any pleasantries.

'Where is what going, my friend?'

'You and Manavi, where is all this going?'

'What do you mean?'

'She's young enough to be your daughter?'

'Yuvraj is twelve.'

I made a drink without bothering to switch on the light. I didn't want Manavi to wake up. Not when Cooper was having this stupid conversation.

'I know that. It was merely a figure of speech or take it as an exaggeration, if you will, to make my point. You think Yuvraj would accept her?'

'What's not to accept?'

'I mean, his dad going around with such a young girl.'

'She's not such *a young girl. And it's not that I've shanghaied her, she's here of her own volition and she's over eighteen. For your information, she's a twenty-eight-year-old woman.'*

'And you are forty-five,' he said sarcastically. 'Laila, twenty-eight, Majnu, forty-five: a love story with a twist. Or should we call it a terrifically twisted love story? In any event, Mahesh Bhatt would kill to acquire the movie rights, don't you think?'

'Forty-three,' I couldn't stop myself correcting him. You don't want a fifteen-year age gap to suddenly increase to seventeen. Two years, at my age, matter.

'Now come on, Jay. Imagine someone of your age and status, the biggest defence advocate in Delhi, the mighty Jay Singh doodling some twinkie's name on his legal pads? Have you totally lost it?' Cooper genuinely sounded irritated.

'What are you trying to tell me, Cooper?'

'I want you to focus on your career, your case. Focus on what you're good at. You cannot afford to lose cases because you squander time romancing a young girl … err … woman.'

I could sense he was enjoying his own acerbic gags.

'Is your problem that I am with a woman, or that she is a younger woman?'

'Forget it. Forget I even mentioned it. In time you'll realize how foolish you've been for carnal pleasures.'

'Carnal pleasures?'

Cooper had been the only outlet to intimately process what had happened in my life. I respected him and appreciated his determination and loyalty to have stuck around for so long. But why did he have to drop by tonight of all nights? How the fuck did he know she was with me tonight? Or did he? This was just another of many things about Cooper that I still didn't know and that he wouldn't tell me. However, for the first time, I felt him invading my privacy. Perhaps, I never needed any before tonight. I wanted to finish with him and join Manavi as soon as I could.

'Why beat around the bush, Jay? Put on 'Makin' Whoopee' *on the player – she'll know your intentions loud and clear – then go jump into bed and have a nookie. What's stopping you?' he chuckled.*

He actually fucking chuckled.

Why was he taking my love as some sort of animalistic lust? But then again, what did Cooper know about love? Try explaining colours of autumn to someone who's visually impaired from birth. Cooper's advice was now getting a bit, well, cloying to be honest. I wanted him to leave before my lovely date found out that a drinking buddy was advising me to stay off her at three in the morning. As if she was some cougar hunting for a teenage me. He was a friend, not my dad and – here and now – I was getting impatient listening to him.

'Look, Cooper. It's no crime dating a younger woman.'

'You're right. It's not a crime, but it might be categorized as a sin. And you, of all people, should know that the two could be different. Everything that's legal does not necessarily mean it's right in the eyes of the Lord.'

Lord? Since when had Cooper become a believer? I wondered if he also had a copy of the Hanuman Chalisa *that he would pull out of his pocket any minute now and start chanting. I wanted to – what's the expression these days? – LOL, but contained myself. Nevertheless, I think he caught the expression on my face even in the dark.*

'What?' he growled.

'Nothing.'

'Don't fucking nothing me. In your heart you know what I'm saying is true. You just don't want to acknowledge it. Do you think I'm here to crack jokes?'

'I didn't say that. I understand your concern, Cooper, but I am carrying on with all the background investigations on the current case and—'

'I know that, you don't have to tell me. You know Talwar is prosecuting, and he isn't someone you can take lightly. You shouldn't count on luck this time; you can always look back and think you were lucky if you win it. And the way you're wasting time you'd have to be really lucky to win it.'

'Do you have any information from the prosecution camp?'

'None. And I am not here for that. You have one of the best guys working for you. I cannot get you anything more than what Bhīma can, and you should know that by now.'

I didn't say anything. I just nodded that I echoed his point. And there wasn't anything to argue where Bhīma's efficiency or loyalty was concerned.

'All I am trying to tell you is that there is no match between you and her. You are still stuck on the music we heard in our college days, when we had some money and company. In the ensuing years, when you struggled to make ends meet, there was hardly a choice of exploring the world and feeding your finer senses. When you got the money and lifestyle back, Michael Jackson had come and gone. Manavi, on the other hand, wouldn't enjoy Zeppelin or John Coltrane or Queen – in all likelihood, she might not have even heard of them; Katy Perry and Lady Gaga would appeal to her.'

He had valid arguments, and that was the foremost reason I always sought his advice. Little had I known that one day he'd start advising me against my wishes. And who knew, in time he might be right. Maybe she had different tastes in music and films and fashion, but how did that matter? I was savouring the moment, and he was yapping about forthcoming years. We were, for once, on different planes. Perhaps on altogether different planets!

I still couldn't fathom why he was against my relationship with Manavi. But I didn't want to argue, to raise voices like we had sometimes done in the past. My immediate concern was not to alarm Manavi, so I conceded. I let him be in control to make him feel happy. I'd need to reflect upon what had put my dear friend off my lovely Manavi later. Was he plain jealous? Of what? Or whom? Or was he thinking that he'd lose me if I had an interest in another human being, especially a younger girl? Like a bolt of lightning, it suddenly occurred to me that I should definitely discuss this with Anita. She might have some insight.

'You know I've been seeing a therapist, Cooper?'

'I know that too, yes.'

'She wants to see you.'

'Why does she want to see me?'

'She thinks you might be able to help her help me.'

'If you think I can help, give her my number. I have no issues, but you know I'm busy, so if she cannot get me, she should leave a message and I'll return her call.'

'Thanks.'

'Goodnight, I should be going now.'

'Who were you talking to?' Manavi was still déshabillé but getting into her robe to come down when I walked into the bedroom.

I almost said a prayer to thank God that she hadn't woken up any earlier and heard any of the senseless conversation.

'Uh … an old friend.'

'At this hour?' She looked at the clock. 'Where is he?'

'He was downstairs, just dropped in for a quick chat.'

'Why didn't you introduce me?'

'He's more a business colleague, my partner, Sam Cooper.'

But Manavi was out of the room before I could complete the sentence. She was back a couple of minutes later.

'Where is he?'

'He was leaving when I came up. He is very vague most of the times. Visits me at random.' Just why I was trying to explain Cooper's untimely visit, even I didn't know.

'Strange man.'

'Let's go back to sleep, honey.'

'Let's go back to bed. I want to sleep with my head in the nook of your arm.'

We made love again, the third time. Whoever said it was an exercise and made your heart do a workout was right. It was one of the most sensational exercises I'd ever done.

Over mushrooms and cheese omelettes served al fresco for breakfast at the poolside, Manavi quizzed me about Cooper yet again. She found it bizarre that my friend decided to pay me a visit without any warning at three in the morning if there was no emergency. Maybe she thought there was some crisis and I was covering it. Furthermore, she found it hard to believe that I did not find it weird. What more could I say? I rationalized to myself that either something like this had never happened in her life or it had occurred too many times with me that I had ceased seeing any eccentricity in a visit by a friend in the wee hours of the morning. I knew neither of us was wrong; it was a question of perspective, so I let it pass. I didn't want to waste precious time, so I feigned it to be a one-off and said that I would speak to Cooper about it.

Manavi insisted on taking a cab back to her place, but I convinced her to go with Bhīma. She ate and left after giving me a tight hug, a long kiss and an assurance that we would repeat this soon. Not once in the entire time she spent with me did she ask why I was seeing her boss. And I appreciated that. Perhaps she knew, but I don't think she did, as such files were confidential and a therapist would be careful not to give access to everyone in their office.

Bhīma returned after dropping his 'bhabhiji' *and updated me on various pending issues. The search for the swami had been contracted, but there was no information on the missing Glock from his Delhi rats. Ergo, he had been in touch with some people in Mumbai – he didn't give me any names and I didn't want any – and was confident we should get some gen soon.*

The first thing I did on Monday morning was call Anita. Cooper's unsolicited discourse was weighing heavily on me, and I wanted to discuss it with her to get it off my chest. I kept it brief and professional with Manavi when she picked up the phone at the clinic, told her I needed to see Anita and would like to drop by. Once she passed the line to Anita, I asked for some time today as something was troubling me. Fortunately, she had a vacant slot in her diary that afternoon and, realizing that I sounded very anxious, decided to see me at short notice. Isn't that what any good therapist is supposed to do anyway?

Manavi looked stunning as usual. She winked at me, but stayed professional in her conduct and extended the same courtesy she had offered me earlier as a client otherwise. I did not have to wait for Anita since she was free at the time.

Everything okay?' she asked after only a few initial pleasantries.

Normal, I would say.'

'Then what put you in this anxious state, Jay? Coffee?'

'Yes, please. Thanks.'

Holding back on the name, I told Anita I had started seeing someone, which was good, as that had engaged my mind elsewhere and reduced my alcohol intake. I told her about the terrific time we had together at my place, and it was all going great till the honourable Mr Sam Cooper arrived on the scene in the early hours of the morning to ruin the party. Obviously, it wasn't possible for me to repeat his words verbatim, but I did the best I could to express that he was grossly displeased about my involvement with this young woman.

'So, is he afraid she might take you away from him, or is it the fact that there is an age gap between the two of you?'

'God only knows. I asked him the same question, but he didn't explicitly respond.'

'Jay, I can empathize with you that someone, even as close as Mr Cooper is to you, drops in without being invited at such an odd hour, particularly if he knew that you had a date, but I can't see how I can help you unless I see Mr Cooper to understand his take on all this. You see what I mean? As I mentioned to you earlier, it would be great to meet with him. He must be able to tell me subtle things that you might have missed. In any event, it would be worth meeting him if only to explore what ticked him off about you seeing someone.'

'Sure. In fact I asked him this time and he told me to give you his number,' I said, pulling out my iPhone. While Anita refilled coffee in the cups, I punched in the four-digit code, dived into my contacts and went straight to 'C' for Cooper.

Cecil.

Chopra.

Another Chopra.

Yet another Chopra.

Choudhari

Another Chowdhary, but with slightly different spelling.

Chakraborty.

Charan.

Chauhan.

One more Chauhan.

Chugh.

Chandal.

Cooper was conspicuously missing.

Maybe I stored him in the wrong place. I looked under S for Sam.

Nada.

Where the fuck had his contact details disappeared?

Had Cooper deleted his own number after permitting him to give it to Anita? It struck me that my phone had been kept in the living room all night, and Cooper could have accessed it easily.

Bastard.

My expression must have changed since Anita caught me fretting.

'Anything wrong, Jay?' Anita quizzed with an uncapped pen still in her hand, waiting to jot down Cooper's number.

'I can't find his number in my phone book, none of the numbers. In fact, his contact details are missing,' I uttered, my brain unsuccessfully trying to work out when Cooper had done this – before or after I left the living room? Had to be afterwards, as he only knew I wanted him to see Anita after our little tête-à-tête that night. So he hadn't left when Manavi had gone looking for him in the living room; had he hidden somewhere to avoid her?

Telling me to act my age and then playing hide-and-seek in my living room.

'When was the last time you called him?'

I sat there. Anita's words hardly registered, though I saw her lips move. I was part wounded, part furious and felt totally let down. Cooper had no bloody right to play with me like that. He may be a damn good friend, but this was crossing the line. Snooping through my phone. Total privacy intrusion. What else had he seen?

My call history? My texts? Checked my albums to see if I had taken Manavi's pictures?

'When was the last time you called Mr Cooper, Jay?'

'Hmm.' I was transported back into the room when Anita repeated the question.

'I can't think of anything right now, I'm sorry. But my contacts sync with my laptop, so I'd be able to send you the number when I get back to office.'

Anita smiled. 'That's okay. There's no crisis. However, do you remember calling him recently?'

'No. As you know, I've been awfully busy, I haven't called him at all in months. In any case, we don't phone each other, we meet face to face.'

'Then the contact might have been erased by accident a while back and you wouldn't know, would you?' She said it more like a statement than a question.

'Yes, that could be right, too.'

She had a point. Was I jumping to conclusions? Maybe.

'Send me the number when you get back to the office and I'll contact him.'

'Thanks. He mentioned that if you cannot get him on the line, please leave a message and he'll return the call as soon as possible.'

'Don't worry, Jay. Just leave that to me. And don't think about this incident too much. Sometimes old friends are only envious about their friendship and don't want their old mates to make new bonds – specifically with the opposite gender – because they fear losing their buddies totally. Actually, it's predominantly a female trait, but it is prevalent across both genders. I'll talk to Mr Cooper.'

'Thanks, Anita.'

21

NOW THAT JAY KNEW ABOUT KUMAR – AFTER LISTENING TO BHĪMA'S tapes and meeting Rita in person – it was imperative that he met his client again, and soon. Besides, with the date for the trial set, the judge appointed and the prosecutor ready, Jay wanted to check if Kumar had any last-minute opinions or reversal of earlier ones. Kumar could easily plead guilty on account of self-defence or Private-Defence, through the provisions conferred under IPC Sections 96–106 that provide protection to both person and property. The provision rightfully extends its sphere to include a reasonable apprehension of threat or danger, which is the root of the law of self-defence. As per law, 'the violence used must be in proportion to the injury to be averted and must not be employed for the gratification of any vindictive or malicious feeling.' Hence, if Gina Pinto had pulled the Glock on Vinay Kumar, it could be legally argued and justified that, feeling a threat to his life, Kumar shot her in a fight. Perfect Private-Defence: it was not retribution.

The accumulated intelligence revealed that Kumar's father was in hot water with the current political party supremo. So, although the self-defence plea could get Kumar acquitted by the court, the party still needed a squeaky-clean candidate. There could be no compromise on that. As such, with Kumar being a suspect and then being taken to court as the accused was already big news. If only Kumar could be somehow portrayed as a pawn in the opposition party's game play – an innocent sacrificial lamb – all sympathies would drastically be in his favour. If everything went well and it could be labelled as a smear campaign against Kumar by the opposition, votes for him would shower like rainfall in Cherrapunji. Sacking Vinay Kumar was easy, and the party chief could do it anytime. It would be even simpler if the court found him guilty.

What Jay needed to know was whether the party ticket meant more to Vinay Kumar than his freedom? Claiming self-defence might destroy his political career, but it *would* most certainly set him free.

'We can put this as self-defence. Some altercation, you guys had a fight, she pulled a gun on you and—'

'I didn't kill her.' Kumar wasn't willing to give an inch. He was confident, edging on cocky.

That, or it would prove to be the biggest lie in the game.

'Let's go through this again, Vinay. For my sake, please indulge me.' Jay laid out the bare bones of the case once again. 'Do you have any idea how the prosecution would attack you and, in turn, me? They'll shred us like confetti. If I was prosecuting this, it would be the easiest case in my career.'

'What do you want me to say, Jay?' Kumar looked up, like he was requesting God to back him up, but his voice lacked the confidence he had displayed on earlier occasions. 'This is a set-up to destroy me, my family, my career. I think—'

'I don't give a rat's ass what you think, Vinay. The time for you to think has run out. It's my turn now, and as your advocate it is for me to devise a strategy to get your acquittal.'

Kumar frowned at being chastized like a schoolboy but jerked his head in agreement as Jay confirmed he was still looking at exoneration.

'Just remember one thing, Vinay. They say crime pays but

it only pays until a certain point. In my honest opinion, crime costs, and when it sends you the bill, it demands payment in hard cash. It doesn't take kindly to delays, doesn't accept credit cards. Justice will be served then and there in the court.'

Both men held each other's gaze. Neither spoke for a full minute.

'I don't think I shall need to meet you for a couple of months, unless something comes to light that has the potential to change the case. I shall be putting forth a motion that you loved Gina, you wanted the child with her and that this must be a set-up. You are innocent. Once I finish strategizing, we should have a session to go through the whole thing. In case you come across something that can substantiate this motion, please get in touch immediately. Otherwise, we proceed as discussed today. Is that okay with you?'

'I get it, and I'm glad I hired you and no one else. When can we discuss your fees, Jay?'

'Don't worry, I won't let you off free.' Jay let out a phony chuckle. 'I'll ask Julie to send the bill across to your office by the end of this week.'

Jay pondered about Kumar for a long time after his client had left the building. If he was honest, something had to give. If he was lying, something still had to give. Unlike whatever anyone has ever told you, there are many grey areas in the law. Exceptions One and Four under Section 300 of the Indian Penal Code were founded upon the same principle: absence of premeditation. However, while Exception One protects those accused when they are totally out of self-control, Exception Four covers the acts committed in a sudden brawl; obviously – and it is spelt out for any ignoramus who does not find it apparent – the brawl or scuffle must have occurred with the person killed. Nevertheless, to establish that an incident wasn't a cold-blooded murder, the defence had to prove beyond any doubt that there was no premeditation or planning, and that the quarrel – with or without weapons – started impromptu, following some verbal altercation or threats that erupted, which led the two concerned parties into uncontrollable rage. All Jay needed to do was prepare Vinay Kumar according to the script: that there had been a fight. Gina's murder would then be classified as 'Culpable Homicide' rather than a cold-blooded murder. But that could cost Kumar up to ten years in jail. However, when Kumar wasn't willing to plead guilty in self-defence, what were the odds he'd agree to culpable homicide? Jay deliberated on it and reckoned that this hearing required some serious work. He was tired now; it was like exhaustion was cutting off the blood supply to the lungs or heart or maybe even his brain.

Their second date was as good if not better than the first one. They left for an overnight trip after work on Friday. Jay, using his contacts, had reserved the Ramji Mahal at the Neemrana Fort-Palace Hotel. Bhīma refused to let Jay travel alone with Manavi. Conscious of the situation, and as consolation, he had privacy glass installed in the car to separate the two compartments and provide space to the lovebirds. The jaunt was successful. At no point did Manavi refer to Jay's sessions or even ask about Cooper's surreptitious visit the other night. The age gap, which Cooper had vehemently argued against, did not hamper the relationship, but then again, this was just the beginning. Manavi did request to meet Yuvraj though, and Jay decided he would certainly introduce her to him when Yuvraj was back for vacation in December.

Back from the trip, Jay delved into Kumar's case. His office had a small ensuite annexe that accommodated a couch, a wardrobe, his bar and a vinyl player with concealed speakers in the ceiling. He was known to spend nights here when he was in the thick of some important case. Between preparing for Kumar's trial, the thoughts of his own mother flashed through his mind. Did she know who had killed his father? If she did, why hadn't she spoken for so many years? Why did she break her silence just before her death? The advocate in him was looking for her motive to reveal the truth so late in life; the son in him was arguing she wouldn't have lied while facing her death. Someone had murdered his father, accused his mother and taken his childhood away.

Commander Kawas Manekshaw Nanavati, an officer in the Indian Navy, was frequently away on duty for extended periods of time. His English wife, Sylvia, fell in love with his close pal, Prem Ahuja. Sylvia decided to divorce Nanavati and marry Ahuja, but he changed his mind at the eleventh hour. When Nanavati returned and found out, he, naturally, went ballistic. As already planned, he dropped his family at the cinema, excused himself and left to deal with Ahuja. En route, he stopped at his naval base, picked up his pistol and cartridges under some vague pretext and then drove to Ahuja's home. As expected, an argument ensued, and Nanavati shot the Romeo point blank. Three times. Then he drove back to the naval base and confessed to his supervisor, who made him surrender to the police.

Any respectable man would have done the same. A Naval officer would obviously be outraged when his own friend stabbed him in the back by having an affair with his wife. To cut a long story short, when the case reached the court, the jury acquitted him. What else were the men and women of a young and free India supposed to do in the 1950s?

Nanavati's exoneration by the jury was dismissed and Bombay High Court re-tried him. The powers that be decidedly abolished juries. That, dear friends, was the day the jury died in India. No one saw the irony that the world's largest democracy did not trust in juries anymore. What do the grassroots – who simply elected governments – know about justice in any event? In countries where juries are still prevalent, the members of the jury, under oath, determine the guilt, or lack thereof, in any crime; the judge is merely a referee. However, in India, where juries have been abolished, the judge has absolute powers. And Justice Alok Nair gloated in his.

Justice Nair almost wore a tiara of peacock feathers. And, since both advocates in Kumar's case were high profile, he did not want them to be under any illusion. He called for a pre-trial meeting with them in his chambers. Neither advocate knew the reason, as this was something that didn't occur regularly, but it wasn't worth disappointing the judge by asking or by not turning up for the appointment. Talwar was waiting outside Nair's office when Jay arrived. Jay walked up to him with his hand out – professional courtesy coupled with the fact that Talwar was fairly senior to him. As they say, if you don't respect your seniors what would happen when your juniors come along? Talwar stood up to shake hands. This was going to be interesting; a voice inside Jay's head told him. A wry smile appeared on his face as both waited for another fifteen minutes before the assistant ushered them in.

'You've never been in my court, Mr Singh,' Nair began. He was a tall, dark-complexioned man in his late fifties, balding and sporting the thick untrimmed moustache that most men from his part of the country – Kerala – usually flaunted. 'Nevertheless, I've heard about you. Please remember: no frivolity or showmanship will be tolerated in my court. I do not make any concessions for personalities or celebrities or politicians. In my court there is only one hero: the truth. And as a judge I only need one thing: the evidence. Is that clear?'

'Yes, Your Honour.'

'And Mr Talwar,' Nair looked over his rimless glasses, 'I expect no distasteful language in my court. If I catch you even one time using unbecoming words, I'll hold you in contempt of court. Is that understood?

'Yes, Janaab.'

'And to both of you, I request you to please avoid extracurricular lines of arguments. If it isn't relevant to the case, don't waste the court's time and mine. Don't play cards you don't have – I want no unnecessary allegations if you do not have evidence to back your claims. Likewise, don't withhold any evidence you have relating to the case either – that's a crime and I will not tolerate that in my courtroom. If I catch either one of you doing so, I can assure you that this will be your last case. I will get you disbarred, and that will only be the beginning. At all times, do not forget you're in my courtroom and not in a theatre. I will dismiss any references to the media on the case. Don't make this a media trial. And for your own good, do not antagonize me by unnecessarily obliging the press with impudent interviews. Am I clearly understood?'

Nods again.

'I have a few weeks scheduled in my diary for this trial. I don't want any excuses to ask for continuances. If your witness doesn't show up, deal with it, change the order and advance the case. No wasting time.' Nair looked at the two advocates daring them to disagree.

Nada.

'I want both of you to exchange witness lists at least one week prior to the trial. I don't like surprises in my courtroom. No holding back any witness, and if you have an unwilling witness, feel free to request for a court order. I'll sign.'

Talwar and Singh looked at each other and nodded: *The schoolboys will do their homework on time, sir.*

'I'd like brief opening statements from both sides, not long diatribes. Is there anything you want to discuss, off the record, before the trial?'

'No, Your Honour.'

'No, Janaab.'

'So we meet in February. You may leave now,' Nair said happily. He had called this little meeting to establish the pecking order for his courtroom. He was the king. The two advocates were mere pawns.

♝

December came and went. Yuvraj was back for Christmas break. Though Jay introduced him to Manavi, he didn't mention what relationship he had with her. He didn't think introducing her as more than a friend was required. What was the rush? He wanted Yuvraj to get comfortable with her before breaking the news. In fairness, they had only been together for just over a month and who knew if they were going to stick together long-term? Manavi didn't mind either. Yuvraj saw her once at home and on another occasion when he went out for dinner with Jay. Manavi and Jay decided it was best that she did not stay overnight while he was around.

♝

Someone always knows someone who knows something. Isn't that how the whole world worked? Raja – Bhīma's informant – had dug up some gen about some other swami who lived in the same area around the same time. According to this other godman's assistant, who still resided in Patparganj and owned a tea stall now, both the swamis had left for Haridwar together in the mid-eighties. He had had no contact with either of them since, except, he had an old sepia picture of this other swami. Now that was a lead. If the two godmen had left together, it was a high probability they might have, at the very least, kept in touch. And since they had a picture of one, it could come in handy to show around and ask for him in Haridwar. However, all the informants could unearth was that the duo had moved to Varanasi after living in Haridwar for the best part of a decade. They were definitely on the right track, which was good news. It was only a matter of time now.

A week later they found the swami. He now resided in the revered holy town of Pushkar: located on the sacred lake, and known for one of the very few existing temples dedicated to Brahma, the creator. The story is that Brahma's wife, in a fit of rage, cursed him that he would never be worshipped, but then reduced the curse, permitting his worship in Pushkar. As such, the town became the king of pilgrimages for Hindus. The swami, after having been to all other sacred places, might have ended up in Pushkar to live around until his end.

22

IT WAS THREE WEEKS UNTIL KUMAR'S TRIAL. GIVEN HIS PAST record, Jay Singh would never have focused on anything else, let alone set foot outside town for any reason, but this was different. This was personal. There are times in everyone's life when all reasoning gets suspended simply because the brain resolves to shut down. Jay didn't quite have a choice; he didn't need to think or decide. He reckoned that if he didn't leave for Pushkar right away, he'd be trapped till Kumar's hearing was over, and he couldn't wait that long. At any rate, with his mind trying to detangle the mystery of his own father's death, Jay could hardly concentrate on the case. Ergo, it was best that he put this behind him quickly. He had to meet the swami.

They started from Delhi at five in the morning, however, the thick morning fog did not let them clear the outskirts until eight. There were a million thoughts competing for space and consideration in Jay's mind all through the 400 kilometres to Pushkar. The godman had travelled to a few locations before settling in Pushkar, but Bhīma had found him. In fairness, the swami hadn't attempted to hide his trail. Jay's father's murder had been such a simple open-and-shut case that perhaps Swamiji hadn't seen the need to obscure or eradicate his tracks. And now that it was so long ago, he might have stopped looking over his shoulder.

Once in Pushkar, Bhīma picked up the local guide from Ajmer – the contact who had located the swami – and drove over the low hills into the sacred city. The sun was retiring for the day and the valley was washed in blushed orange. Jay noted that the place was beautiful, worth visiting for a holiday with Manavi.

There weren't many choices to stay in mid-town Pushkar. Jay checked into RTDC's Hotel Sarover on the banks of the lake. A quick wash later, the three men set out on foot to walk to the swami's abode. The guide showed them the little hut from a distance and Bhīma took him aside to pay for the job. There was no reason for the guide to listen to any of the conversation, or to stick around: the fewer ears that heard the story, the fewer the tongues that wagged.

'How can I help you, child?' asked the godman when Jay knocked on the hut's jamb; there was no door.

Memories came flooding back as Jay looked at the swami. The man looked exactly as he had aeons ago. Not one additional wrinkle, no weight gained or lost. The hair had grown a bit longer and whiter and now hung in dreadlocks. He had a saffron robe wrapped around his upper torso to cover his furry chest. Jay was aware it would be difficult, if not impossible, for the swami to recognize him. Besides his mother's details that he knew, Jay had carried her picture to jog the sage's memory. Just in case …

'I've come looking for you from Delhi.'

'It must be really important then. Sit down.' The swami retreated to let Jay enter. The hut was sparsely furnished and the smell of incense sticks permeated the place just as when Jay had visited him in childhood. It was like Jay had time travelled: same swami, same smell and an all too familiar sparsely filled hut.

Bhīma waited outside.

'Can I get you something to drink, child?'

There was something soothing about the old man that melted Jay's rush of rage as he sat down on a rickety wooden stool.

'Do you remember a Mrs Rani Singh?'

The swami looked up like he was trying to recollect. 'Could you be a little more specific please, child? Can I call you child?'

'Yes, you can. You've called me that before.'

'Oh, really? I didn't realize that we've met before. Please remind me, child.'

'I used to visit you in Patparganj with my mother, Mrs Rani Singh.' Not keen to waste time, Jay pulled out the picture from his pocket and showed it to him.

Swamiji barely glanced at the picture, looked up at Jay and then closed his eyes, like he was attempting to recollect. He then opened his eyes and continued looking at the picture for a while. 'I remember her well. Where is she now?'

'She passed away.'

'I'm very sorry to hear that. When did that happen?'

'That does not matter, that is not what I am here for. Can you tell me why she visited you with me tagging along?' The words dried in Jay's mouth. Asking about your own mother's intentions, being distrustful of the man she visited regularly wasn't easy.

'Is that what brought you here all the way from Delhi?'

'Yes. I've been looking for some more answers, but let's begin with this one.'

'Jayakumar, isn't that your name, my child?'

Jay resentfully nodded. He was getting a bit exasperated with the swami's calmness. Nothing in his demeanour had changed at the mention of his mother's name. Had Jay been an idiot travelling all the way from Delhi?

'What else do you know about your mother?'

'What do you mean?'

'I meant, for instance, do you know you're not her real son?'

The blow hit Jay hard. His face turned crimson with indignation that this lowlife knew Jay's familial descendancy or illegitimacy. For a moment he felt like throttling the swami, but he controlled the urge. He needed the whole truth.

'How the … I mean … how do you know that?'

'That's a naive question, child. That is the only reason she used to visit me.'

'I don't think I understand your reasoning. Do you know my real mother?'

'I can see you are very angry, child. Rage kills all reasoning, so calm down. And no, I do not know who your real mother is or was, and even if I knew that, I wouldn't tell you. Familial relationships are more important than any biological one. Nature is powerful, I agree, but we underestimate the powers of nurture and love. You knew this before you came here and wanted me to confirm that your mother wasn't your birth mother, didn't you? You don't have to answer this question, just ask yourself: why did you bother? You see, Devaki might have given birth to Lord Krishna, but he always regarded Yashoda as his mother, didn't he? Even Balarama wasn't his real brother. We, humans, give undue importance to biological relationships. Yes, your mother wasn't your biological parent. Could I ask you what does it change for you? She loved you immensely. Did you ever feel you were an orphan?'

'No,' Jay answered. Numerous questions sparked in his brain, but he silently waited to hear the man out.

'Your mother was a woman, and every woman I've ever known wants to give birth to feel motherhood. So, despite the fact that she had you, she still wanted to procreate but after all the doctors had thrown in their expensive towels, she came to God for help. That's how she found me. Your father didn't believe in all these holy things, so he refused to participate and also dictated that she not visit me or any other *Maharishi* for this. I'm sure you can understand now why all those visits were a bit guarded?'

A feeling of guilt surged over Jay. He felt petty. How could he have thought anything impure about his mother who never even once let him feel that he was an orphan?

'I am sorry, Swamiji. Forgive me, I thought—'

'Who am I to forgive? It is Him.' The swami pointed skywards. 'I tried my best, with prayers and Ayurveda to help your mother conceive, but I think that God had other plans.'

'Why did you move from Delhi?'

'I am a nomad, child. God gives me a purpose; I do my duty and move on when I get a call from Him.' The swami folded his hands in respect to God.

'But didn't it bother you that my mother never conceived after all the treatment you provided?'

'We humans are mere puppets; we can only do our duty. It is up to God Almighty to give or withhold. Your mother stopped coming, so I figured she must have either lost faith or given up trying.'

'Or maybe she conceived?'

'I don't think so. I believe that she would have at least come to me once to offer her prayers to God if she had.'

'Your believe in God is so strong that you just accept your fate?

'What else is there to believe in? Isn't everything else just mere illusion – we call it *maya*. Do you know why your mother stopped coming to me? Did your father find out and stop her?'

Jay thought for a while. Was there any point in lying? Or concealing anything? He told the godman everything, who merely listened with his eyes closed. In the end, he invited Jay and Bhīma to have dinner with him.

It is illegal to consume alcohol meat, fish or poultry in Pushkar. The swami had prepared plain yellow lentils and cooked some chapatis on an open fire to feed them. It was strange, but for once, without his material comforts, without alcohol, Jay sensed peace. Like some great load had been taken off his chest. He felt deep respect for his mother for not letting him feel like he wasn't her own blood and an equal pang of shame to have thought inappropriately about her relationship with the swami.

They sat on the cold sand outside the swami's hut after dinner. Nothing but the sound of the wind sweeping the fallen leaves surrounded them. There were no other humans, just the three of them. The night sky was clear, the stars shone bright. A *koel* flitted its wings and cuckooed from somewhere up on the tree. Jay felt no haste to leave. He was happy and at peace.

Sipping hot tea, the swami said: 'Child, at most times nothing is in your control, but sometimes, things turn really bad and ugly. I can only sympathize with you, for what you went through. And though I may not be able to help you in your search for your father's killer, what I can offer is prayers at the Main Ghat for both your parents. Please join me at sunrise. You may or may not believe in all these rituals, but believe me, if nothing else, it will give you peace to give closure to a chapter.'

Despite the long travel, Jay had a restless night. The weariness was more mental than physical. He juxtaposed his material success with Swamiji's penury and, for the first time in his life, wondered if he was happy after achieving all that he had aspired to. He had never believed in any scriptural rites, but he got up before sunrise, took a bath, checked out of the hotel and attended the prayers offered at the Main Ghat. Bhīma drove him back to Delhi after that. All along the journey, as the car travelled through the arid land of Rajasthan, and shrubs and cacti raced in reverse while some stray cattle looked up to gawk at the roaring sound of the Audi, Jay was drowned in Jack Daniels and his innermost thoughts. He only felt remorse and guilt. How could he ever have let such despicable thoughts stray into his mind about someone who – not even for a second – let him feel that he was her stepson? Stepmothers were known to be evil creatures who dispensed ill treatment. One of the epigrammatic dialogues of *Sholay* came to his mind: '*Sagi mausi hoon, koi sautelee ma nahin.*' (I am a real aunt, not a stepmother). It is sad that some realizations occur only after a long time, and, in some cases, long after the soul we yearn to seek forgiveness from has departed. Was that his penance? Was that why God – and this was the first time in years Jay had God on his mind, perhaps only because Swamiji had so influenced him – had steered him to the godman? Wish he could go back in time and … and do what? He couldn't stop his parents' wrangling. No. And the hatred he felt for his father overwhelmed him. The way he had treated his mother, physically abusing her. Worse still, the man did not allow her to pursue her single desire to have a child of her own. Although Jay was, now, aware that it was medically impossible for his mother to conceive, his old man had given nothing but agony to her. He had no pointers to figure out if his father was his biological father, but after this Pushkar visit he had no inclination to look for the truth either. Something unprecedented had happened; he felt relieved that that his father had died when he did, though there was no consolation for why his poor mother had got implicated in the hideous crime she hadn't perpetrated. The child in him wanted to look for his biological mother, the man in him denied it. Then the topography changed. The state of Haryana offered lush trees to look at. Jay pondered where he could focus next? One suspect eliminated is also one lead gone. With the main suspect, the swami, out of the frame, Jay was back to square one. On the radio, Barry Manilow was singing his heart out about missing someone *even now*, and *even now* he woke up and cried in the middle of the night. *Ahem!* Jay connected his iPod through Bluetooth and changed the music to Pink Floyd to feel *comfortably numb.*

'Did your guys find the friends of my father who had borrowed money from him?' he asked Bhīma as they were nearing Delhi.

'Out of the two you asked me to investigate, the first one is no more, hukum. The other one is still to be located. He moved out of Delhi decades ago, but we are on it.'

'Thanks, Bhīma. And thanks for the long drive, too.'

Sheeba heard the car in the drive and couldn't contain her cheerful yelping. After petting Sheeba for a long time, Jay fixed his drink and waited for Cooper. There was no prior arrangement, but he waited. And he waited in vain.

23

THE CALL WAS PREDICTABLE, BUT IT NEVERTHELESS SURPRISED Jay. In his sudden dash to see the swami in Pushkar, he had totally overlooked getting back to Anita with Cooper's number. The trouble with some of the new technologies is that they accomplish more than you want the bloody things to and occasionally more than you are actually even aware of. When Cooper's number went missing on his iPhone, little did Jay realize that the deletion would also sync up with the address book on his MacBook via the Cloud. It was a revelation and he felt cheated all over again. Had Cooper known this? Suddenly, all the benefits of technology seemed like a curse as Jay Singh sat brooding in his office about how big an idiot he had been for not keeping Cooper's contact details anywhere else. What happened to the good old world of Rolodex? Or jotting down contacts in the little address book alphabetically? Anyway, he knew Cooper would be back in a week or so. Jay decided to give him a piece of his mind. But why the heck did the sucker have to agree to let Jay give his numbers to Anita? He could have simply refused, and Jay would have understood. It wasn't that Cooper had to comply with everything Jay requested! *Bastard.*

He felt ludicrous explaining the faux pas to Anita, but she, it appeared, had better understanding of the technology than him.

'I expected this, but I thought maybe you kept the numbers elsewhere, too. Anyway, we'll get to it. When you see him next—'

'You bet. The next time I see him, I will physically bring him to you.' Jay knew better. Since he had known his friend, Cooper always had an upper hand in the relationship. He couldn't coerce or cajole Cooper to do anything that he didn't want to. Persuading Cooper? No way. But then, when had Jay tried?

'That's not required. I mean … if Mr Cooper isn't willing, then he is hardly of much use even if he turns up physically.'

'I know.'

'On another note, is it at all possible to relieve Mr Bhīma for a while?'

'For?'

'I'd like to talk to him in private.'

'Talk to Bhīma about what? I've already told you all there is about Bhīma. If there's anything else you want to know about him, I shall fill in the gaps when we meet next.'

'You've got it the wrong way around, Jay. I want to talk to Bhīma about you.'

'What about me?' Jay's curiosity and anxiety both rose like helium-filled balloons. Was this therapist getting too smart for him?

'He lives with you, spends more time with you than anyone else, so it's only natural he might know something that might be of some help to you and me.'

She had a point.

Bhīma would know more about Jay's day-to-day life than Cooper or Ali put together. It might be a totally different matter that Bhīma might not divulge much, given his loyalty.

'Okay,' he murmured. 'When do you want to see him?'

'Well, if you are okay with it in principle, I'll ask Manavi to set something up.'

'No worries, I'll call Manavi and let her know.'

Manavi.

The very thought of her made some of his gloom fade. He gave her an account of his hurried visit to Pushkar and what the swami had told him, and that taking everything he now knew into consideration, he had cleared the godman of any ill feelings or accusations.

'Good. That should ease some of your worries.'

'I am still nowhere closer to the truth.'

'We'll get there.'

As Jay put the phone down, Julie brought in his morning coffee. He requested her to close the door and leave him alone for a while. No calls or interruptions please. He mulled over his conversation with Anita. This little therapy had started overtaking his whole life. What had started as a few sessions for him had begun to involve his friends and associates. And all to understand what they could disclose about him. Nevertheless, what choice did he have? If he did not cooperate with the treatment, the update – he could bet it would go back as a complaint – would be sent to Justice Chowdhary and he understood what the exact ramification of that would be: disbarment. The therapy, however much of a nuisance it was to his schedule, was certainly working; he had started drinking a lot less. But that could also be because he was occupied with Manavi. At any rate, he conceded that he couldn't afford to withdraw.

Bhīma's boys finally hit pay dirt. The news was disquieting, whichever way you looked at it. Seven years previously, Kumar had been accused of killing a young girl who he had been dating. In other words, another mistress. However, his dad being in power was then, used his political muscle and money to quell the case. The victim's mother was bullied and threatened to withdraw the case and then paid off handsomely. She changed her story to one of burglary and stabbing. The FIR against Kumar was obliterated from police files. By any record, the murder did not happen and could not be upheld by prosecution. Nevertheless, if Talwar even got so much as a whiff of the same, he'd most definitely exploit it, mentioning 'the rumour' in front of the judge to influence the current case. The judge would find it all too coincidental to accept that someone might be accused of murder on two occasions, both under similar circumstances and on both occasions with the victims being the accused's alleged mistresses. Sadly, Jay had no way of establishing how much Talwar knew. His intuition told him he should proceed assuming Talwar didn't know, given that his investigative channels were limited to the state and the state had itself destroyed any record of the same; they wouldn't be stupid enough to bring it up and risk any flak or retribution. But a defence advocate had to anticipate every possible move and countermove and plan an attack against it. Yes, the prosecutor could come up with yet another unanticipated and even more bizarre move – the beast of legal battle couldn't change – but there wasn't much choice.

Despite having told Kumar he'd only see him in the week before the trial, Jay knew this outstanding new slice of discovery needed to be discussed. As part of consultations with his defence advocate, Kumar should have revealed this even if the allegation was unfounded. Anyhow, it warranted a tête-à-tête with the flamboyant Mr Vinay Kumar.

♝

'I thought we weren't meeting till later unless something came up.'

'You're right. *Something* did come up.'

'Pray, what's that?'

'Have you ever been accused of bumping off another mistress before Gina, my dear master of encore?'

'No,' he spat out immediately, but then pursed his lips.

Was he was rendered speechless? Had he finally been caught out?

Jay waited till a tight smile appeared on his lips. Was he concealing his embarrassment? Offering an apology? Jay wanted to stand up and slap the idiot.

'Vinay, from now on if you are desperate to lie, lie to your wife, lie to your dad, lie to your kids, your friends and if you can't get hold of any of them stand in front of the fucking mirror and lie. If you fucking lie to me ever again, I'll personally fuck you up. Let this be the last warning.'

'What docs anything from my past have to do with this case? It was a fabricated accusation and I had even forgotten about it till you mentioned it now.'

Forgotten? Who the fuck forgets that they were accused of murder?

Jay wondered what else Kumar had concealed. And what more could pop up before or during the trial? He let the silence hang sufficiently long for Kumar to continue.

'Why is it so difficult for you to believe I'm innocent?'

'I've told you before – it's not me, it's the judge who has to believe it.'

'And why should it be difficult for the judge to believe that I am innocent?'

'You don't really want me to answer it again for you, do you Vinay? All circumstantial evidence points towards you, and the motive isn't lacking far behind.'

'But I hired the best lawyer—'

'I am a lawyer, I don't *make* the laws,' Jay interjected before Kumar would come up with something more ridiculous.

'So what's the best mitigation strategy if this comes up?'

What cheek to ask that.

'If the prosecuting advocate, Mr Talwar brings it up, it would be without any evidence, and my best option would be to quash it and expect the Judge to uphold my objection. No guarantees, but that is the only option we have.'

Kumar seemed to accept that.

'I have received the bill from your office and shall send a cheque,' Kumar mentioned when the meeting concluded and he was about to leave.

'Apologies if I sound crude and candid, Vinay, but please ensure your cheque is cleared before the trial begins.' Jay smiled. He wasn't wont to chasing clients after the case. Vinay Kumar did not qualify for pro bono. In fact, no defendant ever did.

Unfortunately, Bhīma's search for the Glock still drew a blank. It was now only a week for Kumar's trial to commence and he seemed to have exhausted all possible sources. Where had the confounded Glock surfaced from in Delhi? And where had it been dropped after Gina's murder? Jay would be happy with even one of the answers, but Bhīma was struggling. Had they missed something blindingly obvious? After all, sometimes it is merely one missing piece in the jigsaw that can render the entire game hopeless.

Equally hopeless was the progress made on the other front. Bhīma's moles had located the other friend of Jay's father who had owed him a large amount. The old man in question had migrated to Canada long before Jay's father's murder. He had no reason to contract anyone to eliminate the senior Mr Singh, as he had no plans to ever return to the country or repay the money. Then, why bother dirtying your hands? Jay felt bitter that the person had *borrowed* from his father with no intent of repayment but that was in the past. Three suspects down, including the swami. It was now like looking for the proverbial needle to go after the two dozen or more associates who owed small sums of money to his father. Best of luck with that!

♝

The whole day had passed tending to the affairs of the office, processing Bhīma's updates and then there was Kumar's already voluminous case file that was burgeoning with every new discovery of another one of his antics. Jay was worried sick thinking what the idiot might spring next.

It was late, Jay was tired and needed a drink. He thought of calling up Manavi but decided against it for he didn't want to sound desperate. And he didn't want to go home either. Akbar Ali! He decided to go and see his friend, who would surely give some valuable advice in general and, maybe, dispense some counsel on Kumar's impending trial; though it was unlikely he would be willing to help a defendant. Nevertheless, Jay knew, philosophies and doctrines would be discussed, foreign policies of many a country would be thrashed out in a highly inebriated state, which is what his brain needed to evade the building anxiety. The next few weeks, Jay knew from experience, would be very trying and he was sure he wouldn't find any time for an evening with his friend. As per ritual, he picked up a bottle of Scotch on the way.

'Bhīma, the doctor I'm seeing, Anita, wants to meet you.'

'Why me, hukum?' Bhīma sounded genuinely surprised.

'To know more about me.'

'So she wants me to divulge secrets about you, which you, yourself, haven't told her about, hukum?'

'No, it's not like that.' Jay let out a loud laugh. 'Stop the car when you can, and I'll hop by to explain.'

Bhīma took less than five minutes to stop the car at the roadside. Jay jumped out and climbed into the front seat.

'Let's go.'

'Seatbelt,' Bhīma gestured.

'Oh yes, I forgot.'

As the car started to move, Jay let Bhīma safely switch lanes before he started. 'It's not that I have kept any secrets from Anita, no, it's quite the opposite. In fact, I want her to know everything about me so she can help me. She reckons there might be things about me that I may have inadvertently missed and that you might have noticed, as you live and spend time with me.'

'So do you want me to not hold back anything?'

'Use your judgement. There isn't much point in telling her how we conduct business. Some of it isn't exactly law abiding, and you know that. This is more on the personal front. So, if you think something might help me, please let her know.'

'Jee, hukum.'

'And you don't need to tell me everything you tell her about me.'

'What could that be, hukum?' Bhīma jabbed.

'Like if you want to tell her how big an idiot I am ...'

Both men laughed. Jay regarded Bhīma's loyalty as something sacred.

He didn't attempt to convince Bhīma to leave when they got to Akbar Ali's place. As last time, Bhīma dropped him and left to dine at some place close by, where he could get some street food packed for the drinking buddies. He also called Bahadur to tell him to have his dinner, feed Sheeba and not stay up for them.

The day dawned bright, the February sunlight trickling through little fissures between the curtains; the thin rays brought a promise along with the warmth. Jay pressed the buzzer and stayed in bed for some time. Bahadur brought in the coffee and newspaper. He asked Bahadur to open the curtains and let the room soak up the sunlight as he lay in his boxers, reading the same ugly newspaper headlines on politics and corruption that besieged the country. Elections were next year, but with candidates like Vinay Kumar in the fray, what could one expect? This wasn't the country that Mahatma Gandhi had dreamt of; this wasn't the nation a million freedom fighters had given their lives for. However, who was Jay Singh to talk about righteousness and honesty? Even if Kumar wasn't guilty, what moral grounds did he have to contest for parliamentary elections? Well, he had a genetic qualification: a corrupt politician for a father. Then again, wasn't all politics about promoting *mishpocha*? Why point fingers at politicians, when even sons and daughters of film stars were unashamedly promoted? How could a new kid-on-the-block even think of starting? Jay turned the pages to the sports section to check the cricket scores, then proceeded to read the comic strip and fold back the newspaper.

When he showered and came down for breakfast, Bhīma had another blow to deliver. Rita's ex-boyfriend had been traced in Chennai. He was happily married, had two kids and hadn't left the city for anything in the past few years. Another possible suspect eliminated. In reality, he wasn't a suspect; he was merely a remote possibility, a very long shot, but a defence strategy had been jettisoned. The 'burden of proof', of course, lay with the person who brought in the charges: the prosecution. The defence merely has to decline all the charges as it, fortunately, carried the 'presumption of innocence': everyone's innocent until proven guilty. Jay didn't really have to prove anything. That was Talwar's job. Jay would simply shred all theories, witnesses and evidence put forth by the prosecution. In the end, if none of the evidence stuck, the judge would be obligated to squash the case. However, it would be an added bonus if Jay could plant some reasonable doubt or provide an alternate suspect – and that is where Rita's ex might could have fit in neatly; an old grudge settled, a jilted lover's payback – and that was what he was struggling to contrive. He couldn't think of anyone else who could even have a half-decent motivation to eliminate Gina. Jay knew he was surely missing something. And that bothered him. The cliché that 'the whole is greater than the sum of its parts' is more befitting an investigation than anything else. While a lot had been unearthed by Bhīma's troops, Jay needed time to put it all together. It wasn't at all helpful that Kumar's case had come to trial just when he was struggling to untangle the greatest mystery of his life. His brain was struggling to process the two in parallel.

'Bhīma,' he called as he scooped out half-boiled eggs from the cup. 'I am not attending office today. I need time to prepare for the trial next week. Please call Julie and let her know, and ask her to load all files onto the shared drive please. I'll access them from home.'

'Jee, hukum.'

'And as I am at home, you should go over to Anita's office today. I'll speak to her and set up a time.'

'Jee, hukum.'

♝

Bhīma continued to trawl the underbelly of NCR, contacting as many moles as he could to establish the origin of the Glock and yet came up with nothing. In the past, he had never been unsuccessful in providing timely leads to Jay, and hence he was displeased with his failure. What worried him more was if the provider of the Glock had successfully managed to throttle the info getting out. Though it had never happened before, this could well be the first time, and if that transpired, it could be bad for business. NCR was a powerhouse with the entire political royalty living there. You never knew who was connected to whom. And loyalties mattered more than money because money could only get you so far, and it could certainly get you killed if you crossed the wrong lines. Allegiance was sublime. Small felons were happy making trivial amounts with people they had long established contact with rather than being promiscuous and inviting fatality. Who could dare to jump on Bhīma? Oh yes, it bothered him. He was ex-army. Failure wasn't an option. Were his fangs into the unlawful arteries of the city on the wane? Nonetheless, there was nothing Bhīma could do about it.

24

Bhīma was in for a shock when he got to Anita's office at two in the afternoon. The situation hadn't escaped Jay; he had deliberately played the prank on the humble man. When the big man saw his bhabhiji at Anita's office, it was like someone had poured superglue in his mouth, since he had no idea that Manavi worked there. He had never asked Jay where he had met her. Words refused to leave his parched mouth; his eyes blinked uncontrollably. He wanted to turn around and run out screaming like he'd seen a ghost, but his feet were fastened to the ground. He stood there wondering how to acknowledge her.

'Hello, Mr Bhīma,' Manavi eased his anxiety by keeping a professional tone.

'Good afternoon, madam. I'm here to see—'

And now the name of the therapist escaped him.

'Anita, I know. Just wait, I'll let her know.'

Without looking at her for another moment, he walked over to the reception area and filled himself a cup of cold water from the dispenser.

'You can go in now,' he heard Manavi say.

He upended his little plastic cup and, keeping his head down, walked into Anita's office, softly murmuring, 'Thank you, ma'am.'

'Hello, Mr Bhīma,' said Anita as he entered.

'Hello, Doctor.'

'Can I get you some coffee or tea?'

'Nothing, thanks.'

Once they were seated across Anita's big desk, she asked him questions on his background and how he came to be in Jay's life. Bhīma felt relaxed after a while. His heartbeat had settled. This was easy.

'You know why you're here? It's not about you; it's about Jay.'

He nodded, but he was nervous again like she was about to give him a prostate examination.

'Do you know why he's been referred to me?'

'He's not well,' he answered naively.

'Okay, let's start from the beginning. First of all, I need you to read a form and sign it for me please.' She picked up a two-page form kept at hand and handed it over to him. 'This is a kind of – Non-Disclosure Agreement or NDA which states that any discussion we have today, anything I tell you or deduce about Jay from our conversation, stays in this room. We are both bound by law to protect the confidentiality of any illness or disorder Mr Jay Singh has and consequently the treatment, therapy or medication being specified for him. Simple?'

Bhīma speed-read the form – his military training had taught him to. The form was pretty much what Anita had summarized with a bit of legal jargon thrown in. He picked up a pen from her desk and signed it without hesitation. With or without a signed form, betraying Jay was not in his DNA.

'Jay was initially referred to me because of excessive drinking,' Anita started without a warning as soon as she filed the papers. 'Would you agree he drinks more than normal?'

'Normal is different for different people, isn't it?'

Anita smiled and shook her head. 'That's a loyal friend's non-committal response.'

Had she expected anything else? How was he to know how to respond? Jay should have come along with him.

'Did I say something wrong?'

'No, Bhīma. I expected this response. But please understand that non-committal or ambiguous answers will not get us anywhere. You are free to leave whenever you want, you're also feel free to say "no" to anything you don't want to answer. My only interest is for Jay to feel secure, to know that alcohol is not the answer to his troubles. On the contrary, it is one of the key problems.'

Bhīma nodded. Even he recognized that.

'Good. So, could you now answer my question please?'

'Yes, he drinks more than one should, ma'am. I've been in the army and we're known for alcohol consumption, but hukum drinks more than anyone I've ever known.'

'And you agree that cannot be good for his health.'

'Yes, ma'am.'

'Okay. So we, together, need to work towards getting him off this alcohol wagon.'

Nod.

'Does he drink more when he is alone or when he is with his friends?'

'Usually when he is alone, ma'am. He doesn't have many close friends, which I'm sure he would have told you.'

'What about Akbar Ali and Sam Cooper?'

Bhīma was still for a full minute. He couldn't think. He couldn't speak. He could feel his Adam's apple racing up and down involuntarily. His body started itching. He wanted to disappear or, at least, duck under the table.

How much did this lady know?

'Are you okay, Bhīma?'

Bhīma's appointment was for an hour, but Anita buzzed Manavi to cancel the following appointment. He eventually left Anita's office after five.

'Manavi,' Anita came out immediately after Bhīma. 'You were right. Could I talk to you for a mo—' She saw a client waiting and turned to him and offered a smile. 'Sorry to have kept you waiting. Just give me a few minutes to prepare.' She pirouetted and returned to her office.

Jay had asked Bahadur to cook some spicy chicken curry and rice for him. He sat and scribbled notes on his pad till one-thirty and then poured himself a beer with his meal since he wouldn't be working after lunch. Sending Bhīma away gave him complete freedom, not that Bhīma was his mother-in-law who disallowed his drinking routine. Manavi called him at four to let him know Bhīma might be late, which got him worried. What was it that Anita was asking Bhīma? What was it that Bhīma had observed?

He reckoned Anita was sharp enough to know all defence advocates were a bit bent anyway and none was in business to win a fair play award. Moreover, he was confident that Bhīma would not give out any trade secrets. If anything, they'd be discussing his personal life, his personality and how many units of alcohol he consumed. That reminded him that he needed another drink.

Jay sat in the living space, as it was a bit windy outside after the sun had descended below the horizon. He had had one drink too many and could vaguely catch the elusive sound of a motorcycle that seemed like some garage band playing drums far away.

When Bhīma came in, Jay was slouched in the living room after drinking himself into a coma once again. He picked him up, took him to the first floor and tucked him in bed like an infant. As Bhīma lay in bed after finishing dinner with Bahadur, he reflected – Anita was right. And he, too, had been right in enlightening her with what he knew. It seemed right even in retrospect. If Jay could abstain from alcohol – or at least stopped relying on it as a crutch – he was willing to pay whatever price he had to, including being sacked. Given how Jay consumed the poison, it was only a matter of time. And before he shut his eyes to the day, he prayed that Jay be saved before any sort of irreversible damage was done.

25

SAKET IN SANSKRIT MEANS A PLACE CLOSE TO THE HEAVENS; WHY then did the area warrant a seventeen-acre district court for criminal proceedings is an irony lost on everyone. The District Court in Saket is located on Press Enclave Road. The new building houses courts and district and sessions judges, additional district judges and additional sessions judges. Most state prosecutors have chambers in the building, too.

Someone from another planet, or maybe even an alien nation, might have mistaken the place for a film set. In fairness, the number of cameras and the bustling crowds gave every impression of it. However, it was an altogether different setting. The media carried cameras of all shapes and sizes; the larger and better ones, naturally, belonged to the plush television channels while the newspaper scribes hung on to their smaller and cheaper ones. Then there were several denizens who were recording the event on their mobile phones. Just why ordinary people go to the trouble of turning up to see other folks' prosecution would forever remain a mystery. Perhaps, *Homo sapiens* covertly love misery, provided it's not inflicted on them. Some were honest individuals who fancied witnessing the trial of a would-be dynastical politician so as to make an informed decision in the upcoming elections. However, the rogue congregants who constituted a large portion of the crowd and the ones who carried placards and shouted slogans of 'justice' were indeed organized and most definitely paid for by the political party to which their leader, Vinay Kumar, belonged. Politicians love swarms of followers; it affords them a sense of comfort, albeit a false sense, but there you go. The paid crowd was exceedingly raucous, as if their life depended on it; by the look on their faces, their dinner certainly did. For now, the case was making front-page news. If Kumar was guilty, it would make headline news for a few days before fading into oblivion, perhaps the media might even dig out the dirt from his past for all the wrong reasons. If he was acquitted, there was a danger the news could lose its headline spot – doesn't it usually if it's not bad news? – and these supporters were paid to do something to create headlines; the political party would have to ensure that.

Slogans of '*Humara neta kaisa ho? Vinay Kumar jaisa ho …*' (How should our leader be? He should be like Vinay Kumar.) were being shouted.

Really?

Vinay Kumar, dressed in white – probably khadi silk – kurta-pyjama and a saffron scarf, arrived in a white Tata Safari. The driver rushed down to let the leader out; Kumar got down with folded hands raised over his head to salute the supporters. The Cameras flashed as the close coterie circled Kumar on his way up the steps to the District Court.

Arrogance and unashamed ostentatiousness are unparalleled assets in a district court, and Jay Singh had both on display as he arrived at thirty minutes to ten. He was dressed in a seersucker black Armani suit and a black Hermès tie instead of a scraggy, starched-for-the-umpteenth-time white band like his opposite number, Talwar, who in appearance was the exact antithesis of his rival. Jay's polished Audi gleamed as it wheeled to the final spot – to the security barriers – before the chauffeur stopped. Oh yes, it rolled heads. On occasions like these, Bhīma didn't drive; he was the security that the mighty defence advocate required. Haughtiness personified. Bhīma, still in uniform, almost jumped out of the front passenger seat to quickly canvass the area and grant the media maggots enough time to focus their cameras before Jay got down. Once sure that nothing was out of order and there was no apparent threat, he knocked on the rear window to give an all-clear. Jay got out to face incessant flashes – one of the most sought-after defence advocates in the country arriving for a high-profile case was like a celebrity walking the red carpet. He buttoned his coat and waited for Julie to join him. Julie wasn't an advocate; she merely accompanied him to make notes and sway the judge. She wore a black skirt – not too short, not too long – a femme fatale. En règle, women advocates and assistants had a dress code for court attendance, but try telling a woman advocate how – or on this occasion how long – the dress should be and the feminist would love to turn you into mincemeat. In any event, was Justice Nair going to object to a bit of peekaboo? As they would be sat in the courtroom side by side Julie's movements – every flick of her hair, every smile, every crossing and uncrossing of her legs – would be dictated by Jay Singh lifting and dropping his red pen on the table in front, which in turn would be dictated by Talwar's incriminating questions.

Rumour had it that Jay Singh's fee for this case was in excess of ₹5 crores. Why wouldn't the media be there?

'Why do you think Vinay Kumar is innocent?' someone shouted from the crowd.

'Everyone is innocent until you prove their guilt. Anyway, it's not what you or I think; it's what the court decides after I provide the evidence, isn't it?' Jay's response was practised for the media. Even an ant-brain knew that this statement would run every hour on the news channels covering the story. Such ripostes weren't left to chance.

'What evidence do you have?'

'No comment.'

One should know when to shut up.

'If he is innocent why does he require a pre-eminent criminal defence advocate?'

That was something the media had already been speculating for weeks now. And why did Jay Singh take such an open-and-shut case? What was in it for him except defeat?

Jay walked up the stairs behind Julie. Bhīma, armed with a gun, wasn't permitted in the building. As everyone had to go through security checks, he was comfortable leaving Jay on his own when the court was in session. In any event, he had to leave, as he needed to catch up with his informants. He hotfooted out without wasting any more time.

The media forages for such trials and incidents to feed the scavengers. They were there as if this was the event that could shape the nation in the coming decade. *Star News. Doordarshan. NDTV. Aaj Tak. Tehelka.* You name it. Big microphones and even bigger cameras floated around. Given the heat they generated, it was surprising the weather channel hadn't made an appearance. It looked dramatic, like a set from Bollywood, although Ram Gopal Varma wasn't in sight. The crowds had been anticipated, and as such *State versus Vinay Kumar* was to be held in the biggest of the eighty-one courtrooms in the property.

The law of the jungle says that there cannot be more lions than lambs. The other lion, Talwar, was already seated with his papers organized and his assistant – a young prosecutor – sat next to him. Jay acknowledged him with a smile from a distance, walked up and shook hands. Both were good advocates; trouble was both were in it to win it – a professional, stoic resolve, no ill feelings or emotions wasted – and that destined heartache for one.

Vinay Kumar was on bail, and justifiably so, as the state had failed to get any evidence against him but circumstantial. He sat at the defence table, close to his expensive advocate. The tables were all three feet by two, with four chairs for each advocate to sit alongside their team or clients. Jay's was ornamented with a few thick files – to communicate that he'd accomplished a lot of work – and a few reference books, which he had never had to refer to during any trial. Not as yet.

The crowds kept teeming in like flies on a fresh pile of crap and the courtroom was packed. Even struggling advocates stormed in. Ramesh Talwar versus Jay Singh wasn't an everyday affair. It was a clash of legal titans; there would be something to learn, some tricks to pick up or, if nothing else, it would be no less exciting than a T-20 match. There was not a single seat unoccupied; some even lined the back of the room, standing.

The courtroom was called to order when Justice Nair entered a couple of minutes after ten. Nair sat on a high-back wooden chair inlaid with green faux leather that was cracked in places. A black-and-white photograph of Mahatma Gandhi hung behind him. Just why did the poor Mahatma have to witness all the scum and sleaze? But then again, why did the Mahatma have to be on all currency notes either?

The court clerk – a tadpole of a man who looked like he'd been in the courtroom when the British were still around – appeared so time warped, he could stand up and shout '*Angrezon Bharat Chhodo*' (Englishmen, Leave India) any minute. In a meek voice, which only he thought could sound authoritative, he declared that all court proceedings would be recorded, unless ordered otherwise by the judge. He reiterated that court discipline should be maintained and reminded everyone that cameras and microphones or recording devices of any sort were illegal and anyone breaching the diktat would be prosecuted to the full extent of the law. No exceptions.

The opening statement from Talwar followed. It was brief but fiery. Essentially, he summed up with: 'Janaab, Vinay Kumar is a spoilt son of a rich politician who kept a mistress and when she became pregnant, he eliminated her. I will provide evidence that there were frequent fights in Ms Gina Pinto's apartment. Whatever her demands were from Mr Kumar – Money? Marriage? We can only speculate – Mr Kumar had every intention of ending those demands with a gun. He procured a gun, illegally, of course, as a licenced gun could easily be traced back to him and on the said night, he intentionally carried it to her apartment. As anticipated, after dinner and sex, when all his cravings had been taken care of, he must have instigated a fight. In the middle of the verbal confrontation, he pulled out his gun and when Miss Gina Pinto dared him, he fired. He then returned to his home and feigned ignorance about her death when the police got to him in the early hours of the morning. I promise the court that I will provide you with such ironclad evidence that Miss Gino Pinto was shot by Mr Kumar that the defence advocate would not be able to challenge.'

Poor Gina. Heartless Kumar. If one looked closely, the entire game of prosecution and defence is sympathy versus empathy. The poor victim or the innocent accused?

Jay Singh got up to protect the innocent accused, Kumar, in his opening statement, which was brief too. He stressed that his client Vinay Kumar had been set up. 'Your Honour, sincere apologies if you think I'm pedantic, but I actually counted that Mr Talwar used the word *gun* four times. He told this court no less than four times that my client used a gun to shoot the mother of his unborn child. He, however, forgot to mention that there is no gun. Not even a fungible one has been presented. The police don't have it, no gun has been found missing from the victim's house or my client's house, there is no evidence that my client illegally bought or owned any such weapon. So, where is this gun? The fact is that there is none and, unfortunately, the State cannot link my client to the murder in the absence of the murder weapon, unless they plan to produce an eyewitness. Simply put, the State does not have a case. What it has is suspicion based on circumstances, and that is not the same as circumstantial evidence. My client should be exonerated right away. He deserves all fairness afforded under Indian law. Your Honour, I could stand here and say I'll strike off all of the State's evidence, but that would be a lie; the prosecution does not have any evidence.'

The parting sentence was a bit of drollery meant to lighten the mood. There was hushed laughter, but Justice Nair let it go with a stern look at Jay Singh as he sat down.

'You can call your first witness, Mr Talwar,' Nair instructed.

As always, the State's opening witness was the police officer who attended the crime scene first. After taking the oath and going through the elementary motions, Talwar quickly came to the point. As Gina's body was found in a pool of blood that came from the bullet wound in her chest, this was an opportunity no prosecutor worth his wage would let pass. It was a time-tested practice. What better way to start a trial than to invoke firsthand compassion by displaying pictures of a cold-blooded murder and a corpse and let the dead speak for herself through the exhibits? There is no way the defence advocate can cry 'foul' or 'objection'. There wasn't much in the way of verbal testimony by the assistant police inspector. Jay, however, did draw some useless exclamation marks on the pad in front, signalling Julie to distract the judge from the gory pictures and she crossed her legs.

'Thank you, Officer,' Talwar concluded. Then, turning to Jay, he said, 'Your witness.'

A lot of defence is nothing but opposing the prosecution. At the right time. Sit calmly and when you spot a slip-up, tighten the screw till it hurts, till it bleeds; the judge takes notice and the court clerk records it. That's good defence. Nevertheless, Talwar had been cautious in examining the assistant inspector, not letting any slack question hang low for Jay to exploit.

'No questions, Your Honour.'

A wolfish smile crossed Talwar's face.

'Then, you can call your next witness please, Mr Talwar?'

Julie flicked her hair back. The judge shouldn't gather her movements were orchestrated, so she moved regardless of any signal from Jay.

The State's next witness was (surprise, surprise!) the forensic pathologist who had carried out the postmortem on Gina's stiff.

'Your name?'

'Dr Ram Dubey.'

'What's your profession, Dr Dubey?'

'I'm a forensic pathologist.'

'By forensic pathologist, you mean the person performs the postmortem, correct?'

'Yes.'

'How many postmortems have you done for the state, Dr Dubey?'

'Oh, over five hundred, I would imagine …'

'The record says you've done 623, including the deceased Miss Gina Pinto's autopsy.' Talwar held the Xerox of the record he had unsheathed from Dr Dubey's medical vita.

A copy was passed on to court clerk and Jay Singh for perusal too.

Credentials well established.

Using the exhibits from the autopsy, the doctor described how Gina had been shot at gunpoint, just in case anyone in the court had any misconception that Gina had taken her own life. He explained the wound, the probable trajectory of the bullet and whatnot; whichever was the first blood vessel to burst with the slug, it still wouldn't pinpoint the hands of the killer. However, the prosecution always made it a point to display more gruesome imagery to prejudice the judge's eyes. Jay sometimes thought that it was a wasted bullet, as the law had no appetite for emotions – it couldn't afford to assess people based on emotions. Regardless, the doctor carried on monotonously on his findings, how Gina hadn't suffered, as the death must have been *fairly* instant and the direction in which her body would have *probably* dropped. Dr Dubey carefully laced his summations with adjectives and adverbs so as to remain ambiguous.

The camera and science don't lie, and challenging the doctor's testimony would be futile. Jay knew it would merely make a mockery of himself and the defence. He also acknowledged that Talwar would exploit the doctor's testimony to score a huge point.

'Shot at gunpoint, from the front' meant the victim *might* have known the killer. As there was no break-in, either the victim had let the killer in or the killer had the key to the main door. In both instances, it pointed a more than a doubtful finger at Vinay Kumar, who had unrestricted access to Gina's apartment. Heck, it was his apartment. Jay drew a doodle, and Julie moved. There wasn't much Jay could do on this.

'So you think Miss Gina Pinto was shot at close range?'

'Very much so.'

'Then it is very likely the killer was known to the victim?'

'Objection, Your Honour.' Jay got up. 'Dr Dubey has no facts to establish that. This calls for speculation.'

'Objection sustained.'

'No more questions, Janaab.' Talwar didn't fret on the objection; in fact, he would have expected it. Talwar must have thought he had delivered a blow – not so much to Vinay Kumar, but having had a second dig at invoking compassion for the poor victim. That, and the fact that he had surreptitiously embedded a more than possible scenario in the judge's mind: *Victim knew the killer, a sordid betrayal of trust.*

'Do you want to cross-examine the witness, Mr Singh?'

'No, Your Honour.'

Any prolepsis – the anticipation of possible objections in order to prepare answers in advance – that might have burnt lots of man-hours for Talwar was totally wasted. It was 2:0. Jay had let the second State witness walk away without questioning them.

'Okay. The court shall recess early for lunch, then,' ordained Justice Nair. 'Everyone should be back in the court at 2 p.m. sharp.' With that, he got up – so did all the commoners respectfully – and left.

There was only one witness on the list for the afternoon. After being sworn in, the ballistic expert, Praveen Sen, took the court through the lands and grooves of the bullet, the trajectory, the calibre of the bullet and that it was from, beyond doubt, a Glock. All yesterday's news, nothing new or game-changing. The only worthwhile information he presented was that the gun that fired the slug had never been used before.

Jay's eyebrows went up: if it was a brand-new weapon there was a good chance it was bought for the purpose. Why then had Bhīma's moles not been able to trace it yet? He made a note to dig elsewhere.

You cannot leave too many State witnesses without cross-examining, however irrelevant it might seem from the sides. Tear their stories into as many small shreds as possible. Make them appear like idiots or liars. One lying or speculating witness could sire doubt – even it was mere *arrière pensée* – in the judge's mind and that should be adequate. That, and the fact that Jay Singh had left the first two witnesses without cross-examining them. He needed to send the message to Talwar that the legendary *Kumbhakarna* had awakened, and would be paring the witnesses henceforth.

When his turn came, Jay challenged Praveen Sen. There wasn't anything he would gain directly by this line of questioning, but it was obligatory that he confirmed what the expert had just stated.

'Could you, Mr Sen, say with hundred per cent confidence that the Glock used for this murder was new, that it had never been used prior to firing this one shot?'

'Yes.'

'Mr Sen, can you elaborate on how you could establish that?'

'Yes. Using ballistic fingerprinting techniques, it is relatively simple to determine what weapon is used to fire a bullet, as guns leave a mark in the machining process. Firing a bullet causes wear and tear in the machine and every individual piece acquires its unique characteristics after the first bullet is fired. I can vouch that this Glock had never been fired before.'

'Thank you, Mr Sen. Now, coming back to the Glock, what more can you tell us about this gun that might help the case?'

'It's a really compact gun.'

'Compact, did you say?'

'Yes.' Sen sounded enthusiastic. Jay's questioning was employing Sen's intellect. He gloated and carried on. 'As a matter of fact, we colloquially refer to it as a ladies' gun—'

'A ladies' gun?' Jay interrupted him mid-sentence.

'Yes, sir. It is compact enough to fit into a handbag and because of its size it is relatively simple to fire, as it doesn't need a lot of strength.' Sen was at ease now; all was going his way it seemed, with no awkward questions from the defence.

'Oh.' Jay Singh forced surprise. He turned his back to the witness box and began to walk to his desk. Then, suddenly he turned around to face Sen and fired the blow.

'So, it could well have been Ms Gina Pinto's own gun that was turned on her?'

'Objection, Janaab.'

Justice Nair looked at Talwar as if waiting for a reason. It was evident that Jay Singh had gone over the line.

'Janaab, the defence advocate is conjecturing. The State has no evidence that Ms Gina Pinto even owned a gun.'

'Sustained. Mr Singh, do you have any evidence regarding Ms Pinto's gun ownership?'

'Not yet, Your Honour. But we haven't ruled out that possibility.'

'So how do you intend finding that out by questioning my witness?' Talwar barked.

'Mr Talwar, please refrain from talking directly to the defence advocate. Your objection has been sustained. Please be seated.'

Like a dejected kid, Talwar grudgingly sat down, expletives surely bubbling in his mind, Jay could imagine.

'Mr Singh, if you have no evidence, please do not attempt moot theories in my court. Is that clear?'

'Yes, Your Honour', Jay said respectfully. Then he turned to Sen. 'Thank you, Mr Sen, that would be all. No further questions.' As he walked across from the witness box to his desk his brain churned. *Ladies' gun?* Why hadn't he thought about it? Why hadn't Bhīma explored this angle? What might have come across as brusque or rubbish to others in the court had set a new train of thought in Jay Singh's head.

'You may call your next witness, Mr Talwar.'

'Janaab, I need a lot of time with my next witness. May I request the court to adjourn for the day please?'

Nair looked at the clock. It was almost 3:45. 'Do you have any objection to that, Mr Singh?' he asked in an I-dare-you tone.

'Not at all, Your Honour.'

Nair thanked everyone and closed the proceedings.

Bhīma was waiting outside the court when Julie and Jay came out. As Talwar had retreated to his chamber within the building, the media thronged Jay. Anything that they could get that wasn't spoken or produced in court, but Jay knew better.

He parroted, 'No comment' to every question and briskly walked to the waiting Bhīma.

'Bhīma,' Jay initiated the conversation as the black A8 rolled forward.

'Jee, hukum?'

'We *both* missed something.'

'What's that, hukum?'

'What if Julie wanted to buy a gun?'

'I'm not sure I understand the question, hukum. Why does Julie need a gun?' He turned around to look at Julie, who responded with a smile.

'Nah. I mean what if a woman wanted a gun in Delhi, where would she get it from?'

'You mean—'

'Yes. The expert told us that the Glock G-19 – the murder weapon – is a compact pistol, and is loosely referred to as a ladies' gun, which got me thinking that Gina could well have bought it. If we can find that out, it would be a cake walk.'

'I never thought of it.'

'Neither did I, Bhīma, neither did I, and hence, my comment – we *both* missed something. Change the course of the search, we might have a breakthrough.'

'Roger that, hukum.' Bhīma was visibly excited.

'Who do you think Talwar will call as a witness next?' Julie asked after the conversation with Bhīma was over.

'Under ordinary circumstances, I would think any other prosecutor would bring in the ASP responsible for the investigation, but one never knows with Talwar; he's not what you'd call a predictable opponent. He might save the ASP for later; it all depends on what evidence he's got.'

'Who would you call next if you were Talwar?'

'The neighbour who reported the crime, but only if I was confident that he wouldn't make an ass of himself. I mean I'd train him before getting him into the witness stand. Should the three of us go for coffee somewhere before calling it a day?'

'Sure, why not? Though, knowing you, you will probably be up all night preparing for tomorrow,' Julie said.

Julie was right. Jay went straight to the office after the coffee and skimmed through the entire case dossier again. Had he missed anything? On their own, most facts don't mean much; they only start to add up when they're put together and that was precisely what he was struggling with, because some of the pieces were missing. If only the bloody Glock would turn up or, at least, its origins become known. Somehow – whether Kumar was innocent or not guilty – if the Glock could be tied back to Gina, it would be an open sesame. However, with Bhīma's sources of information drying up, the odds were not any better than those of finding a polar bear in Connaught Place. He was still deliberating the ifs and buts when there was a soft knock on his office door around midnight. Bhīma had come by after he had been through the day's logs on all his machines in his office below with nothing new to report.

'Bahadur called from home; should I ask him to reheat the dinner, hukum?'

'What time is it?'

'12:03,' Bhīma said, reading from the clock that hung behind Jay.

'This fucking work can go on forever.' Jay closed the files. Before he got up, he opened the first drawer of this desk and foraged for any alcohol. There was a half-filled bottle of Gentleman's Jack that lay flat in the drawer. He picked it up, opened it, took more than a mouthful and switched off the lights. 'Let's go.'

The two marched out like *Twins*: Arnold Schwarzenegger and Danny DeVito; the only difference being that Jay wasn't bald or round. Bhīma did not think that the bottle in Jay's hand was a good idea, but the vakil insisted sitting shotgun on the drive home. And he was the boss.

'When was the last time you got laid, Bhīma?'

Now, that was the last question on earth that Bhīma expected from Jay or wanted to answer.

'I've asked the team to find out how can a woman procure a weapon in Delhi, hukum.'

'That doesn't answer my question …'

'But I thought you wanted to check if there was any way that Miss Gina had owned that Glock.' Bhīma soldiered on regardless, ignoring the frivolous quizzing.

Jay eventually got the message. He knew Bhīma hadn't been with a woman for as long as he had known his faithful friend. Carrying on with that line of conversation would only shower embarrassment. What was the point? If Manavi hadn't come into his life, what would his own response be to this gross question?

'Sorry, Bhīma bhai,' he murmured.

'Hukum, please don't humiliate me by apologizing.'

Jay took an enormous mouthful and finished the entire Jack in the bottle. 'No, I'm sorry.' Bhīma simply nodded.

'I'm in love, Bhīma. You know, it's given me a purpose in life.'

'I'm so happy for you, hukum.'

'Am I too old for Manavi?'

'Age, as a wise man once said, hukum, is in the mind.'

'The ... n why doe ... s Co .. opa think it's a ffuckin fant ... asy ride?'

Bhīma didn't respond. But there wasn't much point in him deliberating on an answer, for when he glanced towards the passenger seat, Jay had nodded off into his own paradise. Jay had had more than he could handle in a span of a few minutes. To add to that, he hadn't eaten much all day.

'Don't do this, hukum, please don't do this.'

26

COOPER HADN'T RETURNED SINCE THE DAY HE HAD PROMISED TO see Anita for me. Pulled a rather nasty one, leaving me looking like a first-rate idiot. I was fuming, but also getting concerned. It was quite unusual for him not to crop up for so long – it had been almost a month now. That was very unlike Sam. Was he really annoyed with my relationship with Manavi? Annoyed to the extent that he wouldn't see me for so long or anymore? I simply couldn't believe it. That wasn't my friend. It got me worried. What if something bad had happened to him? However, wouldn't that be too much of a coincidence that something untoward had happened to him just when we had a little disagreement? No, I wouldn't even call it a disagreement as any reservation was solely from his side. In time, I knew, my friend would comprehend my perspective and come to terms with my relationship. Ah, how childish of me to even muse along those lines. Cooper was mature enough not to break an age-old friendship on something as trivial as that. Perhaps he was busy. Or travelling? Or maybe he, too, had found a love interest. That would be funny, really rib-tickling. I smiled, but the annoyance of his deleting his contact details on my phone returned. He could have simply declined to see Anita. Why agree to my face like an angel and then buy time to get away now and tackle the situation later? And tackle he did for sure by pushing me under the train, leaving me to explain to Anita how juvenile I had been. What would she think of me? He hadn't played fair with me this time. Although, this was only the first time he'd played dirty. Everyone deserved a second chance, close friends like Cooper definitely did. I promised myself that if he ever did such a grave idiocy again, I'd be the one who'd disappear from his life. Thank you very much. Though, inwardly I knew that I could never afford to part with Sam. Forget what the advertising pundits have told you all along: sex doesn't cause the most formidable adrenaline rush. Fear beats it by a huge margin. And the fear of losing a friend tops many.

I poured myself my umpteenth drink and sat in the living room, looking at the pool, counting my blessings. All my life I had only counted the disfavours my life had meted out and ignored whatever good I had got out of life. Cooper was, indeed, one of the blessings. Akbar Ali. Bhīma. Manavi. Sheeba. Yuvraj. My career – however late it had sprung. I had lots of good belongings in my life basket and all I ever fretted about was the bad part.

Since I had requested Akbar to meet Anita, I was sure that he would have met my therapist earlier in the day while I was at the court representing Kumar. I should have caught up with him after the day's trial, but I was so engrossed in the case and in briefing Bhīma that I had almost forgotten about it. Now – I looked at my watch; holy shit, it was past 3 a.m. – I didn't think it was a decent time to call and wake up Ali. At this hour I'd only get strong expletives: incestuous references or anatomical impracticalities. Not that at a decent hour of the day, he would divulge any confidential gen that he had afforded to Anita about me. And then it struck me, I had court in the morning and I needed sleep too. Or, at the very least, stop drinking or the moustachioed Justice Nair would literally disbar me in the morning. I had seven hours to rest and to be alcohol-free. I drank two litres of water and went back to sleep.

27

IN MANY WAYS, A COURTROOM TRIAL IS AKIN TO THE COMPLEX game of chess. The game is not played on the board; it's played in the mind. The tangible pieces on the board are always a few moves behind, like a delayed live telecast of some game. You need to think ahead, anticipate all possible moves your opponent can make and plan your counterattack for every option. The more accurately you can think like your opponent, the greater your chances of winning the game. If you cannot do that, play snakes and ladders instead because you don't have a chance in hell. If Ramesh Talwar and Jay Singh ever sat down to play chess, the game would be a draw or they would continue till the end of time, for both were very similar in their approach and strategy.

Talwar's next witness turned out to be Gina's neighbour, who had made the call to the police.

Mr Pratap Raj had retired as a professor of botany from Delhi University in the last millennium. An empty nester, his wife and he lived on the top floor of the building that overlooked Gina Pinto's flat across the street. Given his age, his prostate woke him up a few times every night and he, after completing his business, normally wandered into the kitchen for cold water from the refrigerator. To his refrigerator's right was a window, which provided a view into Gina's bedroom. *How lucky!* He didn't normally peep but on the night in question, because the lights in the flat opposite were on after midnight, his eyes gravitated towards her room. And he saw her lying in a pool of blood. Ergo, he was concerned and called the police.

'Approximately what time was it, Mr Raj? Talwar asked.

'Why approximately? I can tell you it was exactly twenty minutes past midnight.'

'How do you know for sure it was that time?'

'I have a little clock-magnet on my refrigerator door, I see the time whenever I open the door. It's an old habit. You see when I was young …' The old man was clearly basking in the glory of being a witness in a high-profile trial. He had all the time in the world. If given a chance, he would have gone ahead and pulled out his wedding pictures to show to the court.

Jay found nothing contentious in his testimony. This wasn't the witness who could hurt. He let Pratap Raj carry on without any objections.

'How do you know Mr Vinay Kumar?' Talwar pointed towards the defence table where Kumar sat.

'He visited our neighbourhood often.'

'How often, Mr Raj?'

'Almost daily.'

Talwar looked towards the defence table again. Kumar's countenance reflected that he did not know Pratap Raj or perhaps never even noticed that the latter lived around Gina's apartment. As Nair's eyes followed Talwar's neck, Jay took the opportunity to shrug his shoulders as if to suggest 'so what'?

'Who exactly did Mr Vinay Kumar visit in your neighbourhood?' Talwar continued.

'Miss Gina Pinto.'

'How do you know that for sure?'

'I have seen him get down from his car and go into the apartment across the street. Sometimes, unintentionally, I've seen him inside Miss Pinto's apartment.'

'How well did you know Miss Gina Pinto?'

'She was our neighbour, so we occasionally bumped into each other.'

'In your opinion, what kind of a woman was Miss Pinto?'

'Objection, Your Honour: "What kind of a woman was Miss Pinto?" Really?' Jay repeated Talwar's words for effect.

'Mr Talwar, does this have anything to do with the trial of Mr Vinay Kumar?'

'Apologies, Janaab. I withdraw my question.' Talwar turned to Pratap Raj again. 'So, you called the police, Mr Raj. What happened then?'

'The police jeep arrived within twenty minutes. I came down, gave my account. Then, they went into Miss Pinto's apartment.'

'Okay. Now let's talk about Mr Vinay Kumar. You said he came to see Miss Pinto *almost daily*, correct?'

'Yes, sir.'

'What time did he usually visit?'

'In the evening, after eight most days.'

'How can you be so sure?'

'Well, I didn't see him coming every day, but his car was parked outside the gate after eight.'

'What time did he leave?'

'Objection, Your Honour.'

'State your objection, Mr Singh.'

'Your Honour, unless the witness stood by the window every night to watch my client Mr Kumar leave, how would he know?'

'Overruled. You can answer that, Mr Raj.'

'But, Your Honour—'

'I just overruled your objection, Mr Singh. Do you have any more?' Nair's tone wasn't exactly pleasant.

Jay was riled, but he realized he better sit down. However, he knew exactly where Talwar was headed. He would very shortly take Pratap Raj down the path to assassinate Vinay Kumar's character – vile, disgusting, adulterer – and the old man would harp on if not stopped and aid Nair conjure up an image of a demon. For that, he needed his opponent to step out of line or else Talwar would be squeezing his gonads in a few minutes.

'Let me repeat the question for you, Mr Raj. What time did Mr Vinay Kumar usually leave Miss Pinto's apartment?' Talwar had dexterously planted *usually* in the question to avoid any further confrontation, despite Nair overruling Jay's objection.

'Around midnight, I would say.'

'And you would know that, how?'

'Simple. I could hear the car start and leave in the still of the night.'

Talwar deliberated on the answer as if this was some new theory from Darwin and needed consideration when all the crafty man was doing was letting the whole scenario sink into Nair's mind: an adulterous man spending clandestine evenings with his mistress.

'So, according to you, Mr Kumar spent his evenings in Miss Pinto's bedroom …'

'Objection, Your Honour. That is not a question.'

'Sustained. Mr Talwar, do I have to remind you that you are not here to suggest or lead the witness in any manner. Please ask the questions, not answer them.'

'Mr Raj, what do you think was the purpose of Mr Kumar's visit to Miss Pinto's apartment?'

'Objection, Your Honour.' Jay shot up. 'Mr Raj just admitted his passing acquaintance with the deceased as a neighbour that he used to bump into occasionally – those were his words. I'm sure she didn't have a tête-à-tête with Mr Raj to confide in him what her relationship with my client was.'

'Objection sustained. Mr Talwar, please take this as a warning to keep your questions in line.'

'Apologies, Janaab.' Talwar bowed and turned to his witness again.

Jay objected numerous times; sometimes when it was logical, other times he took a cheap shot to break Talwar's performance, despite knowing that Nair would certainly overrule his weak objection. Nevertheless, Talwar soldiered on shamelessly till he circumvented the legal framework to extract words out of Pratap Raj's throat that Kumar had an illicit relationship with Gina. The star witness also intimated that in the past few months, there had been some loud arguments in Gina Pinto's apartment, and he had heard the noise from across the street.

'Janaab, Mr Vinay Kumar is a vicious person,' began Talwar as a summary of Raj's testimony. 'He had illegitimate relations with Miss Pinto, although he is married and is a father of two. As Miss Pinto's neighbour told us there had been fights in the near past, it all adds up that there was some disagreement between the two lovers, which Mr Kumar finished with a gun. We can all guess what those disagreements were, can't we? Miss Pinto was impregnated by Mr Kumar, and I wouldn't be surprised if someone told me she wanted her rights – right to marry, right to motherhood, a settled life – which Mr Kumar could not offer, given his electoral dreams. On the fateful night, after his libido was satiated and his brain subsequently returned from between his legs to his head—'

'Objection, Your Honour.'

'Mr Singh, the prosecuting advocate is talking to me, what can be your objection to that? Please sit down. You shall get your turn.'

'According to the records and witnesses so far, Janaab, Mr Vinay Kumar left Miss Pinto's apartment after twelve and Miss Gina was dead between midnight and 2 a.m. I don't believe in coincidences and neither should the court. I shall provide this court with even more evidence to prove that Mr Kumar shot Miss Pinto.' With that, Talwar sat down.

'We'll take a short break of thirty minutes. See you back at 11:30. Mr Singh, do you want to question Mr Pratap Raj after the break?' Nair asked.

'Yes, Your Honour.'

'Mr Raj, please be back in the court at 11:30. Court is recessed.'

Down came the gavel, softly.

♝

'Your Honour, firstly,' began Jay Singh after the break. 'The prosecuting advocate, Mr Talwar has been highly presumptuous in this morning session, by calling my client guilty even before the trial. I always assumed that that edict came from you, after hearing both sides.' Said frivolously, but it struck home.

Justice Nair looked at Talwar. A warning was rendered without words.

'Secondly, the deceased Miss Pinto and my client, Mr Kumar were lovers. Consortium was expected. That my client was seeing Gina on a regular basis, and that they were expecting a child together, is something my client has acknowledged or rather proactively told the court – please refer to the statements filed by me on his behalf. They were having a child together. What more proof does one need to recognize love? An adulterous relationship might not meet the moral code of ethics for some people, but we are not here to discern the good from the bad, the right from the wrong, and this trial is not about the extramarital affair of my client. This trial is about the murder of Miss Gina Pinto and simply because some paramour in some corner of the world once killed his mistress, isn't it inductive reasoning stretched too far to assume all lovers resort to murder? Having an extramarital relationship does not implicate my client in the hideous crime of eliminating the mother of his *unborn child*. The evidence – or should I say the sham – presented so far does not support any probative charges.'

Nair nodded as if in agreement, though Jay had no idea what was in the judge's mind.

Jay turned to the witness box. 'Before we begin Mr Raj, I must remind you that you're still under oath.'

'Yes sir, I know that.'

'Good.'

Isn't it ironical that the oath is only taken by witnesses and not by their advocates?

'How old are you, Mr Raj?'

'I'll be seventy-four this year.'

'It's quite commendable to have such good hearing at your age,' Jay mocked. 'I mean you could hear voices from the apartment *across* the street.' The 'across' was accentuated; morally, it was an unfair remark at a witness in the stand, but Mr Raj had elected to be there. 'Mr Raj, I don't disagree that you have heard loud voices from the deceased Miss Pinto's apartment. However, all lovers have tiffs, but their disagreements don't end by killing each other, do they?'

'Not at all.'

'Thank you, Mr Raj. So, how long have you been married?'

'Forty-seven years.'

'Forty-seven years. Wow! Congratulations.'

'Thank you.'

'Have you ever been unfaithful to your wife?'

'No.'

'In letter and in spirit?'

'Yes.'

The old man was clearly beginning to dislike Jay, which wasn't wrong because Jay was about to throw a screwball. Every veteran advocate knew that if he did not stick to a linear questioning during cross-examination, it more often than not threw the witness off guard; the rehearsal is blown out of water, something the opponent advocate has worked hard on.

'So you've never even had a moment in those forty-seven years when your mind has strayed to another woman?'

'Not that I can remember.' Raj responded straight-faced, though sweat beads had started appearing on his forehead.

'Isn't that just another way of saying "yes"?

'No.'

'No? Mr Raj, I do not like obfuscation. From now on if I ask something I want a clear response of "yes" or "no" please. Let me rephrase my question: have you never at any time in your forty-seven years of married life thought about a woman other than your wife?'

'I might have thought of another woman but—'

'So, it's a yes.'

'Yes.'

'And when you thought of another woman did you want a *rakhi* to be tied by her?'

Pratap Raj's face flushed.

Talwar was on his heels, but the judge motioned him to drop back into his seat.

'Mr Singh, where is this heading?'

'Your Honour, if you could indulge me for a few more questions please …' Jay pleaded.

'Just a couple more, Mr Singh.'

'Thank you, Your Honour. So, Mr Raj when you thought of another woman did you want her to be your sister?' Jay repeated the question.

'It's different.'

'Who or what is different? The woman you thought about with the rakhi or the other one?'

'Objection, Janaab. This is worthless questioning only to badger my witness. I cannot understand what this has to do with the case at hand.'

'Sustained. Mr Singh, please advance the case.'

Jay raised his hands in frustration like he had been stopped from making one of the most important points in the case.

If you think something's made an impression on the judge, leave it at that. Just walk away. Sometimes less is more. If the point is well made, let the rest of your predation go to waste. You're here to win the case, not give a discourse to a demimonde of hippie disciples. Jay had already more than quelled the notion that being unfaithful in marriage could equate to being a killer. By discrediting Pratap Raj, he had successfully sown the seed that all men – even men with forty-seven years of marriage – strayed in their thoughts. It only takes an opportunity to translate that into reality. Net conclusion: Pratap Raj turned into a zero-sum game, a sheer waste of court's time.

'No further questions, Your Honour.'

Justice Nair looked at the clock: 2 p.m. He still had time for another witness, but he seemed put off by the proceedings of the day. 'I have another appointment, so I adjoin the court for the day. See you all tomorrow at eleven.'

Jay was back in his office. He re-examined the whole file closely, pulled out crime scene photographs and looked at them under a magnifying glass. He studied the case for hours, noting each name, drawing a character of witnesses that Talwar had provided; then he made a new flow of activities chart. He analysed the lab reports, the evidence file. Nothing. Banishing the statements recorded, he started to penetrate the bare bones of the case. Statements can be flowery and made up; the reality doesn't change with words. That is the core and that is the truth.

The Glock was still missing.

The phone rang. It was Manavi.

'Got relieved from court early today, sweet cheeks?'

Sweet cheeks?

'Yes, but still engrossed in the case.'

'You think your client is innocent?'

'Sorry, Manavi. This isn't something I can discuss with you.'

'So why don't we discuss something else? We haven't seen each other for some time, you don't even call – are you bored with me already?'

Who said falling in love was all rosy?

'No, baby, just been busy. You know this is an important case, I—'

'Why? How is any case more important than the other?'

She had a point.

'Why don't we have dinner together tonight?'

'Only for dinner? Let's go for a midnight swim too? I'll bring my swimwear and a change. See you at 8?'

'Yes, darling.'

'Bye, sweet cheeks.'

Sweet cheeks?

Jay closed the files, capped his pen, uncapped it and capped it again. His fingers played with the buttons on the telephone for a few minutes before he called for Bhīma.

On the way to the farmhouse, Bhīma updated him. 'There has been an unusually loud fight in Kumar's household, hukum.'

'What? Something more boisterous and louder than the last one?'

'Yes, and Kumar has left the house and driven himself to his friend's house – the same friend with whom he had gone to meet some girl.'

'Aha. Keep a tab on this rutting idiot.'

'Roger that, hukum.'

Bahadur was in love with the fact that Jay was in love. Since the time Jay had called from the office to let him know that Manavi was coming for dinner, he had gotten into a frenzy, cleaned the whole house, the bedroom, the pool … and the smell of prawn curry had driven Sheeba crazy.

Manavi came at 8 sharp – you could set your clock by it. She wore a knee-length red dress cut in a classic shape with a pencil skirt, draped bodice and finished strikingly with off-shoulder sleeves. Whichever way one looked at Manavi, one had to be totally blind to miss the magnetism she exuded. She carried a small tote, a change of clothing as she had hinted.

'Hello, sweet cheeks,' Jay took her in his arms.

'What's with this new "sweet cheeks"?'

'Just a term of endearment; I won't use it if you don't like it.'

'I didn't say I don't like it.'

They were still in embrace while Sheeba encircled them to break up so she could get some attention from Manavi.

True to her words, Manavi ensured they both had a dip in the pool before dinner, not at midnight, though. They sat sipping Rémy at the poolside post dinner before going to bed.

'Please wake me up if your friend visits today.'

'Who? Cooper?'

'Yeah. The one who visits in the middle of the night.' She smiled.

'I haven't seen him since the last time you were here …'

'Is he afraid of me?'

'Extremely scared.'

'Why?'

'Have you ever looked at yourself in the mirror?'

'Do I look scary?'

'No. I mean it must be some kind of a mistake that they let an angel like you get out of heaven for me …' He smiled at his own cliché.

'Are you trying to embarrass me?'

'No.'

'Are you trying to get me into bed with you?'

'That I already have.'

'For your information, Mr Advocate, there is no law against making love again so just shut up and treat me like a real woman and not some angel.'

28

THE COURT WAS AS PACKED ON THE THIRD DAY AS IT WAS ON THE first of the trial. Jay still did not have any concrete evidence that could get Vinay Kumar acquitted. However, if you muddied the waters to a shade of chocolate brown by throwing in enough possibilities, one or the other might stick, he reckoned. And as soon as a doubt became reasonable and acceptable, acquittal would become easier. Nevertheless, if he could find the Glock, he was very confident he could link it back to Gina. How? This was Jay Singh and he could arrange for a witness who would happily accept that he had delivered the Glock to Gina Pinto. Once he could prove it was Gina's gun, there were endless possibilities he could play with. But time was running out. Talwar would soon run out of witnesses, and then it was Jay's turn to produce witnesses and evidence.

Talwar's first witness for the day was Dinesh Patel – the lead forensic scientist, who had swept Gina's apartment for physical evidence. He incessantly explained all the techniques they use for genetic fingerprinting, how they use repetitive sequencing, etc., etc. All generic stuff and nothing relevant to the case. Jay wondered if Talwar had some hidden agenda for having walked Patel down this path.

'The hair and fibre we found in the deceased Miss Gina Pinto's apartment positively belonged to Mr Vinay Kumar,' Patel declared confidently.

'So, it is logical—' Talwar said.

'Objection, Your honour.' Jay stood up.

'Please state your objection, Mr Singh.'

'Logic, Your Honour, could be a set of rules based on one's upbringing or schooling or one's wrong set of beliefs, and hence not necessarily absolute.'

Don't you love how lawyers distort even perfectly logical words?

'Objection sustained. Mr Talwar, please rephrase your question.'

'Yes, Janaab. So, Mr Patel, it can be deduced—'

'Objection, Your Honour. Mr Talwar should ask for facts not the witness' deductions. Based on his short-sightedness the witness could well deduce that this earth is flat, but it won't be a fact, would it?'

A bit of a murmur went around the court. It was another cheap shot, but it struck brilliantly.

'Sustained. Mr Talwar, please continue with the facts and facts alone.'

'Okay, Janaab.'

'Do I hear an attitude, Mr Talwar?' Nair barked.

'Not at all, Janaab, not at all.'

Jay felt like he had scored a small victory. Making Talwar sound contentious and the judge reacting irately simply meant a point in the defence's favour. Court cases were no different to playing cards. Throw in the ace to win the round at any given opportunity. For all practical purposes, this witness' testimony was now as useful as an appendix in a mammal's body. But he knew he couldn't do this too often.

♝

When his turn came, Jay was prepared to further shred Patel's testimony. Opening with simple questions, he shrewdly led Patel down the path that did not raise objection from Talwar and then delivered the knock-out.

'Mr Patel, is it fair to expect that if you did a scene search of my home you'd find ample fibre, skin residue, hair and DNA of mine?'

'Yes, of course.' Patel looked at Jay, then at Nair; his face expressed it was a very stupid question.

'And why would that be?'

'Because you live there.'

'According to Mr Raj – the witness before you, Mr Vinay Kumar practically lived in Miss Pinto's apartment for four hours every evening, give or take. Wouldn't a similar amount of hair and fibres from Mr Kumar be available at Miss Pinto's apartment?'

'Of course, yes.'

'Thank you, Mr Patel. Nothing further. Your Honour, I am not sure why the prosecuting advocate bothered to call Mr Patel to the witness stand. It was a sheer waste of time. Besides Mr Kumar's fibres and hair, he has a full wardrobe and shaving kit, etcetera at Miss Pinto's apartment. All this is documented in the docket we've already submitted to the court. If only Mr Talwar had read the submissions ...' Jay left it at that.

The challenge in the case was that none of the advocates had any evidence. All State witnesses were being thrashed, as if they were novices bowling to Tendulkar. Similar thrashing was expected when Jay got his witnesses on the stand soon.

'Court recessed for lunch. Don't be late for the 2 p.m. start.'

Vinay Kumar's driver was coached and perfected by Jay Singh to sing the praises of his master's character all through the testimony. Also, he would be probed on Kumar's demeanour when he exited Gina's apartment that sordid night in question: did Vinay Kumar look any different? Did he convey any signs that he had just killed another human being? Jay had had three rounds of rehearsals with Puneet, the driver. Nevertheless, given how he had been trashing Talwar's witnesses, he wanted to have another practice session with him. For the first time in his illustrious career, Jay Singh was scared. Petrified, to be honest. Talwar could – and most certainly would – mercilessly massacre every witness he would bring in. A game of equals always gets more vicious and bloodthirsty and courtroom trials, unlike chess, don't ever end in a draw. One wins, the other loses. And victory and losses are more than what they can be on a chessboard. It's a question of reputation of advocates.

'Thanks for sending your friend, Akbar Ali. It was really nice of him. Nice guy, real gentleman. When could we have our next session, Jay?' Anita sounded confident when she called Jay.

'Anything important, Anita?'

'Lots to talk about.'

'Tell me then,' Jay was enthusiastic. 'What is this about? What golden nugget did Akbar Ali deliver?'

'I don't think it is something we should discuss on the phone. When can we meet face to face?'

'You make it sound all so mysterious, Anita. I am most keen to know now …'

'Let's keep it tentatively on Friday evening. Why don't you give me a call on Friday morning and let me know? Does that work for you?'

'Yes, ma'am.'

'Oh, is it *ma'am* now?'

'Why not? If my assumption is correct, I should be in for a treat this time.'

'A real one and we might need some extra time, so I suggest you keep two hours free.'

'Okay, then, hopefully, I'll see you on Friday.'

The afternoon session was called off. Talwar's next witness – the lead in police enquiry – had been called into some other investigation and had sought to be relieved from court duty for the day. Given the circumstances, Justice Nair had obliged; he intended to attend the silver reunion of his friends from college. Nothing could have pleased him more.

29

THE SUN AROSE AND FLOWERS WERE BLOOMING. EVERYTHING seemed to be in order. But something had to give today. Nothing lasts forever, and neither could this case. In all probability, Jay knew, the DSP – Deputy Superintendent of Police of Saket precinct – was Talwar's last witness. He also knew Talwar would press hard to crack open the case with his officer, and that could well nail Kumar. And then factor in that he would get a chance to slaughter each of Jay's witnesses and take the case away.

Jay played with Sheeba all morning. He always felt that her love was as unconditional as the love of parents for their children, never wanting anything in return. In a way he found playing with Sheeba highly relaxing. Then he breakfasted, got dressed and picked up Julie on the way to the court. The trio, the driver inlcuded, arrived at Saket Court well before time. It was only 10:45.

♝

DSP Ashish Mehta was in uniform. He had all the ammunition that was required. Vinay Kumar was the only person with the motive to eliminate Miss Gina Pinto. Correct. Vinay Kumar was the only person who had the opportunity to carry out the job. Correct. Vinay Kumar was the only person who could be circumstantially linked to be at Miss Gina Pinto's apartment at her time of death. Also correct. With motive, opportunity and circumstance having a close threesome, there wasn't anything pending to decide that Vinay Kumar was guilty. Or was there?

DSP Mehta explained all this to the court. Justice Nair's countenance spoke a zillion words. With all the earlier prosecution witnesses, even with Jay's histrionics, there weren't any misgivings about Vinay Kumar's character. He was a married man and, above all, a politician in the making who had a mistress. Forget the evidence; the reality was that Gina Pinto could have been – even without the altercations – a sore point that wouldn't have exactly embellished his political ambitions. That he could have done away with her was understandable, but Justice Nair couldn't have agreed to anything without evidence. DSP Mehta could provide that evidence. His testimony was vital. And he was delivering on that.

Jay Singh had known this. DSP Mehta was the last and greatest hurdle and Mehta wasn't someone he could walk over. But DSP Mehta had erred on a horrendous scale, which Jay knew he would whip till it bled. Sometimes all the defence advocate needs is just one strong point or one miscue on the prosecution's part to assemble the whole defence around it. That Talwar had been slapdash was something Jay couldn't imagine. It appeared more like the DSP would have not agreed to be coached by an advocate. In any event, they had left a wide hole.

Or was it a trap for Jay Singh?

Asking a prosecutorial witness a question you don't already know the answer to could be suicidal. Jay Singh didn't want that outcome. No one likes a surprise being sprung on them. Not in the courtroom where the questioning and answering is for the benefit of the judge. Jay had to approach carefully, craftily and cautiously. He could feel the iPhone in his pocket vibrate when he got up to question DSP Mehta, but he intentionally ignored it. The last thing he wanted was to invoke Justice Nair's wrath for picking up his phone, which was a strict no-no in court. He let the vibration die before he started talking; it was a text anyway, he reckoned. To put a stop to the distraction, he put his hand in his trouser pocket to put his phone on silent.

Taking DSP Mehta around the unsuspecting bend of modest questions, Jay Singh came to the point he had prepared for.

'DSP Mehta, I respect your testimony and your passion towards duty. Full marks on that. However, in the current case of State versus my client Vinay Kumar, do you have any other suspects?

'No.'

'Why not?'

'The motive for Mr Vinay Kumar was so obvious—'

'Unless I'm wrong DSP Mehta, whether the motive is real enough or a mere suspicion is something that the court decides based on the evidence provided. It isn't something that the police should use to take their enquiry on a single track. Shouldn't you have carried on with the investigation in other directions?'

'Then there was circumstantial evidence in this case that Mr Kumar—'

'That Mr Kumar was present in Miss Pinto's apartment? Yes.' Stemming a witness mid-sentence is something advocates always relish. If nothing else, it destroys the witness' confidence. 'Yes, my client was there and he accepts that, but that was for the purpose of love, not murder. It is documented on the file I've submitted to the court already. So, let me ask you once again, why didn't you look beyond Mr Kumar?'

'We didn't think it was necessary.'

'Forgive me because I do not understand this. Because you didn't think it was *necessary* to look in other directions, you focused solely on my client Mr Kumar and ignored all other lines of inquiry?'

'Yes.'

'Objection, Janaab.'

'What now, Mr Talwar? Please state your objection.'

'The defence is pointlessly hammering the witness.'

'Overruled. I don't think so. Please sit down, Mr Talwar.'

Talwar was doing the same to Jay: simply attempting to break the presentation; there was no cause to object so far.

'Let me repeat, DSP Mehta, did you not forsake all lines of enquiry to focus on my client?'

'Yes.'

'Isn't that tunnel vision?'

'Maybe.'

'Maybe? DSP Mehta, you of all people should know what the answer in a courtroom should be – a *yes* or a *no*. Simply answer the question I ask. Please don't wander off into the *maybe* territory. The court has no time or interest in your irrelevant musings and contemplations, please.'

'Yes.' The DSP looked crestfallen.

'And should we attribute this tunnel vision to an oversight or plain incompetence?'

'Objection, Janaab.' Talwar got up again.

'State your objection, Mr Talwar.' Nair looked seriously annoyed.

'The defence is ridiculing a police officer in your court and not coming to the point.'

'Mr Singh, where is this headed?' Nair asked, but Jay could feel the judge had frivolously asked the question only to humour Talwar.

'Your Honour, all I want to state is that the police found it convenient to focus solely on my client and ignored the rest. It was a faulty investigation from the beginning and, now, given the delay it has caused, it has given ample time for the real killer to get away comfortably. For all we know, he's sitting in the audience enjoying this trial.' Jay rolled his eyes across the court to labour his point.

A low laughter passed in a wave.

'Order.'

'Your Honour, it was short-sightedness on the part of the investigating team. They were so myopic that they did not look beyond the obvious motive; they saw Vinay Kumar as a paramour, a benefactor. They found Gina pregnant, and they used some algorithm to come to a rushed conclusion that my client was the guilty party. They did not even bother to look further. In truth, they did not look for the murderer. They looked at my client and made it their agenda to make him the fall guy.'

Nair looked at Talwar who appeared miserable.

Jay realized his initial assessment was correct: the imprudent, smartass DSP hadn't been coached by Talwar to counter Jay. Too late now.

'Your Honour, the lack of any other suspect does not in any manner prove that my client is guilty. That is prejudicial and my learned colleague should know that. I have no more questions for this witness.'

'Mr Talwar ...?'

'Janaab, all that Mr Jay Singh has tried to accomplish here is find faults in the police procedure, which is far from the trth. The police did not have any agenda; they don't have old scores to settle with Mr Kumar from some previous life. Why would they even want to railroad him? The defence's arguments are absolutely ridiculous and merit no serious consideration. I hope the evidence provided by all my witnesses and especially DSP Mehta is rock-solid and enough for the court to establish that Mr Vinay Kumar cold-bloodedly shot Miss Gina Pinto. I urge the court to award the accused the toughest punishment this court can afford. I have no more witnesses, Janaab. The State rests.'

'Well then, we can all go home early today. See you in court on Monday at 11 a.m. sharp. Do any of you have any other court proceedings at that time?'

'No, Janaab.'

'None, Your Honour.'

'Good, because I would have asked you to cancel them anyway; the court is recessed.' Nair gave a cunning smile and banged down the gavel.

Jay pulled out his phone the minute Nair left the court. His privacy settings meant all he could see on the screen was that there was a message from Bhīma. Sending a text when Bhīma knew Jay was arguing a case in court meant it was important. He quickly typed in his passcode and read the message: '*Urgent: I am outside the court.*'

The only urgent information Jay Singh was in search of at this moment was the Glock. He rushed out.

Bhīma was waiting. When Jay and Julie got into the car, they noticed that the driver had been discharged of his duty and Bhīma was at the wheel. After all, there was only so much one could trust a temporary driver with.

'What is it, Bhīma?'

'The Kumars had a rather ugly row over Gina last night. I couldn't catch the entire thing, as it must have started in some other room that isn't bugged, but there was mention of a Glock a few times during the whole incident. An ambulance was called in just before midnight and Rita was taken to A&E at Max Hospital. She's obviously not admitted the truth, the authorities were told that she fell down the stairs.'

'That bastard looked cool in the court. Not a hint of any of this mess,' Jay cursed.

'I should have caught it last night, but we left the office, and hence I picked it up only this morning.'

'There's absolutely no reason to blame yourself for it, Bhīma. It could just be an episode of domestic violence and it might have nothing to do with us, except for the fact that *Gina* and *Glock* were mentioned in the same argument. I need to see Rita when she's alone. Track Vinay Kumar and let me know where he goes from the court. If he isn't going to the hospital, let's drop Julie and take me there.'

'You can drop me here, I'll take a cab,' Julie said forthwith.

'Are you sure?'

'How long have you known me, Jay? I wouldn't offer if I didn't mean it. It's more important to go see Rita than to chauffeur me around. In any case, I'll bill this to that son-of-a-bitch Kumar, so why bother?'

'Thanks, Julie. Bhīma, please stop at the next taxi stand.'

They dropped Julie and Bhīma left the car parked at the taxi rank. He took out his master control computer from the boot and got it online using a 4G dongle. Jay needed a drink but controlled himself. If he were to rush to Max to see Rita, he didn't want to smell of alcohol. There was one thing Jay couldn't tolerate and it was wife beating. He had seen it all too closely growing up in his own dysfunctional home and what it had led to. It was still an open wound that wouldn't heal; it was déjà vu. Almost instinctively, his hand went for the bottle of vodka in the pocket of the front seat as if it was some panacea that would sort all his problems. He took a swig. Then another.

'Kumar's gone straight to his office, hukum.'

'Let's go to the hospital, then,' Jay said as he capped the bottle and placed it back. A faint smell of alcohol was one thing – though he was confident vodka wouldn't betray him – but he wanted to be clear-headed when he spoke to Rita.

The instructions were clear: Bhīma would stay in the lobby area, sitting inside Café Coffee Day opposite the reception, pretending to read a book while actually keeping an eye out for Kumar, just in case he bothered to turn up. Jay took the elevator to the floor Rita's private room was on. One phone switched on for Bhīma to monitor for any trouble upstairs, the iPhone in his pocket if Bhīma tried to reach him.

Intubated, with her right eye blue-black and stitches on her upper lip, Rita lay comatose. Jay remembered her as the inebriated yet beautiful woman he had met when he gone to see her at their residence. Her large almond-shaped eyes were sad even back then and made Jay wonder why she stuck around with the bastardly husband who was clearly a fucking swine. Rage built up inside him as he saw her through the little glass window in the door. He couldn't decide if he should knock and wake her up or return later, but the nurse came by.

'Looking for someone?'

'Yes. Rita Kumar.'

'And you are ...?'

'An old friend.'

'Let me see if she's awake. Who do I say is here to see her?'

'Jay Singh.'

'Wait a minute.' The nurse softly opened the door and tiptoed in. She was back in less than two minutes. 'You can go in now, Mr Singh.'

'Thanks.' He waited for the nurse to exit before he went into the room. *I should have at least brought her some fresh flowers*, was his first thought.

'Hi.' Rita forced a smile.

'Hi, how are you?'

'Fuckin'tastic, as you can see. What brings *you* here, Mr Advocate Jay?'

'I wanted to see you, talk to you.'

'Oh, I thought you were taking me up on the offer I made you last time—'

'Shhh!' Jay put his finger to his lips. 'I know you weren't in your senses when we met last time, Rita. And you shouldn't feel embarrassed by anything you said when we met last. I am a heavy drinker myself and I know that sometimes, in that state, we inadvertently end up saying things we don't mean. Sometimes it is a mere slip of the tongue and sometimes it is out of sheer spite. I know it all ...' He again raised his finger to his lips as he saw her lips quiver. 'I know you're hurting so let me speak, please. As I was saying, I know your behaviour stemmed from the humiliation you've been through at the hands of your philandering husband ...'

Tears started rolling down her face. She still did not close her eyes or look away. She, of all people, knew the truth. Perhaps she figured there wasn't any point in pretending that he wasn't stating facts. Or perhaps it was regret for how she had behaved with him last time around.

'Sorry to be blunt, Rita and do tell me to shut up or ask me to leave as I have no right or reason to interfere in your married life.'

'Who told you I was here?'

'I've got sources. I don't take up a client without knowing all about the client or his idiosyncrasies.'

'You won't tell who told you?'

'I never rat out a rat. It can be fatal for my business. And me.'

'So you're here for what exactly, Jay? You don't expect me to believe you're here to console me for what happened last night, do you?'

'I can't, even for a minute, think you're dumb enough to believe it even if I said that. So, no. And though it's none of my business I wonder why you go through this shit?'

'Could you raise my bed a bit please? It's a bit inconvenient to lie straight and concentrate …'

Jay bent down to press the lever that elevated the head of the cot. It was then he saw her closely and realized she had taken a much more brutal walloping than what he had initially seen through the glass pane of the door. There was also a little blood clot on the white of the right eye that was blackened all around. Images of his own mother flashed before him. He could have killed his own father for that; he could kill Vinay Kumar for this, he knew. But he did not let his mien reflect any of that.

'Is that okay for you?'

'Yeah, thanks. Would you like some tea or coffee?'

He shook his head.

'It's not a bother at all. I don't have to make it. I just need to press the buzzer. I was extremely unpleasant to you last time so let me make it up to you at my loving husband's cost.' She attempted to smile but it was quite obvious she was in pain.

'I don't need anything, but if you want some, please feel free.'

'Gin and tonic?'

'I've got some vodka in my car,' he jabbed.

'Should I come down or would you bring it up here for me?'

He let the joke dangle there. It was good the lady had a sense of humour despite evidently being in physical agony and the discomfort of knowing that this wasn't the first or the last time her husband had awarded her some serious abuse. But he wanted to come to the point before Vinay Kumar or any of his cronies made a surprise visit.

'Could I ask you something?'

'Here comes out the advocate from behind the man,' she chuckled. 'Go on then, ask.'

'You admit you were nasty to me last time, right?'

Nod.

'I know you were drunk, but still, may I ask why you were so foul? Why with me?'

'Because you are his friend.'

'For the record, I am not his friend. I am his advocate.'

'Same thing, isn't it? Friends save your ass when you are in trouble; you're his saviour too.'

'And you don't want me to save your husband?'

She looked away and didn't answer for a couple of minutes. The silence screamed in the room. From the window towards which she turned her face, Jay could see the sun getting ready to withdraw for the day. It would still be a couple of hours though before it totally abandoned this part of the world and slipped into absolute shade. A foursome of pigeons had descended on to the window ledge to provide company to Rita for the night. Thankfully, the car horns blaring at ground level were only a faint noise on this higher floor; they lacked the harshness to disturb sleep.

'Save my husband for whom? He doesn't care if I live or die. Why should I care?'

'Why don't you just leave him then?' Jay was uncomfortable discussing her marriage, but he reckoned he needed to swim the tide to get to the other side for the truth that he came to see her for.

'They are a very influential family.'

'I know that.'

'What do you know about Vinay?'

'You tell me.'

'You know he's done this before?'

'What … put you in A&E?'

'No. That he's been accused of killing another one of his mistresses before Gina?'

Jay knew the bastard had snookered him. The entire search Bhīma had done had been true. Kumar had escaped the last time.

And with Jay's defence he would be acquitted yet again. That hit him. That hit him bad.

'Does Vinay know you're here?' She had a worried expression on her scarred face. 'Please be honest.'

'No. I came here of my own volition. And you're free to shoo me away and not talk to me. Anything you say is off the record.'

'I'll tell you everything if you promise to stay with me for dinner. We can chomp on the sad hospital sandwiches.'

'Okay.' Jay was aware Bhīma would have heard the conversation, and hence calculated that he would take longer than initially assumed.

♚

Jay left Rita's room after nine. She told me him more than he had come looking for. The truth had killed his appetite and the sad sandwiches had hardly bothered him. The only thing he didn't know after what she had told him is how could he walk away from his client? This wasn't the first defence case where he knew his client was guilty. If truth be told, they all fucking were. It was not a defence advocate's business to side with the truth. But deserting Vinay Kumar now would mean he could kiss his legal practice goodbye. All that he had worked for would be gone. Why should he give it up for Rita, whom he had met barely twice in life? For someone who did not want to stand up for herself? He could sense his blood flow a bit faster than usual: the adrenaline was picking up pace. A loose end had tied itself up. He sneered as the elevator carted him to the ground floor, partly for even letting such a silly and scrupulous thought stray into his mind, but predominantly because he knew he would walk all over Talwar on Monday. This case was over.

'Bhīma, did you hear that?'

'Rita owns the Glock.'

Talwar had left a big void in his search – the gun – and Jay would jump into that void and tear the State's case.

'Yes. The locker, as she mentioned, is under the bathtub in the main bathroom; one of the tiles underneath moves. The code is 9-5-1-0. The house is locked and the kids are with their grandfather. Check when Kumar is away, retrieve the Glock and change the security code on the locker so Kumar cannot open it if he tries. I don't want him to do anything stupid should he open the locker and find it missing. I'll speak to him later. Please also ensure that none of the locks are compromised. Kumar should not be able to figure out that there's been an intruder in his house. Then, I want a ballistic expert to run a test to confirm it is the same Glock that was used to shoot Gina.'

'Jee, hukum.'

'Finally, I need someone who should be ready to testify in court that he supplied the Glock to Miss Gina Pinto. We'll pay more than his five years' earnings in one go, and I'll defend him *pro bono* – he's looking at no more than three to six months, I promise.'

'Roger that, hukum.'

'Let's go to Ali's place. I am too excited to sleep now.' It resurfaced that he hadn't spoken to his friend since he had seen Anita. But by the time they got to Ali's place, Jay had finished off the vodka. Ali only had to tell him once that he wasn't going to reveal his conversation with Anita and that it was for Jay's own good that he let her complete the analysis.

What was the fucking rush anyway? Wasn't he meeting Anita tomorrow?

They talked about everything except Kumar's trial. Ali simply did not want to hear anything about it or give his opinion. Jay was feeling ecstatic and his spirits were triumphant, which was enough to divulge that he had found the evidence to defeat Talwar yet again. While Akbar Ali was happy to see his friend celebrate, he was unhappy to know that truth would fail again. It was a fucking mockery of the legal system.

'One day, we might be against each other in court. What would you do then, Akbar?'

'Never. That day you'll have to decide if you'll be my opponent or my friend. But why bother about hypothetical situations, my friend?'

As there was no court appearance for either advocate on the following day, they partied till three in the morning, munching on packed *aloo-paranthas* that Bhīma had brought for them before leaving to get the Glock.

♝

The sun, which Jay had seen sinking from Rita's room, was beginning to wake up and colour the sky when Bhīma drove past the gate of the farmhouse. It was 4:30 a.m.

'We got the Glock and I've arranged for it to be sent for testing, hukum. We'll get the result by Sunday evening.'

That was all Jay heard as he walked up the stairs. He was too drunk to ask anything or even thank Bhīma.

30

I COULDN'T SLEEP DESPITE THE FATIGUE AND THE INTEMPERANCE, and I attributed it all to my anxiety: the sweet smell of victory. Most people only complain that they lose sleep when they are sad; they always overlook the point that exhilaration can kill sleep equally mercilessly too. When I say I couldn't sleep I mean I didn't have a deep one. I knew Cooper visited me, as there was drink on my bedside and he had turned on music – metal, Black Sabbath to be precise – at a fairly high volume and as 'War Pigs' *marched on, it numbed me in and out of sleep. I had desperately wanted to catch up with Cooper for a while now to confront him for making me feel like a complete and utter idiot, but I didn't quite have the strength. There was way too much alcohol in my system. Besides, confronting is never a happy job and even in my stupor I could grasp that I did not want anything to ruin my mood. There would always be time for such little skirmishes later. Why bother?*

I distinctly remember finishing my drink before these thoughts carried me into slumber, but when I woke up, my glass had been refilled. Why was he bent upon getting me drunk? The asshole must be sitting somewhere in the living room below and grinning. I decided not to touch any more alcohol.

I opened my eyes at noon. The little stream of sunlight pierced my brain like a strobe light. It wasn't a hangover; I was still drunk. Headache, nausea and dizziness enveloped me the moment I put my feet on the ground. I couldn't even stand. I pressed the buzzer for Bahadur and ordered fried eggs, sausage, bacon and hash browns along with coffee. All this on the morning I was supposed to be seeing my shrink who was trying to make me quit alcohol, or at least reduce its intake. Sheesh!

Sheeba came in wagging her tail with gusto; if I was in bed till noon, she knew I wasn't going to work. If I wasn't going to work then it was playtime for her. How could the poor thing know that her master could barely walk, let alone play? I offered her the best alternative – I got her in my bed, cuddled her and snoozed for a few more hours.

I finally woke up to find my body rested. My head still wasn't totally clear but clearer than what it was at noon. The greasy food had done some good to my system. Sanity was on its way back.

And then the phone rang.

'Hi Jay, are you coming to see Anita today at six?'

It was the honeyed voice of Manavi. My Manavi.

'Shit, what time is it?'

'It's five-thirty, Jay. Are you okay?'

Something in my voice must have indeed given away that I wasn't.

'Oh, I must have overslept a bit.'

'Just a bit? It's five-thirty in the evening, sweet cheeks. You sure you're okay?'

'Sorry, I was partying last night and only came home in the morning.'

'That must be some party – why wasn't I invited?'

'Boys' night out.'

'So can you make it here by six?'

'Is it possible to reschedule for later by any chance?'

'She can't do any later today. Anita wanted a two-hour session with you and if you're not here by six, I'm not sure it's going to work. Hold on, let me check with her.'

I heard the synthesized sucker music when she put me on hold. Sheeba was back in the room. So was Bahadur with another cup of hot black coffee. I gestured to him to draw the curtains and let the daylight come in; well, whatever was left of the day now. Manavi was back on the line.

'Unfortunately, as I mentioned she cannot do today. She can do ten, tomorrow morning. Does that work for you?'

'Yes, please. And please apologize to her on my behalf.'

'I'll pencil it in. And that's not all; I'll make sure you make it on time, sweet cheeks.'

'How?'

'Because I'm coming over.'

'Now that's what I call full-service.'

'Early dinner on the patio and then we'll make love.'

I flushed red. Cooper was right in a way. I was too conservative for Manavi. She was the one saying my lines.

'Should I send Bhīma to pick you up?'

'Nope. I'll be there by seven. Why don't you have a shower and wash up by then?'

'Good idea.'

'See you soon.'

Click.

I pulled myself out of my bed with great effort and then struggled into the shower and let the water rain on me for more than half-an-hour, then shaved and got dressed for my love.

She arrived on time. Always fresh like a newly plucked flower, she was dressed in a white unevenly hemmed dress that provided fluidity to the flow. She had added a tan leather belt to define her flawless silhouette. The lace-up sandals added four inches to her height.

Gorgeous. I wondered how much longer I would have the pleasure of seeing her.

She kissed me on my lips when we embraced.

It was a sublime evening. The food prepared by Bahadur was amazing as always. I ate like a pig; my stomach, or maybe the liver, needed it. The lovemaking was earth-shatteringly good – with some alcohol still in my system, my libido was heightened and reflected in my performance. I have to admit this was the best lovemaking in my life so far.

We lay in bed, naked.

'You look excited,' Manavi turned towards me with her head elevated by her arm. Her other arm played with the greying fur on my chest.

'I am.'

'May I ask why?'

'I am excited to have you next to me, sweet cheeks.'

'Ha, liar! They say you shouldn't lie immediately after making love. Are you withholding something from me?'

'Not at all. It's just that I've cracked the all-important case that I am currently arguing in court. It should all be over on Monday, I think.'

'Great.' She bent down and gave me a kiss. 'Well done you, congratulations! Don't worry, I won't ask for details.'

'Thanks, sweet cheeks.'

Cooper was bloody wrong. This was bliss. This was true love. How could the age difference be any deterrent between two people who love each other? We still understood each other. After all, Lady Gaga must have listened to Queen's 'Radio Ga Ga' *for inspiration. What did that old fool know?*

'Are you sure you want to see Anita before your big day at court?'

'Why should that be an issue?'

'Don't know, I was just wondering. Why not get over with the trial and then see Anita, just in case ...'

That came as a surprise. First it was Anita being cryptic and now Manavi. What was it?

'Nah. Unless you know something that I don't, and you're holding something back from me—'

'Nothing. I was just teasing you ...'

Something in her tone didn't feel right; she was definitely hiding something.

'Why do you say that? You're making me nervous, Manavi.' I turned towards her and elevated my upper body to face her.

'Oh, forget it. I was just being a sentimental fool. After all, I'm a woman, and it's our prerogative to be sentimental, isn't it?

'I love you, my girl. But what about you getting bored of an old dog like me?'

'Maybe.'

She was a tease.

'Marry me.'

No, I hadn't planned to say this. Before I blurted out those two words, marriage hadn't even occurred to me. But suddenly the fear of losing Manavi had taken over my mind.

'What?'

'I said, marry me.'

'I heard that. Do you really mean it? Are you proposing to me?'

'Yes, without concealing anything.' I gesticulated towards both of us, lying bare.

We moved towards each other and kissed. She moved closer, put her head in the nook of my arm and we dozed off sometime around eleven, which by last night's standard, was an early tuck-in for me.

Manavi hadn't brought any change along. When I woke up, she was wearing one of my shirts over nothing. She looked hot. I was still in bed when she came over and touched my lips with hers. 'I love you, Jay. Promise me whatever happens, you will never stop loving me.'

She left before breakfast.

I had breakfast in my room jotting down all that I needed to do tomorrow – the day before I presented the Glock. It would be an uphill task to introduce a witness I hadn't mentioned in the file I had handed over to Talwar. I'd have to send a request to Justice Nair at least an hour before the trial began, explaining why I was presenting a new witness at this stage of the trial. Okay, we found the Glock and subsequently traced the rogue who supplied it to Gina. The logical question would be: how and where did we find the Glock, which the entire police force had been looking for? I'd have to think of a plausible story. So, what if we prove the gun was Gina's? How did it exonerate Vinay Kumar? Kumar had already categorically refused to accept a manslaughter charge on self-defence. But in light of what I knew now, and with the Glock in my possession it would be worth speaking to him again tomorrow. If he still declined my recommendation then, he wouldn't be totally in the clear. However, it would be difficult for the prosecution to prove his guilt categorically either. If Gina owned an unlicenced Glock – the very Glock that was used to shoot her – then it presented an opportunity to anyone who visited Gina that night after Kumar left. It could definitely not be proven that nobody called on her that night. Worst case, Kumar might not be found innocent, but given the reasonable doubt he couldn't be labelled guilty either. Of course, anything could go wrong, but that was what I'd tell him tomorrow – that was a chance he took if he wasn't willing to plead guilty on account of self-defence.

I made my notes, called Bhīma and asked him to pass them on to a junior advocate in the practice to get it all typed up and be at Justice Nair's chamber at nine on Monday morning to request him to allow a last-minute witness. And send the Glock over to the police station tomorrow night after the private ballistic expert gave a conclusive report. In any event, it was crucial evidence and it belonged to the State.

I washed, got ready in blue jeans and white-T – God I dressed like a younger man these days – and left for Anita's clinic.

'Bhīma, we've got a lot to accomplish between now and tomorrow evening if we want to win this case,' I reiterated to him in the car as if the big man didn't know. My biggest worry was that because of this new evidence and the plea to present a witness last minute, Talwar might ask for an adjournment. Tricky.

31

I WALKED INTO ANITA'S CLINIC TWO MINUTES BEFORE THE appointed hour, paced up to Manavi's desk and blew her a kiss. So bold! She looked every bit a professional and not the siren that was with me the night before.

'Good morning, again.'

'Good morning, Jay. Anita's waiting for you,' she said with a mischievous smile, pointed towards the door.

The aroma of fresh coffee was the first thing that hit me when I got inside Anita's therapy chamber.

'Good morning, Jay,' she said, looking up at me, and smiled as she poured the coffee. 'I'm glad you could make it.'

'I sincerely apologize for the goof-up yesterday, I didn't mean to miss the appointment, but I was totally zonked out when your receptionist called.'

'Apology accepted. Or should I say it was accepted last evening itself.' Anita gave me one of her customary disarming smiles that I was now familiar with. 'Coffee – black, no sugar, as usual?'

'Yes, please. Thanks.' I slumped into the easy sofa I had got used to relax in whenever I was in her office.

'So, how are you feeling today, Jay?' Anita took her therapist chair next to me. I noticed she didn't hold her ubiquitous pen in her hand, only a thin folder.

'Same old, same old. A bit excited, as I believe we've got a

breakthrough in the current case, but otherwise everything else is the same.'

'Still drinking as much?'

'Sometimes, yes. Anita – what is this about? Why do I get a feeling that you have some rather significant news that you want to tell me but you're being ambiguous or withholding it?'

'No, I won't withhold anything, that wouldn't help.'

'Okay, then, give me the bad news … why do I drink? And then tell me the mantra: what can I do to quit?'

'Who said anything about bad news? First off, there's no bad news. Secondly, I have no magic potion that I can sprinkle on you and make you a teetotaller.' She shrugged to make it sound frolicsome when she had said it in all seriousness.

'I didn't mean …' I didn't know what to say next. Anita – and Manavi – had hyped up this meeting to such a crescendo that impatience was getting the better of me. I decided to keep quiet for a while.

'Thanks for asking Bhīma and Akbar Ali to have a candid chat with me. It was really very helpful.'

'Well, it was up to them. I only requested them as I knew I would be the one who'll benefit, not them.'

'You will have to excuse me here, because I did some further digging into your past without your explicit permission. All in good faith, though.'

'Carry on, Anita.'

I couldn't care less if she dug around for dirt on me. I – and I mean Bhīma and his men – did that all the time without any permission obviously, and therefore I should be the last person to object.

'Alright, then. Let's go back to you first year at college. Do you remember any one particular incident that you found really difficult to recover from or even come to terms with?'

Where was she headed? How far back was she looking to go?

'Nope. The only such incident that I can recall is the dreadful night we've already spoken about, but that happened right after my third year. True, it is something I have lived through and never recovered from.'

She nodded. 'I know about that, and we'll come to that in a minute too.'

'Could I have some water, please?'

What was it with me? Was I scared of where she was taking me? Did I know which memory was she asking me to dredge up? Was I stalling by asking for water?

'Yes, of course.'

She had a small refrigerator under her desk that I didn't know of. She pulled out a bottle of chilled Bisleri from it. 'Do you need a glass?'

'No. This should be fine. Thanks.'

I quaffed down the bottle in two large swigs. We settled into the routine again.

'Sorry, you were saying ...?' I broke the silence.

'I was referring to an incident that happened in your first year at college. Maybe not any longer, but was there something that you regretted for a long time?'

Not sure how many people have even heard of a View-Master, but at this moment it was like I was staring into one – frame by frame, and each frame was vibrant. Another truly sordid incident that had occurred during my first year at college seemed like it was recurring now: Five of us freshmen in the first term sat drinking in Bihari's place – we called him Bihari as he came from the eastern state of Bihar – but the guy's name escaped me at the moment and something told me it wasn't of import here. We had split sometime after midnight and walked to our respective rooms in separate wings of the hostel. And though all five of us were close friends, it was one of them who

I was thick with, and his room was across the swimming pool. The janitor had found his body floating in the pool the next morning. I could never get over it. For the next few months, all I thought was if only I had walked with him that night, the outcome would have been different. Whether he slipped that night or just went in for a dip, in the intoxicated state that he was in, we will never know.

I could feel that Anita could see pain in my eyes, but I stubbornly stopped it from flowing out by strongly ebbing away any moisture.

'But what does that prehistoric incident have to do with anything?' I blurted out.

'Maybe nothing, but I need to make sure of everything. Hope you don't mind?'

'Not at all, please carry on.'

If nothing else, she had aroused my curiosity to such a heightened level that I was happy I wasn't a cat. For my own sanity I wanted to hear her logical deduction.

'So do you remember a friend of yours drowning?'

'Yes, I do. It isn't a memory I prize, which you can well appreciate.'

Anita waited for a second since my last sentence was articulated in a softer than usual tone, like I was still reminiscing.

'Do you remember ever having any discussion about the dysfunctional marriage of your parents with this friend of yours?'

'Oh yes. As a matter of fact, if I came from a "dysfunctional" family – as you just mentioned – he came from a totally defunct one. Fortunately, or unfortunately, his parents had had a bitter separation. His dad was an alcoholic too and he did remark, more than once when he was drunk, that he could have killed the sorry bastard if the separation hadn't materialized when it happened.'

I was suddenly on a roll. Once the old memories flooded in; it was as if I was in some kind of a trance, narrating everything to Anita. Don't ask me why. Maybe I reckoned that all had been bottled up in me for years needed a release.

'And you both were quite close, right?'

'Very thick.'

'So did you believe him?'

'Believe him? In what way?'

'Did you even for a second believe him that he could have actually killed his father if his parents' marriage hadn't broken up when it did?'

'Oh absolutely, no doubt about that. But why do you ask that?'

'We'll come back to that in a second, Jay.'

Anita got up, pulled out two bottles of water and gave one to me. After taking a tiny sip, she sat down again.

'What do you know about schizophrenia, Jay?' Her tone changed to a more business-like-doctor-like now.

'Split personality? You mean a Jekyll and Hyde type of thing? I think it's more prevalent in stories and cinema than witnessed in real life, but then it could just be that I haven't met anyone who's been diagnosed with it.'

'You're correct, but only to a certain extent. It happens in real life more than normal people know about it. Schizophrenia can be best described as a sort of breakdown of thought processes – it can thwart one's emotional responses to people or situations or things, or all of the above. The first symptoms, usually, occur in early adulthood and, if undetected and untreated, they can prevail for a lifetime. It may or may not be accompanied by other visible indicators like social dysfunction, which, in your particular situation, is clearly not the case. You are socially adept and professionally successful—'

'Wow-owow-owow,' I abruptly came alive. 'You're not telling me I'm schizophrenic or something are you? You didn't call me for this long session and take me all the way back to my first year in college to convey this to me?'

'Hang on a minute, Jay. Be patient. You've paid me to analyse you, so let me do my job. You can choose to ignore everything I say,

seek a second opinion or forget all about it when you walk out of the door.'

'Okay, ma'am, go on,' I said, though I wanted to laugh. If I was, actually, schizophrenic then it meant someone else was drinking, wasn't it? Good for me!

'Schizophrenia is a continuum, but the two ends of the spectrum could be extreme. It's a sequelae – an abnormality nevertheless ...'

She paused for some reaction from me there was none. I couldn't focus on what she was saying, nothing registered anymore but I nodded like an idiot to give her a feeling that I was making some sense of deduction. All I wanted was for her to carry on and conclude this little pub-quiz. Perhaps she expected me compute the information she had so far expounded into some kind of a logical theory and relate it to myself. If that was the case, it certainly wasn't working.

'Am I making any sense, Jay?'

I looked at her blankly.

'Do you remember the name of the friend who drowned in the swimming pool that night – the one we spoke about just a short while back?'

I drew a blank. I seriously drew a blank. Despite the visuals of that evening still being in high definition, the name of my drowned friend, like my Bihari friend, eluded me. In fact, put under the spotlight by Anita, I couldn't remember anyone's name at this given moment. No one's. Honestly, if she had asked me I'd have had trouble reciting my own full name.

'No,' I muttered sheepishly as if lapse of memory was a serious crime.

'Let me jog your memory, Jay.'

She finally opened the skinny folder she had on her side, took out a sheet of Xeroxed paper and handed it to me. 'Sameer Kapoor, his name was Sameer Kapoor. Does that ring any bells?'

The clanging started as if an entire tribe of Rastafarians had started performing some percussion carnival inside my earlobes.

'You don't mean ...'

'Good to know you are on the same track as me whether you believe it or not, Jay.'

I kept quiet. I wanted to see where this was leading.

'Could you describe your friend Cooper to me?' Anita brought me back into the room.

'Eh?'

What the heck did she mean by that?

'I mean what does he look like? Features? Height, weight, complexion, hair? Anything that you can tell me?'

'Why'd you want to know that?'

'Just humour me for a minute.'

I dived into the recesses of my brain but failed to come up with anything; I couldn't conjure up even a single vivid glimpse of Cooper that I could describe to her. And then it occurred: Cooper always came unbidden and always in the middle of night or in the small hours. Especially, on the nights I was heavily drunk. I had never seen his face. And now when I was asked, naturally I couldn't summon up his appearance.

Anita was sharp. She saw me struggling.

'Do you remember what you called your friend, Sameer Kapoor in college?'

'Sam Kapoor.' Flash! The name came to me now.

'It isn't a million miles away from Sam Cooper, is it?' Anita did not hold back this time.

She waited for what she had just said to sink in, for me to digest before carrying on.

'Are you saying ...?'

'Yes. Sam Kapoor is Sam Cooper. He exists only in your mind, Jay. He does not exist in this world.'

That was a blow. I wasn't sure if she was hallucinating or I was, but I patiently listened as she carried on.

'There are known cases in psychopathology that are very similar to yours. Some people are directed by a voice that doesn't exist – they imagine someone talks to them, gives them orders or suggestions; others suffer from pareidolia – they actually see people and things that aren't there. There was a Nobel Laureate called John Nash—'

'Are there any statistics?'

My mind was just not accepting this jargon and hence, I thought if I asked general questions on the topic, it might further alienate me from such claptrap.

'Look, Jay. Here's the thing: statistics cannot give a diagnosis. What it can do is provide the trends, maybe predict a probability, but each case is different. We are talking about humans here, not machines.'

'Why me?'

'It's not some singing competition won or lost on the performance. It's a disease looking for the weakest cell to strike at. No one ever told you that life was meant to be fair; it was your assumption, and you know what they say about assumptions, don't you? So, I could turn your question around and ask you why shouldn't it be you? Or I could answer it for you: maybe because you were strong enough to handle this.'

'Hold on a minute,' I almost cried out. 'I just remembered that I'm not the only one who's seen or met Cooper. Cooper has to exist, he's a partner in my law firm, Bhīma's met him and though I hate to break someone's confidence, for a past few months I've been dating your assistant, Manavi, and he – Cooper – once came in her presence too. What do you have to say about that?'

'I was expecting you to come up with this earlier. And don't worry about Manavi – I know you two are dating. However, trust me, I've talked to Bhīma about this. He's never met or seen Cooper. What he has seen, though, is you talking to yourself in the middle of the night sometimes.'

'You're kidding me, right?'

'You think I run this outfit and charge people to kid them? Absolutely not, Jay. Why would I do that? It's the truth, unfortunately. Even Manavi confirmed you were talking to someone in the living room, but when she rushed down to check, there was no one.'

'That's because he had left by then.'

'Quite the opposite, Jay. The reason she didn't find him that night was because he wasn't there in the first place.'

I shrugged in frustration. How was this fucking possible?

'Alcohol is a huge stimulant, as it reduces the brain's efficiency. You must have noticed that Cooper only visited you when you were drunk, really drunk and practically out of your senses? If you were to plot his visits and study the pattern, you'd find he only visited you in those times.'

I had already summarized that in my mind; that was irrefutable. The truth was now dawning on me. I went quiet for a moment looking for any other argument or evidence of Cooper.

'So why does he visit me? I didn't hurt him. Does he mean any harm?'

'Cooper doesn't mean harm, no. He doesn't interfere or advise either. You do. You imagine he is the one telling you, talking to you. Hallucinations can be audible or visual. In your case it's both: you see him, you talk to him and sometimes, you only sense his presence after he's gone because something's changed when you have no memory of doing it yourself. You just don't have any memory of the things you've done when you wake up, like someone else has made another drink for you or changed the music.'

'I cannot, even for a minute, believe this. However, if I extrapolate your deduction ... you think ...'

I couldn't think. My head spun even faster now. I tried reaching for the staccato memories of the night that my dad died, the ones that had haunted me every day since. But somehow, some moments were evading me. Or were they? Were they missing or was there some part that my subconscious preventing me from getting into?

Time stood still for a while as if the entire universe was waiting for my answer.

And then the memory of someone else being in the house that wretched night nagged me again like a little street urchin who wouldn't leave till you handed over some change to him. In this case there was no change to be given or any shoe to be polished. The burnt-out memory simply wouldn't go.

'Yes. Maybe he did something for you. Maybe he wanted to help you out of the misery you were in, experiencing severe altercation between your parents. Remember, by your own admission, you were so drunk and stoned that night you have no memory of anything. All you remember is that your father was dead when you woke up and your mother was holding the knife. She, obviously, knew who the killer was; that's precisely why she wanted to save him.'

'You don't really think I stabbed my own dad, do you?'

She didn't say anything. Instead, she smartly waited for me to rationalize what must have happened. Suddenly, it all made sense, like pieces falling into a jigsaw. It made sense why my mother must have wiped off all the fingerprints off that knife. She wasn't shielding anyone else. She was protecting me. Me? And, even in the end, she had told me not to go looking for the killer. Why? Because she knew the truth would wreck me.

'Did she know Cooper?' I asked.

'No, she was completely oblivious of Cooper, Jay. As I told you, no one knows Cooper; no one ever knew Cooper.'

I might have been known as the greatest, most-revered, most expensive defence advocate in the country. But the levee broke. The tears came unannounced, uninterrupted and shamelessly. Incoherent ideas and a welter of memories flew past me, even scenes from the weary past were scattered around in fragments now and I had no intention of picking any of them up. Everything moved past me as if someone was fast-forwarding a reel faster than I could consume. Hysteria was just a block away. Instances of my interaction with Cooper took over.

How he was always a step ahead. How he always knew what was happening in my life. He knew my mother had died even without me telling him. He hinted that if I looked harder, I might find her innocence buried somewhere. He knew the music I liked and the food I ate and the places I visited. He knew when I went on my first date with Manavi. And now, a shrink was telling me there was no Cooper? What about his telephone numbers that he erased from my iPhone? God! That struck hard: I never had Cooper's numbers or address in any of my address books. It was my imagination all this while. His unexpected outburst at seeing Manavi, too, became obvious. If she were to be with me all the time, he'd be caught out. So it was my own alter ego telling me that?

My thoughts strayed to my mother: an epitome of sacrifice. She suffered my dad for years because she wanted to be near me. Me, who wasn't even her biological child. I mistrusted her when she visited Swamiji when all the old woman ever wanted was her own child. And then, she stood by me in the direst of times. She didn't have to take the blame. She didn't need to confess and to be convicted. She didn't have to live the rest of her life incarcerated in a mental asylum. She did all that for me? An ungrateful stepson?

I was in a self-induced reverie. I had waited twenty-seven years to uncover my father's killer only to find … No, I couldn't complete the sentence, not even in my own mind. How could I?

I have no idea how long I sat there, running all the permutations and combinations to come up with something that could emphatically convince me that all this wasn't happening and this was one shitty dream. That this was a non sequitur based on some weird and perverted inference that was all fucked up.

'Jay?'

I heard Anita's voice, softly calling me.

'Jay, are you okay?'

I nodded. I knew if I spoke the words would come out wet. Or I might break down once again. Through the thin film of cascading tears, I saw her walk to her desk and pull out another bottle of water and bring it to me.

'What next?' I asked after downing it all. 'Without Cooper, I'm a broken man.'

'I won't let the truth break you. I will help you overcome Cooper.'

'Will he go away?'

'Cooper will never go away. You will have to overcome the delusion. Have you heard of something called psychokinesis, Jay?

I shook my head in ignorance. The tears had dried up, but I knew they could return any minute.

'Psychokinesis refers to the power of the mind. People are known to move things merely by thinking about it. All you need to do is to use it to overcome your illusions.'

'It's easier said than—'

'I know, Jay, I know. Trust me you aren't the first case of this kind that I have consulted.'

She paused for some time, letting me chew on all that she had explained.

'Do you know which is the fastest animal in the universe?'

What was this now – another pub-quiz?

I kept quiet waiting for her to answer and give me the example or analogy or whatever she wanted to. I couldn't care less.

'Cheetah. It can reach up to a speed of over 110 kilometres per hour. What chance do you think a deer has to escape the predator? But God works in mysterious ways. The cheetah can only achieve that speed in short bursts of, maybe, a little more than half a kilometre and the deer only has to run faster than the cheetah for that long.

It sure is difficult, but it isn't impossible. It was a wrong choice of words on my part to tell you that Cooper will not go away. Next time you see him, just ignore him. You have to consciously realize he isn't there, even if you see him. In time you will leave him behind and his presence will cease to matter.'

'If I could go back in time, I'd say "no" the first time I was offered alcohol. Since after that I am not aware at what point I could have walked away. I guess after the first few times, all of this was inevitable.'

'You can't live the rest of your life in guilt, Jay.'

'Do you think I murdered my father?

'No. What makes you say that?'

'But you just said …'

'I didn't say anything about your father. I've only deduced that Cooper is your alter ego and even that is one of the several possibilities in a hypothesis – an assumption within an assumption. There is no evidence, no witness. I could be completely wrong. However, if you were to ask my opinion as a friend …'

'Go on, Anita.'

I got up and walked up to her desk, opened her little refrigerator and pulled out two bottles of water. I passed one to her and sipped on the other one. I wanted to show her that I was getting back into my element.

'I think your mother already paid the price for your father's death. I don't think she'd be happy,' Anita looked up like she was talking to the heavens, 'if you still went around digging. What would be the point? Who would you do this for?'

Maybe Anita made that theory up, I don't know, but I value her effort. I appreciate that no therapist could confirm what had happened that night. In fact, no one could confirm except the one person who had been present in that house that night. Me.

But I didn't argue.

I was supposed to be out by noon, but when I looked at the clock it was 4 p.m.

'I've ruined your entire day.'

'Don't be funny. I feel happy to have shown you the—'

'Light?' I humoured. 'Thanks, Anita, I owe you one.'

'You owe me nothing. And this isn't your last call here. I want to see you later in the week to give you a detailed plan on how to cope with your delusion. From then on, we'll meet once a month.'

I gave Anita a hug before leaving.

By the time I exited Anita's office, Manavi had left for the day. I knew she'd call later. Back in the car it occurred to me that I was crying again. I pulled out a tissue and wiped my face. My eyes met Bhīma's in the rear-view mirror; he had surely seen me crying but he looked away. Thank you, Bhīma, I wanted to say – for understanding, for talking to Anita, for so many things – but I knew my voice would break if I spoke.

Manavi called, but I explained that I was tied up with my work – the trial – and so it would be an unnecessary commute for her tonight and tomorrow. I'm pretty sure she understood I wasn't 'me' today. She got it. See, Cooper was wrong, she was smart – and then it struck me: there was no Cooper. Why, then, did I tell myself the other night that Manavi wasn't good for me when I knew I loved her and had even proposed to her? If you find the last sentence confusing, just imagine how blurry the lines are between Cooper and me? How could there be no Cooper? And now that I could discern, how could there be no 'me' other than just me?

Later, I sat wondering what was true. Did I love Manavi or did I not love her? I didn't even know that anymore. It was like I was watching myself from a distance, observing myself. That this malaise would be my shadow for the rest of my life depressed me.

I bet the gods were fucking laughing.

I didn't have dinner. I couldn't. I asked Bahadur and Bhīma to dine and pack it up. I beheld the amber liquid in the half-filled Jack Daniel's bottle for a few seconds, and then took the bottle of what I'd considered ambrosia for more than half my life to the sink and drained it. The disease had to end. The best way to avoid temptation was to kill it. My jaded mind still warred firmly to not accept the reality. In some ways, I was thankful that the hours that had vanished from my memory were crawling back now. The black hole was filling up drop by drop. I can't say I remembered everything, but I knew enough to put the pieces together. Jay Singh – the best defence advocate in the country – was also his own father's killer. As was predictable, sleep gave me a wide birth. I slipped into it briefly (was it sleep or pure exhaustion?) but drifted out of it most of the night. Sheeba stayed in my room and, watching me toss and turn in bed a few thousand times, she jumped into it to join me.

32

SUNDAY WAS A BIZARRE DAY FOR ME AS I WAS TRYING TO COME TO terms with myself. I guess melancholy was expected after being hit by the harsh reality. Emotions fluctuated like the voltage in a small town. I was angry one moment and scared the next. Anxiety, bitterness, loss and annoyance were in a confluence and battling simultaneously.

And then that miserable feeling of inevitable professional defeat took over everything else. Losing Kumar's case was a defeat for the advocate, winning and setting him free to kill someone else or even abuse his wife was a defeat for the human in me. Oh, I so badly needed Cooper for advice. One thing led to another, and the memories of Cooper's numerous visits over the years trickled in. How had I missed all the signs for years? Decades, actually. Why was I never suspicious? Why hadn't I made the connection? Leaving Cooper behind would be like leaving a piece of me behind. Whether he was the cause or the consequence of my problems didn't matter; we had to part. It had to be done; the conflict of the soul had to be laid to rest.

She didn't call, but I got a text from Manavi asking if I was fine and if I wanted her to come over. It was an indication that she knew – if not fully, at least in some part – what Anita had analysed; she had provided some feedback too, hadn't she? Last night, she had only come over to ensure I made it to the session. No, I didn't think there was any contrivance there; she wanted to do what was best for me. I knew she loved me and I loved her too. Tonight, however, I made a polite excuse that I was preparing for the trial. She texted me back wishing me luck.

For the first time in years, I was internalizing my feelings without alcohol. I thought of my mother and father. Of happier times and how the political climate of the country had changed everything for us. I remembered the few holidays together as a family. The trip to Kathmandu, to Mussoorie. And the one time we went to Mumbai, I clearly remember walking by the sea between Ma and Dad, holding their hands on each side before the sudden downpour started, and my Dad picked me up and we ran for shelter in some arcade. I had been too young then to remember what part of Mumbai it was, but that didn't matter. Unfortunately, when the money dried up it was as if the happiness dried up too. What if ... I repressed the train of what-ifs straightaway. Such ruminating thoughts were of no value other than for self-pity. Nothing ever changed, and nothing could change now.

I thought of leaving my legal practice, getting married to Manavi and moving someplace else. Goa? Abroad? But it sounded too much like a Bollywood flick.

Eventually, I brought myself to dwell upon my strategy for the impending trial tomorrow, only to quickly grasp that there was no way out of this case. I couldn't just walk away and not turn up at the courthouse tomorrow. Justice Nair would fry my ass; make that deep-fry. And if I showed up, how could I lose a trial as big as this that had the media's spotlight from the word go? Losing it could be career dampening at best, career suicide at worst. Defence cases would start moving elsewhere. No one would want a defence advocate who'd deliberately lost a trial in the limelight – it would be tantamount to going off to sleep when on stage. No one could be the best forever, not on reputation alone. One defeat and the world would start forgetting the successes. If they overlooked, the media would rub it in. The all-conquering advocate Jay Singh losing a trial of this magnitude meant losing the stripes it had taken me a lifetime to earn. Besides, even if I decided to lose how could I? It was a moot point to debate and to fret, so I jilted the whole argument. It was a waste of time. What was the point of considering a move I couldn't make? There were far bigger problems to think about than Vinay Kumar. My mind was still not at rest. I pondered this and I pondered that: all hopeless, pointless things. Then I quelled the futile thoughts, switched off the lights and went to sleep.

33

SLEEPING LATE HAS A LOGICAL COROLLARY: WAKING UP LATE. IN Jay's case it wasn't something he had consciously strived for; his mental disposition had disallowed his mind to rest. He was still in bed at noon, struggling to get his thoughts together. A lot had transpired yesterday; more than most humans could handle. The reality had begun to penetrate his brain. There might have been a few loose ends, but he knew it would all iron out at its own pace. He wasn't going to fret about the little things that weren't even palpable at present. His mind segued to figure how Anita had come up with this absurd hypothesis to begin with? What gave? But then, most hypotheses started as being absurd; isn't that the reason why someone dug further to ascertain or invalidate them? It didn't matter anymore; he didn't give a flying fuck. He knew the truth, and that was all that mattered. It was a satirical serendipity of kismet: he had spent twenty-seven years yearning to find the killer whom he had prevented himself from knowing.

Absorbed in his own despair, Jay couldn't care less about Vinay Kumar or the case. He didn't even bother to make calls or prepare for it anymore; he couldn't inconvenience himself for anything. His mind was too weary. For years, Jay Singh's sole focus was his career. Nothing ever came between him and his cases. The focus was split or shifting, and he didn't know how to pull it together, nor did he have the desire to. Sunday passed with him lying in bed; he didn't even get up to wash, didn't leave the room at all. Bahadur brought in the meals and Bhīma checked on him a few times. He watched a bit of television. The news on Vinay Kumar's case told the viewers that the Glock – the murder weapon – had been found. So, the police had released the information to the media. However, they hadn't revealed where it was found and who had turned it in. Jay could see the tweets from viewers scrolling on the bottom of the television screen conveying what was on their minds. All useless guesswork, he knew, even when he was out of sorts. No one knew the truth, and no one might ever know.

Bhīma called him in the evening to say that the private ballistic expert had confirmed the Glock found in Vinay Kumar's home matched the marks on the bullet mentioned in the police report. There was no reason to second-guess anymore.

'Ask your boys to stop all searches Bhīma, and you can disconnect the wiretaps too.'

The truth was out; there seemed little point in listening to Kumar anymore.

'Jee, hukum.'

Before Bhīma left, Jay also asked him to stop his adjutant from approaching Justice Nair on Monday morning to file a plea for a new witness as they had discussed earlier.

Bhīma, of course, must have wondered why, but didn't question him.

Rita Kumar had been honest when she had confided in Jay that on the night of the murder, Vinay Kumar had beaten her up and taken away her handgun. The more he thought about it, the more it hurt Jay's head. The conniving bastard had snookered him, after all. Under the circumstances, there weren't many choices he had, being the defence advocate for the devil. It was all part of Kumar's plan from the beginning. Kumar's real motive for hiring

Jay Singh wasn't that he was the best defence advocate in town; it was because he was also known as the one with few morals. It was precisely for if and when the advocate figured out the truth, he shouldn't become hostile. Kumar had been sharp; he knew the rules and he knew how to twist them.

By the time he left his house for the court on Monday morning, Jay Singh had decided what he wanted to do. And he had resolved how he would do it. He knew that there was the letter of the law, but there was also its spirit, which he had ignored for far too many years now.

♝

In all respects, Talwar was a match. If Jay had any misgivings, it was his culpability. Talwar had anticipated how Jay Singh would play his innings in the court. Vinay Kumar's driver would be first. He had, obviously, heard that the Glock had been found and deposited with the Saket police station. His own sources had also figured out that Jay Singh himself had sent the weapon to the police, though he had no evidence and hence couldn't broach the subject in the court, he knew that well. Talwar had expected a call from Nair or, at least, from Jay's office to update him of the developments, a.k.a the new witness – he was prepared to fight that firmly and ask for an adjournment till his team mined the details. Gaining time, he knew, was crucial for Vinay Kumar, given the upcoming elections – but he heard nothing from either of them.

As usual, Talwar arrived at the courthouse first. He hadn't come early for the trial, though; his chambers were in the same building.

♝

The mighty Jay Singh arrived thirty minutes before the trial was to begin. The court and its surroundings looked no different today. It was crowded with people who had come to witness the media-labelled trial of the year or decade. Some others waited for their own trial or that of their close ones. Some wished their kin got pardoned; others prayed that the felons pleaded guilty for their agony to be over. No one looked happy. Anyone who has ever run around to get anything done at any courthouse knows that despair, fear and anxiety are permanent residents there. No one could look happy, except the advocates. But then, they aren't the ones who have to speak the truth or face the consequences.

'Who's your first witness, Mr Singh?'

'Do you know that the murder weapon has been found, Mr Singh?'

Jay disregarded the questions from the media and walked up the stairs alone. Julie wasn't at his side today. For a moment, as Jay entered the courtroom, he thought he saw Cooper sitting at his desk, with his head buried in a file. He stopped and consciously turned towards Talwar.

'Good morning, Mr Talwar.'

'Good morning, Mr Singh. Is everything okay?'

'Oh yes, just thought I should say hello.'

Jay figured his countenance might be giving away his mental temperament. When he rotated one-eighty again, Cooper had left and Vinay Kumar sat in his place. Jay quickly kept his bag at his desk and rushed to the men's. There were still twenty minutes for Justice Nair to arrive and he decided a face wash couldn't hurt anyway.

The courtroom was once again brought to order at the arrival of Justice Nair.

'The prosecution rested when we recessed last, so unless

Mr Talwar has to say anything new, we can begin the proceedings with the defence.' Nair looked at Jay.

'No more witnesses at this moment, Janaab, but as you might know the police has recovered the murder weapon. In light of this discovery, my team would like to do some searches, so I'd like to request the court to retrieve my earlier statement.'

'Do you want time now, or would you want to reserve it for after the defence, Mr Talwar?'

'Ideally, we should adjourn this trial till I complete my search, Janaab, unless my defence colleague has any lawful objections.'

Justice Nair anxiously looked at Jay.

On any other day Jay would have pounced and spat out an objection. But he didn't. He was preoccupied. His eyes couldn't focus; his mind was miles away collecting his thoughts. Something was wrong. For a moment even he thought about letting the case adjourn – it would better than losing it.

'Mr Singh?' Nair called out break Jay's reverie.

'Your Honour,' Jay stood up as if on cue. 'The prosecution's task is relatively easier as they have the support of the entire State's machinery that has documented the charges in the first place, so I would request that we progress the case, at least for today, and see if the new evidence is of any consequence at all.'

'Objection, Janaab. How can the murder weapon be insignificant in a murder trial?' Talwar stood up. He was clearly annoyed. If not for Nair in the room, he would have surely showered some expletives on Jay.

'Overruled, Mr Talwar. Let's progress. Mr Singh, please note that if I find any evidence that's detrimental to the State's case on account of this new discovery, I'll be forced to adjourn the trial or maybe even ask for a retrial. Is that okay with you?'

'Your Honour, I promise you will not need to do that today.'

'Objection, Janaab—'

'I already overruled, Mr Talwar. I am the judge here and I have decided to progress the case for now. Please sit down. Mr Singh, let's proceed. You may call your first witness.'

'Thank you, Your Honour. The defence calls the defendant, Mr Vinay Kumar, as its first witness.'

There was a soft murmur in the courtroom. Even if you did not hear them talking, all lips were moving in amazement. Defence advocates weren't known to call their own client – the defendant – as a witness; it was a high-risk strategy because the prosecution would not spare a sitting duck. Jay had gone against the odds by calling Vinay Kumar to the box. Maybe he was sure Talwar wasn't prepared for it and might be thrown off track. Talwar certainly looked shocked. He whispered something to his assistants. Scribes scribbled the unconventional move. Whatever the outcome of this strategy, it would definitively be picked up by the media. This was masala!

Vinay Kumar sat stunned, like someone had slapped him without a warning. Jay had not given any inkling about this radical move, not prepared him for the questioning or for defending himself against Talwar. However, he got up, gave Jay a blazing glare and walked to the witness box to take the oath.

'Mr Vinay Kumar, what do you do?'

Kumar knew the routine. He didn't need any preparation to sing his own praises, he did that dazzlingly, then moved on to impress how his dad had served the electorate and how he intended to do so if he won the forthcoming elections. A right messiah of public. 'I know this is a conspiracy—'

'We'll come to that, Mr Kumar. I promise to give you the chance to explain yourself—' Jay cut him off, only to be interjected by Talwar.

'Objection, Janaab.'

'What is it this time, Mr Talwar?' Nair asked, shaking his head; he didn't look happy or sound pleased.

'Janaab, the defence advocate should ask questions to the defendant that are pertinent to this case and not use court's time to allow Mr Kumar to run an election campaign here.'

'Sustained. Mr Singh, please ensure all your questions to the defendant are germane to the case.'

'Absolutely, Your Honour.'

Talwar appeared contented. First, with Nair permitting Jay to proceed despite his plea of adjournment and then being stumped by Jay's curveball – bringing Kumar into the witness box – Jay knew Talwar would run an 'objection-campaign' throughout the defence testimony. What other options did he have? He would pounce at every remote chance before Jay Singh took the case away from him. If there was a panic button at his desk, Talwar's finger would be on it.

'Mr Kumar, could you tell the court where you were on the said night?'

'I was with Gina.'

'By Gina, you mean Miss Gina Pinto, the deceased, right?'

'Yes.'

'By your own admission you had dinner with Miss Pinto that night, like all other nights, then had an amorous evening before you left her apartment. Am I right?'

'Yes.'

'Unfortunately, the time you were at her apartment overlaps with the time window that the autopsy report mentioned as the time of Miss Pinto's death. The State's entire case, therefore, rests on inferences drawn due to circumstances; circumstances that you and Miss Gina Pinto had a relationship that some society members might disapprove of, that she was expecting your child, the best gift of love—'

'Objection—' Talwar barked.

'Sustained. Where is this headed, Mr Singh? I reminded you that do not let this be an opportunity to run recommendations for your client.'

'Apologies, Your Honour.'

As Jay turned towards Nair to apologize, the larger-than-life picture of Mahatma Gandhi that hung behind the Judge came in his line of vision. It was at that moment Jay Singh knew that his allegiance to the Devil had to end. His guilty conscience was looking for redemption. His mother wanted an answer. All women who had faced a fate similar to his mother's needed an answer; Rita Kumar demanded an answer; Gina Pinto demanded an answer. Jay shook his head pejoratively. The marks he'd seen on Rita's face at the hospital were a chilling reminder of what he had seen on his own mother's face years ago. Correction: on his *stepmother's* face who had given her life away for him, her stepson, and for what: to defend brutes and fiends?

'Are you okay, Mr Singh?'

He heard Nair's voice in the background.

'Yes, Your Honour.'

'Then please continue.'

'Mr Kumar, could you please tell the court what firearms you and your family own?'

'I own a Colt Defender, and I have the licence to carry it.'

'Is that all you have?'

'Yes, to the best of my knowledge.'

'To the best of your knowledge?' Jay Singh repeated slowly as if he was musing on the sentence. 'That's an interesting statement. So, you reckon, there could be a possibility – however remote – that someone else in your family owns a firearm and you don't know about it?'

'Yes.'

'And who could that be, Mr Kumar?'

'I don't know what I don't know.' There was a strain of hostility building in Kumar's voice. His body language was changing too.

'Let me refresh who all live in your house then, Mr Kumar. It's you, your wife Mrs Rita Kumar and your two children. I wouldn't expect your underage kids to play with guns. So that leaves us with your wife and you. You, of course, don't own any other firearm, as you've just told the court, so that leaves only your wife. Now, let me simplify the question. Does your wife own any firearm – handgun, pistol, any kind of weapon?'

'No. She does not have the licence to own any kind of firearms.'

'See, that is where it gets tricky, Mr Kumar. I didn't ask you if she had a licence or not. I asked you does she own a gun?'

'It's possible ...'

'Possible could mean it's likely and it does not rule out an impossibility, does it?'

'I guess it doesn't.'

Everyone in the courtroom looked spellbound now. Jay Singh was playing tough on his own client, which could mean only one thing: that he would, in a minute, spring a real googly on the prosecution. The only thing that the media or the audience could predict about Jay Singh was that he was unpredictable. And that made him a fierce opponent. You couldn't fight what you didn't know, he was very much like the *Doosra* in cricket: unreadable. You fail only because you can't read which way the bloody thing would turn. They were waiting; some even had their mouths open. It was about time he did a one-eighty.

'Are you sure, Mr Kumar?'

'Yes, absolutely.' Kumar tried to utter in all confidence, but his face was flushed red. The composure seemed to be leaking out of him like water out of a broken bucket.

'Mr Kumar, are you aware that the Glock in question – the one that fired the fatal shot into Miss Gina Pinto's body, the one that has been recovered by police this weekend – belongs to your wife, albeit without a licence?'

'Objection, Janaab,' Talwar charged. 'This is something the State has no knowledge of …'

'That's all, Your Honour. The defence rests now.' Jay had a hard time trusting his own voice, but he said it in as calm a voice as he could muster.

Talwar looked at Jay in disbelief.

Justice Nair appeared shocked.

Kumar let out a long breath indicating he was fucked. Pure and simple.

It was like Jay had removed the pin and handed the grenade to Talwar. A shark doesn't need more than a speck of blood to be drawn to its victim. He knew Talwar would, in a moment or two, recover from the premature resting of the defence and realize Jay had handed over the accused to him on a platter. The rest would be easy, as Jay had reached an agreement with Rita that if required, she would come to the court for testimony. Jay was confident that Talwar would surely finish the case and bring it to its honest and swift conclusion. It was payback time for Vinay Kumar. And if Rita Kumar had lied to him, Talwar was still the best hound to smell it out. Truth would, in any event, triumph.

More than anything, it was the only true valediction Jay could offer to his mother in heaven.

'The court shall recess until tomorrow after lunch.' Even Nair wasn't stupid. He grasped what was unfolding too. 'Mr Talwar, I give you twenty-four hours to do all your searches on the murder weapon and collect any and all evidence you need to conclude the case now that the defence has no more witnesses. I look forward to the closing statements from both advocates tomorrow evening.

Furthermore, I cancel Mr Vinay Kumar's bail and order that he to be taken into custody with immediate effect—'

'But, Your Honour—' Kumar pleadingly looked at Justice Nair and then at Jay Singh. The membranes in his throat sounded dry like a squeaky door suddenly run out of grease. He was royally fucked, if there was any such thing.

'Mr Kumar, please do not speak when I am talking. I cannot put the entire trial in jeopardy. You are a now clear flight risk from my perspective. You remain under oath and shall be brought in for cross-examination by the State in this court at 1 p.m. tomorrow. Is that clear?'

'Yes, Janaab.' Talwar couldn't have sounded any happier. He shared his entire joy with the courtroom.

'Any objections from you, Mr Singh?'

'None whatsoever, Your Honour.'

Kumar looked helpless as he saw the bailiff walk towards him to take him away. He turned around and glared at Jay but didn't utter anything.

'You threw away a winning case, Jay,' Talwar told Jay as the latter was walking out of the court.

'I saved my soul. Not a bad bargain, is it?'

'You know you won't get a single defence case when this thing gets out?'

'I don't think I care anymore, Mr Talwar. I trust you to ensure that whoever is guilty gets what they deserve.'

'You can count on me, Jay.'

'Thank you, Mr Talwar.'

Evading the media and the crowds, Jay trudged out from the rear of the building. Bhīma was waiting there.

There's an immense difference between losing a game and throwing it away. Jay Singh had thrown away an inconsequential game. And he was happy. Failure had never tasted so sweet before.

But calling it a failure was to consider merely one dimension in life. Jay had won on several other levels. And it was time for penance. He knew that once conscience grows its legs, a defence advocate has to exit the game: even if you invite both of them at different times of the day, God and the Devil simply won't dine at the same table.

34

THREE MONTHS LATER.

Yes, it takes a long time to dismantle an empire – however deceitful – you've built over the years. I went from being the country's greatest defence advocate to just another advocate in a chair outside Tis Hazari courts. Whether I descended or ascended was a matter of moot debate; I gave it all up the day my conscience stirred. Gone were the days of my black suits by a couturier. Now, I prided myself in doing the right thing. Sometimes you define yourself by what you decide in split seconds. As I realized nothing was career-threatening once you decided to give it up of your own volition, for your own good.

I spent the last three months doing what I thought was important. First off, I had to protect Yuvraj. I had taken his responsibility when I wasn't a crooked man. It was a promise I made to a dying mother, and there was no way I was going to break that. I set up a fool-proof trust for him that would support him for the rest of his life. His upbringing, all his education till the time he post-graduated or some such. If by then he couldn't make it, it was his kismet and his problem.

Bahadur decided to retire and return to his country. I, too, couldn't see what he would do if he had decided to stay with me. I wrote a single cheque that would take care of him even if he decided never to work for a single day of his remaining life. Of course, he could go back to Nepal and spend it in one go on a Blackjack table in a casino. That again, would be his kismet and his problem, though he didn't look the kind.

My experience has taught me that often the timing of things you really want in life is pure shit. I had really started looking forward to spending time with Manavi, just being with her, had even started envisioning spending my entire life with her as my wife. God knows that I loved her and shall do so for the rest of my life. But, love, like priorities, can change. It was a difficult conversation, but in the end, I was successful in explaining it to her. She was young and had her whole life in front of her. I was winding down, so to speak. She had been through heartbreak before and when she realized I was asking her to leave me, the dam broke. She had stayed at my farmhouse for a week, but I refrained from making love to my girl. Had I known back then that I would never make love to Manavi again, I would have savoured the last time more. No regrets, though.

I convinced her to follow her dream of going abroad – to the US – to study interior design. If, after finishing the course, she still decided to return, I would wait. I knew well that in the three years she spent at New York School of Interior Design studying for an MFA, I would be long gone from her memory as a lover. She might still remember me as a benefactor, someone who paid for her education and made her realize her potential. I would be a good chapter in her life, and I was happy to support her any way she wanted later. Except financially, of course, because I would have no money subsequently. I held some of the most prominent personalities by the gonads and made them write the best recommendations they could, and got her admitted in the coming fall. I went shopping with her for her clothes all around town. I remember the day Bhīma drove us to the Indira Gandhi International Airport in Delhi to see her off. It was extremely difficult – almost impossible if you ask me – to let go of someone I loved so much, but I remained strong for her, promised her that I would visit her in the New Year. I knew it was a false promise, but what the heck! This wasn't the first time I had lied; but it would be one of the last times, I promised myself.

Passing time has been known to throw dust on memories. At some fucking point, your imagination and memories blend so much like the waters of the oceans that it's hard to discern which is fucking which. Did that really happen, or was that something I'd conjured up? My love for Manavi felt synonymous with fiction now.

Did it ever happen? Was it a dream or did we really make love?

All those things that had once mattered to me seemed frivolous now. I sold the farmhouse. You'd be surprised to know that it sold within hours of being advertised. I offered it as-is, didn't want to remove much chattel from there except my personal stuff, especially my music. No, not the expensive system, I only wanted the music, so I sold my entire vinyl collection and made-do with my iPod. The Audi was a quick sale too. After paying for Yuvraj, Manavi and Bahadur, I donated all the money to the Jaipur Mental Hospital. They were the ones who had taken care of my mother when I had turned away.

Bhīma was worse than a dog when it came to loyalty. He refused to leave me. After a million conversations, I gave up. He told me in as many words that the only way I could get rid of him was to pump bullets into his massive chest. So, in the end, the two stayed on with me: Bhīma and Sheeba. Sheeba: what choice did the poor old girl have? The only two men she ever loved were Bhīma and me. If she was uncomfortable with the destitute life without air conditioning or mattress, she never showed it. Our parsimony was acceptable to the old girl. Knowing Bhīma, he was the last man on earth to complain. And I? It was all my doing, so I don't think I had any right to moan or whine.

The three of us lived in the shanty next door to Akbar Ali. Bhīma, Ali and I took turns at cooking every night. It was a simple existence. Bhīma was the best cook amongst us. He seemed to have learnt some skills in the army and then later by watching Bahadur.

All four of us went to the Tis Hazari courts every weekday morning without fail. With age having caught up and the traffic in the city becoming unruly by the day, cycling was a forgone thought. It didn't even occur to us. Plus Sheeba couldn't ride a bicycle. With my riches denuded, we pooled and bought an old and battered Ambassador. It didn't have air conditioning, and the rattling silencer more than made up for a CD player and the horn.

The best part was that everyone who worked alongside me, when I was a fuck-all nobody, was still there. Stories of my giving up a gold-studded career only enhanced my integrity amongst the community. If they envied me when I was a successful defence advocate, they revered me now. They had no idea what wrongs I had done to get to where I had got. I guess my success covered all the ignobility. Obviously, some laughed at me for giving it all away. No one knew why and no one bothered. Why should they? We quipped and bantered and laughed like old times.

A few people thought I was crazy, others even said so to my face. You know, at times I wondered too. Not sure if you've experienced this, but sometimes it takes a while for reality to hit, like in my case. However, when it hit me, it hit really hard. I realized I was just about as important as a speck of superfluous dust; persona non grata Jay Singh. I had been decadent, deceitful, a scoundrel and a legal liar; an outlaw who had been authorized to practise law for a long time, but I was no better than the people I defended – the filthy criminals. It was good that my conscience awoke when it did and I had no regrets. At any rate, if not for my conscience, the alcohol would have got me disbarred from being a defence advocate. The end of my career was in a way a relief. The cognitive overload was becoming a burden. I needed a hiatus from running for years, like a marathon runner needs rest after an event.

In some weird sort of way, the game of test cricket is the best metaphor for life. There is a second innings. You get another chance to redeem yourself for all the mistakes you make in the first one. I was playing my final innings. I realized I had become too big an advocate, and it was time to grow and evolve as a human being now. That day in court I had broken a fundamental principle, the one I had lived by as a defence advocate: 'Every man has a right to a fair defence and consequently a fair trial.' Something in me knew that was all nonsense and that Vinay Kumar deserved to be incarcerated for the murder of Gina, after having escaped arrest for his first murder, which I now believed he had committed; justice had to be served. It was a fallacy that most people believed: that if justice was delayed, it was denied. The cliché is fabricated and wrong.

It might have taken a long time, but it had finally clicked. Talwar dug till he got to the evidenced truth. Rita was innocent, as she had confided in me. Kumar got fourteen years in the lock-up. It wasn't my way of getting even with Kumar, and I can swear upon God Almighty that I didn't do it out of spite because he had screwed with me. I merely let it happen as I felt that was the right thing, the honest justice.

Then again, who are we to judge?

My self-aggrandizement was certainly over. My worldly possessions were very few, my needs and wants were even fewer. Simple maths. Material belongings could no longer trap me when I ran out of life. It was no longer important what sound system I listened to the music on; it was important who I listened with. Leonard Cohen sounded even better in Akbar Ali's, Bhīma's and Sheeba's company.

I had spent my whole life so far wishing the nightmarish evening that led to my father's murder had never occurred; I knew I'd spend the rest of it trying to forget it. The pain wasn't assuaged, but at least I could see clearly now. A ring of the unknown had been lifted. Not the kind of closure I had expected but a closure nonetheless. What changed, however, was I had stopped licking my wounds; I had ceased to feel guilty for what happened almost thirty years ago, reining in being sorry for myself. The pain didn't vanish. But it ebbed away each day and I felt content … at last. I had spliced my life together. It was now a diorama and not a set of disparate broken pictures.

My biggest challenge – and how it all started in the first place – was to give up alcohol. Reacquainting with a sober life wasn't easy; it wasn't impossible either. The day I decided to give up alcohol it felt like an impossible task. In time, it was just another thing to give up. When I gave up everything else, I also gave up alcohol. That alcohol was the only intoxication I was suffering from was a fallacy. Actually, I soon realized there was nothing to 'give up'. I just quit. I spent evenings with Akbar Ali – he stopped drinking too – and we still chatted and argued till the wee hours of the morning, but we both remained sober. And we still had a lot in common. In fact, we had more in common now that I had returned to the right side of the law. We enjoyed life. We had an anthem we always listened to when we got together: 'Comfortably Numb' *by Pink Floyd.*

Everything had evened out in the end for me. I was a simple man with unlimited dreams. I had reached the peak of my career, which I had always aspired to, only to learn it wasn't worth it. But I had to get there to know that it wasn't there. Happiness and contentment are indefinable words; each one of us finds them in different places.

I sat under a tree, an advocate of the people, for the people, not only for the ones who could pay. Unlike Faust, I had decided that I would no longer provide my services to the Devil.

I dissolved Cooper & Singh – I couldn't think of ending my association any other way. The rechristened Singh & Son was put under a trust. The partners there were caretakers until Yuvraj decided what to do with his life. If he decided not to be an advocate, the entire firm would go to the partners. Should he become an advocate, his share would be sixty per cent that instant.

Mentioning Cooper reminded me to tell you a little about him.

Some memories are best kept locked in the bottom-most drawer. I put as much distance as I could between him and me. I ignored him even when I saw him. And I saw him a lot in the initial days. Maybe he got the message eventually, because he stopped visiting me. I had finally dismantled the bond. The first time he encountered me, he held my eye and asked, 'Are you happy, my friend?'

'You tell me who is?' I responded with a humourless smile and walked on.

I still see Cooper every now and then but we don't talk. I'm very sure he feels let down that I don't make any attempts to be social. He might even think I am capricious, but I don't care. As Anita had explained, the deer had run too far ahead for the cheetah to catch him now. I was over Cooper, I knew he was an illusion; an imaginary friend like Calvin had Hobbes. And for the record, I don't blame Cooper. In fact, I don't accuse anyone of anything anymore. I just hark back to the facts every time I get that feeling. I did think of turning myself in but then decided against it. Ma had already paid the price for the crime. It wasn't a case of my tail between my legs. As Anita had warned, it was an assumption within an assumption; it wouldn't go very far in the legal framework. Worst case: they'd think I'm loony and I'd be incarcerated in a mental asylum for the rest of my living years, just like my mother.

♝

You want my summary?

Heaven and Hell are both on earth. You choose where you want to end up. Do not even carry any belief other than this. This is it. This is life.

Justice. It isn't something humans are capable of dispensing. That's Shiva's job. He is anything but fickle. Shiva solves all the mysteries about God and death, heaven and hell, truth and dishonesty. They're all here, in this world and He takes that weight upon his cosmic shoulders. As I mentioned earlier, I was always only a speck of unwanted dust, irrespective of what I considered myself in my hey-years. The time had now come for Him to intervene.

Brahma, Vishnu, Shiva. The Creator. The Protector. The Destroyer.

Shiva, supposedly, has a third eye on His forehead which He had opened for me at the right time and destroyed everything that I thought was imperative.

Remember Shiva does not wish for apocalypse; He does not destroy because He wants to; He destroys only when there isn't any other option left to exercise.

I had lost it completely when He took over. My karma had invoked Him to intervene to save me.

I have rehearsed these lines countless times since that ill-fated night, and if I ever meet Shiva the only question I would ask Him when I see Him: why me?

I know Anita had already answered it for me, but I still yearn to hear Him tell me: 'Why not?

Epilogue

For a country that only treated politicians, cricketers and film stars as celebrities, it was quite extraordinary that every single newspaper – from *Times of India* and *Hindustan Times* to the useless, most insignificant rags – carried it as the front-page headline. Bad news, as always, was more titillating and better masala:

'Noted Defence Advocate Jay Singh Shot Dead'

Once a premier defence advocate, he was seated under the tree one afternoon when his karma caught up with him. They pumped all six bullets into him, not leaving anything to chance. Someone wanted him to be silenced forever indeed. Unfortunately, if he had survived this attack, there were many more who wanted him dead. Not surprisingly, he was only good for them till he was bad. Him changing sides wasn't acceptable; not to people who couldn't afford to let their secrets be out in the open. Whether he would ever reveal anything about his former associates or not wasn't a risk they were prepared to take. It was his ridiculous decision to give up everything that God – God? – had bestowed on him; it had to be him who would have to pay the price. It wasn't anything new or unusual: as they say, people who live by the gun …

You break an agreement, you pay back. You pay back with interest. Compounded interest. Jay Singh's payback time occurred six months after he quit his flourishing practice of lying legally. The enemies caught up with him – the alleged connections or associates whom he once protected and who, in turn, protected him. Ironical? Life is an endless series of ironies in every respect when you look at it closely. When you turn your enemies into friends, they make the most loyal of friends. Regrettably, the converse is factual too: when friends become enemies – by chance or choice – they become the fiercest of enemies. Logically, you don't leave them any choice since you know too much about them. Jay Singh knew too much. A little man with big ambitions, what if he someday decided to turn into a state witness, now that his conscience had apparently awoken. That he will always be on their side was a tacit agreement. And if one side had broken that agreement, the other side would end it too; unfortunately, they ended it in the only manner they recognized. You can call it vengeance or you can call it justice; it's again a matter of perspective. In any event if he weren't going to defend them anymore, what use would he be to them anyway? It was an occupational hazard. Don't they say, you can't drown and die if your kismet says that your end has to come with a bullet?

Anyway, his jig was up. His life had met its purpose. He died on the spot, painlessly and contented.

A lot of people were around but apparently no one saw the killers. When it came to crime, the city always slept. No one ever saw any crime happen, let alone reporting it or testifying in a court. What have they done to the country? Why are people afraid of protectors and justice?

Shiva, the ever-friendly god, ensured Jay Singh didn't carry the baggage in his next birth.

Bhīma could never absolve himself; he had only walked a few metres to get hukum a tea. He carried Jay's ashes to Pushkar, as the latter had desired when the two had visited Swamiji. He only returned to Delhi to pick up Sheeba. The two retired to a simple life in the shadows of the Creator: Brahma.

Yuvraj stayed in his hostel.

If there was one error of judgement on Jay's part, it was that he had assumed that in time Manavi would forget him. She is the only person who annually visits Pushkar to spend time with Bhīma and Sheeba, and to be in the place where Jay eventually found peace. She believes his ashes are still in the air, she can see him in the sunrise, she can see him in the lake.

Jay Singh might have gone for the rest of the world, but he still lingers on in the memories of Sheeba and Bhīma and Manavi.

Acknowledgements

'A person often meets his destiny on the road he took to avoid it.'

Jean de La Fontaine

Déjà Karma was first published in 2015. It was my third book and my first foray into the legal-psychological territory. Although the book was well received by readers and critics, it went out of print by the year's end and, for a whole host of reasons, it did not get republished until now.

The media at the time deemed the book, a legal thriller (also gave me a moniker for life) and they were not entirely wrong. What everyone missed, however, was that the book was a whole lot more. It is the story of a troubled man, a successful lawyer psychologically broken by traumatic events from his adolescence, struggling to build a bridge between his past and present, completely misjudging that – in his case – the past and present are better kept disjointed. And as though he isn't already besieged by problems, his professional success has made him an egomaniac, a narcissist.

Until karma comes calling …

I have a lot of people to thank:

Nidhi, my wife, my partner in crime.

Mita Kapur and the entire team at Siyahi.

Teesta Guha Sarkar, Shreya Gupta and the Pan Macmillan India team.

Sidharth Jain and the team at The Story Ink, who I know would love to take this story to screen.

I very much hope you enjoyed *Déjà Karma*. If you want to get in touch and share your thoughts, please do so on email/Facebook/Instagram. A review on Amazon and/or Goodreads is always very welcome.

Many thanks for reading.

Love, lots of it.

Email: vishdhamija@gmail.com
FB: www.facebook.com/VishDhamija
Insta: vish_dhamija